I0591504

ANTIPODES SERIES BOOK 4

CIRCLE OF PROTECTION

ANTIPODES SERIES BOOK 4

CIRCLE OF PROTECTION

T.S. SIMONS

4 Horsemen
Publications, Inc.

4 Horsemen
Publications, Inc.

4 Horsemen Publications, Inc.
1497 Main St. Suite 169
Dunedin, FL 34698
4horsemenpublications.com
info@4horsemenpublications.com

Typeset by Autumn Skye
Cover Design by Jen Kotick

Library of Congress Control Number: 2021951215

Print ISBN: 978-1-64450-380-5
Hardcover ISBN: 978-1-64450-953-1
Audio ISBN: 978-1-64450-378-2
EBook ISBN: 978-1-64450-379-9

Caim is a Gaelic word meaning sanctuary or circle of protection.

To those who form my Caim, thank you for the ongoing encouragement, love, and support, and for believing in me, especially when I didn't.

Kerguelen Islands

Melbourne

August Island
Auckland Island
Bellcamp Island

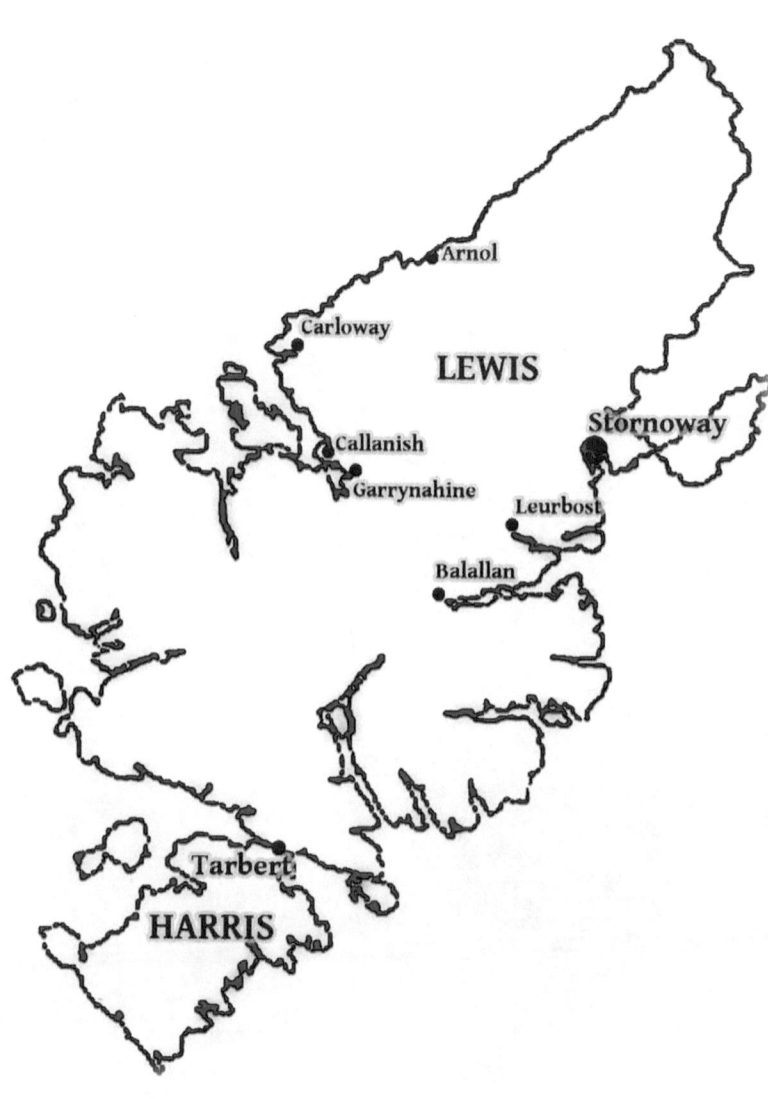

Arnol

Carloway

LEWIS

Callanish

Stornoway

Garrynahine

Leurbost

Balallan

Tarbert

HARRIS

CONTENTS

ACKNOWLEDGEMENTS:

BOB - THANK YOU. For everything. Your support means the world to me. Even if you don't like cats!

Debra St. James, Chelle Pimblott, Serafina Jax, Stevie D Parker —thank you for the chats, the support, the friendship. You are all goddesses among women. I am so blessed to have you in my Caim.

To all the wonderful people who have bought or recommended my books, and even waited patiently for the next in the series—thank you. I can't tell you what it means to me that people enjoy my work. The feedback you provide is invaluable and keeps me going.

Special thanks to Alison FG, Fairlie, Dani, Kelly, Caitlin, Izzy, Steph, Helen, Tracey, and Rae.

Hayley Ramsey Editorial—the blurb queen. Once again, thank you.
If you enjoyed this book, it would mean a great deal to me if you could spare a few minutes to leave a quick review on Goodreads, Amazon, Bookbub, or any other platform.

GoodReads:
www.goodreads.com/author/
show/20861749.T_S_Simons

Amazon:
www.amazon.com/T-S-Simons/e/B08MT6YYDL

Bookbub:
www.bookbub.com/profile/t-s-simons

CHAPTER 1

FEELING MY WAY THROUGH the darkness, I moved cautiously to avoid stumbling over a carelessly discarded toy and cracking my shin against the solid timber furniture that crowded our home. At well past midnight, it was blissfully silent, and the children tucked up in bed. Bone deep weariness after assisting a long and challenging labor propelled me to my own. Hopefully Isla would check on the mare and her foal in the morning, leaving me to sleep.

Kicking off my boots and dropping my clothes in a heap on a nearby chair, I couldn't suppress the audible sigh that escaped my lips as my weary head finally connected with the pillow, careful not to wake Cam, who was sleeping soundly beside me. Never had I been so pleased to be lying down. Closing my eyes, I willed sleep to overtake me.

Short, sharp trills punctuated the still night air.

"What is that frigging noise?" I muttered as the screeching continued unabated, like a bird announcing the approach of a predator. I rolled over, burying my head under the pillow, praying it would stop.

Cam stirred enough to kiss my protruding neck, then lifted his head, alert.

"That's the..."

"Alarm!" we chorused, sitting bolt upright, my pillow tumbling to the floor. That harsh noise could only be one thing—the proximity sensor. We hadn't heard it since we had set it up years earlier, and I scarcely recalled the sound of it. Flinging back the covers, I staggered the two steps to my still warm clothing on the chair as Cam snatched at yesterday's clothes carelessly discarded on the floor. Still pulling arms through sleeves, we ran to Illy and Luca's house, Cam several strides ahead of me. Thumping coming from their home, bare feet on floorboards, echoed through the crisp night air.

"Bloody hell, who approaches an island in the middle of the night?" I grumbled as I joined him on the doorstep, and Cam knocked lightly. Functioning with no sleep was not a strength of mine, especially not when tumbling out of bed unceremoniously. Cam kissed me, glancing down at my unbuttoned jeans.

"Hurry and finish getting dressed! If Luca answers the door, he'll see more of you than any of us are comfortable with!"

My groggy, half-asleep mind pictured the times Luca had seen me naked, or barely dressed, in the years we had traveled together—coming out of a shower or daring me to go skinny dipping with him in a lake on a domed community—but my brain couldn't form the words. Fortunately, Illy answered the door, looking disheveled but alert as she tied her heather gray robe, long dark hair falling across her face. She ushered us inside with her usual chirpy tone as I hurriedly finished fastening my jeans, socks and shoes still in hand.

She was my best friend, and I adored her, but right now, I hated her. How could she possibly be happy to see us at this hour? Once inside, she steered us toward the study and closed the door so we wouldn't wake their twin girls. Allison and Summer were six, a few months older than our youngest, Thorsten. Our bonus baby—the child we had when we thought we had finished having children. Louis and Katrin could look after the younger two if they woke and found us gone. Xanthe was our sensitive child and often had nightmares, waking screaming in terror.

Luca had turned off the alarm and barely acknowledged our entrance, busily hooking up the larger surveillance monitor as we crowded in. Standing behind him as he fiddled with cables and camera feeds, we strained our eyes, watching the dark shadow slithering on the single screen. As my eyes adjusted to the darkness, I could just make out a sizeable white boat mooring in the harbor at Stornoway.

"That's not anyone from Newgrange, is it?" Illy asked as she returned and thrust a steaming mug in my hand, and a matching one in Cam's, but we all recognized the question as rhetorical.

"Fuck," I muttered, not removing my eyes from the screen.

Luca was studying the craft carefully, muttering under his breath. "I don't recognize it."

We all stood watching the screen, waiting for someone to appear on deck and tie up. A minute passed. Two.

I grunted at Cam, knocking back the contents of the cup in one gulp. "We'll go. Ils, can you watch ours?"

Waking any of our other friends at this time of night would make us most unpopular, not to mention unnecessarily scare people. Cam's sister Sorcha and her partner, Di, lived with their two children on the opposite side of our home. Isla and Fraser lived between our place and Illy's, Jamie and Jacinda farther down the valley. Any of them would assist, but all had young children and would almost certainly be asleep.

Illy smiled at me. "Of course. I'll head down while Luca keeps watch. Are you sure you don't want one of us to go?"

We had discussed this scenario often when setting up the alarms in both our homes—what we would do if someone approached Lewis, our protected community. Self-sufficient and isolated, we loved the sense of belonging here. Everyone looked out for each other, lending a hand. That sense of interconnectedness extended between all residents.

Seven years ago, our community had severed ties with the outside world to prohibit the intrusive and controlling influence of the team of scientists at Clava, near Inverness. Wanting to dictate our laws, our trade, but most sinister of all, planning to force us to have children with a scientifically selected partner, the scientists in the two controlling communities of Clava near Inverness on mainland Scotland and Auckland Island off the coast of New Zealand had devised and implemented a selective breeding program to reproduce key genome sequences and ensure their survival.

"No," I sighed, more than a little grumpy by the unexpected early morning call out. "We'll go."

Illy grinned at Cam. She knew me well enough to know I desperately wanted to go to bed, but we had promised. When we had established our security systems and protocols, we had agreed it was less threatening if Cam and I responded to any unplanned visitors. Illy and Luca had been military personnel before coming here whereas Cam and I were civilians. After all, it could be anyone. A similarly isolated community existed in Newgrange, Ireland, another community not part of the Collective, the association of domed communities. More protected settlements existed on the mainland of the UK and several on the Scottish islands of Orkney and the Shetlands, although they were all now part of the Collective. People occasionally came to visit, or we went to them, but never without notice.

Luca grimaced as he sipped from the mug that appeared tiny in his enormous hands.

"I have repositioned the cameras and satellite. I will be watching. You remember the distress signal?"

Luca handed Cam one of the few remaining operational hand-held two-way radios. We had originally taken a large supply on one of our raids on the mainland and spread them out across the community so people could always contact each other. With the original rechargeable batteries failing, and no way to replace them, the remaining functional units were a precious resource.

"We do. Come on, honey. We will need to move to make it before dawn, and it will be slow going in the dark."

"They couldn't have thought to visit at a reasonable hour?" I grumbled as our golf cart chugged slowly up the hill in the dark, out of our beautiful valley of

Roseglen and toward the original and largest settlement of Garynahine. The lights on the cart were
barely strong enough to cast a shadowed light on the
dirt track. "Who do you think it could be?"

"No clue. If they are strangers, they won't be able
to see the geodesic dome openings in the dark. They
will probably wait on their vessel until first light. We
have a little time. They may not know we have been
alerted to their arrival."

He slipped an arm around me as he drove, and
I snuggled close. We approached the dock slowly as
the dawn light tinted the horizon a pretty pink gold,
making everything glow warmly. But I was in no mood
to look at sunrises. It was clear that this was no one
we knew. No one had radioed ahead to announce their
arrival. Friends would have arrived in daylight, not
caring that they could be seen by us and likely by the
surveillance teams on Clava.

Standing upright as we slowed, I cupped my hands
and bellowed, "Who are you, and what do you want?"

I felt Cam jolt from beside me. He shot me a sly
grin in the dim light as he killed the ignition. He loved
it when I played the role of commander. I felt his hand
cup my bottom.

"Now!" I boomed, making him remove his
hand rapidly.

CHAPTER 2

AS THE FAMILIAR FACE drifted into view, faintly illuminated by the dawn light, I sucked in my breath, recognizing Jorja's long, dark hair and exotic features. We had enjoyed our weeks on Clava, the easiness of it all. Sharing a home with Jorja and Bridget had been wonderful, but we had sensed that something was off. Despite their offers of support, of relocation, we had made the difficult decision to return home to our family and friends, only later learning that we had been fed a drug to keep us compliant. The final straw that had seen us sever all communication had been learning that they had infected our friend Diana, along with several others from non-complying communities, with cancer, believing that if their doctors saved her, we would join the Collective.

What we hadn't known then was *why* they had chosen us all. We always knew that we were selected to ensure the survival of humanity. The part we hadn't known was that we were expected to take part in their forced breeding program. Instead of conforming like most of the other communities and choosing a life of connectedness, better technology, and resources, we had chosen to isolate ourselves and set up security systems to alert us to possible intruders. We had lived in peace, but hypervigilant, so we were wary of what tricks they could be up to now.

"Why are you here?"

"I..." Jorja stammered but quickly recovered her composure. "Freyja. Campbell." She nodded at us, a smile on her face, although I noted it didn't reach her eyes. "It is good to see you."

"I wish I could say the same." Jorja sensed the warning and flinched. "Why are you here?"

"We ... that is, Bridget and I came to talk to you."

"Talk to us? You couldn't have radioed? Let us know you planned to drop by for a cup of tea in the middle of the night and scare us all?"

"Well, the matter we wanted to discuss is a little ... delicate."

"Delicate? I'll tell you what is delicate—learning that you and your friends were planning to breed us like pedigree dogs. Discussing our genetic profile over drinks, scribbling notes, and planning who to partner us up with. Treating us like science experiments."

"I..." she stammered.

"Tell me," I snapped, not wanting to listen to feeble excuses. "Are you an endocrinologist? A fertility specialist? All that time we lived together, you knew what they planned for us, and you said nothing?"

"I am." Her long black hair fell across her face as she looked down at her feet.

"Why didn't you tell us?" I was seething. "You told us you were a doctor." I felt Cam's reassuring hand rest on my shoulder.

"I *am* a doctor."

"You deliberately deceived us!"

"Because that part of the project was still secret. No one was supposed to know. Even I didn't know all of it then—truly. They chose me to help couples conceive, to ensure that we all survived, and we all wanted that. I swear, I knew nothing about the selected partner part. Honestly. And I *am* a doctor. I just specialized, that is all."

"It was a massive omission." Cam spoke calmly from beside me. "You stitched us both that day and said nothing. Not to mention all those evenings we spent together. We trusted you. Thought you were our friend."

Jorja shrugged forlornly. "They bound me to secrecy. My loyalty was to the project. Then."

"Then?" I questioned, picking up on the pertinent word.

"I guess you could say that things have changed."

"Spit it out. Why are you here? And why now?"

"Bridget and I have two children."

"Okay ... so what?" I snarled, not in the mood to offer congratulations. "We have four. What is your point?"

"As the girls grew, we knew something wasn't right."

"What do you mean, not right?" Cam cut off my next comment, suspicion dripping from his words.

Jorja stepped back onto the deck, calling, "Bridge? Girls!" through the open hatchway.

Bridget emerged from the lower deck, holding the hands of two blonde girls, the glow of the early morning light illuminating them. She hadn't changed. Her brown wavy hair was longer, tinted with gold, and she was slightly more curvaceous. I gasped audibly, and I felt Cam's body tense beside me. These two girls were so similar looking that it was apparent that they had the same parentage. But that wasn't what had made me react. These two girls were the spitting image of our daughters: Katrin, Xanthe, and *me*. My mouth hung open. Judging by the gurgling noises beside me, Cam was also struggling to form words.

"As I thought," Jorja spoke quietly, but with an unmistakable note of sadness. "They look so much like you."

"*How*?" I finally gasped when I had regained control of my speech, still staring at the girls standing on the deck of their vessel, the light glinting from their hair.

"If we had never met you that time on Clava, we would never have known. We would have thought it suspicious but wouldn't have taken it further. Neither of us are fair in coloring, especially me, but we assumed they had the same donor father. But as the girls grew, we saw more and more of you in them. We discussed it at length. How on earth could our children look like *you*? Eventually, we landed on only one logical answer. You are their mother."

A pain shot through my chest, making me exhale sharply. Bridget smiled wanly at me as she and the girls made their way over to us, and I tried to hide the pain. The girls couldn't have been more than six but looked exactly like Katrin had at that age. How little Xanthe looked now.

"Hi Freyja, Cam. Meet Ruby and Scarlett," Bridget introduced us kindly. The girls hid behind her, scared at meeting these new people.

"Can you say hello, girls? These are our friends. The ones we were telling you about. They are from Australia, too."

"What do you want from us?" I snapped, exhaustion and shock making it sound more venomous than I had intended. Bridget recoiled but regained her composure. One girl looked like she was about to cry. She looked so much like Xan. Instinctively, I wanted to hold her close and protect her.

"We came to ask you questions if that is okay."

Cam, being a better person than I, and realizing that we couldn't stand here all day with exhausted and emotional children in crumpled, dirty clothing, gestured with his chin.

"Come on. You can stay with us while we sort this out."

I openly glared at him. I was in no mood to be gracious, and under no circumstances wanted them in my home, but equally recognized that I couldn't just leave them here, exposed. Scowling, I helped Cam load a bag each on the cart with a promise to collect their remaining items later. With the girls balanced on their mothers' knees, we began the long jolting journey home. The conversation was stilted as Cam tried to make small talk, pointing out places of interest. Jorja and Bridget were visibly uncomfortable, the girls plainly terrified. We had been friendly once. A long time ago now. But we had been deceived and learned the true nature of why we had been chosen. They had been an active part of that deception, and I wasn't the forgiving kind.

Xanthe and Thorsten rushed out to greet us as we came over the hill into Roseglen. I heard Bridget gasp from behind me as we neared our home, and she saw our daughter, her long blonde hair streaming like ribbons behind her. A daughter so like her own.

"Oh ... my ... God!" I heard her breathe from behind me.

"God had nothing to do with it," I muttered.

We sent Illy home pleasantly, but she gave me the look. "We will talk. Later."

We fed the children breakfast, chatting pleasantly about our friends who had come to visit. Louis alone sensed the underlying tension. He watched them suspiciously, glancing at the girls, his eyebrows furrowed, but remained silent. After sending the children outside to play, we sat Jorja and Bridget down in our cozy living room with a second coffee. Jorja was more discreet, but Bridget could not take her eyes from Katrin and Xanthe throughout breakfast. Thorsten was darker, like a mini-Cam in appearance. Louis was not my biological child and looked like the few precious photos Cam had of Laetitia with her chestnut brown hair and exotic brown eyes. But the girls looked just like me. Tall, blonde, and with sparkling emerald-green eyes that betrayed their feelings long before they spoke.

"Out with it."

Jorja spoke first, holding Bridget's hand. "It was a few years ago when we noticed how alike the girls were. Looks but mannerisms too. And idiosyncrasies that neither of us possess. We talked, of course, but we had needed donor sperm, so we just assumed that was it. It made sense that the girls had the same father, so they were actually related. We accepted it until one day, when she was three, Ruby rolled her eyes scornfully at something I said, and looked so much like you, Freyja, that my heart stopped. I questioned my colleagues, and they assured me I was mistaken. They were our own eggs and donated sperm. We believed them ... for a time. After all, this was my team. But it didn't sit right with us. We sensed something was off.

As you know, my parents immigrated from Iran when I was a child. They are both dark-haired, and dark hair is a dominant gene, so the chance of me having a blonde child with light eyes is almost impossible. But they were still toddlers, and kids change a lot, so we watched the girls closely, thinking that they would change as they got older. But what we saw was more and more of *you* in them as they grew. We pushed, and my colleagues denied it, until I threatened to perform DNA tests. Finally, they admitted the eggs were donated from a desired genome, and the girls were full siblings."

Slumping on the couch, the toast in my stomach formed a solid mass.

"How?" I asked weakly. "How could they have taken them?"

"That is the million-dollar question. Without your knowledge, they likely couldn't have. Do you know anything about IVF?"

"Not really. I mean, I learned the basics in my undergrad degree and saw it performed at some of my student placements, but I have never put it into practice. Life as a vet here is a little more rustic."

Cam shrugged helplessly. As an agriculturalist with a specialty in food security, reproduction in humans wasn't his area of expertise.

"How IVF works is this. In a normal month, you produce one ripened egg. The team in Melbourne may have been extremely lucky and been able to harvest an egg from you when they conducted the selection tests in Melbourne. But that doesn't explain both Ruby *and* Scarlett. During IVF treatment, you are injected with a hormone cocktail that makes you produce more ripened eggs. It is these that are retrieved. But this process is delicate and takes even me half an hour, and I have performed the procedure thousands of times. We typically retrieve ten to fifteen eggs in one surgery, sometimes as many as twenty if we use more drugs and time is limited, like in women about to undergo cancer treatment."

"Okay, so how did they take them from me then?" I wiped the sweat from my brow, willing the nausea not to overtake me. Cam, seated beside me, had his arm around my waist protectively.

"Well, that is the thing. The entire cycle takes at least fourteen days. Usually longer."

"But I haven't been in a hospital or anywhere else for fourteen days. Unless they did it while I was on Clava, but even then, I would have noticed." I looked up at Cam for confirmation.

"You weren't away from me for longer than a few hours, and even then, we were in the same building. Just attending different briefings."

"Did you have any siblings or close relatives?" Bridget asked.

"No." I shook my head, my nose crinkled. "My parents were alive when the pandemic hit, but in their fifties. They weren't candidates. My sister passed before I left for August, and all of my cousins and distant relatives were in Norway. But any of them could have survived, I guess. We weren't close."

"Did she?" Cam spoke gently, turning to look me directly in the eyes. "I thought you said your sister was brain dead, but alive?"

I stared at him, dazed.

"You told me she was a shell, the life had gone, but she was still alive the day you said goodbye," Cam whispered, not wanting to distress me, but loud enough for them to hear.

My feet hit the ground, and I was out the door. I heard the empty mug from my lap bouncing along the rug behind me. I was running, but I didn't know where. The thoughts, images, and nightmares filled my brain, overflowed, and tormented me as I ran faster and faster. But I couldn't escape the horrors of seeing her lying there, trapped in that bed for life. Alive, but not *her*.

Holy fucking hell. No. They couldn't.

But who was going to stop them? The nagging voice pricked at me. *The world was dying. Who would have even noticed? One comatose woman missing. No one would know. Or care. But why her?*

A backup genome for you, the logical part of my brain interjected. *Like Sorcha and Kendra, and all the others on the mainland protected communities. They wanted a backup for you, in case...*

In case I refused to participate. The brutal force of that reality struck me like a blow to the pit of the stomach as I realized that my refusal to be part of their plans had caused this. I slowed, dropped my head, and fought to keep the nausea at bay.

Sitting beside Loch Acha Mor, I watched the sky change color through the dome, from blue to purple, the orange and pink tinge of dusk, silver, and finally black. I sensed movement behind me but was too shellshocked to look up.

Luca's enormous frame scrambled to sit beside me on the small rocky shelf and not slide into the lake. He propped there, not speaking, for the longest time. He was just ... there. I dropped my head onto his shoulder and let go. His strong, muscular arms came around me and held me as I sobbed. For letting her down. Abandoning her. The tragedy of her life and for what they had likely done to her. Exhausted, I slumped onto him. Luca scooped me up like a child and carried me home, depositing me into Cam's care. The house was quiet, and I heard the front door close. The tears started again as I raged, and cried, and eventually fell asleep.

"How could they?" I sobbed when I woke during the night, and Cam held me as my body shuddered with the agony. Reliving the pain of her death—but she wasn't dead. I truly believed she hadn't survived long after the pandemic had struck. *Had they just harvested her eggs before they left, or was she still lying unconscious ... somewhere?*

"What else did Jorja say?" I finally asked.

Cam spoke haltingly, not wanting to distress me further. But that ship had sailed. I had already imagined all the indignities she might have suffered. I had watched helplessly as I envisioned the medical procedures they had inflicted on her poor, lifeless body. All in the name of science.

"Perhaps sensibly, rather than ask any more questions, Jorja and Bridget took it upon themselves to do some research. They didn't find much. Many records were classified or redacted. But they learned there had been many anonymous donors of eggs to women who couldn't conceive. Donor Seventeen was the donor to both Jorja and Bridget. Likely it was planned, maybe luck. They don't know. But they learned that Donor Seventeen was the egg donor of five fertilized embryos. Full siblings. What they didn't know was whether that donor was *you*."

"Five?"

"Five."

"Holy fucking hell," I muttered, my brain whirring. *If it wasn't me, then it must have been her. Was she on Clava? More likely Auckland Island. That was where Bridget and Jorja had lived and had their girls. Was she still being used as a guinea pig? Or had they just taken her genetic material before they left Australia, to be used in case I refused to take part in the breeding program? That made more sense if they only needed a few eggs.*

Despite it being the middle of the night, I couldn't stop the torturous images flickering before my eyes. I could see Kat's face clearly, her beautiful long blonde hair fanned out over her white pillowcase, glowing in the sunshine that streamed through the window of her small private room. How she had looked as I had left her, the day I said goodbye. Two years she had lain there since her accident at only eighteen. After the pandemic, I genuinely believed she had perished. Maybe she had.

"Do they know?" I asked. "Is she still alive?"

"They don't. They have come a very long way to tell you this, Frey. They took those girls through the portal to Clava and then sailed here. They wanted you to know."

"Why now?"

He shrugged. "Likely they didn't know before. Their girls are only six. They change so much in the early years."

"They look so much like our girls," I whispered. "So much like Kat ... and me."

"They took a chance coming here. What if they are your children, and you wanted them back?"

"No. Even if they are, I could never do that to a child. Take them away from the only parents they have ever known."

I lay there, my mind racing, unable to think clearly, unable to slow the random thoughts galloping through my mind. Like a whirlpool, I felt giddy, unable to slow the world down. Desperate for the thoughts to stop, I pulled Cam's face to me in the dark and kissed him, insistently. Forcefully, I pushed his shoulders down, straddled him, and stripped off the old thin gray t-shirt of his I used as night wear, dropping it off the side of the bed. He pulled back to look at me, confusion furrowing his dark brows in the dim moonlight.

"Now?"

"Now!" I demanded, my lips crushing his. I needed this. To not think. To let my body take over and silence my chattering mind.

Cam was warm and powerful. Cradling my face between his large, roughened hands, he kissed me with so much tenderness that I bit his lip out of frustration. I didn't want gentle. I wanted to be driven, to be oblivious to my pain, just for a short time. I didn't want to make love; I wanted him to take me. Responding to my provocation, he wiped the drop of blood from his lip, and with a gleam in his eye, deftly flipped me onto the opposite side of the bed. Gripping both of my hands firmly in one of his own, he used his weight to pin me to the bed, his hips forcefully crushing mine, and stretched my arms above my head to hold them against the bedhead. I writhed violently, kicking and squirming, and he held me there, firmer. His muscular legs atop mine kept me still. He knew what I needed. To feel alive. To focus on the physical so I could stop my thoughts from tormenting me, even just for a short time. I gasped as he filled me, not caring who could hear me. Forcing myself against him, I wanted him to take control of me—body, and mind. Focused on him, I finally stopped thinking. He pushed me to the brink until I could bear it no more. He released my hands as the familiar warmth flooded me, and I wrapped my arms around him as I moaned. Holding him tight, he joined me, quivering as the waves surged through him.

"I love you," I whispered as I tumbled into unconsciousness, still safely entangled in his arms.

"Not as much as I love you."

CHAPTER 3

BREAKFAST CONVERSATION WAS MONOSYLLABIC and communicated chiefly in grunts and gestures. Unable to look at the children, too nauseous to eat, I gazed into the swirling depths of my cup. Cam bustled around making toast, but even his attempts at conversation were stilted.

"I'm so sorry," Bridget said. "We always knew this would be difficult."

I sniffed, indicating I had heard, but wasn't prepared to engage, especially not with the children here. They were abnormally quiet. Normally they were raucous and silly, constantly needing to be reminded to eat with cutlery, not to be rude to each other. But today, they sensed something was wrong and stalled, making Cam sweep them out the door to school.

"Like you, we always knew we were chosen. Part of that was for our skills, but the other part was to help repopulate the earth. We genuinely thought we were doing the right thing," Bridget said as soon as Cam had closed the door.

"Forcing people to have children? How is that the right thing?" I demanded, jerked out of my trance. Even with a little sleep, I was in no mood to be sympathetic. Cam had told me as I dressed that upon hearing of their arrival the previous day and me taking flight, our close friend and neighbor Isla had screamed and locked herself in her house, terrified of the thought of being forced to have more children. With four of her own, the idea of being forced to mate with a selected partner was repugnant on many levels.

"We knew we were chosen for our genome," Jorja explained. "All of us. I knew my job was to help couples have children, especially same-sex couples like us. I didn't know about the selected pairs, I promise you. That is beyond anything I knew. That made me sick, but what could I do? We had two babies of our own by then. We were expected to work, and we needed the support, so they neatly trapped us."

"Well, *we* didn't even know about the genome selection part, so you knew far more than us."

Jorja nodded grimly. "But we had no idea why. Truly. Mapping genomes and ensuring that all healthy genotypes survived makes sense. You are a scientist. Surely you can see that. Ensuring that we maintain the healthiest samples of the most diverse gene pool to secure the best chance for future generations is critical. Plants and livestock too. Didn't you wonder why the communities are so diverse? People from all nationalities and cultures? When you think that only a few thousand people survived, it was critically important to choose the best samples possible."

"All the communities are very multicultural," I admitted, thinking of Di's Chinese ancestry, Isla's

Indian mother, and even Jacinda's Maori heritage. "I can see that."

"That is what we thought my role was—to ensure that each genome survived. Logically, that was through having children. As a fertility specialist, I thought they chose me to help people who couldn't conceive. Sometimes mixed-race couples struggle to conceive naturally, or the rhesus factor can be an issue."

"Rhesus factor?" Cam asked.

"You know how you are told you are positive or negative with your blood type?"

Cam nodded.

"That is the rhesus factor. It is a protein found on the red blood cells; you either have it, or you don't. It can cause issues if a rhesus-negative mother carries a rhesus-positive child. It can be fatal for the child. There are also some blood type incompatibilities. They can be treated if caught early."

"These women you treated as part of the program— were they all artificially inseminated?" I asked, feeling nauseous. The toast I was nibbling on was doing little to ease my gurgling stomach.

"No. They were all given the choice of conceiving naturally first."

"Shagging a stranger, even though they were in a relationship with someone else?" Cam supplied helpfully.

"Well, yes. You could put it that way. Natural conception is a far better option. IVF works, but it involves a lot of synthetic drugs and is very time and labor-intensive. It also isn't great for your body long term. We can time ovulation fairly precisely, so for most pairs, it only took the one time."

"And that is where the drugging people part was helpful?" Cam asked.

Jorja's eyes dropped. Bridget looked away.

"We didn't know about that either, I swear," Jorja said.

"We worked it out after we left Clava," I replied, unable to keep the animosity from my voice. "We both felt sick for days, then it wore off."

"They were feeding it to us, too. Again, we didn't know. Honestly, we ate what you ate, remember? They didn't treat us any differently," Bridget added, placing a protective hand on Jorja's leg.

"Well, I hope they gave the conceiving couples some privacy," I sniped. "Or did they observe that, too?"

Bridget grinned unexpectedly. "No. That part was very discreet. Dark rooms and lots of privacy. Often even the love partner didn't know who the other person was. It was better that way."

"I have to ask—how were the pairs chosen?"

"I had no part in that. The geneticists made that decision. My role was to help them conceive, quickly, and with minimal intervention when they brought them to me. If we could impregnate a woman and send her back to her own life and just monitor the pregnancy, that was the best outcome."

"Best for whom?" I muttered under my breath, but Jorja ignored my barb.

"All we knew was the pairs were not in the same community. Many were in the partnered, antipodal community, though. They didn't want love matches to cause issues in the production of breeding selected children."

"That makes sense," I admitted reluctantly. "After all, if they forced me to have a child with someone, I would prefer not to see him every day when I went to get bread."

"Do you know who the partners were for each of us?" Cam asked.

"No. That was top secret, well beyond my clearance level. However, Bridget found notes that they deliberately separated people who had hit it off during the testing phase. They noticed you and Callie got along, so they sent you to different communities."

"Why would they do that?" Cam asked. "Were we supposed to be a pair?"

"Unlikely. It was just that they thought if you started as a couple, then you wouldn't take the time to become part of the community. You would be focused on each other and not on establishing networks and friendships."

"That makes sense," Cam admitted. "Although I never felt about Cal that way, or she about me. We are friends, nothing more."

"How would you know that about Cam?" I quizzed, my mind whirring.

"We were given copies of your files when you stayed with us. They wanted us to know a little about you. Our job was to befriend you, get you to stay."

"I see." I could see—with crystal clarity. We had been set up the moment we stepped foot on Clava.

"And you? What was your role?" I asked Bridget, boring holes into her face, making her squirm as she squeezed the curvature of her cup.

"Initially, it was to communicate with the off-shore communities. Provide enough carefully curated information to keep everyone calm and want to make their new life a success. Give them enough information about the world they had left without inciting panic. But I knew there would be a greater role to play when they activated the antipodes, and people could travel through the Nexus."

"Convince people to be unfaithful?"

"Look, I get it," Bridget snapped back, slamming her cup onto the table. "It is repugnant no matter how you look at it. But as I keep saying, I didn't know when we met you on Clava. Neither of us did. We just thought they had chosen us to help ensure that we all survived. The details we didn't learn until after we had the girls—when they knew we couldn't go anywhere."

I felt my face flush, guilty for provoking her.

"What do we do now?" I asked, allowing my voice to soften. "You are here with the girls. They let you go."

"Not exactly. We asked for another secondment to Clava and waited over a year for it to be approved. Settled in, started work. Did nothing to attract attention. Then we escaped late one night, using one of the electric cars. We took a boat from Inverness and made our way here. They could see us by satellite, but we kept moving and hoped they wouldn't follow."

"We have seen no sign of anyone in pursuit," Cam told them. "Illy checked."

"Can we try to access their systems?" I asked Bridget.

"I have some idea," she admitted. "They likely changed protocols after we absconded, but I have some clues. The patterns and such. I set them up."

"Illy can help, too. I'm sure Tadhg would assist if needed," Cam said, looking at me, worry lines etched in his face.

"I need to know," I replied, looking at him and ignoring our guests. "Do they have *her,* or did they just plunder her for her genetic material and leave her to die?"

"I don't know," Jorja said. "But likewise, I need to ask. These girls are likely your blood. Your nieces, if not your daughters. What role do you want to play in their lives? Do you want us to leave? Do you ... want ... *them*?"

I had given that matter a lot of thought as I had sat beside the loch. Louis was not my biological child, but he was my son. Kendra was Cam's biological daughter, but she wasn't his child.

"I would like to see them grow up," I intoned, enunciating each word, "in a loving, stable home. But they are not mine. That home is with you. If you choose to stay here, and I can see them sometimes, that would be okay. One day, when they are old enough, I want them to know all of it. My sister, where they came from. But you are their family, the only parents they have ever known. I could never take them from you. And no. I don't want you to leave."

Relief washed over both of their faces as they both slumped in their chairs, the release softening their features.

"Let's see about finding you somewhere of your own to live," Cam suggested kindly.

CHAPTER 4

"YOU CAN'T POSSIBLY WANT to leave the girls," I sputtered incredulously upon hearing their announcement. "They are so young, and we will be gone for months. Ocean travel is the only way. There is no way we can travel via one of the antipodes without them knowing of it."

Luca, around his daughters, was a teddy bear. I had watched the hulking, military-hardened man of six feet, six inches take down several men single-handedly when we were traveling to new communities. A formidable opponent, yet around his children, he turned into mush. Those girls batted an eyelid, and they had him—hook, line, sinker. Cam and I had watched as they had ridden him like a pony, served him mud-cake at a make-believe tea party, plaited his hair, and dressed him up with scarves and ribbons. He was putty in their rather manipulative hands, and he knew it.

Illy was the bad cop. Despite being tiny in stature, she had a booming, commanding voice. She was the parent who disciplined them, put them to bed, and made them brush their teeth and eat their vegetables. We would regularly see her raise her eyebrows at Luca across the table, expecting him to co-parent when one girl did or said something inappropriate. Instead, he would drop his chin and dissolve, unable to tell them off. Allison, known to all as Ally, was the ringleader. Small, like her mother, and intelligent well beyond her years, she was cheeky and conniving but with such a mesmerizing smile that no one could stay angry with her for long. Summer was the muscle, taller and more solid in build, and the one who often got caught, even though it was evident that Ally had put her up to it.

"They are six," Illy responded curtly. "They will be fine. Thorsten is even younger. You are leaving yours. Why is it any different?"

"I know, but this is my sister. I need to go. You don't."

"We do." Illy was resolute. "You are the family we chose. Family are the people who love you, even when you don't love yourself. We do this together."

The sense of relief washed through me as I leaned over to hug her, my muscles softening. This would be much easier with Luca and Illy along, especially as Illy had lived on Auckland Island for the first few years. She was familiar with the layout and operations, which would be invaluable.

"Thank you," I whispered, fighting back the tears. "This means more to me than I can say."

Since we had deactivated the antipodal point on Lewis, Illy had steadily become the sister I had lost. My best friend and confidante. The person I trusted most, aside from Cam. We shared our laughter, tears, and dreams. If I needed to bitch about someone and know it would never be repeated, Illy was my person.

After I had lost Katrin, I had never had a female friend. But I loved having someone on my side, who knew the real me and loved me, in spite of it.

"Our pleasure." Illy smiled at me. "Now, I estimate Auckland Island to be about 15,000 nautical miles from here. How fast can the *Eurydice* go?"

"Not fast enough." Mentally calculating the distance and speed, I said, "If we took a larger vessel from Edinburgh and could run it at thirty knots, we could probably do it in around three weeks."

"Yes, but we know from experience we use about a liter an hour at that speed. We would need to stop and refuel a hell of a lot," Luca said. "Even a few years ago, the places we could access clean fuel were becoming limited. We need to plan this carefully, know how fast we can run her. Stop at larger ports that likely still have reasonable stores."

"We do," I said. "We will need to run her slower, which is more economical. In places, we can. But on a larger vessel, we can only travel around 1500 miles without refueling."

"What is the longest leg?" Cam asked. "Africa to Kerguelen, if I recall?"

"It is. But we can't stop at Kerguelen. They will alert Auckland that we are coming."

"From South Africa, or perhaps even Mauritius, surely our best bet is to head to Freo," Illy suggested.

"Free-oh?" The quizzical look on Luca's face was priceless.

Illy laughed in her charming, lilting manner. As one of the few non-Australians in Roseglen, Luca still struggled with Aussie slang. Di especially loved to tease him with colloquialisms and Aussie rhyming slang, which she would drop randomly in the middle of a conversation just to gauge his reaction.

"Fremantle," she spelled out with a cheeky grin. "A large port near Perth on the West Australian coast. And one with yachts, I believe."

"There is a large yacht club in Fremantle," I confirmed. "Several, actually. I've been there for sailing competitions and regattas. We should be able to get fuel. Also, any spare parts we might need. It is an excellent choice."

"Can we get from Africa to Fremantle on one tank?" Luca asked.

"We would need to travel slowly across the Indian Ocean," I mused. "But I don't see we have a choice. There isn't much in-between. Nowhere where we can refuel. Not without being seen."

"Don't we have an even bigger problem?" Cam asked. "They will see us coming. Weeks before we get there, they will know we are on our way. It isn't like there are fleets of vessels out there anymore. They will soon spot us."

"I'm onto that," Illy replied with a grin. "I sent a coded message to Tadhg, and I am waiting for his response. Between us, I am fairly sure he can either cloak us or position their satellites so they won't see us coming."

"How will you do that across the Indian Ocean?" I asked Illy, amazed.

"Not us. Tadhg. If he tracks us either with a beacon or one of the satellites he controls, then he can ensure that their satellite misses us in their sweep. It won't be hard. Just think—one boat in the enormous Indian Ocean is a microscopic speck. Unless they know we are coming, they are unlikely to spot us. Think of those passenger planes that went down in the ocean in our lifetime. They were impossible to find. They shouldn't see us if we are careful and avoid communities that might alert them to our movements. The bigger issue is getting home, especially if they know we have visited. But again, Tadhg has offered to help in any way he can."

Cam nodded. "Thank goodness for Tadhg."

"Do they use drones?"

"They do, but only when looking for something in particular. Drone range is also limited, most under ten kilometers."

"Sunny, what about a more basic camouflage?" Luca said, looking at Illy thoughtfully.

"What are you thinking?"

"Painting the upper surfaces of the boat blue, so it isn't as visible from the sky."

"That makes sense," Cam admitted. "Kind of like those houses in Switzerland with grass roofs. Bombers couldn't see them from the sky as they blend in with the landscape. If we paint the vessel blue, it will mostly blend."

"That is an enormous bloody job," I replied in disbelief. "And a lot of paint."

"Let's get some helpers then. There are paint stores in Stornoway. If it was stored properly, there is no reason it isn't still usable. Besides, we only need to paint the top deck."

Part of me was horrified. It was vandalism to splash paint over a multi-million-dollar vessel. But equally, I was pleased to think that it might afford us a little protection from the spying eyes of Clava and Auckland. Making a silent promise to return the *Eurydice* to her former pristine white state upon return, I followed Cam to the sheds.

CHAPTER 5

SORCHA STOPPED ME WITH a wary look as I headed home the next day after hours of supervising painting crews and loading the *Eurydice*. Luca had suggested that an uneven job was actually better than a perfect paint job as it would blend in with the moving waves better. Probably just as well. Most people were slapping it on, and there was quite the party with music and free-flowing beer.

"Illy told me about your mission. Do you want us to look after the kids?"

"That would be wonderful." I had wondered how I was going to ask them to care for our four. Popping over after dinner one night and dropping that bombshell wasn't exactly ideal. Cam and I hadn't left Lewis since we last went to Newgrange. After our return, I had vowed never to leave again. But last time we only had Louis and Katrin. Now we had Xanthe and little Thorsten too.

"But between our four and Illy's girls, how will you cope?"

Sorcha grimaced at the thought of six additional children. "We will probably split them between our place and Fraser's. Isla takes no nonsense. I can't see that Jacinda would cope with Illy's monsters, and yours would be happier with us."

As a mother of four, Isla had the control of a seasoned regimental sergeant major. Sorcha also tolerated no foolishness from the children. In many ways, I felt she would have been a better candidate for the military than Illy. But Jacinda's children, Aroha, Kara, and Rangi, were quiet, compliant children. Nothing at all like Kat, Ally, and Summer. Jacinda would never cope with needing to yell to have instructions acknowledged and the constant battle to get them to do anything without an argument.

"Freyja, I have something I need to ask," Sorcha spoke haltingly, making me look up at her from where I was connecting the bike to the charging port in the shed.

"Anything," I said and meant it. We could only make the journey to find out the fate of my sister because of Cam's. If we had any doubt that Sorcha and Di would care for our family, this trip wouldn't be possible.

Sorcha looked at me, assessing something. I closed the shed door and turned to her.

"What is it?"

"If you find the lab," she said, her usually powerful voice dropping to a whisper, "and there is a sample there labeled Tomori Hajime, and you have a way to carry it... can... can you bring it back?"

I furrowed my brows in confusion. It took me a moment to realize what she was saying.

"Tom? Sam's dad?" I asked softly. I had never heard his full name.

She nodded gravely.

"Destroy it or bring it back?"

Sorcha tossed her long red plait dismissively.

"Di and I have spoken at length, and we feel that if there is a possibility that we can give Sam a full brother or sister, then we should at least try," she said, so quietly I couldn't believe it was Sorcha speaking. "But transporting cryo-preserved samples is not that straightforward, so you may find that you can't."

"Done."

"Who knows?" A wry smile crossed her face. "In your absence, we may decide that it isn't what we want to do. I'm not getting any younger. But I don't want the option taken away—if you know what I mean. If there isn't a sample, or it doesn't work, then at least I will know for certain. But I can't live knowing that I had the chance and did nothing. Tom was a good man, and he was a wonderful father. I owe him this."

"I understand. I will do everything I can for you."

"Maybe there is something I can do for you," Sorcha continued.

I looked at her quizzically. "Besides caring for six additional children for several months?"

"We would always have done that. We will curse you and complain, but we would always support you. You know that. What I mean is … if she is there … your sister. I can give you something … to end it. Quickly and painlessly."

Struggling to keep control of my face, I froze. I hadn't thought that far ahead. I was still hoping that they had taken a sample from her in Melbourne, and she had died all those years ago. But I recognized the logic in what Sorcha was saying.

Sorcha was studying me in that cool, assessing manner of hers.

I nodded grimly. "I would like that."

"Consider it done."

CHAPTER 6

"SIT," ILLY ORDERED, STARTLING me. From the serious look, I suspected where this was going.

"We need to tell you what we learned. Thanks to Bridget's intel and Tadhg's skills, we hacked their servers again, and we are reasonably sure we know where she is," Luca said after checking that we were alone and none of the children had crept back inside.

"Kat? Where?"

"There is a facility at the edge of the settlement. A laboratory, I guess you could call it. But inside, there are twenty-five patients."

"Patients?" I questioned, trying to keep my voice low, despite my heart pounding so loudly I thought it would burst from my chest.

"Specimens is how they are described," Illy corrected. "Katrin is listed as number seventeen. We don't know for sure it is her or just what they took from her. The labeling is sufficiently vague. But you need to be prepared, Frey. The terminology in the records, combined with the small number of staff we can see rostered to the facility around the clock, indicates it is likely to be actual people."

I lifted my chin, feigning confidence. "Are you sure? We can't exactly go roaming around in the dark, checking every building. Jorja says that Auckland has a significant settlement. Clava did."

"Auckland is not dissimilar to Clava. But I spoke with Nasir and Magali today using the COFDM so that we couldn't be overheard. They remember this building too. It is at the far edge of the township in the medical zone. As you may have recalled from Clava, all the medical buildings are together, the educational buildings co-located, and so on. But none of us ever went inside this particular building, nor were we told what it contained. We all asked, of course, but were told top secret or some bullshit. I'm fairly sure I was told storage facility when I asked. It is the only building that none of us have seen inside, even doctors like Magali and Nasir. They are hiding something significant there."

"What about Jorja?" I asked softly. "Has she been inside?"

"I didn't ask," Illy said. "We can't trust anything she tells us. I didn't know either of them well when we lived there. She has no loyalty to me. Don't be fooled into thinking she is telling you everything."

Cam and I had liked Jorja and Bridget when we stayed with them at Clava. But now... We accepted a lot of events that had occurred were beyond their control, but we still weren't entirely sure of their allegiances. They had come here to tell us about their girls and the other children of the same egg donor. But could we trust them? If Illy didn't, and she was a very astute judge of character, then we would be well advised to follow suit.

We spent the next week preparing for our departure. We were quite open about what we had learned, and everyone we spoke to was shocked to hear that there were back-up genomes. While they had known of the isolated communities in Australia since Cam went to get Sorcha, many questioned if samples were taken while they were unconscious during the testing phase. Sorcha, Di, Cam, and I were all processed in Melbourne, but we had no way of knowing if the Edinburgh-processed residents had also had genetic samples taken.

Luca, Isla, and Fraser described their testing as similar, including waking from the full-body scan, Isla with the same cramping as me. Before being offered her role, Illy had undergone far more invasive testing but with consent.

Lewis residents treated Jorja and Bridget cautiously. They were strangers and had appeared in the middle of the night with children who bore an uncanny resemblance to my own, although we had said nothing about their parentage to anyone outside of Roseglen. No matter how it appeared—that they were here with good intentions—we had thought the same of Angus once. Cam and I spoke at length about what to tell the children, but in the end, we told them a sanitized version of the truth. They were all under ten, and we didn't want to scare them, but there was no other logical explanation for why we would be away for so many weeks. Louis, understandably, was distraught but held it together for his siblings, although Cam and I worried about the anxiety simmering beneath. Knowing his mother had gone *out there* and never returned was a terrible burden for a young child.

Jorja and Bridget temporarily moved in with Aidan while Cam arranged for an old farmhouse to be renovated for them at the end of our valley, a few kilometers from our own. Isla still would not speak to them, although Di, Fraser, Jamie, and Jacinda were pleasant enough. *In time...* I thought. *She will come around.* The vehemence of Isla's reaction had surprised me. While she had four children and was adamant that she would have no more, she hadn't relaxed at all since they had arrived. I had tried to talk to her, but she had clammed up, refusing to speak about them.

"I'm worried about Isla," I confided in Cam as we cleaned up after dinner, the children all in bed. "She won't leave the house. She is so scared of Bridget and Jorja."

Cam shrugged before responding. "Can you blame her? I suspect it is the combination of being kidnapped herself to be a slave combined with what she thinks may have happened to your sister that terrifies her. She has been scared since Illy told us about the selective breeding program. Now here they are ... with those girls as proof."

Returning from Mousa with the rescued women, my concerns at that time had been for Cam, dangerously ill and grieving for his wife, and then for myself, learning I was pregnant. I hadn't known Isla then.

"Was she traumatized about what happened?"

"I can't believe you are even asking that. She had the three girls then. She spent those days on their boat, petrified, believing she would never see any of them again, knowing precisely what they would do to her when they reached Mousa. Watching her best friend be murdered and knowing they wouldn't hesitate to do that to her. Then Jorja arrives, and she learns they may be keeping your sister captive for equally repulsive reasons. It isn't a stretch."

Isla was competent and sharp. Strong-willed and highly intelligent. I had rarely seen her vulnerable side. But having been held captive myself, with a young child, I understood.

"I'll speak to her tomorrow," I promised as I turned out the light, and we padded down the hall. "Not that it will do any good."

"It will." Cam turned to face me. "Just knowing that you struggled with the same emotions after being held captive at the farm. She adores you."

"What?" I asked incredulously. "No, she doesn't!"

"And you tell me I am blind." Cam yawned. "Can you not see that she would do anything for you?"

Unsure how to start the conversation with Isla the next day as we wormed sheep, I muttered, "I am so sorry to be leaving you with all the work and our kids."

She glanced up at me, her mouth opening slightly.

"What if they have her?" I asked, letting the fear creep into my voice as I turned to reach in my bag and avoid eye contact. "I keep seeing her lying there. Even after all these years, I still get flashbacks of being tied up myself in that filthy shed, helpless, with a baby at home, and knowing what they wanted to do to me. Well, the sexual stuff. I had no idea about the cannibalism at that point."

Isla exhaled audibly through pursed lips.

"It took me years to stop having nightmares," I confessed and saw the fear darken her beautiful, tanned face. "That absolute terror of being restrained and knowing I had a baby at home depending on me."

"Me, too," she admitted, tears filling her soulful brown eyes. "Why have we never had this conversation before?"

"I am sorry, Isles. I should have checked in. On all of you."

"I don't think I have ever thanked you enough for what you did. I know you feel awful that you couldn't save … Laetitia." She faltered on the name. "But you saved the rest of us. Cam, too. He would never have survived that time if it wasn't for you."

Waiting for me to give the signal, Isla released the sheep and grabbed the next one.

"Can I ask something?" she asked softly, her glossy black hair falling forward and obscuring her face momentarily.

"Anything."

"Katrin is his child, isn't she?"

"She is."

Isla nodded knowingly as I administered the dose.

"It is complicated…" I started to say, lest she think ill of me, but she cut me off.

"There is no judgment from us. We thought Cam and Laetitia were made for each other. They were so happy…"

My heart lurched as she spoke, a lump of vomit coming into my mouth, and I needed to turn away.

"…until we saw him with you. Fraser and I have spoken about it many times. Cam loved Laetitia. You know that. But he is whole because of you. He worships you, and together you are a formidable team. You challenge him, bring out the best in him. It is you that makes him the man he is. We can see why he chose you."

"Thank you," I whispered.

"The way you love Louis," she continued, flicking back her hair and looking directly into my eyes. "We worried about that initially, especially after you had Katrin. But you just accepted him and treated him like one of your own."

"He is mine," I confessed. "He is one of my own heart. I know I didn't give birth to him. But Cam and I wanted children all those years ago when we lived on August. We were torn away from each other. But Louis has always been mine."

"I can see that. Well..." she slapped the sheep on the rump, and it ran off bleating, "we will happily share the load until you get back."

"Can I push the friendship and ask that you feed Jam?" Although they had a cat of their own now, one of Jam's kittens from a few years ago, Isla was always willing to feed our beautiful girl.

"Of course. She will be the easier one. Did you hear we are caring for Ally and Summer? You might need to bring back a stash of Prozac!"

"Thank you. It means so much to me that I can do this, knowing my family is taken care of."

"Frey, I still have a family because of you. They still have me. I would do anything for you."

As we kissed the children goodnight, they stalled terribly, knowing it was our last night. Louis was stoic. It wasn't the first time we had left him, although he barely remembered the last time. Being strong-willed and determined, Katrin jutted her chin out and promised to watch the younger two and not let Xanthe bring random animals into the house. She would relish the role of surrogate parent. Thorsten didn't understand what was going on, but sensing his siblings' change in demeanor, he took longer to fall asleep than usual. It was Xanthe who cried until I thought her heart would break. I lay beside her in her tiny bed, stroking her hair, talking to her, reassuring her until she finally wore herself out. Slipping out of bed and closing the door as softly as I could, it was late when I closed the door to our room.

As soon as I entered, I sensed something was up.

I watched him pacing as I slipped out of my clothes and prepared to pull on the old t-shirt I wore to bed.

"What is it?"

He reached out his hand and took the top away. I couldn't read the dark look on his face as he backed away from me. I stood at the side of the bed, naked.

"Is something wrong?"

He was somber. Something was eating at him as he started pacing again. Cam had Asperger's syndrome and struggled to read emotion. It took him more time than most people to process his conflicts and communicate what he was thinking.

Making a split-second decision and vaulting over the bed, I was at his side in a shot.

Anxiety had taken over. I could see it. But he couldn't form the words from the maelstrom in his mind. Jerky in his movements, he couldn't maintain eye contact or communicate his thoughts.

Dropping to my knees in front of him, I forgot my kneecap still hurt when I kneeled on it. Too late now.

Running my lips and tongue up the insides of his leg, I felt him quiver and gasp. His hands came down to rest on the top of my head as I forced him to take his mind off his troubles. A soft moan escaped his mouth, and I doubled my efforts. His strong arms lifted me and spun me around, finding my mouth as he pinned me to the wall.

As we lay on the floor, covered in our doona and cushioned by pillows, he whispered, "You know, we are about to spend months on a boat. We should probably sleep in the bed."

"I don't care where I am as long as I am with you. We have slept in caves, in dead forests soaked in our own blood, and on yachts. Even on hideous hospital beds beside each other. No matter where you are, I feel safe."

"I needed that."

"I know. But why?"

Cam exhaled like a deflating tire as he sought the words. "I hate goodbyes. They never used to bother me. I used to want to get away from people, from events, and return home. But now, after losing you, after Laetitia, leaving my parents, and what happened to us in Inverness ... I am always fearful of what could happen. Saying goodbye to the kids tonight and watching them so distressed ... I am scared I will never see them again. That something will happen to you ... to us. I'm not sure how many more people I can lose."

"We will be fine. They will be fine. We are doing it together this time," I soothed as I massaged the tension from his shoulders. "I won't leave you again."

"Promise me?"

"I promise."

CHAPTER 7

"**I CAN'T BELIEVE I** have never noticed that you still wear a wristwatch!" Cam teased as Luca reached for his water bottle. "Didn't the battery die years ago? Mine snuffed it when I lived on August. I still wore it out of habit for a while, but I have no idea where it ended up."

I saw the flash of pain in Luca's eyes before he responded. Illy placed a hand on his arm. She had seen it, too.

"Before I left for my first international deployment, my mum bought me this watch. It is nothing flash. But it was far too expensive for her to afford. I suspect she went without food to pay for it. She said she wanted me to have a little piece of her. She knew I couldn't take much, but I could wear a watch even when in uniform. It was perfect. I would always wear it when I was on patrol. Just a touch through my jacket would remind me of her strapping it on my wrist. It stopped running years ago, and I keep it in a drawer, but I still put it on sometimes and think of her, just for a moment. It felt right, searching for Freyja's family, that I bring this token of my own."

"Your father?" Cam asked. Illy and I glanced at each other. We knew this story. After several weeks at sea together, we were comfortable enough with each other to ask almost anything, even family secrets.

Luca half-smiled but answered readily enough. "That knob? I don't know who he was. I mean, I know his name, of course. It is on my birth certificate. There were some photos, so I knew what he looked like. But I never knew him. He walked out on us when I was a few months old, and we never heard from him again. Went back to Italy, mum thinks. As I grew up, I made up all sorts of stories to fill the void—a war hero who died in battle. A god from another realm and had to return home to protect his world. A foreign diplomat who traveled all the time and did important work. Most of the kids at school had two parents, and I desperately wanted a father. Mum never spoke negatively of him, not once. She just said that we should all follow our own path in life, and he was following his. He was just a loser. The idea of caring for a child was too much, putting someone else's needs above his own. So, he bailed. My mother, though. She was my everything. It was just the two of us. She worked three jobs to care for me and provide me with opportunities. Pay for my schooling, my sports, camps, the enormous amount of food I ate. Never once did I feel like a burden. I changed my name from his, Alessio, to hers, Cadman, before I enlisted. He had never been part of my life, so I didn't want to wear his name on my uniform. See it every day. I bought her a brand-new car with my pay from my first international deployment. It was no Audi convertible," he flashed a cheeky look at me, "but new. It was the very first new car she had ever owned. I still remember the look on her face when I arrived at her flat and handed her the keys. Her eyes sparkled like diamonds. She used to sit in it, just to breathe in the new car smell. She was my world..." Luca stared off into space.

Illy touched his arm. "We named Ally after her," she said, although Cam and I already knew this. Allison after Luca's mother, and Summer, as Luca's nickname for Illy was Sunshine, often shortened to Sunny, which suited her personality perfectly.

"What happened to her?"

"When I was on my second deployment, she passed suddenly of a heart attack. Got up in the night and collapsed on the bathroom floor. With no one to help her, she died there. When she didn't show up for work, they sent someone around to check on her. She was never late. Rarely took a sick day. I never got to say goodbye. By the time I heard, her friends had already planned the funeral. We had very little family. My CO woke me in the middle of the night. I thought we were under attack, and I just about shattered his nose in the dark. He broke the news, then left. I was gutted. I was lying in my bivouac, feeling like my heart had been ripped out. It took me a long time to accept that she would have passed, whether I had been there or not. It was out of my control. But I wasn't there to say goodbye, and that was the part I couldn't deal with." Luca touched the face of his watch again and stared out the window.

The pain carved in Luca's face made my heart hurt, and I spoke to change the subject.

"For my father's fortieth birthday, my mum bought him a hideously expensive watch—a Breitling. I was about ten. I still remember the party at the yacht club, the jazz quartet playing in the far corner, looking glamorous, all wearing black. Adults were standing in small groups, talking, many out on the deck that overlooked the ocean. Men in black tie, women in beautifully colored dresses, swishing around elegantly. From where Kat and I sat, on chairs at the far wall, watching everyone, it looked like a rainbow had exploded and the room filled with color interspersed with black. Fairy lights hanging from the roof. Servers were flitting around, looking like penguins, serving food from silver platters around the room, but ignoring us. One server made sure she brought us food as she made her rounds, but the rest acted like we weren't even there. What I remember most, and vividly, even now, was dad showing it off, proudly— the light sparkling on the glass. The look on his face was one I had never seen before. He was beaming at my mother. He was *happy*. He didn't look at her like that. Never looked at Kat or me like that. My parents rarely showed emotion—and absolutely never in public. To show emotion was poor form. Everyone gushed over it, and I remember thinking that it must be important to give expensive gifts, so people knew you loved them. Maybe that was why he had never looked at me that way. I didn't have money to buy him something to make him proud. All the art projects I made at school and gave him. He smiled, but it never reached his eyes. I never saw them displayed or on his desk. Not like that watch, which he wore daily. It took until I met Cam on August to realize that the value doesn't matter. It is the thought behind it."

"How expensive is expensive?" Illy asked curiously.

"Oh, around twenty-five thousand dollars Australian. I overheard mum telling people. Even as a child, I knew it was a lot. And I readily admit I didn't know the value of things back then."

"For a *watch*?" Cam was incredulous. "That is more than my first car!"

It was Luca who responded. "Luxury goods have ridiculous price tags. It is a whole other world. They are of exceptional quality, but ultimately, it is a status thing. I was planning to buy a Mont Blanc watch myself after my third deployment. Fortunately, I didn't make it that far."

"Well, we can likely find you one in Perth. There were luxury shops there," I noted.

"A flat one," Illy chipped in cheekily.

"No." He lifted Illy onto his lap and lay her back against his shoulder. "It took a pandemic for me to work out what is important. My Sunshine and my daughters. Possibly my coffee machine. I'm happy just to look at this one." He waved his left wrist in the air. "Just for old times' sake."

"My mum always made a fuss of my art projects," Cam said, smiling at me. "I remember a hideous clay coil pot I made in art in primary school. Fired, and painted yellow on the outside, bright blue on the inside. Badly painted, I should point out. Lopsided and wonky, but she kept it on her desk and stored pens in it. By my teen years, I begged her to throw it out. It was embarrassing. She refused. Said she loved it."

"My parents did the same," Illy said. "Dad ran a cord with pegs on it along a hallway in our house. Mum would pin up my artwork from school and only take it down when the whole thing sagged or was coated in dust. I made a painted plate one year. Mum used it as a spoon rest in the kitchen. The painting on it was so bad I could barely tell what it was. One of our cats, apparently. But mum used it every day. I packed it in my storage unit when they passed. She loved it, and I couldn't bear to throw it away."

"Goodness, my parents always looked like I was handing them a gift-wrapped cat turd when I produced my school artwork," I said, making them all laugh uproariously. "By late primary school, I just ditched it on the way home so I wouldn't need to go through the rigmarole of them pretending to like it. Kat kept trying to impress them, though. Paintings, craft projects, Mother's and Father's Day gifts. It was almost a game in the end, trying to get them to gush over something you could tell they found cringeworthy."

"Oh, what about home economic classes?" Illy laughed. "I remember taking home a sunken, soggy apple tea cake and my parents telling me how delicious it was!"

Cam added, "Overcooked baked pretzels for me. Rock hard. They were awful, but my parents ate them anyway. I'm surprised no one chipped a tooth."

Luca, returning to the conversation, added, "We weren't quite so posh. It was just called Cooking at my school. Most of ours was learning how to cook a basic meal, and we ate them at school. Lots of vegetables, I recall. But the paper-thin chocolate chip biscuits I still remember. I misread the recipe and put in a cup of butter instead of half a cup, so they spread in a single thin layer across the tray. I failed, but mum still ate them."

"I served my mum undercooked merengues once," I confessed. "I had spent too much time chatting and didn't give them enough time to cook. Because we had to finish up and clean the kitchen before we left for our next class, I had no choice."

"What did she do?" Cam asked.

"Took one bite, and it stuck to her teeth. She tried to maintain a smile and placed the rest on the plate, telling me she would save it for later."

"Binned?" Luca guessed.

"Definitely. Mum rarely ate sugar, anyway. Sugar was the devil in my house."

"Really?" Illy asked. "I loved baking with my mum on weekends. We often made cupcakes or something for me to include in my school lunch. For every special event, we would bake a cake. It was our time. Something we did together."

"You know, we should introduce Mother's Day and Father's Day," Luca announced. "I'd love to see what our kids come up with."

"Well, at least there are no kilns, so no crappy clay pots," Cam breezed. "I'm safe."

"Oh, I might have a chat with Di and see if she can think of something creative," I twinkled at him. "Then we will all watch your face as your darling children hand it to you."

"I will love it, regardless."

The funny part was, he would. Every drawing or painting our children brought home from school, Cam loved. He made a point of looking carefully at everything they handed him, considering it like it was valuable art, framed and hung in a gallery. He would always ask about some aspect of it, even when I could tell that he had no clue what it was. The child would always leave feeling proud, valued. I wished I had that skill. I always seemed to ask the wrong question, and the relevant child would respond indignantly, horrified that I couldn't identify the blob. But Cam had a knack of knowing what to say and the proper accolades. *What are our children up to now?* Glancing out the window, I saw it was mid-afternoon. It was night in Scotland, and they were likely asleep at Sorcha's house. Closing my eyes, I could picture them asleep, looking angelic. Seeing them sleeping triggered the memory of the last time I had seen Katrin, unconscious, lying in a sterile bed with white sheets, surrounded by machines, catheters, and colostomy bags. The muffled noises of the facility she called home. Nurses, patients, and visitors clattering outside her room on the slippery gray lino floors.

As the others teased each other about school art projects and home economics classes, I slipped out of the room to the bathroom. But instead of returning, I made my way up to the freshly painted blue deck. Pulling out one of the white timber deckchairs, I dragged it to the railed edge and gazed out to sea. Images of my children, my sister and my parents flickered in and out like an old movie. Stagnant images, joined together, but fragmented.

"You okay?"

Jolting out of my trance, I glanced up to see Illy studying me, her nose wrinkled in concern.

"Shitting myself," I confessed, trying to maintain a cool façade.

"What are you scared of?" Illy asked as she dragged another deckchair alongside me. The aquamarine ocean before us was blissfully calm, only the occasional white cap visible on the surface as we glided peacefully. I could hear Luca and Cam laughing raucously in the living room.

"Everything. Being seen before we even get there. Finding the building but not being able to get in. Guards. Finding her there. Not finding her. Honestly, all of it."

I saw Illy's head nod in my peripheral vision as we both continued to stare across the vast blue expanse, contemplating the magnitude of what we were embarking upon.

"Well, let's tackle those one at a time. First, Tadhg and Jake are monitoring around the clock from Ireland. Auckland has no reason to think we are heading their way, and as Tadhg rightly pointed out, we are a camouflaged thirty-five-meter-long yacht in millions of square kilometers of ocean. Even if they knew we were coming, the chances of them seeing us are minuscule. It is like looking for a grain of sand at the beach. Next, I know the building. I haven't been inside, but I have seen it. I know exactly where it is, how to get there and away. And you may not know it, but Luca is a master at breaking and entering."

Grinning, I nodded. I had seen Luca's skill in action. Nothing got between the man and his goal. I had wondered more than once if he had set his sights on Illy and not the other way around.

"Guards we can take care of. Again, Luca has some experience with that, and he tells me you have some skills in that department, too. What this really comes down to is your sister. That is the unknown variable. We will get you there, get you inside. But there is no guarantee she is there or that she is alive. This isn't a rescue mission. It may well be that they just have her genetic material. My question is, does that make it easier for you?"

Shrugging, I stared out at the sunlight reflecting off the water, wishing I had brought my sunglasses with me as the occasional dazzling flash blinded me. *Would it make it easier to know she is already dead?*

"What is Auckland Island like?" I asked, partly to break the silence.

"Very similar to Clava," she admitted. "Everyone lives in a single village with paved streets and street lighting—lovely homes with picturesque gardens and flowers. Mine had tulips and daffodils, lots of calla lilies, in a range of colors, including a beautiful dark purple, almost black one. I used to love having fresh flowers in my kitchen. Homes are filled with all the modern conveniences that we no longer have. Modern shared facilities for engineering, science, and agriculture are built around the periphery: schools, hospitals, laboratories, offices, and large storage facilities. Small electric cars to get around. It is a community, to be sure. But it is cold and sterile at the same time."

I knew what she meant. Clava had been wonderful to visit, but after I left, I could see the disadvantages and why Illy had chosen to leave. Lack of privacy, being forced to undertake work you may ethically disagree with. No diversity. No crazy neighbor with the ramshackle house, overgrown garden, or bathtubs used as dubious art features in their front yard.

"Did you ever regret it?"

"Leaving, you mean? Not for a nanosecond. I felt ... free. When I lived on Auckland, we were still in the establishment phase—setting up hospitals, finishing the buildings, landscaping, and planting out the orchards and greenhouses. From a work perspective, we maintained communications with the communities, working toward a time when we could introduce them to each other. Foster support and trust. We all genuinely thought we were doing the right thing, saving people. That was our focus, our goal. And we were. Initially, I believed that all the settlements looked the same as ours, had the same resource allocation. It didn't take long for me to work out that was far from reality. We had better resources, equipment, facilities, and better-trained specialists. That never sat well with me, but I assumed, erroneously as it turns out, that those resources were limited. Thus, they were centralized and would be deployed to the communities when they were needed. I convinced myself that it made sense. After all, not every community needed an oncologist or a geological engineer. For only a few thousand people, one was enough and could be deployed when required. Then, in our third year, we heard about the massacres occurring on Gibraltar and Great Barrier Island near New Zealand. Everyone talked about it. I kept waiting for them to deploy a team to assist … but they didn't. I tried to raise it several times; I even volunteered to go. Great Barrier Island wasn't that far, and we had vessels, but they shut me down fairly abruptly. I was told, 'it wasn't my role to interfere.' That was when I questioned why we were even there. If we had the capacity to assist, and had been told that our role was to ensure the survival of humankind, then why weren't we helping?"

"What did you do?"

"Stopped questioning but started paying more attention. Became a nuisance, I guess. Then, when it was my turn to travel to Clava, I was thrilled. I thought it would be different there. Perhaps it was just Auckland that had an elitist feel. Besides, despite being born there, I had never been back to Scotland. I was only two when we left, so I don't remember it at all. My parents always wanted to, but they sold everything to emigrate. Airfares from Australia were prohibitively expensive, and they never had the opportunity to go back."

"And?"

"Within hours of arriving, I was in heaven. I loved the physical environment at Clava. Walking through the cairns was breathtaking. The climate, the mountains, the forests. That crisp mountain air that smells like pine needles. Even the snow-capped hills in the distance, outside the dome, of course. For the first few months, I was blissfully happy. But soon enough, I battled with the sense that we had been established as an elite—the ruling class. I told you before that my father was a fisherman before he left Orkney? My mother, a teacher? She taught in a tiny single-teacher school on Orkney with only a handful of children. Australia gave them opportunities and provided me with a wonderful life, but I never forgot where I came from. They were part of a tight-knit community, but they moved to Australia, gave up everything they knew to give me a better life, even if it meant going without luxuries themselves. Dad bought a coffee roasting business and worked long hours but built his reputation on being honest. He took the time to get to know all his customers, and they came back because of the relationships he forged. They were simple folk who never looked down on anyone. My parents always taught me to treat people with respect; you never knew someone's backstory, what challenges they had fought to overcome. They treated everyone with courtesy. Bus drivers, cleaners, people waiting tables. They were humble people."

"A world apart from my family."

"Ashton had accompanied me and a few others to Clava. He knew I was unhappy. I kept asking to visit my ancestral home, and finally, he relented. I guess he thought that a trip to Orkney would... I don't know... settle me? Make me realize how good I had it? So, they let me go. But what I found there was probably what I had subconsciously sought. A genuine community of people, much like what my parents had left in search of a better life. But what I learned on Orkney was that *they* had a better life. Families, friends who worked together. Shared the raising of children, meals, and the everyday mundane chores, even cleaning the communal toilets. Sure, they struggled. People got sick and occasionally died. It was dark and cold, and with nowhere near the level of comfort we had before, or the level of resourcing that the communities enjoyed on Clava and Auckland. I secretly resented that, yet it was blatantly clear that they were happy."

"So why didn't you stay?"

Illy paused. "Even on Orkney, I had doubts. About my purpose. I had been chosen to help all the communities, facilitate trade, assist negotiations when they came up. Comparatively few people had survived, less than ten thousand, and I couldn't do that from Orkney. So, I returned as I had promised."

"But it didn't last?"

"It didn't. After I had that exposure to my humble origins, I questioned what was important. It was a tough time; I will be honest. Ashton tried to set me up with half a dozen single men, gave me challenging and interesting projects. Programs that would help people in the future. But nothing could fill the void."

"They rolled out six different men on a silver platter, and you didn't like *any* of them?"

Illy rolled her eyes and looked across the ocean. "More, now I come to think about it. All lovely men. Interesting, intelligent. From a variety of backgrounds and with diverse skills. Any of them could have been an excellent match. One or two I really liked, had a lot in common with. But it was the *why* that I resented. I knew he deliberately wanted to hook me up with someone so I would stay. If I fell in love, I would be obligated to contribute to the community and have children. I pushed back. Then, I learned how some communities had been allocated better facilities and resources than others. I didn't know about the Nexus and the Collective back then, but I was suspicious and recognized that those resources that should have been provided at settlement were now a bargaining chip. Why give to some and not others? It irked me. Why would Clava have access to a reliable electricity grid and deny the outer islands the same resource? I didn't know what they planned to use as the trade-off, but I guessed it was something big. It went against my moral compass, so I left."

"Just like that?"

"Well, as I recall, Ashton sat me down in his living room with a cup of tea and some freshly baked short-bread and tried to reason with me. He asked about my concerns, and I told him. He tried to explain there was a greater purpose, that it needed to be done slowly. There was a plan. I told him I disagreed with the plan and that all people should be treated equally. He argued that all people were treated equally, all communities were established in the same way. I pointed out a long list of things that were inequitable. Then he got frustrated, which I admit I did nothing to alleviate. I may have goaded him a little. Finally, he lost his temper and, in a rather demeaning manner, towered over me, told me to, 'do your duty, and be a good little lady. For the sake of the project.' I came rather close to smashing his glasses. I threw my cup against the wall, told him where to shove his commission, went home, and packed."

"Luca warned us once never to call you little lady. But I didn't know the backstory! Oh, how I wish I had seen that!" When I had finished laughing, I asked, "Do you ever regret accepting the offer to come? The original offer, I mean."

"I did, in the early days. My parents had passed, but I had my cats. A small circle of friends. A career. But the world was going to perish. That was exceedingly obvious. I knew why they chose me—they made that very clear—but I still harbored feelings of guilt for all of those who didn't make it."

"You are very much like Cam in that way," I confessed. "He struggled for years with that. He suffered terribly from survivor guilt."

"He told me when he met me on Orkney. We had a lot in common back then. Mothers who migrated and worked as teachers. That mixed Scots-Australian upbringing."

I sensed the reticence as she said, "Did I ever tell you that for a short time, I considered a life with him?"

Tipping my head to the side to look at her and flinching as the sun struck my eyes, I grinned. "You don't need to feel guilty. He told me everything years ago. Besides, you are brave finally confessing you slept with my husband while we are on a yacht in the middle of the Indian Ocean. I'm significantly larger than you. I could throw you overboard with minimal effort."

"I wondered. But..."

"It is fine, really. I have always known about you and Cam. Though I wondered how long it would take you to tell me. Now that we are so close, I can see you would have made a wonderful couple. You have a lot in common. More than he and I, in many ways. I only hated you ... until you hooked up with Luca. Okay, maybe a little longer. But not much."

Illy snorted at that. "I don't blame you for hating me. But he only ever had eyes for you. Even when he married Laetitia, he still loved you. He just hadn't worked it out. He was so lost when I met him. He just needed for you to find him."

"Do you mean that?"

"Absolutely. Now, back to you. What are you worried about?"

"What if she *is* there?" I whispered, my voice shaking unexpectedly. "What if I can't end it for her? What if we get caught?"

Illy turned to me and held my hands in her dainty ones. I always felt so huge and clumsy beside her tiny form, like a giant smothering a fairy.

"Would you like to cast a caim?"

"A ky-em?" I repeated, confusion furrowing my brow.

"A caim is a circling prayer used by the ancient Celts. My father taught me when I was very young. For years I was bullied at school for being so tiny, having an accent, and using strange words, mostly colorful Gaelic swearing picked up from my father. Kids used to pick me up and put me in rubbish bins, drop me in bushes, and push me quite a lot. Pipsqueak was my nickname for many years. My father showed me this ritual for protection ... as well as enrolling me in karate classes." Illy grinned at the memory. "The word caim is Scots Gaelic. It means sanctuary or protection. It is derived from the root word meaning circle."

"How do you do it?"

"A caim is casting an invisible circle of protection around yourself. Like a circle of light, you draw it around your body with your hand. It reminds you to be safe, even in the darkest of times. I used to do it before an exam or going into a potentially dangerous situation, even hostile negotiations. I did it before getting on the ship when we departed for Auckland. I disappeared into the loo and cast a circle. Just to be safe."

"Really?" I asked, careful not to sound disrespectful. It sounded a little pagan, especially for Illy. She was the most practical person I knew, aside from myself and Sorcha.

"Logically, I know it isn't magic, but it is focusing on your intent. In my work, knowing what success looks like is the most important factor in succeeding—identifying the goal and focusing your intent on achieving it. Then breaking down the steps and tackling them one at a time. If casting a circle makes you more confident, it is worth it, isn't it?"

"You are my best friend. I trust you implicitly. If you derive benefit from it, then I will try anything you suggest. Can you teach me?"

Sometime later, I broke the comfortable silence, Illy's hands still in my larger ones, my long fingers wrapped around hers. Glancing up at her, I asked, "Do you think Lewis is a caim? A circle of protection ... for us, I mean?" It may have been the ritual or being with my friend, but I felt more at peace with the mission I was about to undertake. My stomach was less jittery, and I felt more settled and focused. I tried to clarify my thoughts. "The dome itself protects us physically but the island, too. We are isolated, safe from dangerous situations."

Illy considered for a moment before responding.

"No. The island and dome aren't the caim. The *people* are. We all chose to be there, to protect each other. We form the circle, the extended family unit. We care for each other and keep each member of our family safe, even in the darkest times. Like when Laetitia died, when Di became sick. The community could never make up for the loss, but the circle bonded around each other, interlinked, knit ever more tightly."

I nodded in agreement. I liked that analogy.

"Circles have been known to hold power for millennia. Women's circles symbolize equal power. King Arthur's round table, where all the knights had a voice. Even a simple ring. It is equal in strength and beauty. No one part is stronger or more beautiful than another. Circles are cast to contain energy or form a sacred space. Think of the stones at Callanish, Clava, and Stonehenge. They are all circular and deliberately constructed that way. No sides and all parts have the same value. That is how I think of our community on Lewis. All people are valuable and all equal."

"Have I ever told you how blessed I am that you came into my life?" I whispered. "You are my family, Illy. You, Luca, your girls."

Her tiny arms engulfed me, and in that moment, I felt protected against whatever was to come.

CHAPTER 8

MY STOMACH CLENCHED PAINFULLY as I sat at the table, watching Luca make fettucine. With time in abundance, Luca had returned to making pasta from scratch, something I loved.

"I wish Jam were here." I sighed.

"Why?" Luca asked as he rolled the dough through the cutters. "There are no mice on board. Well, not that I have seen."

"Jam had a knack of knowing when I needed her. She would sit on me, purring. Just stroking her was a comfort."

"I miss Max and Lily," Illy said as she hung the freshly cut strands on the pasta tree. "They were so intuitive and always sensed when I needed them. I am glad to have Millie and Mollie," she rushed to say, recalling that I had upset a few people on the waiting list for kittens by giving her two, "but I could never replace my first fur babies. I hope Isla is looking after them all."

"She will," I assured her. "Isla loves cats. Did you always have cats?"

"Ever since I can remember. We even had one, Herring, a tabby boy we brought from Scotland with us. I remember my mum laughing that the neighborhood cats likely couldn't understand his accent."

"No dogs?" Cam asked.

"No. My parents were cat people, I guess. I have never had a dog."

"I wasn't allowed to have any pets."

"You said that once before," Illy asked. "Why? You had a big house, didn't you?"

"We did. But my parents insisted pets were a burden. They traveled, worked long hours. After all these years, I genuinely believe that they wanted nothing that could make a mess. Our house was so white."

"*White*?" Luca questioned mockingly as he kneaded the next ball of dough.

Ignoring him, I continued speaking to Illy. "The walls, the carpets, the furniture. Everything was crisp and clean and white. So bloody Scandinavian. Lots of timber and glass, but that cold, sterile look. Glass fronted wine storage room. Pristine white kitchen. Carefully curated artwork on the walls, but not allowed to touch anything. It was like living in a museum. The perfectly manicured lawn that couldn't be spoiled with something as repulsive as dog shit. Nothing at all like my home with you." I smiled at Cam, reading a book opposite me but not really focused. With four children, many more who dropped in daily, and a cat, plus the odd lamb or other creature, our house was a home. Warm and inviting, but messy and lived in with muddy footprints, clothes strewn around, and dents in walls.

"What would your parents think of our home?" Cam asked curiously, putting his book down on the table, careful not to lose his place.

"They would be polite to our faces but likely horrified behind our backs," I confessed. "My mother carried antiseptic wipes and wiped down the toilet before she used it. Carried little bottles of hand sanitizer. When we traveled, even to third-world countries, for dad's work, we always stayed in the five-star hotel that the expats stayed in. No local bunkhouses for us."

Cam grinned. "I miss all the pets we had growing up: cats, dogs, fish, even guinea pigs at one point. They were all family, and I loved them all."

"I had a cat once," Luca said, in a voice that indicated there was a story there, making me look at him expectantly as he wiped his hands of excess flour.

"We lived in a flat, so a dog was difficult. Of course, I wanted a dog. All the other kids at school had dogs. I desperately wanted one. But no. I get a cat. One day I tried to walk the cat, but that ended badly."

Illy smirked. She had clearly heard this story. But Cam and I egged him on.

Luca sighed dramatically, his muscled chest rising. "Hornet was a rescue cat, a big ginger tabby boy with a white patch down his front. Maybe four or five when mum and I adopted him from the shelter. We suspected he had belonged to an older person who had died. He was overweight, loud, demanding, and opinionated. He just smeared himself around, fat lump of lard. We found his fur everywhere. You couldn't eat without first checking for ginger hair in your food. As well as company for me, Mum got him as we had mice in our flat, and she thought he would catch them and keep them at bay. But no. He just lay there on the sofa and watched them run past. I used to tease him, tell him they were his buddies, and he had named them. He loved to lie on my chest when I was in bed. Very possessive. Anyway, one Saturday afternoon, when mum was at work, I decided to walk him, like a dog. He was bigger than a Chihuahua or a Fox Terrier, so I thought, 'Surely it will be fine.' Note to self: It wasn't fine. He hated the rope lead I tied to his collar for a start and arched his back to get it off. Dug his feet in, and I dragged him for a few meters before he started to walk, realizing that I wouldn't give in. We made it half a block before we saw a dog—an enormous bloody Alsatian. The owner couldn't control the dog and let go of the leash. The dog lunged at Hornet. Hornet climbed me like a tree, leaving every exposed inch of skin scratched and bleeding. Shredded my shorts and t-shirt. So, the dog is jumping up at me, barking, slobber flying everywhere. Hornet is perched on my head like a Russian ushanka hat, yowling and screeching, and I'm also yowling and screeching with blood running in rivers down my face, blinding me."

Cam and I laughed hysterically at the image this provoked, but asked, "What did you do?"

"There was a crowd forming in a circle around me. Watching. Assholes. Finally, a man got a hand on the Alsatian's collar and pulled it away. I managed to retrieve Hornet off my head, not without incurring a few more puncture wounds in the process. Someone brought a box to stuff him in. I would have been happy to see him get hit by a car at that point. The paramedics arrived, and I was taken away in an ambulance."

"What happened to poor Hornet?" asked Illy, her eyes opening wide. "He was just scared. You never told me that part!"

"Oh, nothing. My mother retrieved the fat lump from the neighbor later on. I note you didn't ask about my sixteen stitches, did you? Sheesh, Sunny. You and cats. At least I know where I stand in the pecking order." Luca sighed in disgust.

"Did you ever try to walk him again?" Cam asked, unable to control his mirth.

"No. And he lived to a ripe old age." Luca swilled the rest of his wine and poured another glass before rolling out the next batch of dough. "But he repelled the mice after that, so I guess that was a small win. And at least I had a pet. Even if they did make a mess," he taunted. "We couldn't have that in your perfect white castle, could we, princess?"

"I am not a..."

"Did Freyja ever tell you about her towel fetish?" Cam interrupted my protestations.

"It is *not* a fetish!" I retorted, lowering my eyes in warning.

Illy's eyebrows raised, and Luca just chuckled. "Nothing would surprise me about Princess."

My eyes narrowed as I growled, "I ... am ... not ... a ... princess!"

"Sure."

"Go on, tell us," Illy urged, a wicked smile on her lips.

"When she first moved in with me, Freyja insisted we have matching towels."

"Why?" Illy asked.

"It is the definitive sign of coupledom, apparently."

Luca roared with laughter. "See. Princess! I suppose they had to be Egyptian cotton in pristine snowflake white, too? No skiddies?"

I broke in. "This isn't fair. Everyone I knew before I moved to August had matching towel sets. I thought it was a standard thing. I found it jarring that my towels were white and Cam's blue."

"The funny part was," Cam interjected, grinning mercilessly, "my parents had different colored towels so they could tell the difference. I had seen matching towels in catalogs and display homes but didn't realize it defined who we were as a couple."

Realizing I couldn't win, I relented. "Fine. So, we had matching Egyptian cotton towels on our own personal rail. Yes, we replaced them regularly. Guests always got a new towel and a new cake of soap. My parents even had two basins in their bathroom. His and hers. Are you happy?"

"What did you do with the old soaps?" Illy asked, astonished.

"Thrown out, I guess. I know. The thought of it horrifies me now. But it was the sign of a valued guest. New towel, new soap, and crisp white sheets."

"You ironed sheets?" Luca's mouth dropped open.

"Well, not me personally..." I tapered off, realizing how this sounded to someone raised in a tiny two-bedroom flat.

"Your housekeeper ironed sheets?" Luca couldn't restrain himself from using his posh accent. The one he used to ridicule me.

"No, we didn't always have a housekeeper."

"But you had an ironing lady and a cleaning lady?"

"And a gardener? And a pool boy?" Cam added.

"You are not helping."

"So, tell me about the matching towels again?" Luca teased.

I pursed my lips, realizing he wasn't going to give this up. "I just thought that if we were a couple that we should have matching towels. That's all," I muttered, not really wanting to be heard. "I don't know about you, but we were allocated two when we arrived. Mine were white. Cam's were blue. I wanted to see if we could get new ones. You know, so that we could start our lives afresh with fresh sheets and towels."

"New sheets, too?" Luca's hilarity filled the room. "What, were you worried he had farted on them?"

"Many couples do that," Illy interjected, defending me. "After all, if you have been with someone else, it makes sense to start a relationship fresh. New sheets are a symbol of a fresh start."

"Well, I'd like to think Cam washed them in between shags," Luca butted in.

"There wasn't anyone before Freyja," Cam interjected. "And I told her that. Many times. But she still demanded fresh sheets."

Luca guffawed as my face reddened. "If you could see some of the places I have slept, Princess! Bedbugs, rats, you name it. I even shared my bed with cockroaches on one memorable occasion. I'm surprised she didn't run a mile when she found your sheets weren't 1000 thread count, Cam."

Cam glanced at me to test the waters before responding. "They weren't exactly polyester! Maybe not to her luxurious standards, but they were cotton. I remember asking one of the cotton growers on August why the linen was pure cotton, and she said it was so that it could be recycled. Pure cotton sheets and towels could be shredded and converted to cotton fibers. The fibers are woven back to thread and used again."

"I didn't know that," Illy said, glancing at me and seeing my reddened cheeks. "That is interesting. Do you know if they do that on Lewis?"

I smiled gratefully.

"Oh yes," Cam continued, always happy to talk about anything agricultural. "Wool too. That was why most of our products are made of cotton, linen, or wool. Everything can be re-used. Nothing is wasted."

Luca, unable to restrain himself from having one last dig at me, asked, "So, how did you recycle your single-use guest towels, Princess?"

"We used them as pool towels," I muttered, flushing vigorously.

CHAPTER 9

MOORING THE *EURYDICE* A few kilometers off the coast as the sky turned from purple to black, we sought something to do. We had timed our arrival for the dark phase of the moon, fortunate that the days were shorter here at this time of year. Illy was familiar with the location of the settlement, and we deliberately moored several kilometers out, on the far side of the island, just in case a random person out walking caught sight of us arriving in the dim moonlight. Luca had advised 2 AM as the time when most people were asleep and the best time to avoid detection.

We sat and talked after dinner, but the conversation was stilted, and no one wanted to numb our senses with alcohol. After a period of uncomfortable silence, Luca suggested a game of cards and retrieved a pack from his cabin. Luca was a gun at cards, and he and I had spent many a night playing poker, blackjack, and as many games for which we could remember the rules. We both had a competitive streak and had argued over the rules many times. We had always planned to find a book with the rules to prove each other wrong, but somehow never did. Several hours of hilarity ensued when it emerged that Cam not only did not know how to play blackjack, but his face showed every thought as it flitted across his mind, resulting in him losing every hand. Bemoaning his constant losses, I eventually let him in on the secret.

He scowled at me. "You could have told me sooner. I would at least have tried!"

"Come on." Luca stood. "It's time to gear up."

Launching the inflatable dinghy, we paddled to the coast, stealthy and silent. It didn't take long to find the dome opening. Illy had known the location of some, and that they were three kilometers apart, so it hadn't been hard to calculate. Luca had brought obsidian scalpels, sourced during one of the medical raids on the mainland, just in case. But we weren't here to hurt anyone. With Cam firmly gripping my hand for moral support, we crept through the thick foliage at the edge of the village, the lights in the distance making it so obvious that Luca didn't even need to switch on the single torch we carried.

The austere gray brick building with small, high-set windows loomed silent and ominous at the edge of the settlement. Straining my eyes, I could see Illy pointing it out to Luca in the darkness. Luca, dressed in black and his face smeared with the coal dust we had collected from our beach fire a few days prior, went first, testing a rear door. I had to strain my eyes to see him. He camouflaged so well and moved with the agility of a cat. Locked. My heart sank. Damn. We watched silently from our concealed position in the foliage as he tested every door and window, finally finding a high window ajar. I watched with astonishment as he swung himself up and onto the tiny ledge with more nimbleness than should have been possible given his size. Unable to fit through the opening, he returned for Illy. Holding her above his head like a feather, she slipped her tiny form into the opening and disappeared into the dark. Cam and I waited nervously at the edge of the forest until we saw the door open a crack.

Creeping into the lab unseen, I saw Illy gesturing to Luca that there was a single guard. A nurse, perhaps? Keeping our backs to the walls, Cam and I heard a minor scuffle and thud emanate from the adjoining room. Illy and Luca returned, looking grim. A quick glance behind them showed the man unconscious on the floor. Illy nodded at me. It was safe.

They weren't even valuable enough to have a team of nurses. I sniffed angrily, equally feeling foolish. More staff would be impossible to overpower and would jeopardize our chances of finding anything. Luca and Illy disappeared up the hallway into the offices, seeking records, paperwork, learning about Bridget and Jorja's children and how many of them existed. What procedures they had performed here. A long corridor divided the building, and tiny rooms ran off each side. Peering through the windows, I could see that each room contained a single bed. Cam and I crept along the hall, my small, black, crossbody bag banging lightly against my thigh. Cam stopped outside number seventeen, marked in simple lettering on the white door, beneath the half-glass window. Cam glanced at me in the dim light. *Am I ready?*

I nodded, not wanting to break the silence. He pushed the door open, and we entered.

CHAPTER 10

SHE LOOKED SO *OLD*. The thought skipped in my mind like a scratched record after Cam had turned on the bedside lamp. Leaning against the doorway, fighting my flight instinct, I couldn't bring myself to step fully into the room. That would make it real. Even in the coldness of the tiny artificially lit room, she looked far older than her laps around the sun. Thirty-four, I calculated, mentally subtracting from my own age. And nearly half of them, not alive at all. Her hair was brittle and white-gray, so thin that it was bald in patches. Her skin had a sickly yellow tinge, gray on the extremities. Always slim, now she was a breathing skeleton with paper-thin skin overlaid. She looked nothing like the vibrant, loving sister I remembered. *It isn't her,* part of my brain wheedled, convincing me we had made a mistake.

As I stood motionless in the doorway, Cam returned to close the solid door behind me and carried a chair from the opposite side of the room to Kat's bedside, careful to avoid the machines surrounding her. He took her limp gray hand with harshly clipped nails in one of his and spoke kindly.

"Hi, Katrin. It is lovely to meet you. I'm Cam."

A sob escaped my lips, and Cam looked up at me. My hand covered my mouth as I gulped and tried to pull myself together. In the time since Jorja and Bridget had arrived, and I had suspected her fate, I had visualized this moment a million times. But now that I was here, and she was within speaking distance, I was paralyzed, leaning against the door for support.

Cam smiled down at Kat and kept speaking in the low, soothing tone he used when one of the children were scared or injured.

"Your wonderful sister and I married twelve years ago. Even I can't believe it has been that long. It feels like yesterday that I saw her for the first time, and she stole my heart. She is the most amazing woman, but you know that already. We have four beautiful children, two girls, and two boys. Our eldest girl is named after you. Katrin Rose is her name. She is eight and a cheeky and highly intelligent young lady who keeps us on our toes! She looks so much like you, like her mum. We live in Scotland now, where Freyja is a vet, and I am a ... gardener," he said, glancing up at me with a smirk, making me smile through my pain. Angus had belittled him, calling him the gardener behind his back, and I sometimes teased him, calling him that, usually in bed—when I was trying to provoke a reaction.

"We live in the most beautiful part of the world—a small island in the North Sea. There are archaeological sites like stone circles and ancient Norse brochs but mountains and fields of purple and silver heather as far as you can see. Our house is nestled at the end of a closed valley, surrounded by grassy hills and a stunning blue lake where we source our water. Our children have the most wonderful life, roaming the forests and fishing in streams. Playing with the animals and taking long walks. We love it there. Everyone works together and cares for each other. I love your sister so much, as I know you do. She is the most astonishing person I have ever met. She has saved my life several times. I wish you could meet our family. They so badly wanted to come and meet you."

Cam's focus shifted from the skeleton in the bed. *Do I want to say something?*

Gliding to the end of the bed, unable to take my eyes from her face, I froze, unsure what to do. Cam smiled encouragingly.

"Hi, Kat," I tried to say cheerfully, but it sounded flat, forced, even to my own ears. "It is me, Frey. Goodness, I have missed you."

Cam stood, and gratefully, I took his seat. With my hand on her arm and looking closely, I could just make out the glimmer of the girl she had been, beneath the painfully thin, fragile discolored skin and protruding bones. A thin white cotton nightdress sagged unbecomingly across her collarbones. Her high Nordic cheekbones were still prominent. But her once lively green eyes, now dull and glassy, were wide open and staring. Tiny memories of helping her try out makeup flickered in my mind. Picking out sunglasses. It was still her. I held her hand, cringing as I felt the bones, distinct and too close to the surface. As I spoke, I warmed up and spent the next half-hour filling her in on the highlights of my life. Meeting Cam on August, our first night together at the springs. I told her about our weddings, both of them. All about our children and our lives. My hopes and fears. My sorrow for not knowing she had been here all this time. My regret for not coming sooner.

Between tears, I lay my head on her sunken stomach, hip bones protruding. She never had the chance to be fat. Jorja's girls flitted into my mind, and I lifted her gown to confirm the pattern of parallel scars crossing her stomach.

"I have my own war wounds," I confided, displaying my wrists and telling her about my cesareans for our children.

As I slowed in my storytelling, Cam returned, entered the room silently, standing at the end of the bed while I finished. He looked at me expectantly, sympathy in his eyes. *Do I want him to do it?*

I shook my head silently. *No. This is mine to do.*

"Goodbye, Kat," I whispered, choking back the tears. "For the rest of my life, I will wish I could have done this for you years ago. I'm so sorry for letting you suffer. I love you so very much."

Removing the syringe from the cloth pouch in my bag, I uncapped it and slowly injected the clear liquid into her upper arm. The needle slid in like I was inserting it into a tub of butter, with no muscle to offer resistance. Recapping the needle, I replaced it in my bag. I held her hand, memorizing her face as her heart rate slowed and finally stopped. Cam hurriedly switched off and unplugged the monitors as they emitted loud beeps. With my head laid on her sunken chest, I sucked in my top lip and exhaled forcefully, fighting to hold it together. Cam tapped me lightly on the shoulder. We needed to go. I touched my lips to her cold gray forehead in farewell, held my lower lip between my teeth, inhaled, and didn't look back.

Exiting the building and creeping from the lab to the dock passed in a blur. Cam's arm steered me, the only anchor keeping me from drifting. As we neared the dinghy, Illy came out to meet me and held the dome access hatch open. My lip trembled; she could see me fighting to keep control of my emotions, even in the dim starlight. She looked expectantly at Cam, and I sensed him nod beside me. It was done.

"Let's go," she mouthed.

I stared back at the dome, faintly illuminated in the moonlight as Luca paddled. The image of her, dead, permanently etched in my brain. Cam helped me board the *Eurydice* as Luca lifted the dinghy, securing it in place. My feet shuddered as Illy started the engine, and we putted quietly some way out to sea. After a few minutes, Luca, now at the helm, killed the engine.

"Ready?"

Unable to nod, I blinked acquiescence.

Cam lifted me to my feet, stood behind me, holding me against his chest, his arms securing me in place. The click sounded in the darkness as Luca remote detonated the charge. The white-orange flame flashed for an instant under the dome, illuminating the curvature of the sphere and everything protected within it, and then was extinguished. In the dark, we couldn't see the dust. I trusted Luca had done his job well. The lab was gone, and all the records and samples along with it.

"Thank you," I mouthed as he leaned in to engulf me in a hug, wedging me between himself and Cam.

"Both of you." Illy, on my other side, supported me, too. I had the best friends in the world; I had no doubt about that. My husband, Illy, and Luca. They had all accompanied me across the world for a mission involving *my* sister. But in doing so, they had proven themselves to be my family.

Luca left us to pilot the *Eurydice*. Gunning the engine unexpectedly, we sped off through the night. Illy led me to a deck chair and forced me to sit. Cam lowered himself beside me. She handed me a glass of whisky, and I sat on the upper deck, twisting it in my hands, flanked by my friends. It would be a long time until we could stop safely, and we needed to get as much distance between us and Auckland Island as possible while it was still dark. Luca had already plotted a non-direct route in case they had drones with night vision capability.

Illy looked at me, wanting to ask how I was, but knowing instinctively that there was no adequate answer to that question. I had just killed my sister. To save her from a worse fate, I tried to convince myself. Dying at my hand was preferable to what they had done to her, would have continued to do to her. Better than dying in an explosion. At least this way it was peaceful and calm and with me holding her hand. But I had done it. Ended it. Killed her.

Cam was silent, his face twisted and torn. Illy could see it as well. I knocked back the glass in a single gulp.

"It's late. Let's go to bed," I announced stonily, standing. Not that I wanted to sleep. But I didn't want to talk either. At least in bed, I could be tortured alone.

CHAPTER 11

"HONEY, I NEED TO tell you something."

"I gathered that. You have that look."

"I have tortured myself over whether to tell you, but ultimately, we have never kept secrets from each other." Cam paused, unable to say what was on his mind.

I waited, unable to ask.

"While you were … saying goodbye … and I was poking around, I found something."

I watched his face contort. "What?"

"Her medical records."

He handed me the centimeter-thick manila folder he had hidden under his shirt. It was warm and smelled of him.

"The top page," he whispered, sitting beside me on the edge of the bed, looking at his feet. Ugly feet, he always called them, with his middle toes longer than his big toe—Louis' feet.

A consent form. For Katrin's body to be used for scientific research.

"On the back," he said, slightly louder, as my mouth hung open.

There were two signatures, neatly printed in blue ink on the bottom of the form: Claira Jorgensen and Magnus Jorgensen. Handwriting I would have recognized anywhere. I barely made it to the bathroom before the vomiting started.

"I'm so sorry," Cam whispered as he held back my hair and embraced me as I crumpled onto the floor. "I wasn't sure whether to tell you or not."

"No, you did the right thing." I wiped my face with the towel he held out to me. "It is important, I know. It's late. You must be tired, and you need to relieve Luca soon. Let's go to bed."

CHAPTER 12

BLACKNESS SWALLOWED ME, SUCKING me down. Forcing my eyes open, I couldn't focus, couldn't see past the end of the bed. Her shadow was lurking, ominously. Judging. *How could they?* How could they have allowed those monsters to subject her to ... that *degradation*? She was their daughter. Their child. Did they consider her expendable? And if they thought that of Kat, what did they think of *me*? Jorja had said that the substitutes were only used if the primary candidate refused or died. Most weren't needed. Was this *my* fault? But what would they have done to her if I had consented? Killed her sooner?

The steel band squeezed tighter around my chest with the realization that this situation was indeed my fault. Had I never left August, they would have caught me in their net, the selective breeding program. Had I chosen to stay with Angus, they would have forced me. By refusing to participate, they did the one thing worse than forcing *me*. They forced *her*. An unwilling and unconscious victim. The lowest of the low. *My* selfishness. My non-compliance had caused them to do this to her. Is that why all those patients were there? As spares, in case something happened to the chosen genome? Many of the spares were alive and living in isolated communities on the mainland. People like Sorcha, a spare for Cam, and Di's cousin, Kendra. But clearly, some were merely genetic material, kept alive, barely. Just in case.

Five embryos, Jorja had said. Her children. My nieces and nephews. But how could I ever watch them and see anything other than how she had looked tonight, lying there, helpless, hooked up to machines? To breathe for her, to feed her, to keep her alive. But that wasn't living.

Cam kept coaxing me to leave the cabin. How could I? How could I let the light shine on my face? She lived alone in that dark, cold cell. One tiny window, high in the wall, her only view of the world, but cruelly, too high to see out of. No one to speak to her, to tell her what was happening. How had they transported her there? Had she been frightened? Still an eighteen-year-old girl trapped in that withered old woman's body. She had never had a serious boyfriend. Never attended university, held down a job, or had a family of her own. That weekend, when she had left me, had been only a few weeks after she had finished high school. She never lived to see her grades. Receive the formal letter advising in neat black print that she had been offered a place in her dream architecture degree. So how could I let the light in when she was forever trapped in that permanent state of hell?

She was here. She kept crying for me. I could hear her voice in the dark, calling my name. It was a child's voice. *Frey-Frey*. She called me that when she was tiny, standing in her cot calling to me. She was always there for me when mum and dad weren't. Every afternoon after school. We would walk home from the tram stop, and I would help her with her math homework. She would tell me about the girls being mean to her, and I would confront them. Intimidate and threaten them. She would confide in me about the boy she liked at the boy's school nearby. He was in the same year level, and the schools met up for co-ed sport one day a week. We would whisper and giggle, looking up his phone number and home address. Once, we even followed him to tennis training and watched, just to see him sprint after the ball in his tight white shorts. She looked up to me, and I let her down in the worst way possible. First in Melbourne, and now, here. Fourteen long years. A single tear ran down my cheek. Was that how long she had been in that room? Her eyes were open. Could she see? Did she know what was happening to her? Injecting her. Operating on her to harvest her eggs. How many times had they cut her open? Many, judging by the crosshatching of scars. The thin white lines evidence of their invasion.

"Honey." His voice was gentle, laden with concern. But I couldn't open my eyes, focus on him. All I could see was her face behind my eyelids. Her poorly cut, brittle silver hair fanned on the stark white pillow, balding at the back. Calling to me. Begging me to save her.

"Frey!" More insistent this time. I refused to look at him, knowing that seeing his disgust would destroy me. How could he not be repulsed by me? I had let her down. He had traveled across the world to save his sister. I had let sub-human monsters use mine as a science experiment—a living corpse.

"This isn't your fault, honey. You didn't do this. You didn't know."

A tear leaked from the inside corner of my eye; I felt it run down my nose. Damn. Now he knew I wasn't asleep. I felt him blot it gently with a corner of the sheet. I felt his large mass lie on the bed behind me, holding me, trying to comfort me. Somewhere, the logical part of my brain knew he was concerned. Fearful for me. Disgust consumed me for what I had done. Not for ending her life, or what passed as it. But that I had left her there for *years*. Goodness knows what else they had done to her during that time. What other experiments they had performed.

An involuntary sob escaped as my chest convulsed, and I felt his arms tighten. He said nothing. He was just ... there. The dam walls burst, and the tears poured out. I couldn't ease the stabbing pain in my chest, piercing me as I stared into the gaping black hole that was my life.

When I woke, he was gone, and I was alone again. I staggered to the bathroom. When I finished, I glanced into the mirror and recoiled at the image staring back at me. Dull, sunken eyes. Greasy, stringy hair so dark it wasn't clear what color it was. My cheeks hollowed out. I snorted. I wondered if all the guys who had wolf-whistled at me through my life would find *this* attractive. *But Cam would. Cam still loves you.* A tiny voice tried to float through the thick muck to the surface. *He loves you no matter what you have done. No matter what you look like.* If no one else got it, Cam did. He knew what unrelenting grief was. He knew that there were no magic words, no quick fixes. She wasn't better off. It wasn't meant to be, or any other ridiculous expression people tell you in a time of grief to make themselves feel better. Nothing can make you feel better when you suffer such an agonizing loss. Pain cannot be overcome. It is just lived through. Cam, who had lost me, then Laetitia, understood. He had stood on the brink of the abyss, twice, but had pulled himself back.

I lifted my arms to push my hair out of my eyes and traced my fingers abstractedly across the faded mesh of white and purple scars that ran along my inner arms. The web was still prominent, even though it had been years since I had inflicted these on myself, trying to escape from being bound and left in a shed. The long purple one, the length of my forearm, was even older. As I stared at my arms, the numbness made me hollow. Chilled. I flicked one scar roughly but felt nothing as my fingernail hit the raised tissue. I tried again, harder. Nothing. As the tiny stream of light filtered past the closed curtains, I wondered if it would hurt if I opened one. *Would I ever feel again?*

Moving toward the bed in slow motion, I sat on the edge and pulled the Swiss Army knife from my bag. Sluggishly tracing the sharp tip along one long cut, I stared unblinking as the redness pooled on the surface. Large blobs in places, thin drips in others. I looked abstractedly at the stain, feeling distant. It was like paint smeared across a canvas, the runs uneven. Drips falling where the paint was thickest, running down a wall. I couldn't feel it. I was removed. An onlooker. It wasn't mine. I did it again, following another line, pushing more firmly this time, but still with no feeling. The pattering sound as drips rolled off my arm onto the floor permeated the haze. *It sounds like rain,* I mused, dazed, the woolly-headed-ness threatening to submerge me. Drown me.

Amidst the fog, I vaguely heard the cry of alarm as he surveyed the scene and dropped to his knees in front of me. Kneeling in my blood. He looked at my face, his distress palpable. Unable to focus my eyes, mired in grief, I dropped the knife dumbly, and he flicked it under the bed.

"Your beautiful arms! Freyja, please! Please come back to me. To the kids. They need you. *I need you.* Honey, I can't lose you. Oh God, Freyja, I love you so much. Do ... not ... leave ... me."

Staring down at my arms, unable to focus, unfeeling, I just sat there, disoriented. I wondered if it was possible to stop breathing just by willing it. Closing my eyes and concentrating really hard. Slowing my breath to a complete stop.

I heard him stand and rummage around in the drawers, clothes being dropped on the floor in his haste. He thrust something under my nose, grabbing my chin forcibly and pressing me to look.

"*Look!*" he bellowed at me. "See what our children did for us. For *you!*"

Through the haze, I looked. My vision blurred, but I still recognized the book of drawings they had made of us, our family. Smiling. Happy. Their gift to us as we had left on this voyage. One of Jam. Several of our home on Lewis. The scribbled childish drawing Thorsten had done of our family. The letters from Katrin and Xanthe, in their neatest handwriting, describing how much they loved us and would miss us. Louis's detailed watercolor artwork of our home nestled against the mountainous green and purple backdrop. Thorsten had cried as he handed the book to me, wrapped in recycled brown paper. We had never been away from him before. Going *out there*, on a boat, for weeks, was beyond his comprehension. Xanthe had been hysterical. Her cries echoing around the cabin as Sorcha held her tightly when we pulled away from the dock. I gasped aloud as the pain radiated from my arms and sobbed my heart out as Cam dropped the book and folded me in. He held me against his solid chest, staining him with my blood.

After an eternity, I pulled back and saw the mess I had made. Really saw. To myself, and to him. Not just the physical mess coating both of us. But his face. He had aged years since we had left. His eyes were sunken, and his skin tinged with sleeplessness. Even his hair had silver tinges at the temples. He was in agony, tortured.

"It's alright," I whispered. "I'm alright."

He studied my face. He knew it wasn't true. I wasn't alright. I knew I never could be again. But he was here, sharing my pain. I watched his face dissolve with relief, knowing that I had stood on the precipice, as he had before me, but hadn't taken that irreversible step. I sat there, dazed and motionless as the blood dried, smeared all over my arms and clothes. Weak and wilted. Even breathing was a challenge that exhausted me.

"Are you okay if I leave you for a minute?" His voice was filled with concern.

I blinked unconvincingly. He buzzed around, filling the bath with boiled, bottled water, never leaving me for more than a few minutes as he carried pots filled with water. Illy and Luca must be helping him, I realized, dazed. He stripped me off, leaving my blood-stained clothing in a puddle on the floor, carrying me like a fragile ornament, and laid me in the bath.

Lovingly, he washed my hair and combed it out. He used a soft cloth to clean my wounds, carefully wiping the cuts. As I soaked, he cleaned the floor and stripped the bed, changing the linen, removing my clothes. I turned over my hands and looked at my fingertips, wrinkled from the water, the whitened whorls and arches protruding.

As the water cooled, he returned and lifted me out. He sat on the end of the bed, with me across his legs, and dried me, slowly and carefully, watching me cautiously, fearful of speaking. The haze still engulfed me. Cam gently dried my hair, then disinfected and bandaged my arms. Wrapping me in a clean towel, he laid me back on the cool bed. The worried look in his eyes made mine fill with tears again. I reached for him, and he collapsed on my chest, holding me as I realized the anxiety he had held in for days.

"How long?" my voice croaked, rusty from disuse.

"Six days."

A tap sounded at the door, and I strained to focus my exhausted eyes past him to see Illy standing in the doorway, desperate worry ingrained in her delicate features as she tentatively held a tray of food. She looked at my face, saw me look at her, and it cracked, tears streaming down her pale cheeks.

"I thought we had lost you," she sobbed.

Weakly, I lifted my bandaged arms to her, and she crossed the room in three tiny steps. She placed the tray on the floor. Cam lay on one side, and Illy lay on my other, curled into me, sobbing with relief as I stared up at the ceiling. Without me noticing,

Luca had arrived and now sat at the end of the bed, watching us all. Watching the light reflecting off the water dancing on the white ceiling, I realized how lucky I was.

"I'm so sorry," I whispered into the silence, icy waves flushing my hollow veins.

"No!" Illy responded sharply, sitting up with a jerk. "You will not apologize! Even the strongest people grieve. Grief is an intensely personal journey. There is no right or wrong way to experience loss. Do not be sorry. You have suffered an immense loss and shock. Healing is a path we all need to travel in our own way, and there is no correct period of time that it must take. We are just so grateful that you chose to come back."

"Bloody psychologist," Luca muttered, making Cam snort.

CHAPTER 13

"WHERE ARE WE?" I asked when Luca and Illy had left us alone, recognizing the sensation that the boat was gently rocking at anchor.

"Adelaide. Partly as we needed to refuel, but also as Auckland is searching madly with drones and satellites. Tadhg and Jake are tracking their signals around the clock, so it made sense for us to lie low for a few days and make things easier for them. From the sky, they can't tell that this yacht has people aboard; the guys have seen no evidence that they have heat scanners. Tadhg believes they never thought they would need them. So, they are crazily searching the ocean, and we are happily camouflaged, moored among other yachts, even with our blue paint job. Adelaide not being a logical place to look, we are also hopeful that they won't think to look here. Luca and Illy have taken the opportunity to load up the vessel for the trip home. Why? Do you want to go ashore?"

"No." Ordinarily, I would have loved a land visit. I had adored being landside when Luca and I were traveling with Angus, but right now, even brushing my hair was a challenge I didn't feel capable of.

"Did you go ashore?"

"No."

I didn't need to ask why. Instead, I ordered in as forceful a tone as I could muster. "Go. Take a long walk. Get things for the kids. Please. I am fine. I promise."

Cam's head dropped to the side, surveying me. I knew I had hit the nail on the head.

"Please. Louis and Kat are growing so rapidly. We need shoes and warm jackets, especially. Can you get a few sizes? I couldn't find anything suitable in Freo."

Standing, he paused. "Will you come with me?"

"No. I don't have the energy for that. Please send Illy. I would like to talk to her."

Our mission accomplished, the journey home was calmer, instilled with a sense of closure, although none of us were happy about what we had done.

"I can't believe she laid in that bed for *years* like a piece of meat," I confided in Illy one night when I had enough strength to climb the stairs to the main living room. Cam and Luca were piloting the vessel in the dark to avoid detection, Tadhg and Jake still making minor adjustments to the sweeps performed by the satellites controlled by Clava and Auckland. "That is what took me to the brink. Learning that my parents had signed her over to them, and they kept her alive, living like that. They jabbed her with needles, harvested her eggs, showed her no love, likely never even spoke her name. It makes me sick to think of her enduring that for so long."

Illy's arms came around me, and I knew she understood.

"What did you do while Cam and I said goodbye?" I finally asked, not wanting to dwell on Kat and what I had done.

"We found the records," she said simply. "All the samples, lab reports. And ... we helped the others pass."

"Others?" I asked dumbly.

"The others like your sister. Twenty-five, including her. All women. We turned off the machines. None of them were alive when the building collapsed. We would never have done that. But I saw the condition they were in."

There was silence as I took that in. Lab rats. All of them.

"Did you find Tomori's material for Sorcha?" I asked to break the melancholy that had descended over us.

"We did. It is in a container in my room. A small, cryopreserved Dewar jar with liquid nitrogen."

"Is it still ... viable?" I asked cautiously. "It has been a long time."

"Stored correctly, cryopreservation is viable indefinitely." Illy shrugged. "So yes. Likely the options are there."

"How are you storing it?"

Illy smiled. "While we were waiting for you, we located a small portable freezer to transport and store the jar to get it home safely. That is why I was on the other side of the dome. I had taken it to the dinghy. We were just waiting for you."

"I am pleased. For her." I forced the words out. It hurt to speak them. I *was* pleased for Sorcha to have a choice. It was the sense of positive emotion in the current circumstances that I couldn't endure. "And the rest of us?"

"All of us from Australia and New Zealand had genetic material there. Even me," Illy said grimly. "It makes me wonder if Clava has a similar facility."

"Likely," Luca added, making me look up to see Cam and Luca paused in the doorway.

"What happened to it all?" I asked. "The samples and records?"

"Destroyed," Illy finished smugly. "Even before Luca's handiwork. We opened every container and destroyed every sample. If they planned to use their backup genomes, they won't now. They still have their electronic records. There was no server room. But the samples are all gone."

Cam and I looked at each other, and in that way peculiar to married couples, we knew that both of us were happy with that outcome. Not that we didn't want genomes to survive; we recognized the importance of that. We just genuinely believed that people should have free choice regarding who they had children with.

"The guard!" I blurted. "I forgot about him! What happened to the guard?"

"Oh, I dragged him well clear and propped him up against a tree," Luca reassured me. "He will have woken from the explosion with a mighty headache. But no lasting effects. I know how hard and where to strike. Just so they sleep for a while."

I smiled at Luca. I suspected I had no idea of the depth and breadth of Luca's skills, and I had known him for years.

He saw me considering. "And, in case you were wondering, only that building was razed. Nothing else was affected. Dust and debris but no smoke. Jakob and Tadhg tapped the feed of one of Auckland's drones, so they saw the debris. Only that building. See," he said pointedly to Illy, "I told you it wasn't too much."

Illy rolled her eyes and ignored him. "We learned something of interest, though," she said, in a slightly odd tone.

"What?" Cam shot a glance at me as his fingers gripped mine more tightly, concerned I would go down the rabbit hole again.

Illy caught the look. "Nothing like that," she assured him hurriedly. "This concerns you, actually."

"Me?"

"They have isolated the Mousa Moss, and they have successfully replicated it in laboratories."

"Replicated?"

"They collected samples after you alerted the team on Clava to the plant life on Mousa. They have been working on it for years, trying to grow more, I guess. But the exciting news is that the moss neutralizes the protozoa. It allows other vegetation to grow within three square meters of a single patch of moss."

"That is promising," I said. "That also explains why different plants were growing on Mousa."

"It does."

"Why is moss special?" Luca asked. "Isn't it just a plant, too?"

"Not really," Cam explained. "Most plants are cellular. That is, they have cells that move water around from the roots through the plant itself. Moss is non-vascular, so it doesn't have cells that move water. A sponge is probably the best way to describe it. Moss soaks up water instead of moving it through the plant. Each patch of moss is composed of hundreds of tiny moss plants packed together, but they don't have roots. They cluster together so they can hold water for as long as possible. Moss can only live in places that are always wet, like riverbanks and the north of Scotland."

"Something in the sponge neutralizes the protozoa. Maybe it is the non-vascular nature of it or the lack of a root system. I don't know and judging by the little I had time to read, I don't think they do either," Illy said. "Maybe that is why they used the term replicate, not grow. They have tried many other species from all communities that have living moss, but the variety from Mousa is the only one that appears to have the neutralizing effect. For now, that is all we have. No rush, but we printed those files, so you can read them when you are ready."

"It is a great breakthrough," Cam admitted. "If the moss can neutralize the protozoa and allow plants to grow in its vicinity, it means we can start re-greening the planet."

"But it doesn't mean it is safe for us, does it?" I questioned Cam.

"Not at all. The protozoa are still toxic to us, but what this means is that other plants will live outside the domes. If we can re-green the planet slowly using the moss, it means that when the protozoa are finally extinct, the job will be less daunting."

"But when will that be?" Luca asked. "Not in our lifetime, I presume?"

"Likely not," Cam confessed. "Probably not in our children's lifetime either. It will take a long time for the protozoa to die out, I would think. Especially one as widespread as this. But this gives us hope we can resettle. One day."

"I'm not really sure I ever want things to go back to the way they were," I admitted. "I love the life we have now."

"There were so many things I missed," Luca said unexpectedly as he stared off over my shoulder into the distance. "Did you know that is why I agreed to go with you and Angus on your explorations when you first arrived? I couldn't quite let go of the life I had once had. Lewis was mundane and boring, and I was desperate to escape. Two years as a builder was enough. It wasn't quite the same as the construction I had done before, building temporary housing in a war zone. I was grateful to be chosen; we all were. But I loved those years traveling with you. Meeting new people, I felt like I had a purpose. Then I met the sunshine of my life."

Luca paused and looked at Illy with so much love that I nearly swooned.

"It took meeting my Sunny to realize that I was constantly seeking my self-worth from external sources. While I was in the military, I sought approval from my superior officers, rank, and even income and possessions. Being accepted in the SAS, passing the training: those things proved I was a success. No matter how well I did on something, I felt like I should have done better. I set harder goals and forced myself to achieve them. I pushed myself to do better than everyone else. Life was a challenge, and I kept setting the bar higher. Then I took your sister and Di to Clava, and ... my life changed. The girls came along, and I can't imagine life without them. I still remember the exact moment when I realized how my mission had changed. Sunny was in the clinic. It was perhaps a day, maybe two, after she had them. I was watching my girls sleep, all three of them, and this overwhelming sense of responsibility dropped me like a punch to the jaw. I knew, at that moment, my only job was to protect them. Not because they were weak—we all know that isn't the case. But because they were worth protecting. Nothing else mattered. That was nearly seven years ago. I have my girls, and my life is complete. I never want to go back to feeling like I did for so many years. Empty. Like I wasn't enough."

"You will always be *enough*," Illy stressed, snuggling into his side, then looking over at Cam and me on the opposite couches. "All of you. You are enough. That is the greatest gift we can give to ourselves or each other. Confirming that we are enough."

"Thank you. For everything." Watching the stars dotting the sky like a tapestry through the open window, reflected in the still surface of the ocean, I curled into him. We were cruising, that peaceful sense of natural motion. We had left Adelaide where the others had salvaged as much food, bottled water, medication, equipment, and supplies as they could, also taking time to find gifts for the children and our neighbors, without whom we could never have made this journey. Cam had proudly presented Luca with his much-wanted Mont Blanc watch, amidst general hilarity. The long slow leg from Australia to Africa was ahead of us with nowhere to refuel.

"What did I do?" he asked, confused.

"Oh, I don't know, nothing much. Traveling all this way with me helped me blow up a building and say goodbye to my sister. You were wonderful with her, by the way, and I am so grateful. I was paralyzed when I saw her there. She looked nothing like the sister I remember. It was like a copy of her, a poor quality, cheap copy. But you just stepped right in and spoke to her like you had known her forever. Thank you, truly."

"She is your sister. I just thought about what I would say if we had met at a café or restaurant, if you and I were together in the old world and you had introduced me to your sister. It is no different."

The likelihood of Cam and I being a couple back in Melbourne was minuscule, but now was not the time to remind him of that.

"It was you that brought me back. I couldn't see my way out of the hole," I confessed, struggling to form the words. "It was dark and dank, and I was trapped, numb. I couldn't *feel*. Even doing this." I raised my bandaged arms. "I felt nothing. I thought I was dead. I was someplace else. Not here. Even now, I see her face flash in front of me for no reason. I feel like I am still trapped in that pit, unable to get out."

"I've been there, honey," he murmured. "When I lost you, I was in such a dark place. I never thought I would find my way out. I endured six months of hell searching for you before I finally sought to end my pain. I know what that torment feels like. There is no shame in it, and there is no shame in needing to take as much time as you need. Some people never see the light again, so I am glad you have."

"I'm not sure I am there yet. I keep seeing her. Hearing her cry."

Cam spoke so softly I had to strain to hear him. "I used to hear your voice when I was searching for you... Crying, calling out to me. I would run in the direction

I thought it came from and search until I dropped from exhaustion. But I never found you."

"How... how did you get past it?"

Cam paused, and I winced.

"Laetitia?" I asked, trying not to choke on the name. While logically I knew he had been married, happy with another woman, had a child with her, it still physically pained me to think of him with someone else when I had spent those years alone. It was enough that I saw her face every time Louis walked into a room.

"Not exactly. She was part of it, to be sure. But it was more than just her. It was Fraser, Isla, Hamish. The entire community on Lewis. They just accepted me, made me one of their own. Even Jam, in a way. The day I started to let you go is the day I found her. I think she was sent to me to help fill a tiny part of the void losing you left in my soul."

We had been married this second time for years. We were closer than ever, but a niggling part of me still resented those years he spent with Laetitia, and I had been alone. Still, I tried.

"I'm glad you found her." I steeled myself, so the emotion didn't break through. "I'm pleased she helped you."

Cam was many things, but stupid was not one of them.

"Thank you," he murmured as he nuzzled my ear. "I know that is hard for you to say, but without her, I doubt I would have survived losing you."

Not wanting to dwell on Laetitia, I asked, "Illy told me before we arrived on Auckland, about a Scots concept called a caim. Have you heard of it?"

"I think so. It is a circle of protection, isn't it? There was a band with that name. Mum had some of their music."

"That's it. Well, Illy and I were talking, and she told me about it. I suggested Lewis was like a caim, a circle that protected us from the other communities, kept us safe. She said that she thought it was the *people* on Lewis that were the caim. They bonded together to form a network, a ring if you like, and protected each other."

"She is right," Cam replied. "From the day I arrived, wet and bedraggled, they welcomed me. I haven't thought about caims in years."

"I didn't feel that at first. But I also recognized that I aligned myself with the wrong person. I just saw him as my ticket home. I chose well in that respect. He was the best person to get me back. I just didn't know about … the rest."

"Well, you don't need to worry about Angus anymore. Nor about the community on Lewis. They all love you and treat you as one of their own. My darling, what worries me now is how much weight you have lost." He ran his hands down my ribcage, which admittedly had bones protruding at all angles.

Not wanting to dwell on my weight, I kissed him ardently. The crisp night breeze blew through the room, cooling his heated body.

"Really, it means a lot to me what you did," I breathed.

"Oh? How much?"

Throwing off my top, I displayed the new burgundy lace lingerie he had sourced in Adelaide. Cam exhaled deeply.

"Oh, *that* much!" He smiled naughtily, like a child caught with a cookie.

Kissing his toes and feet languorously, I slowly worked my way up his body, kissing and running my mouth along his legs. Taunting, teasing. His back arched as I reached the insides of his thighs, pausing to take my time.

"Oh God," he moaned as his body tensed and then quaked, his face embedded in the pillow.

CHAPTER 14

REFUELING AT VARIOUS ABANDONED ports along the way and avoiding the domed communities, we made it home in just under five weeks. Weeks of pain, heartbreak, but time spent with my husband and friends. Luca and Illy had always been close to us, but now we were inseparable. Finishing each other's sentences, sharing meals. We sat up each night, talking, always with two of us awake and operating the vessel. Luca and I had been friends for years, but now we connected on a different level. Two couples who shared their dreams, talked about their fears, revealed their secrets, supported each other, and propped each other up when times are tough. As we rounded the west coast of Ireland, despite my desperation to be home, I was surprised to feel sadness about returning to Lewis and living in separate homes.

Tadhg had sent us encrypted messages along the way. While the scientists on Auckland had openly named us, they hadn't spotted our vessel, thanks to Tadhg's minor adjustments to their satellite passes, which had gone undetected. There had been surveillance cameras in the facility, and the footage was shared. Tadhg had also intercepted radio traffic to each community, asking each to watch for us. None had and reported as much. As no one on Auckland had died in the explosion and the guard had been recovered unharmed, the manic stream of communications had slowed by the time we neared home, making us feel almost safe. We were comforted by the fact that Tadhg and Jakob had targeted Auckland with their missile systems, something we could not do from Lewis.

"I need to train someone else on the system," Luca noted several days before we arrived home. "Just in case something ever happened to Sunny or me, we need to implement a backup plan."

Luca was larger than life. I couldn't see any reason he wouldn't live to be ninety. But took the point.

"I'm happy to learn," I offered, "but perhaps you should also teach someone who doesn't live in Roseglen? Just in case."

Illy agreed. "The likelihood of us ever needing to use the systems is minimal. But we have them, so it makes sense for others to know how to use them."

"Who will you ask?" Cam queried. "Someone with military knowledge? You are fairly few and far between. I don't know anyone other than Jake."

"Agreed. But no. Military training isn't essential. It is quite simple. Likely Aidan could do it."

"But would he?" Illy questioned. "He is a fairly gentle soul."

"Hamish?" suggested Luca. "He lives in Garynahine."

"You don't think his Declaration of Geneva won't affect him?" Cam replied. "Sorcha certainly takes the part about maintaining the utmost respect for human life seriously."

"Is that like the Hippocratic Oath?" Luca asked.

"It is. The Hippocratic Oath sets out the historical role of the profession. In Australia, the Declaration of Geneva was adopted years ago as the values and standards of the profession."

"What do they take in the UK?"

"I'm not sure," Cam admitted. "I'm just suggesting that Hamish may have issues with targeting another community with ballistic missiles. Perhaps one of the hunters is a better choice."

"Leave it with me. I'll find someone."

Sleeping in our bed proved impossible once we arrived home. Children were all over us twenty-four hours a day, hanging off our legs and on our laps at mealtimes and pleading to come to work with us. I had grown used to just the two of us, and these little people in my bed affected my sleep. But it was temporary. They had missed us as much as we had them. But when I woke on the third morning with a child curled up in my armpit and another wedged between Cam and me, my stiff neck and sore back were beginning to think they could love us during waking hours only.

After sleeping on a yacht, I missed the tranquility of the ocean, that gentle drifting motion, the wind blowing through the window, and the scent of salt and surf. Here, life was so *noisy*. Chickens clucked around in the morning, noises reached us from adjoining houses, or a blanket of chatter echoed outside our door each morning. Cam, proving himself far more tolerant, took Louis and Thorsten to work with him in the greenhouses, leaving the girls with me. We had missed Louis's tenth birthday in our absence, and being permitted to miss school was the best gift ever. By the third day, having them underfoot all day meant I could get nothing done, so I sent them to school to accompany Illy on her rounds.

"Have you decided what to do?" I asked Sorcha, meeting her on my way to Illy's house.

"Not really," she admitted after a pause. "But I can't help but feel like I need to try. Just to see what happens. Illy says the sample is likely fine, so we have some time."

"This isn't like trying to bake a cake," I said jokingly. "Success is pretty permanent."

"It isn't successful baking I am worried about. What if I get emotionally invested in this, and it is unsuccessful? I'm forty next year."

"If you want this, you should try. Have you asked Jorja? She is an IVF specialist."

"Actually, I had forgotten," Sorcha admitted. "We just use her as part of the general med team. We are rostered on different days, so I don't see her much."

"Deliberately?"

"Maybe. Do you think she will help me?"

"*I* will ask," Illy's crisp voice interjected from behind me.

I smirked at the interruption. No one refused Illy when she wanted something. Not even Luca or Sorcha. In fact, the only people immune to Illy were her children. Those girls were stubborn, determined, and opinionated. Bloody hard work, as Cam secretly described them.

"I know enough to realize that it is unlikely to be successful," Sorcha admitted. "The age of the sample, my age. And if it doesn't work, then that is okay. At least I know I tried. But not yet. I'm not quite ready to go through that all over again."

"Jorja is very good at what she does," Illy said. "If anyone can make it work, it is her. She was chosen for a reason. Everyone chosen to be on Clava or Auckland excels in their field. They had a choice, you know. They chose the best."

"Well, they chose you."

In our absence, Jorja and Bridget had left Aidan's farm and moved to the end of our valley. They weren't trusted, but no one made their lives difficult either. Bridget shared the communications load with Aidan, although our communications were limited now, primarily to Newgrange and the few other communities who stayed in contact like Orkney and the Shetlands. Di spoke to her cousin Kendra on Kiewa once a month after they had set up a radio following Cam and Di's visit many years ago and learning about the many other communities. We occasionally heard news from August or Bellcamp, but the contact was lessening as the years passed. After our trip to Auckland, I had no doubt messages would be non-existent.

"How are they?" I asked Sorcha cautiously. I should visit, but honestly, I couldn't bear seeing their daughters, the image of Kat still fresh in my mind. They looked so much like my own, so much like Kat, their biological mother.

"They are fine. They accept living here is hard for you. Bridget asked me if they should leave. Is that what you want?"

Sorcha and Illy watched me. I had considered it many times—how much easier it would be not to have the reminder of my sister's captivity and torture in my face. But Scarlett and Ruby were my nieces. They were loved, and that was the best I could ask for.

"No," I admitted. "I don't think I will ever be ready to see them or form a relationship with the girls. But I am glad that part of Katrin survives. Even if it is not how I wanted it to happen."

"Bridget has offered to teach at the school here when you are ready. Free Di up to go back to horticulture."

The logical part of my brain recognized this as an excellent solution. Cam, Jamie, and Fraser were struggling with the workload, and Di was a valuable asset. The school itself was closer to Bridget's home, and I suspected she would be an excellent teacher. While I wasn't ready for Scarlett and Ruby to socialize with Louis, Kat, Thorsten, and Xanthe, I had little choice.

"It is fine. That is a good idea. Cam would love to have Di back."

"Good." Illy climbed up onto her cart, empty, ready for the day's trade. "We are headed there first. You can tell Bridget yourself."

CHAPTER 15

"YOUR HOUSE IS NEARLY finished!" I called across the garden as we approached, more to break the ice than to engage in meaningful conversation.

"Ahh, hello! Wonderful to see you both home! Did you find what you were looking for?" Jorja asked, not looking up from the garden bed she was digging.

Illy was off the cart and had rounded on her before it had even come to a complete stop.

"You knew she was there!"

"No! I just meant..."

Illy's hand on her throat and Jorja's face turning purple made her rapidly revise her story.

"Alright, I knew!" she gasped as Illy's eyes, black as thunder, glinted dangerously despite only coming up to Jorja's shoulder.

"Tell us everything," Illy growled menacingly and relaxed her grip slightly, gesturing with her free hand toward the low rock wall edging the garden.

"I was in charge of the reproductive program," Jorja admitted. "For both communities."

"From the beginning?" Illy snarled.

"Yes. But when I met Freyja on Clava, I didn't know about the forced partnerships. That wasn't a lie."

Taking one look at Illy with her eyebrows raised and eyes glinting, Jorja appealed to me.

"Bridget and I were senior officials. They wouldn't let you stay with just anyone. You needed to be tested. Your skills and your loyalty. Both to each other and the program. There were empty houses on Clava, yet you never questioned why you were placed with us?"

I shrugged. We hadn't. We had been grateful for Ashton accepting and accommodating us, especially with the gruesome news we presented to him at our first meeting. We were still shellshocked ourselves. It was also still new between Cam and me; we were just desperate to be together. We didn't mind where. I caught the glimmer of mischief in Illy's eyes. She remembered reading the reports about Cam and me being intimate in public. I tried not to blush, knowing that Jorja and Bridget would also have been briefed on our extra-curricular activities.

"We loved spending time with you. It was us who vouched for you, wanted you to stay. That was genuine."

"When did you learn? About the forced breeding?" I asked, reeling from the revelation.

"We were brought into the inner circle after the Nexus came online, after we had returned to Auckland. They had lost several key players by then, so they briefed us earlier than scheduled. To allow for potential fallout, I guess."

"Me?" Illy asked coolly. She had known Jorja and Bridget on Auckland, although not well. I knew without a doubt that her loyalties lay with me now.

"You and Magali. Both of you defecting was a monumental blow to their plans. They earmarked you to play key roles, and being women yourselves, they thought you would both want to assist other women in having children."

"Their plans?" Illy asked. "Who are they?"

"Ashton, Angus, and Derek. The three of them were behind it all."

"Derek? That worm?"

"That worm was a highly renowned genetic engineer. He was top in his field in modifying genomes," Jorja advised.

"How did I never know that?" Illy asked incredulously.

"He was the silent partner, and his skills weren't required until much later. Ashton was known, so he stayed on Auckland. After working as a settlement advisor, Derek went straight to Clava to work as a lab tech, despite being Australian. No one knew. Angus wanted to start out in one of the communities to get a feel for when they would be ready for the next phase—opening the portals to form the Nexus and getting everyone to sign up to the Collective. Once everyone agreed, they would begin selective breeding and later genetic engineering. But they knew it would take quite a few years to be ready."

"Hold on," I interjected. "You just said that like they are two different things."

"Well, that is because they are," Jorja explained. "Selective breeding has occurred in some form for hundreds of years—dog or horse breeders choosing animals with certain traits or characteristics so that a particular attribute is enhanced. Royal families marrying off cousins. In this scenario, it meant choosing people with certain genotypes and phenotypes and ensuring they reproduced to ensure those genes survived. But those genes occurred naturally, like me having dark hair. What genetic engineering involves is making a direct change to a person's genome in a laboratory. Editing the genome if you like. Let's say that you were the perfect candidate, but you had the gene for Parkinson's disease. They could edit your genome by disabling that specific gene."

"Holy hell, they are playing God."

Jorja shrugged sadly. "That is why we needed to leave. The problem was, when we found out that part, the girls were less than a year old. We had nowhere to go and didn't want to take babies through the portal. So, we waited as long as we could. But it made us sick. Modifying people. Trying to create the perfect human."

I turned to Illy. "What was your role supposed to be in all of this?"

"I knew none of this. I bailed well before they told me this part. I was uncomfortable about forcing communities to join the Collective, withholding supplies, and basically starving them of resources. That, combined with the surveillance, was enough for me to know that it wasn't anything I wanted to be a part of."

"They thought anyone who was a scientist or military would see the importance of it. You were both, so your leaving blindsided them. And I can see the logic, or ... at least I could," Jorja hastened to add. "They had carefully mapped out characteristics and traits and ensured that only the healthiest specimens were chosen. Of the seven billion people alive, only a fraction of one percent of the world's population survived. The testing was highly detailed. Genome, physical health, skills, and intelligence. Those people chosen to survive were the best of the best, biologically speaking. From my scientific perspective, that made sense. I mean, you wouldn't breed from sickly cows that passed those traits onto calves, would you?"

I could see the logic. I always could. It wasn't until I met Cam and had Katrin that I saw differing viewpoints with equal clarity.

"We always knew that our role was to ensure the survival of humanity, and both Bridget and I supported that. What we didn't know was that they had planned to force people to reproduce with each other. We knew that each of us would need to have a child. For Bridge and me, that wasn't a philosophical problem. We wanted children, and we always needed a donor father. We were told that we would be given handpicked genetic material." Jorja sighed. "While we would have preferred to choose, we were at their mercy. Unlike you, we couldn't just have children ourselves. We knew that every person here had been carefully chosen to filter out inherited diseases and were highly intelligent. It wasn't quite like playing Russian Roulette."

"I can see that," I confessed. After all, if it hadn't been for Cam, Di and Sorcha wouldn't have Kendra. I also knew what it felt like to be desperate for a child.

"When did you realize it was my sister who was their biological mother?" I asked, the words choking me.

Jorja paused and looked at me appraisingly before responding, assessing if I could deal with the truth. A glance at Illy's stormy face was enough to make her relent.

"I worked in that facility, but mostly in the labs and offices. I am sorry to say, to me, they were just specimens. Cadavers. I never went into those rooms until Bridget and I became suspicious about the girl's parentage. Then I went searching. Looked at the person in the bed. Read the chart and realized who I was looking at. She looked like you and had your surname. I knew about the backup genomes by then, so it all made sense."

"She was a living person. So were all the others. Not specimens," I seethed.

"I know that ... now. But at the time, they were just genetic material. No different from any other lab or facility I have worked in. You tend to be quite detached in medicine. You focus on the illness and the cure, not the person."

"You lied to me. You told me you thought they were mine. Why didn't you just tell me she was alive?"

"I couldn't tell you without admitting I had been part of it. That I could have done something, ended it for her. But that would have made us a target. We would do anything to keep our girls safe. We honestly thought you would work out we were senior when Bridget slipped and told you she was in charge of communications. But you didn't, and we thought we had dodged a bullet."

Sitting on the grassy patch beside the new vegetable garden Jorja was planting, I stared out across the vast blue sky. I wasn't sure how I felt about these people—knowing that they had access to my sister for *years* and did nothing. This woman had played an active role in exploiting her, had likely been the one to harvest her eggs. She had been privy to the most controlling aspects of their plans and hadn't spoken out. When they had arrived here, they had deliberately lied to me, told me they thought the children were mine. Why? Illy and Magali had left when they learned what the Collective was about. These women had said nothing. But they had children, very young children, which Illy and Magali did not. Was that the deciding factor? Did wanting to protect your children force you to make different decisions?

"And now?" Illy asked, seeing me conflicted. "Where are your loyalties now?"

"Bridge and I just want to raise our children in peace. We have discussed it at length. We like it here, but we will go if you want us to. Since we had the girls, our focus has shifted. We used to live for our careers, the mission, and our roles in the project. But after they were born, we became responsible for these tiny people. We knew our needs came second. Everything we did was about them. That was when we had doubts. But we managed to juggle it, at least for a while. When we worked out their parentage, that was the turning point. The point where we knew we needed to protect these children and protect them from people like us who wanted to manipulate them, control their lives. One day, they will be forced to be part of the program, and the thought of that made us physically ill. We chose to be parents. There was no way off Auckland Island, not with young children. The few vessels there were always off on missions, so we waited. Requested another for a secondment to Clava and waited until it was approved. Then ... we just walked out."

Illy and I glanced at each other. Many times, she and I had spoken about this: how becoming a parent changes your outlook, how the hard and fast logic softens slightly when it is overlaid with the emotion of being responsible for another life.

"I understand," I admitted. "I was focused and logic-driven…until I had Katrin. Then the prism through which I saw the world changed slightly. I can pinpoint the precise moment, too. She was asleep in my arms, and I was holding her tiny pink hand in mine. She hadn't been well, cried all night. I was exhausted, yet I realized I was now solely responsible for protecting this person. It was my job to guide her, protect her so that she grew up to become an adult. Give her life experiences. She needed me, and my choices weren't about me anymore."

"For me, it was when I saw Luca hold our girls for the first time." Illy sighed. "They were premature, as you know," she said, looking at me. Illy's pregnancy had been high risk. With her carrying twins and being so tiny in stature, we had all worried about her. She was enormous and very unwell. Sorcha had induced the twins early to save them, and they had all spent weeks in the clinic under constant supervision until they were well enough to leave.

"I was lying in the clinic, drugged to the eyeballs, terrified and overwhelmed and wondering what on earth I had done. Across the room, I saw this enormous man in an armchair with two tiny baby girls, asleep, wrapped in blankets, one in each arm. The look of sheer awe on his face shattered any reservations I had. We were a family. The mother lion in me rose, and that was it."

Jorja smiled wanly. "You do understand."

We sat in silence as we replayed our harsh induction into motherhood. No manuals, no guidance. Just wham! Parent.

"There is one more thing I need to tell you. Then that is it. That is all we know," Jorja said, pulling me from my trance. She took a deep breath and let it out. "We found reference to one more full sibling to Scarlett and Ruby. Grown by a surrogate, like us."

"You said that there were ... five." I gagged on the last word.

Illy placed a reassuring hand on my shoulder and spoke. "That is true. Five fertilized embryos were created from your sister. But only three were implanted. It was in the medical notes Cam found."

Illy had no reason to lie to me. The notes Cam had found that proved my parents had damned my sister. The notes that were sitting under my t-shirts in my bedroom dresser. The records I had never read beyond the first page.

"If you destroyed the lab—" Jorja spoke cautiously, and a quick nod from Illy confirmed this, "then there is only one left."

"Where?"

"We don't know. We looked. Really, we did. We found no trace on Auckland or Clava. If there is another full sibling to our girls, we would like to know. To meet him or her. It is important to us that these children know each other. But those records were erased before we went looking. There is a record of the child's surrogacy, redacted, of course, and the child is roughly the same age as our girls. But that single record is all we could find. It is possible the child didn't survive the pregnancy or birth or died soon after. But we just want to know."

Illy and I continued her rounds in silence, jolting along the track. Guilt consumed me. I was supposed to be helping; it was harvest time, the busiest time of the year for her. She had wasted months helping me, and she had brought me along today to help, not to wallow in self-pity.

"What will you do?" she asked as we reached a smooth section of road.

"Do?"

"Do you want to find the other child?"

I had thought of nothing else for the past few hours but still had no clue.

"Let me summarize," Illy said in her typically forthright manner. "Your choices are: One. Recognize that there is another child out there, likely borne of your sister. This child is no more yours than Ruby or Scarlett. So, you acknowledge that fact, reconcile within yourself that you will play no role in their life, and wish them well. We have seen nothing to make us believe that Clava or Auckland would harm a child. Two: try to track down this third child, and, assuming they exist, leave your family here again. Then you need to work out what relationship you want with that child. Three: we ask Clava outright, although given that we just destroyed one of their facilities and the remaining two embryos, I really don't think that is a viable option."

"Likely not."

"I guess the real question is, how much do you want this? You will always wonder. But do you want to leave your children a second time?"

"No." The word came out before I had even consciously thought it. "No. I never want to leave them again. Di said Xanthe had nightmares for weeks after we left. One of the children in Garynahine told her about Laetitia. She spent the entire time we were gone thinking that would happen to me, and she would never see me again. I couldn't do that to her or Louis. He fretted the entire time. No, I couldn't put them through that again."

"Well, there is your answer. But do you want us to find out what we can? It might not be much or anything at all. But we can try."

"I would like that. I need closure. For Kat's sake."

"Consider it done."

CHAPTER 16

PICKING THINGS UP AND slamming them down, I was irrationally angry. After this morning's surgeries, I was supposed to be sterilizing equipment, but a dead weight was burning in my chest, refusing to be dislodged. Dropping the scalpels and forceps in the bucket of steaming water, the clanging echoed around the room as scalpels and other tools bounced from the metal surface.

Cam stood in the doorway, watching me cautiously. "Are you okay?"

"Fine," I snapped as the surgical scissors clanged in the metal bucket.

Cam paused hesitantly, then stepped inside, closing and barring the door behind him. I barely noticed him, unable to overcome the overwhelming need to destroy something. Tear it apart with my bare hands. Smash something. I slammed my hand down on the cold stainless-steel surgery table, trying to suppress the urge to explode.

"What is it?"

I had woken feeling tired and cranky, snapping at the kids for minor things, and unable to eat. As the day had progressed, my mood had worsened. The solid mass growing in my chest was gnawing at me. My jaw clenched, and I had a headache forming, a dull throbbing behind my right eye.

"Tell me." Cam was beside me, his large, warm hand on my arm. I shook it off like an annoying fly.

Cam had learned from our earlier marriage not to touch me when I was angry. He retreated to a safe distance and watched. Unable to communicate my feelings, I felt the heat boiling me from the inside, choking me, blocking the words. Cam stood back and watched as I threw things.

"Your sister?"

Turning off the boiling pot, I turned, glaring. "No."

"What is it then?"

"Stop bloody interfering! I'm fine."

Cam maintained his calm expression. "Jorja?"

My eyes narrowed to slits at the name as I hissed, "*I don't want to talk about it.*"

Cam nodded slowly. "Illy told me she knew all along."

I rounded on him. "I can't believe they kept this from me. They *knew* she was there. She *saw* her. They could have helped her at any point in the *years* they knew she was being held there. They let us go all that way without preparing me for what I would find. Then she finally tells me that there is another child of hers out there, somewhere. And she knew! She always knew! But that isn't the worst part. My own family did that to her. They are responsible for this. They subjected her to that degrading life. Slashing her open, abusing her. Handling her like she was a piece of meat!" I was blathering and didn't care. I slammed my hand down on the table again for emphasis, the pain reverberating up my arm.

"Your parents couldn't have known what they planned to do to her."

"Does it matter?" I fired back, shards of ice piercing him with my words. "They signed her up for medical research. She was their daughter, and they handed her over like a steak at a barbeque. They didn't give her a second thought when they admitted her to the nursing home. They just kept living their precious lives. They couldn't possibly let a simple matter like their daughter being comatose impact their all-important social calendar."

"You don't know that. They may not have shown their feelings to you, but they would have been distraught at losing their daughter in that way."

"You never met them," I pointed out angrily. "When I told Mum I was leaving forever, I had to ask her to come home and say goodbye. Beg her is probably more accurate. Do you know what she said? 'You are an adult, Freyja.' I was barely twenty-two. Dad didn't even bother leaving his precious conference, not even for a day. He was a few hours away by plane, and he didn't even bother coming back. I meant nothing to them. You are assuming all families were perfect, like *yours!*"

"Maybe," Cam replied, not taking the bait. "But they may have been misled, too. Think about it. The world is ending; everyone is dying. Your older daughter is gone, but at least you know she is safe. We know from Sorcha that life after we left was nothing like we had ever experienced. Maybe they thought the scientific purposes were to help save people from the pandemic? Could they even have thought that she could save people like you?"

I didn't want to consider this. They had signed the consent forms, made her a lab rat.

"No! Someone is responsible, and it is them. Without them signing those forms, this would never have happened!"

"You know how persuasive the government teams were," Cam continued in his low, calm voice. "Your parents were practical, logical people, weren't they? If they thought Katrin's life might save others, they would have agreed, wouldn't they?"

"Maybe," I growled. "They believed in organ donation. They would have seen it as being for the greater good."

"Perhaps it was? Scarlett, Ruby. They wouldn't exist if it weren't for Katrin."

Fury exploded within me at the mention of my sister's children, and the simmering volcano erupted.

"They exploited her! For *years*, they abused her. I cannot, *will not,* believe it was for the greater good. It is my fault, too! I could have made sure she was safe before I left. I didn't. I had time. I arrived at the facility in Melbourne early. I should have spent that time ensuring she was safe. Safe from *them*!"

Cam fell silent. I knew what he was trying to do. Make me forgive my parents. But I couldn't. I wasn't ready to forgive. They had sacrificed my sister—she whom I had loved above all others.

"I will never, ever forgive them," I seethed, my skin alight. "Who knows what those lab techs might have done to her? Alone and paralyzed. Abused her? Raped her? I know from the scars on her stomach they cut her open more than once. No. I don't care if they are gone. They are not my family."

Even through the flames consuming me, I could sense Cam's disagreement, but he wasn't prepared to argue with me.

"What? You think I am cold because I refuse to forgive my parents? You have always thought I was a cold, heartless bitch, haven't you!" I shoved him hard in the chest, my face flaming, rage consuming me.

Cam didn't react, just stood solidly, watching me. "They are still your family. No matter what they did."

"No!" I hit him again. "Those monsters are no relations of mine!"

He caught my arms as they struck at him a third time, folded them in, and held them against his chest.

"They are your parents, Frey. They did what they thought was best."

"You are a mindless fucking idiot! You know nothing! They may as well have done this to her themselves! Tied her to that bed and abused her! Hacked her up and used her for spare parts!" The red beast had taken hold and wasn't letting go. I fought him to release my arms, thrashing and kicking.

Cam pushed my back hard against the single brick wall of the shed, pinning me in place. His mouth found mine and kissed me hard, stealing my breath.

No. I squirmed and tried to push him off me. Anger still had the upper hand. The rough bricks gouged my back, but he was larger and stronger. I was engulfed by his body, trapped between him and the wall, and fought to get away. *No. Not now*, my brain raged.

Yes, now! My body responded as my heart began to beat faster, and the tightness around my chest loosened just a little. His body pinned mine to the wall. His hands were on my breasts now, and my temperature cooled slightly as he lifted my top over my head and dropped it on the dusty floor. His lips were demanding, and mine responded without my brain wanting them to. He picked me up effortlessly with one arm around my waist, still thrashing, and sat me on the surgery table. I felt my jeans loosen, sliding down my legs, his lips not relenting in their passion. As he laid me over the table, I felt the cool air hit my legs, the icy surface making me convulse. I sucked in my breath as he touched me. I wasn't fighting him anymore. Now I had a new goal. He was teasing me: touching, stroking, caressing. Fury rose in me once more as his fingers played with me.

"Fucking do it *now*," I demanded, sitting up and slapping his hand away. He grinned.

"No."

A soft growl escaped my lips, taking him by surprise, but he ignored me. As he continued playing with me, the frustration in me rose.

"Now!" I ordered. I wanted him, or I would tear him apart. Either were entirely feasible options.

"Not ... yet."

All the air went out of me as the warmth of pleasure rose and overtook the anger.

"Please..." I begged, and I felt the half-grin quirk his mouth.

He was within me before I could think, and I was complete. No longer was emotion controlling me. Now it was desire, passion, and overwhelming love for him that drove me. And drive me he did. I forgot everything else as I focused on the sensation of togetherness. Fury had propelled me first, but now the heat of desire overrode everything else.

"I needed that." I nibbled his ear. Curled up in the corner, old blankets under and over us, we lay on the straw in each other's arms. I felt as safe and protected as I had the first time.

"If all of these wonderful years with you have taught me nothing, my beautiful, hot-headed wife, it is never to argue with you when you are in a temper."

"I'm so sorry for being awful to you."

"It was the anger talking. It is okay."

"No, it isn't. All those years I spent alone, I replayed every argument we had. I beat myself up a thousand times for each harsh word I said to you. If only I had known what would happen, I would never have spoken to you in anger. So many nights when I was alone, all I could think about was *that* was how you remembered me and our time together. Angry. Difficult."

"I never thought of those times. I only remembered the wonderful moments we spent together. At the springs... at home ... in bed." He punctuated this last comment with a hand sneaking around my bottom. "Even just curled up on the couch, reading or talking. I regretted none of it. I just knew how fortunate I was to have you, even for the short time we had. I think we needed that time on August, to love and to learn. So, we could have this time."

"Happy?" I asked cautiously, my bitter words of the past hour still lingering overhead.

"Deliriously so. Every day I wake beside you, I thank whatever deity brought you into my life. Twice." He kissed me gently as my hands explored his broad, muscular chest and worked their way down the flat expanse of stomach to his hips. "Come on. The kids will be home from school soon and will come looking for us."

"They can wait. Besides, the door is locked."

CHAPTER 17

ASSESSING THE TIME FROM the sun's position midway down the sky, I finished inserting the last stitches in the lamb's leg, grumbling to myself, "Tell me again why I am doing this?"

Because your daughter adores this frigging lamb, and you can't bear to make her sad by telling her you cooked it up for supper was the honest answer. Animals here were livestock, not pets. But Lambie was to Xanthe what Fred had been to me. She adored this motherless lamb, and Lambie followed her around like a dog. Many a night, I had found Lambie hidden in Xan's room, curled up on a blanket. This time, Lambie had cut her leg on a fence trying to get to Xanthe while she was at school. Xanthe had been distraught, tears streaming down her face until Di had carried Lambie to me. Fortunately, I was home. It was a nasty wound. I knew Xan was lurking outside, waiting. Despite my frustration, part of me knew how she felt. Poor Fred. Even after all these years, I still missed him. He had been responsible for finding the cave with the antipodean portal but also for me falling through it. He didn't deserve the end he got. I hadn't met a goat since with Fred's personality.

I grimaced at the time I was wasting, the burden of other urgent tasks needling me but finished cleaning up. Stitching was slow and messy work. Wondering how we would manage Lambie when she grew into a fully grown sheep, I lifted my head as shouts in the distance entered the shed and echoed around the walls. I strained to hear the words. It was a female voice.

"Sorcha! Cam! Is anyone here?"

The vet clinic door faced the opposite direction where I could see the children playing in the yard between our homes but not down the valley.

"Louis!" I called, glimpsing his brown hair outside. "Who is that?"

He popped his head in the door. "It's Bridget," he hissed, fear in his eyes.

To Louis, these women were still people from out there. No matter how many times we told him that Illy, Cam, and I were also from out there, he remained fearful. I couldn't blame him. *Perhaps he had picked up on my reticence*, I thought, making a mental note to be friendlier to them in front of him.

Finishing off, I checked on her one more time before placing Lambie in the pen to sleep off the anesthesia and washed my hands. As I stepped outside, I saw the relief in Bridget's eyes as she came into view.

"Thank goodness you are here!" she exclaimed as she assisted Jorja up the dirt path. Jorja was as white as a ghost and hopping on one leg, each movement making her look like she was going to vomit or faint. Their girls were bringing up the rear, huddled together. Every time I saw them, I had flashes of my own girls and needed to look away.

"What's up?" I asked, dropping the hand towel.

"Jorj slipped and fell down the back steps. She has broken her leg. I can see the bone poking through the skin." Bridget looked rather unwell as she described the wound. I had pegged her as the faint at the sight of blood type when we first met.

"Why didn't you just call us? One of us would have come to you."

Bridget's face dropped. "The radio slipped out of my hand. I was washing dishes as Jorja fell and screamed. I picked it up, and it smashed on the flagstones. We only have one, and the girls were too scared to come and get one of you, so we had to walk."

Fighting to keep my face neutral, I went out to help them and assisted Jorja into the clinic, briskly shooing Scarlett and Ruby off to find the others, asking them to pass on the message to Xanthe that Lambie would be fine. While not a medical clinic, I could at least get her off her good leg and potentially minimize her pain. Bridget had already cut down her pants, which were flapping around as she hopped. Once laid on the table, I could see the problem immediately.

"That's nasty."

Jorja grimaced and spoke, her voice trembling. "I know. The tibia is broken and protruding. I think the fibula might be broken too. It isn't possible to operate on myself, and we have no equipment, anyway."

"Well, you looked after me once. Perhaps it is my turn."

Bridget looked stunned, despite my assurances. "Where is Sorcha?"

"Sorcha was called out to a childbirth a few hours ago," I advised. "Out here in the wilderness, they don't tend to be quick. Because you wanted the day off today, Di finished up school early to help Cam and Fraser. They are all up at Garynahine, tending the greenhouses up there. They were rather neglected in our absence."

Bridget flushed at the reference to our absence.

"Illy is out catching up on her rounds, Luca at the whisky still, Jamie and Jacinda took some of the children out for a picnic and picking wild herbs, and Isla is supposed to be on a day off as she didn't get one while I was away. So, we have a couple of choices. All the carts have been taken for the day, but Isla and I can assist you to the clinic at Garynahine. One of the doctors may be there, but it is a very long way to walk. The alternative is Isla and I assist you here until Sorcha or one of the other doctors arrives. But I warn you, it will probably be at least two hours. Possibly longer."

Bridget looked horrified. Jorja nodded grimly.

"A broken bone is a broken bone, whether in a person or an animal," she assured Bridget. "The treatment is the same."

Bridget didn't look convinced but gave her consent.

"Louis! Can you get Sam? I need him to find his mother."

Louis disappeared and returned a few moments later with Sam's dark head appearing over him.

"What do you need?"

"Can you radio your mum? She went up to the Adams' farm. Petra is in labor."

Sam's face fell.

"What is it?" I snapped, harsher than I intended at his lack of action. "We need her or one of the other doctors."

"Mum took the only working radio. She is expecting another call, so she took it with her. She is the only one on duty today."

"Well, we have two, don't we? It might be at our place or Illy's?"

"We used to. Remember how the other one won't hold a charge or something? Uncle Luca said it was useless."

My stomach lurched. He was right. I was alone with a woman desperately needing surgery. Jorja was looking worse by the second. My brain snapped into action.

"Right. Well then, you need to take a bike. It is a long way. Do you know which way to go?"

Sam nodded and slipped off to the charging shed.

"Louis, I need you to take another and ride to the clinic at Garynahine. See which doctor is second on the list, find them, and get them here as quickly as you can. Can you do that?"

Louis nodded. "But first, get Isla, will you? I am going to need her help."

Exhaling, I knew I could rely on the boys. Trustworthy and mature, they would both get the job done. Damn. Why had Jamie and Jacinda chosen today of all days to take their kids and Isla's on a bloody walk to collect herbs for her naturopathic practice? I could have used their help in wrangling the remaining kids. Naturally, Jacinda had taken the more compliant children, leaving me with mine and Illy's.

"Those with spirit," Di had said when she learned which children Jacinda had left behind to attend school.

"Those that don't do as they are told!" Illy had promptly rebuked her.

"Kat! Kendra!" I called, and the two girls appeared in the doorway.

"You are in charge of the younger ones. Ruby and Scarlett are here, too. Keep them happy and fed. There is bread in the kitchen. Honey, too. Thorsten might need a nap if he is looking tired or starts getting cranky. This could take some time." I looked over at Bridget. "Are you sure you are okay with this?"

Bridget looked like she wanted to object, but Jorja piped up feebly, pain etched in her face. "It is fine, Freyja. I want you to do this. Sooner is always best. Please, do what you can."

I recognized this as trust, both in my skill as a surgeon, albeit a veterinary one, but also in me. She had deliberately withheld information from me, and although I had been home for several weeks, I hadn't entirely forgiven her.

Isla appeared at the door, wearing a flour-covered apron and drying her hands.

"What's u..." She trailed off and recoiled as she saw Jorja on the table, Bridget standing opposite. Despite Bridget and Jorja living only a few kilometers away, at the head of our valley in a refurbished croft with their girls, Isla was still uncomfortable around them both. Still, I noticed she had thawed somewhat.

"I need your help, Isles. Jorja has a broken tibia, likely a tib-fib."

Isla's crisp Scots accent echoed through the shed. "Branched out, have we? Wee lambs and coos not exciting enough for you anymore?"

I smiled at her characteristic dry humor. "No. But Sorcha has been called out to a birth, and I have no way to get Jorja to the main clinic without causing her significantly more pain."

Good flickered for a nanosecond across Isla's tanned face, and I struggled to maintain my calm countenance.

Bridget looked up at Isla, pleading in her eyes. "She is in pain. Please, can you help her?"

Ever the professional, Isla crossed the room in a few strides and stood beside me.

"What do you need?"

Within an hour, Isla and I had Jorja prepped, sedated, and were slowly working on opening the jagged leg wound. Bridget had refused to leave her, making me revise my opinion somewhat. She held Jorja's hand, speaking softly to her, even though her partner couldn't hear her. Isla glanced at me. I needed to realign the bone and insert a rod. *Am I ready?*

I returned the look. This wasn't an operation we routinely performed here, and I was aware of the risks. Mostly, we hatched and patched. Few animals were worth the rehabilitation required for an internal splint. But I knew how, having performed one on Mike's prized stallion a year ago, and we had the equipment thanks to the many explorations and raids on medical and veterinary clinics over the years. Sorcha also kept extensive supplies here, just in case there was an emergency, and she didn't have time to get to the main clinic in town.

"Right then," Isla instructed Bridget firmly. "Hold her hand. You will need to watch her eyes and warn us if she moves. She must remain perfectly still. You need to alert me quickly if you see any movement now, so pay close attention."

Jorja was out cold, and Isla was highly capable of managing the anesthesia. This was more for Bridget's sake, and I appreciated Isla directing Bridget to look away from the action. I had put up a sheet for a little privacy. Watching orthopedic surgery was brutal, especially if it was someone you loved. Bridget turned her chair to face Jorja, and Isla grinned at me from behind her face mask. With a few sharp maneuvers, I realigned both bones. I was sweating terribly. Now for the problematic part: inserting the rods and pins. I tried to hammer quietly while Isla clattered things around on the steel trolley in an attempt to muffle the noise.

An hour later, we finished cleaning the ragged wound and inserted the last stitches. Feeling fatigued, I wished I could sit down. It had been a long time since I had needed to focus for so long on something so complex. I looked up at Isla. She smiled.

"Bridget," she said softly. "She will be fine. She will need lots of help for a few weeks. But she will be okay. Freyja here is an excellent surgeon. Wasted on animals she is."

Bridget's eyes filled with tears of relief. "Thank you. Thank you so much."

Recognizing that it was peaceful outside, I looked over at Isla as I turned to clean up, "Can you check on the kids? They are awfully quiet."

The silence registered, making her eyes pop in fear. Isla bolted outside, not even removing her gloves and mask. The memory of Louis's head wound haunted her, no doubt. They would be fine. Kat and Kendra were sensible girls. They wouldn't allow anything to happen. Besides, there were eight of them. What could they possibly get up to?

As I sterilized the instruments and monitored Jorja, I strained my ears. I could hear Isla calling, sounding ever more frantic. Fear rising in my chest, I checked on Jorja's blood pressure as I stripped off my surgical apron.

"Can you watch her?" I asked. Bridget looked up at me, confused.

Dashing out the door, I could hear Isla up at Sorcha's house, calling. No point going that way. Heading down the main path, I looked in our home. Silent. Checking under every bed and in every cupboard, it was soon apparent that they weren't here. Checking all the sheds and outbuildings, I marched briskly down to Luca and Illy's.

"I should be with Jorja," I simmered. "She isn't even conscious yet. When I find those bloody kids..." But Illy's house was empty, too. Frustration was turning to worry. *Where the bloody hell did eight kids go?*

As I turned to leave, I heard a faint thumping. Standing silently, I tuned my ears. Yes, in the pantry. Something was there. Swinging open the pantry door with a jerk, I braced myself to find eight kids jump out and scream "surprise!" Instead, I was speechless when I looked down to see Kat and Kendra on the floor, trussed up like chickens, back-to-back and gagged.

"What the...!" I dropped to my knees and removed Kat's gag.

"Who did this?" I thundered as I helped them both.

"Summer and Ally," Kat whispered sheepishly.

"You let two six-year-old girls tie you up?"

"They tricked us." Kat was mortified, her face flushed. "We were playing hide and seek. Then they suggested we play a game called Houdini. He was a magician. He could escape from being tied up and underwater, too."

"I know who he was," I growled. "Get on with it."

"They tied us up, and we were supposed to escape. Then it was someone else's turn. Except they tied us up tight, laughed as they shoved us in there, and ran away."

I tried not to smile. I could picture Illy's girls doing this. Conniving little minxes.

"Where are they now?" I asked, a little more kindly.

"We don't know. They shoved us in there and ran away laughing with the others." Kendra sobbed. Kendra was a softly spoken, quiet girl. Being locked up likely would have distressed her. I put my arm around her.

"It is okay. It was only a game. How long ago did they do this?"

"We don't know. It was dark in there, and we couldn't talk," Kendra cried. Kat, who was older and a lot tougher, just shrugged.

"An hour, maybe. I don't know."

Remembering that time I was tied and left in the dark near Inverness, I was pleased she didn't appear too badly affected. At least she knew someone would find her in Illy's pantry.

"Come on. Let's find them and..."

"What's going on?" Luca spoke cheekily from behind me as he entered the kitchen, Illy close behind. "Stealing my coffee, are you?"

"Your daughters," I snapped back acerbically, "tied up Kat and Kendra and ran off with the little ones."

"How on earth did they know how to do that?" Illy asked, amazed.

"I taught them." Luca looked shamefaced. "They asked me how to get untied if they were ever tied up, so we practiced tying each other up and escaping."

"Well, they neglected to tell these two how to escape. Gagged them and left them in your pantry. I will be having words when I find them. Now, where are they? They have Xanthe and Thorsten. Scarlett and Ruby, too. How far can six kids have gone?"

Isla burst through the door, visibly distressed. "I can't find..." she started, then stopped as she saw Kat and Kendra, her shoulders slumping. "Ah, you've found them!"

"No, just these two," Illy told her without explanation. "We need to find the others. Where have you looked?"

Splitting up, we searched. Illy and Luca went one way, Isla and I, the other. I had no time to think about Jorja now. I was frantic. Out of my mind with worry. *Where are they?*

Despite being nearly seven, Summer and Ally had the attitude of children who were much older. Both of them were highly intelligent troublemakers. Combined, they were like a pair of teen web-hackers.

"When I got my hands on them!" I seethed.

Isla glanced at me and saw my face, recognizing that this was fear speaking.

"It will be alright," she soothed. "They are just playing. Lost track of time. You'll see."

I appreciated her calm demeanor, but it did nothing to appease my frayed temper.

The sun was setting rapidly, the orange orb just hanging on before it dropped below the horizon. We still had no idea where they were. The sheds, houses, school were all empty. We had searched the valley floor nearly to the crossroads at Leurbost. Glancing up at the beautiful colors of dusk, Isla and I hurried back up the road past Loch Acha Mor. I stopped dead, blinked, and looked again.

They had built a makeshift raft out of pieces of wood, branches, and reeds. Even from the roadside I could see it was rickety and unlikely to bear their weight for much longer. All six of them were floating in the middle of the loch, scrunched up in the middle of the raft as the edges dipped below the water's surface. They had taken nothing to act as oars, drifted out, and now had no way to get back. None of them could swim well. We had always intended to teach them but never found the time. Isla and I began the descent down the grassy bank to the loch.

"Xanthe!" I called. "Thorsten! Don't move! We are coming!"

Out of the corner of my eye, I saw Illy and Luca approach the other end of the loch, the sandy bank where they had likely launched from.

Thorsten, hearing my voice, stood up and waved frantically, calling, "Mumma!" Precariously balanced on the rickety raft, the corner tilted, and he pitched forward, falling headfirst into the loch as the others held onto each other, screeching as one side of the raft dropped below the water.

"He can't swim!" Running down the bank, I kicked off my shoes and waded waist-deep in the freezing loch, ready to dive, but my focus was redirected when I heard an almighty splash to my right. Luca, fully clothed, was already three strokes across the loch and heading for the raft at high speed. Xanthe was wailing, the others crying, their hands protecting their ears from the shrill cries. Even from here, I could see that Summer and Ally were clutching each other, terrified.

Luca reached the raft and looked around. There was no sign of Thorsten. Isla grabbed at my upper arm as I backed out of the reeds and watched, trembling, unable to breathe. Luca duck dived, and I saw his booted feet in the air as he submerged. The loch was bitterly cold and deep in the center with very little visible in the murky water.

Luca surfaced, gasping for breath as the children screamed.

"Stay there. Sit down!" I could hear Illy instructing them, but they were too hysterical to listen to her.

Luca surfaced a second time, gasping and spluttering, angrily pushing wet hair from his eyes and taking a deep breath before going under again. I dropped to my knees in the muddy, shallow water, unable to lift my eyes from the scene unfolding before me.

When Luca's dark head broke the water's surface, he had a small, limp body cradled in his arms. I could hear the girls screaming from where I kneeled in the mud but had no attention for the noise. I couldn't breathe as I watched Luca treading water in the middle of the lake, Thorsten balanced on one of his enormous forearms as he blew in his lungs. Nothing. He lay there like a limp rag doll, his favorite red fire engine t-shirt billowing across the surrounding water. Floppy and lifeless. The sob escaped my lips. Isla's elegant, tanned hands rested on my shoulders, but I barely registered her touch. I couldn't take my eyes from the still form of my son.

Luca lifted Thorsten onto the raft and swam, towing it to the shore where Illy stood. Isla and I ran to meet them, still bootless. I didn't feel the sharp rocks as I ran. All I could see through the blur was my child's blue, lifeless body.

Illy was helping the other children off the raft, and Luca was kneeling in the mud, performing CPR as we arrived. I dropped beside Thorsten's head and wanted to sob, hold my son. But I knew CPR. *Focus Freyja*, I berated myself, and positioned my body to enter the two half breaths as Luca finished compressions. Luca paused, and I exhaled. Watched the tiny stomach rise and fall, then breathed again. Luca resumed chest compressions, and I heard Thorsten's ribs crack. *It sounded like a zipper*, I thought abstractedly as the popping sound filled my ears. Luca didn't flinch. Neither did I. He could survive broken ribs. He couldn't survive if we didn't resuscitate. Luca compressed, I breathed. I could vaguely hear Illy, Isla, and the children somewhere behind me, but had no capacity to think about them right now. His skin was taking on a bluish-gray tinge, and I steeled myself to focus on the timing. *Breathe*—compressions, breath, compressions. Then under my hands, he jerked, coughed, spluttered, and projectile vomited a sizeable volume of water onto his chest.

Luca, acting quickly, rolled Thorsten to his side. Careful not to let him sense my distress, I spoke to him, calm and soothing. Enveloped in a cotton wool cloud, I scarcely registered anything as Luca carried him home, leaving wet boot prints along the path, the others in his wake. I walked at his left elbow, speaking calmly to a crying Thorsten. Isla was carrying my sopping muddy boots, I noted. The cool air penetrated my soaked jeans like needles, but I didn't care. The girls were still crying: Xanthe, Ruby, and Scarlett in fear of what they had seen, Summer and Ally likely terrified of the consequences. But I was in no fit state to comfort them. I could hear Isla soothing Xanthe, Ruby, and Scarlett behind me, although I couldn't quite pick up the words. Alive. He was alive. But what damage had been done? What was it—three minutes without air? It had felt like an eternity he had been underwater. Then unconscious.

Night had fallen as we walked back to Roseglen, a sliver of stars twinkling in a cloudless night sky through the transparent dome. Lights were on in several houses as well as the vet clinic, indicating Sam had returned with Sorcha. Hearing the commotion generated by crying children, she came rushing out of the shed where she had been tending to Jorja. I heard Illy briefing her on what happened, and Sorcha assumed command in her natural manner, ordering Luca to take Thorsten to our home and Sam to take all the girls to Di and clean them up.

Lying him on our cleared dining table, Sorcha examined him thoroughly and looked up at me, my lip quivering, just holding it together.

"He is lucky," she pronounced after an eternity. "The coldness of the water likely helped. The body shuts down the extremities, squeezing blood to the body and brain and slowing the heart rate. His ribs will heal. I will x-ray them tomorrow. It doesn't look like there will be any lasting effects."

I exhaled, and my shoulders slumped forward, unable to maintain the weight any longer.

"He will need to be closely monitored," she warned, "and will need oxygen to ensure he doesn't develop hypoxemia. I'll set it up."

Sorcha sent Illy and Luca away, ordering Illy to send my children home. Luca's help was enlisted to move Jorja to Sorcha's home and remain under observation for the night but passed on instructions that Bridget and their girls could go home. As I stood dripping on the kitchen floor, Sorcha stripped a frozen, exhausted Thorsten, rubbing him briskly, avoiding his chest, and dressed him in his favorite warm flannelette pajamas. The blue ones with bugs on them, I noted. He loved those.

When Cam arrived home a short time later with Louis, filthy and exhausted, Thorsten was sitting up in our bed, oxygen mask fitted, his sisters waiting on him. Cam looked at me, puzzled, my jeans still wet and mud-spattered, and his mouth hung open. Sorcha, seeing my distress bubbling over, filled him in.

"Those little..." he fired up, but Sorcha placed a calming hand on his arm.

"I suspect Illy will put an end to their trouble-making. At least for a while."

Cam simmered down slightly, crossing the room to check on Thorsten. Seeing he was fine, and rather enjoying the attention, he embraced me.

"Oh fuck, Jorja!" I gasped, remembering my patient.

"That's okay," Sorcha said. "I have taken care of that. You did a damned fine job there. Better than most of the med team. We might call you up to help us when we are overworked. We need an orthopedic specialist."

I heard Sorcha slip out the door as I collapsed in his arms.

CHAPTER 18

"WHAT HAPPENED TO JORJA?" Cam murmured as we lay in bed, unable to sleep. Thorsten was asleep on a trundle on the floor.

"Slipped off her doorstep. Snapped her tibia and fibula. It was a nasty break. Especially the tibia. It will take a long time to heal."

Cam shuddered. "Sorcha said you did an amazing job. That is high praise from her. No one meets her exacting standards. So, does that mean you have forgiven them? For lying to us?"

"Not really. I would always help someone in pain, and Jorja needed help. The longer you go without orthopedic surgery, the greater the risk of complications. Truthfully, I don't think I will ever forgive them, but I sort of understand why they did it. If they had turned up here with those girls and told me the medical team on Auckland were holding Katrin captive, and she had known for years, I would have been furious at them. Refused to let them stay. Questioned why Jorja hadn't done something to save her. By lying to me, I took the time to work through it all. The girls couldn't have been mine. They assessed that I cared enough about Kat to go myself. But mainly the reason they lied to me was to protect their children. The reality is, they didn't need to tell me at all. I have been oblivious for years. They could have stayed on Clava and lived a far more comfortable life. Either there or Auckland would be a safer place to raise children with far better medical treatment and superior opportunities. I believe Jorja when she says that they left so that their daughters would be free, wouldn't be caught up in the selected breeding program."

"You are a wonderful woman."

I sniffed derisively. "I just started with, 'I don't think I will ever forgive them.' I am no saint. Luca, on the other hand, we owe him. He just plunged in and saved them all. Not just Thorsten. They all could have drowned if he hadn't been there."

"How did Isla cope?" Cam asked.

"Fine, I guess. It isn't like her children were even there."

"After all these years, and you never asked her about her life before we came here?"

"Of course I have. She told me her parents were both doctors, and they encouraged her to go into veterinary science, not medicine, because of the unsocial hours. They met at university in London and then moved to Aberdeen. Isla was born in Scotland but sent to boarding school in England."

"Yes, they sent her to boarding school … after her younger sister Rashna drowned while they were on holiday visiting her mother's family in India. Isla saw it happen. She was only young, maybe five or six. They were playing near the pool in the hotel, and her sister slipped, banged her head on the concrete, and fell in.

Isla has never learned to swim herself. Her mother also couldn't swim. Isla is terrified of the water."

"Ahh, fuck. No wonder she hung back. Why did she never tell me?"

"Maybe she didn't want you to know."

"How did you?"

"Lae told me. I suppose Isla confided in her. Lae couldn't swim either, although she was never given the chance."

"Not even at school?"

"Her mother couldn't afford the swimwear or the lesson cost. She also lived in Glasgow. Not Australia. Not exactly summers at the beach and every town with a swimming pool like home. Swimming programs as part of the school curriculum. Not all of us grew up with a fully maintained pool in our manicured gardens, darling, with a cabana and a scantily clad pool boy bringing us cocktails."

"Holy crap. Can you imagine the fear in them both when the raiders took them?"

"I suspect nothing I can envisage can come anywhere close to how petrified they must have been. I can't even come up with an equivalent. Fraser told me she still wakes screaming, remembering that time."

"I don't understand the fear of water, I admit, but the memories of being held captive I can understand. Do you remember what it felt like when we were kept prisoner at the farm?"

"I do. Sometimes, for no reason at all, I get flashbacks of being hung from that butcher's hook, wondering if it was possible to die from the pain. But it is likely that is why she never mentioned it to you. You saved her from the raiders, along with the others. You saved yourself and me from the farm. She didn't know you well, and she probably didn't want you to see her as a victim."

"We have had this conversation before we went to Auckland. Why didn't she tell me then? I would never see her as a victim."

"It doesn't matter that it isn't the truth. It is her perception. Think about it. She watched her sister die, helpless. Then, in her parents' grief, they sent her away, likely in an effort to keep her safe, but what she felt was punished. The raiders kidnapped her and kept her on a boat from which she knew there was no escape. Even if she could get untied and jump overboard, even if the water wasn't toxic, she couldn't save herself. She couldn't swim, and they likely would have killed her before she made it over the side. She was a prisoner in more ways than one. Crippled with fear. Then you arrived, all guns blazing, and saved the day. She didn't know you well when you came after me in Edinburgh. So, when we came back full of stories of how you had saved yourself and rescued me, complete with scars as proof, she couldn't compete."

"It wasn't like that. Anyone would have..."

"No, they wouldn't. Most people, my love, would have been paralyzed with fear the same way Isla was. Most people do not have the cool level-headedness that you possess. Most people could not plan their way out of that. Think of all the skulls we saw. Hundreds. Probably thousands by the time they excavated the pits. Not one of those people managed what you did. Likely no one before us ever got away. Those monsters would have been caught sooner if they had. You, my warrior goddess, are a phenomenal woman."

"I wouldn't say that. Seeing Thorsten unconscious was the most terrifying moment of my life. I truly thought he had drowned."

"He is your child. Anyone would have been scared. But judging by the state of you when I got home, you were planning to swim after him?"

"Luca got there first. I'm so glad he was there. I can never thank him enough."

"So, you would have swum out to him yourself. Then you helped with the CPR. I don't know many people who could do that on their own child, but you did, even when his ribs snapped. Illy told me you didn't even flinch. Likely you make Isla feel inadequate. She can't swim, and you don't hesitate to dive fully clothed into an icy lake to save six kids. You are a hero, and that is how Isla sees you. Is there any wonder that she doesn't tell you about her fears?"

"I'm no hero. How do I deal with this? Make her see I am nothing special?"

"You don't. You don't need to fix problems, Frey. Just be aware of them and be there."

"That is stupid advice. Who told you that?"

"Two people, actually. A psychologist of mine told my mother once that it wasn't necessary to fight my battles for me. When I was bullied at school or people treated me badly, mum would always want to fix it. Mum and Sorcha are so alike. Mum would rage in on her high horse, demanding a meeting or that something be done. Fired off an angry letter demanding answers. But this woman made mum stop and think. Instead of responding, 'How can I fix that?' she told her to just be there for me and say, 'That must have felt terrible.' Just be there emotionally and let me deal with it. Goodness, mum struggled with that." Cam smirked. "I used to watch her fighting with it. Sitting back and doing nothing wasn't her way."

"It isn't Sorcha's either. It is what makes her such a good doctor. She sees a problem, and she fixes it. She was wonderful with Thorsten, by the way. Just took control. There aren't many people who would order Luca to do something, but she did, and he complied."

"There is no way we can express our thanks to him, is there?" Cam murmured, thinking aloud. "He saved our son. I owe him an enormous debt. Although I suppose it was his daughters that took him out there and tied Katrin up."

Not wanting to dwell on the recalcitrant twins, I asked, "You said there were two places you learned it wasn't necessary to fix problems."

Cam paused, and I knew the answer.

"Laetitia?"

"She taught me the value of standing back and taking it in. Just being there for the person, in many ways, is better than trying to solve their problem."

"She was very different from me, wasn't she?" I phrased it as a rhetorical question, but he answered it anyway.

"In some ways, you couldn't be more different. But in others, you are very alike. Your loyalty to your family and friends in particular. You both place those you care about at the center of your world, and they know, without doubt, that they are loved."

"Do you?"

"Every minute of every day."

CHAPTER 19

CAM HAD THAT DISTANT, unfocused look as he gazed out the window, his coffee going cold clutched in his hands.

"Got something planned for today?"

Cam pulled his attention away from his thoughts to look at me. "Just the usual. You?"

"I'm heading up to the north-eastern crofts. Probably my last trip before winter, and no one has been for a while, so I might be late. Can you organize dinner for the kids?"

Cam nodded. "Could you swing past town?"

"Sure. I need to get some supplies from the warehouses. I used a lot of my consumables on Jorja last week. Why?"

"Well, I am sure she appreciates it. She is home now, thanks to you. Do you think we could ask Bodhi for a large supply of meat?"

That wasn't at all what I was expecting. I raised my eyebrows mid-bite of buttered toast. "Why? Got a sudden hankering to be a raging carnivore? Not feeling the urge to convert to veganism?"

Cam's wandering attention focused on me, and he grinned. Neither Cam nor Luca could deal with the predominantly plant-based diet we ate. Both moaned for meat at least twice a week, Luca more so. Even while traveling, Luca had a ravenous appetite, largely unsatiated with canned food, pasta, and rice. Fortunately, he was a superb cook. Jamie, since meeting Jacinda, had become vegetarian. Several times, in the privacy of our home, Cam had griped that Jacinda was slowly murdering him. "She may as well ram a carrot stick through his heart," he had muttered. But Jamie appeared happy, and their children were thriving.

"I'm thinking that it is time we hosted a celebration, a Thanksgiving, if you can call it that. A party. You know, our way of saying thank you."

"For Luca, you mean?" Luca had bluntly ordered me the day before to stop thanking him for saving Thorsten's life. His daughters were responsible, so he was happy to have done what he did. I had agreed but still didn't consider that words were adequate for the gift he had given me.

"Luca loves meat. He would love a barbeque, or a dinner, although we couldn't invite Jamie and Jacinda if you are planning a roast."

"Absolutely, for Luca. The man lives for food. But … it is for everyone, really. If you think about it, many people have enabled us to live the life we have. My sister and Di, Jamie, and Jacinda, even Fraser and Isla have picked up the load so many times. But outside of Roseglen, Hamish and the entire medical team picked up the slack when we needed Sorcha here. Going back a few years, the people who helped when Louis sustained the head injury. Those who supported me when

Lae, Isla, and the others were taken. Everyone who helped when we went to Edinburgh, to Newgrange. Every single person here, in some way, has supported us. Helped us. I can't think of a better way to say thank you than to host a party—can you?"

I could see where he was going and nodded. I swallowed my mouthful of toast. "It is a great idea," I acknowledged but addressed the elephant in the room. "Won't you struggle with so many people in your home?"

"Yes," he admitted, "but it will be by choice. There is time to prepare. I'm also not thinking in our home. I doubt I could cope with that. Initially, I thought of lunch but realized that by the time everyone got here, they will stay for hours, so dinner makes more sense. Those with young children might go home early. But I accept we will have guests, at least for one night."

"I could clear out the vet shed, and people could bunk down in there?"

"That is a great idea. We can put on a big breakfast the following morning, and everyone could be on their way?"

I smiled at his enthusiasm. Cam was friendly, not social, as he phrased it. He found it confronting and uncomfortable to have people around, especially lots of people. This must mean a lot to him.

"When would you like to do this?"

"A few weeks? Fall equinox? People need time to get organized, and we need to arrange all the food and such."

"How are you planning to feed so many people? Our kitchen isn't that big. We can barely cope with cooking for eight or ten people for Christmas with that tiny oven." I was no cook. Cam usually did the cooking when we entertained. But half the community?

"It will take some work, but I am thinking of a fire pit. Digging a pit in the ground, heating stones, and cooking meats and vegetables. I can't see any other way to feed so many people. A hangi, the Maori call it."

"They are fabulous. I have been to a few myself when my family traveled across the Pacific. Lots of communities have a similar method. I remember a fantastic bougna our family went to in a Kanak village in northern New Caledonia. Fish, chicken, cassava, and lots of root vegetables I had never tried before."

"That's it. Jamie gave me the idea."

"Jamie was talking about meat?" I asked curiously.

"Not exactly. We were talking about celebrations, and he mentioned he had been to a few before he left New Zealand. It got me thinking. It would be nice to host an annual event. Something that brings everyone together."

"What about the smoke?"

"We can avoid generating a lot of smoke, Jamie tells me. While traditionally, the Maori used fire to heat the rocks, it is the hot coals that form the underground steam oven. We can get the biogas quite high, so if we heat the rocks in the ovens overnight, it should have the same effect. A small amount of smoke will be produced when we open it up, but it will be minimal and mostly steam."

"Are you sure you want to invite everyone?"

"I figure if we are going to the trouble of digging a pit or two, we may as well make it worth our while."

Standing and placing my dirty dishes in the sink, hoping one of the kids would wash them, I turned to him.

"I will ask Bodhi. But you may need to come up with a better name for your gathering. Thanksgiving has negative connotations for native Americans. Much like Australia Day to indigenous Australians. Not that there are any native Americans here, but we have worked hard to leave offensive traditions behind."

"Really?"

Not really having time to explain in detail, I suggested, "What about a harvest festival? I assume you want music and entertainment as well as food? Many cultures hold a harvest festival to give thanks, both to the earth for her bounty, but also it was a way to celebrate each other and recognized the season's hard work before the long winter hours."

Cam considered for a moment. "I like it. The Roseglen Harvest Festival."

Weeks of grueling preparation led to the big night. Children ran around happily, playing in large groups. Parents collectively shared the load, keeping a watchful eye on them all and jumping on silliness before it got out of hand. All the Roseglen residents were busy. I had been tasked with ferrying vegetables, meats, and other items to be cooked from the cool rooms to the pit. On one of my trips between the house and hangi pit, I overheard Luca giving Ally and Summer a lecture about playing appropriately. In the lull, Ally enquired, in the sweetest voice possible, "What is appropriate play, daddy?"

Thorsten's tiny voice piped up in the pause, "Well, no tying people up. Unless you are a grown-up, and

155

it is con-sen-shoo-all." He sounded out the strange word. "Then it is okay, isn't it?" he asked in a very earnest tone.

Luca and the children were out of sight, down the side of the shed, and I paused, juggling a tray laden with potatoes. Luca's strangled response, and the sound of girls giggling, made me freeze, wondering whether I should intervene. Out of diplomacy, and recognizing he was the guest of honor, I decided against it. It was just as well Luca couldn't see my face. He would have lost it completely, but I made a mental note to taunt him when we were next alone.

Guests had started arriving around midday, wanting a good place to set up their swags for sleeping that night. We had spent days clearing out the vet shed, the bike storage, and the hay shed, and by late afternoon the bedrolls, blankets and sleeping bags were lined up like a refuge center after a bushfire. Despite Cam's initial belief that people would want to go home, everyone was here and intending to stay. All the original residents had come, plus the extras like Illy, Cam, Sorcha, Di, and me. Most had paired up and had children, more than doubling the original settlement. Guests had taken over every spare inch of floor space in our house, Illy's, Sorcha's, Isla's, and Jacinda's. Even Jorja and Bridget, at the head of the valley, had agreed to accommodate ten guests in their small home. But no one minded. While we had held Christmas Eve gatherings at Garynahine, we had never had a full-community celebration like this before. Not an all-night affair with feasting and dancing.

The musically inclined residents set up a small, cleared area behind the tables and took turns playing the guitar, violin, or singing. Toby brought his bagpipes. The noise hung in a low thrum, making it hard to hold a conversation without shouting. The atmosphere got louder and more out of hand as the night progressed, aided by the free-flowing beer, wine, and spirits that had been procured on a recent trip to the mainland. Hamish and Luca proudly cracked open a barrel of one of Hamish's original vintages of whisky, now well cellared and ready to drink. Luca had taken over distilling upon his return here, but Hamish had never entirely relinquished his original role, much to the chagrin of the medical team.

Crowds gathered in various locations. Many were seated on chairs around the hangi, enjoying the warmth and glow of the stones. For most, it was the closest thing to an open fire they had experienced in over a decade. Others sat in small groups, farther away from the noise of the musicians, trying to catch up on news and socializing. Couples lay on blankets under the trees, enjoying the atmosphere and a day away from chores and work. Everyone had come, and no one had anything to do except enjoy.

The hangi was the pièce de résistance. An audible "ahh" rose from the crowd as everyone watching was awed by the full roasts of beef, lamb, and pork being raised from the pit. Several large fish, too. The glow of the embers illuminated the expression of longing in many faces. Trays of roasted vegetables had been roasted in a separate pit, in deference to the few vegetarians here. Juliette unwrapped trays of fresh bread, the fabulous smell mingling with the aroma of roasting meats. She must have been baking all day. Cam and Jamie had placed large bowls of mixed salads on the serving tables, which I suspected Luca would fastidiously avoid, despite Illy's best efforts to coax him to try something green.

After the carving, punctuated with cheers from the crowd, Cam came to find me, and we lined up together amidst the laughter and merriment. The line was long and slow, but it enabled us to speak leisurely to people we rarely saw. Everyone appeared happy, grateful for the opportunity to get together, even if just for one night. Cam's glass was filled several times as we waited in line, I noted, trying not to giggle. Cam was so caught up in conversation, straining over the noise of chatter and music that he barely noticed, sipping as he chatted. By the time we reached the platters with our empty plates, Cam was decidedly less steady on his feet.

"I'm sch-tarving!" he pronounced.

"You're drunk!" I responded, nudging him with my elbow. "Just as well you aren't in charge of the pit anymore! You'd fall in!"

"No, I'm not," he slurred as he tried to pick up a roast potato with the tongs and missed. He furrowed his brow. "Slippery little buggers."

Plucking the tongs from him, I deftly loaded up both plates and steered him away. At least I had worked out why the queue had taken so long. More than one person appeared to be having difficulty with the serving utensils.

Hearing Cam sloshing the drinks behind me as I juggled plates, I scoped out some seats in a quiet spot a little farther away from the main group where we could talk without needing to yell. Illy waved at me, and I took our plates over to join them, dropping them off and returning for the chairs. I tried not to make eye contact with Luca. I wouldn't be able to keep a straight face if I asked him why my youngest was asking about the consensual tying up of people. But Luca took one look at Cam's plate, lifted Illy to her feet, and dragged her off to join the long queue at the table.

"Mind our seats, will you?" Illy called as he swept her off her feet down the path.

Cam tucked into his meal with gusto, and I watched him, eating my own, trying not to grin. As he finished, he looked up and caught my eye.

"What?"

"Hungry, are we?"

"Starving. I've not eaten since breakfast. And that was coffee and an apple."

"Come to think of it, I don't think I have either. I've barely seen you in days."

"Goodness. Between digging and checking on the pits, collecting and heating rocks, clearing out sheds, setting up bedding, ferrying chairs and tables, collecting the food and drinks, borrowing cups and furniture from every house on Lewis, I'm shattered."

"Completely shattered?" I asked coyly, emptying my glass of wine, the slight sense of wooziness enveloping me. Perhaps I had drunk my fair share, too.

Removing my nearly empty plate from my hand, Cam placed them on the ground and took my hand, pulling me to my feet. Disappearing around the side of Sorcha's house, he found a dark spot between the window and the door and pushed me up against it, kissing me insistently. Hearing the chatter and laughter very close by, I pulled free.

"Here? Now? Someone will see us!"

"No, they won't. Did you not notice that all the parents have disappeared into dark nooks and crannies? Every quiet space is taken. I suspect we may be responsible for a surge in the population in nine months." The kissing resumed as his hands roamed lower. Wearing the only skirt I owned offered no resistance to a determined man on a mission.

"Do you not want to go home?"

"There are fifteen bloody guests in our home. How private do you think that will be?" he hissed in my ear.

Lifting my skirt and pulling my panties aside, he found his target, and I gasped as he speared me like a fish against the wall. With nowhere to go, my back slammed against the mudbrick. Unable to concentrate on anything else, I threw my arms around his neck as I felt the hardness of him consume me. My toes curled, and knees buckled as the tension tightened my legs, suddenly unable to stand.

"Shh!" he whispered, covering my mouth with his own. "Someone will hear you."

Not caring in the slightest about my tender back, I rolled my head back and felt the wave of pleasure rush through me. His weight pressed against me, he shuddered, then convulsed as he held me against him.

"God, I love you," he murmured.

"I love it when you are drunk," I whispered as I nibbled his earlobe. Cam so rarely drank to excess. He didn't like relinquishing control, and drinking often fed his anxiety. But when he did ... sometimes it made for an interesting evening. Staggering away, we found a patch of grass under a tree and lay in each other's arms.

"You couldn't have found this spot first?" I teased gently, stroking his chest. "I'll have bruises for days."

Sweeping the hair off my face, he gazed into my eyes. "No, I couldn't. I needed you, that second, or I would die." The world dissolved as he cupped my face between his hands and kissed me. Everything except his eyes faded to black, and I lost track of everything and everyone.

"I still remember our first kiss in the grotto on August," I murmured as he ran his hands over the slopes and curves of my hips and waist.

"So do I. After you finished trying to drown me."

"I wasn't trying to drown you. I wanted you to jump me. Almost drowning you was just a bonus."

"A bonus!" He tickled me behind my thighs, knowing I was immensely ticklish there. Squirming and laughing, he gathered me in as I convulsed.

"That first night in the springs, making love on that rocky ledge, I thought I would burst. I was so filled with desire for you."

"So was I," I confessed. "In that moment, I knew you were the one." Curling up with my head on his chest, I admitted, "I only took you there because I was lonely. But I left there that night feeling something so powerful. You stirred in me feelings I hadn't felt in a long time."

"What?"

"Safe."

His arms tightened as I spoke again.

"I came very close to running away from you. Telling you we had made a mistake and kicking you out. Banning you from my special place."

"Why didn't you?"

"Honestly? Because we ended up on the far side of the pool, naked. I would have needed to swim back across, dry off again, and get dressed."

"Why was that a problem?"

"Because my resolve to kick you out wouldn't have lasted that long. You were lucky we didn't end up on the cavern side, or I likely would have. Had we been at your place or mine, I almost certainly would have kicked you out of bed. But kicking you out of the cavern, naked? You might have been seen, and then my secret place would be mine no longer."

"I still don't get it. Why would you have kicked me out?"

"Because it was strange and overwhelming to someone so used to being independent. I was scared if I let you, you would hurt me."

"I will never hurt you. Not deliberately."

Laying in his arms under the coolness of the tree, I could just see the stars twinkling beyond the dome. I wondered how differently my life could have turned out if the pandemic had never spread. Would I have made a life in Melbourne or somewhere else? Would I have met someone, eventually? Been happy? Or would I have continued sleepwalking through my life, insulated from others?

"Honey, you can't fall asleep here." The gentle shaking of my shoulder roused me.

"Hmmm?"

"Frey! We can't fall asleep here. People will wonder where we are. Come looking for us."

"So ... tired," I groaned, fighting to force my eyes open.

"Me too."

"Why can't I sleep?" I muttered, somewhat annoyed at being woken. "You said everyone was sneaking off. What difference does it make?"

Cam gently lifted me from my lying position. "There is suspicion, and then there is removing all doubt." He kissed me, and my arms snaked around his neck as I tried to get my seated balance, still half asleep.

"Come on. Let's do one round, get the kids to bed, and get to our own. We have served up the meal, and everyone has seen us at least once. The party is likely to go on most of the night. No one will notice if we head home. Besides, we are cooking breakfast, remember?"

Grumbling slightly, I recognized this as a good plan. We may as well go to bed early. We would be woken throughout the night with guests arriving, stumbling over things, and clattering around our home. Then again, we were here to thank people for helping us. Perhaps it was a little rude to disappear mid-event.

Slowly we rose, cleaning leaf litter and grass from our clothing. My hair felt like a bird's nest with dirt, leaves, and grass caked through it. As I ran my fingers through it, I felt Cam freeze in the dark beside me.

"Mumma? Dadda? Why are you on the ground?" Xanthe's shrill voice pierced the night.

"Just taking a rest, sweetheart," he assured her in a low, calm voice, stepping forward to block me as my face flamed. Thank goodness she couldn't see me rearranging my underwear.

"It was getting very loud. We just wanted to talk. But now it is your bedtime. Where are your brothers and sister?"

"Thorsten is with Louis and Sam. Kat is with Kendra," she wailed. "They left me, and I couldn't find you."

"Well, you found us now," I soothed, stepping out of the shadows. "Come on, then. Let's find everyone and get you all off to bed."

"Already?" The whining took precisely two seconds.

"Yes. It is well past your bedtime already, so don't start."

It took over an hour to make our way around the main group, thanking people for coming, for their friendship, for their donation to the immense feast. Locating each child as we made our rounds, we sent them off home amidst much grumbling. I noticed the desserts dwindling rapidly and badly wanted to sample some. But Cam didn't let go of my hand as we spoke to friends, neighbors, family. Luca and Illy had disappeared, the four chairs sitting silently in the dark. Finally, the end was in sight. Our front door was propped open, people streaming in and out. Slipping in, we greeted several friends staying over, checking on each of the children. Thorsten was asleep, out cold on a mattress on the floor of Louis's room. Creeping around him, we could see that Louis was awake, fighting sleep, but alert enough to wish us both goodnight.

"Love you, Mum. Love you, Dad," he murmured as he snuggled under his blankets to block the raucous noise from outside the house and the clattering from within.

"Sleep well." I kissed his exposed forehead. Kat and Xanthe looked angelic in the next room, snuggled up together in Kat's bed, Thorsten's and Xanthe's spaces filled with guests. Neither stirred as we entered, but we kissed them both.

"We are so blessed." Cam closed the solid door to our room, and I watched as he rolled up our jackets to block the noise drifting in from underneath.

I sank onto the bed, unable to remove my shoes. I sat and looked at them, willing them to fall off my feet. Cam, seeing my exhaustion, grinned, barely visible in the dark. Within seconds, he had me naked and under the covers, slipping in himself.

"Why blessed?" I asked belatedly. "Many people would say that we have been dealt a crappy hand in life. Pandemic kills our parents and destroys our world. We are whisked away to a place with limited resources, and we work ridiculously hard just to survive."

"Because we are surrounded by people who care about us. Don't you think that is the meaning of life? To be happy. To recognize how blessed you are to have what you do and not constantly be lusting after things you can't have?"

"What have you lusted after?" I yawned, closing my eyes as the pillow engulfed my head like a soft, fluffy cloud.

"In my life, many things. Cars, objects, experiences. But now … only you."

Too tired to respond, I drifted off as the hands, warm on my stomach, kept me safe.

CHAPTER 20

KATRIN CALLED OUT TO me as I walked the final leg back to Roseglen, and I slowed, waiting for her to catch up.

"School finished?"

"Yup."

With the continual population explosion, the school down the valley had been expanded several times with children from all nearby crofts and small settlements attending each day. A decent walk from our home, but the children didn't seem to mind. The morning and afternoon chattering could be heard from some distance.

"Where are the others?"

"Left."

"Oh. Why are you late?"

Kat's manner was that of an early teen, either monosyllabic or using her cutting tongue, much like me at the same age. She was regularly required to stay behind after school and help clean up as a consequence for back chatting or insulting someone, usually in a very colorful way. Many a night Cam and I had laughed hysterically in the privacy of our room, hearing of her creative and descriptive insults, usually very apt. Kat just rolled her eyes and said nothing. It didn't matter. I would hear from Bridget when I saw her next.

"Mum, what did you want to be when you grew up? When you were my age, I mean."

I paused before responding. Not that I didn't have an answer. I did. Many of them. But how did I explain to a nine-year-old that life in Australia, then, had been so very different to life here, without it appearing like I was gloating? Frivolous things like movie stars, singers, ballerinas, and models. Like all girls, I had been through a phase enamored of celebrities, social idols, although mine had been geared more toward sporting champions. Even that concept I could never explain to her. She watched me curiously. Realizing I needed to give her an answer, I gave her a variation of the truth.

"I had a lot more choice back in Melbourne," I admitted. "I admit to being fortunate. I attended excellent schools and had the opportunity to be anything I wanted."

"Why did you choose to work with animals?"

Laughing as we walked, I explained I had been good at math and science, but for a long time, I didn't like people very much. "Animals don't complain."

Kat nodded sagely. "Sometimes, I think Auntie Sorcha doesn't like people very much."

I chuckled at her intuition. "I can't say you are wrong, although please don't say that out loud, for goodness' sake. She is an exceptionally good doctor. She has saved your life, mine, and your father's."

"She saved my life?"

"The night you were born. The birth wasn't straightforward, and she saved both of us. I will always be grateful to her for that." *Especially as she blamed me for having a baby with her brother* remained the unspoken part of that sentence. But many years had passed, and Sorcha and I had an excellent relationship. Had it not been that Cam was her brother, and Illy and I were close, I suspected we would be even closer. Sorcha and I were very similar. For the millionth time, I wished I had met Cam's parents. I had gleaned enough that his mother was fiery and quick-witted, much like Sorcha, with a highly attuned bullshit meter and absolutely no tolerance for time-wasting. His father he spoke less of, but I gathered had been more like Cam. Quiet, loyal, and always there to support those in need.

I drew my attention back to Kat. "So, what do you want to be, Missy Moo?"

Kat scowled, hating it when I called her that. "We talked about it at school today with Miss Bridget. Different jobs and how we could help others."

"Oh. What did you come up with?"

"I think I want to be a doctor, like Auntie Sorcha."

Kat and Sorcha would likely murder each other, I thought, but spoke supportively. "That is a wonderful thing to do, to help other people. And the others?"

"Louis wants to help grow things, feed people, like dad. Xanthe wants to be a writer and write children's books."

I smiled hearing this. That would suit Xanthe to a tee. I could envisage her sitting in a shed, writing stories about animals, much like Beatrix Potter.

"And Thorsten?"

Kat grimaced. "He didn't understand the question and kept insisting he would be a firefighter. We kept explaining that we didn't have them here, that we didn't need them as there is no fire. But he started to cry, so we let him."

"Where on earth did he hear about being a firefighter?"

"Well, he has those pajamas you got him, the one he wears as a t-shirt."

"Ahh, of course."

"And Miss Bridget has some books with pictures. One has pictures of police, fire, and ambulance. Thorsten loves that book and reads it all day."

"Oh, I see. Well, lots of children in Australia wanted to be police, firefighters, or paramedics. Your grandfather, dad's father, was a paramedic. He saved lots of people."

Kat's eyes popped wide. "Were you always in danger?"

"What do you mean?"

"If you needed police to save you from bad people, firefighters to save you from fires, and paramedics in ambulances to save you from accidents and being sick, was it such a dangerous place? Even Aunt Illy and Uncle Luca protected people, being in the army. They carried guns and killed bad people. We don't have any of those things here, and people don't die."

Fighting to retain the neutrality on my face, I wondered how much was too much to explain to a child, albeit one wise beyond her years.

"Well, for starters, a lot more people lived before. Millions. Tens of millions. Cities were far bigger than anything I can describe, some bigger than all of Lewis.

Lots of people lived in small apartments. Have you seen apartments?"

"You mean those tall buildings that look like boxes stacked on top of each other? Where they only get a small window to see out of?"

"They weren't that bad, but yes. Lots of people lived in those. Or houses like ours. Some people didn't have a house. They traveled in caravans, and some people were homeless. It was a very different time."

"People had no home?"

"Some," I admitted. "Often they had no jobs, therefore no money and nowhere to live."

"Why didn't you help them?" Her eyebrows raised to her hairline in horror as the volume and pitch raised. "How did they eat? Miss Bridget told us that everything cost money in the old times. If they didn't work, how did they buy food?"

This was rapidly getting us into complex territory. "Things were different—then. People didn't look after each other the way they do now. People looked after themselves, their own family, and friends. We worked hard to make money. There were so many people, sweetheart. I guess there was a feeling that we couldn't care for everyone, so we didn't. Everyone just looked after themselves."

"Were lots of people homeless then?"

"Not really. Quite a small number, I guess. I never really thought about it."

"But if each family helped one person, would that have fixed the problem?"

I could see where this was going. "I guess..."

"So why didn't they?"

"Because it just wasn't what people did," I admitted, somewhat sheepishly, remembering. How many times had I walked past a homeless person on the streets of any city in the world begging? A ratty sleeping bag or stained blanket behind them. A note scribbled on cardboard, asking for help. I had traveled extensively for my age and accepted that these problems plagued every modern society. How many times had the pungent smell of an unwashed body struck my nose, and I had cringed and looked away? Once, I had seen a scared teenage girl begging outside Flinders Street Station with a suitcase and her cat, evidently thrown out of home.

"Some people helped. Daddy and Auntie Sorcha's mother used to help people all the time. Invite them for meals. Buy them clothes. Then there were larger groups that provided housing and meals. Helped them find a job."

"But you didn't? Your family?"

I sighed. "Sweetheart, I am going to tell you something very difficult to admit, and something I am not terribly proud of. My parents were not always kind people. My parents both helped others in their own way. My mother was a special type of doctor, and she helped people with their problems. Not like Auntie Sorcha or Jorja. She wasn't that kind of doctor, but she helped many people. My father helped people in other countries, poor people, but he didn't do the work himself. He was an economist, an academic—a clever, special kind of teacher if you like. But I never saw either of them help a homeless person in their own city. I guess they both felt that they helped in their own way … and they did. So, because they never did it, I never thought to do it either. Does that make sense?"

She nodded, but I could see she didn't get it.

I tried again. "I guess many people felt the problem was too big for just them, so they did nothing. Other people did a lot."

"But there were still problems?"

"Definitely. I guess many people thought that was why they paid tax, and the government should deal with the problem. That is why dad and I love it here so much. Every single person's job is to help each other. No one starves. No one is homeless. And despite what Thorsten thinks, we don't need police, fire or ambulance, or the army. Or many other things that we needed then. Maybe it is just because there are far fewer people here. But mostly as we are a family and care about each other."

"We learned about government at school, people who set the rules. What is tax?"

"Ah, that is another thing I am glad to leave behind. It is like what Aunt Illy does. You know how she runs her business? People trade what they grow or make, but she keeps a small part for herself as payment for making the trade? That is like a tax. But it used to be that people went to work and earned money, but they had to pay part of their money to the government. That tax paid for schools and roads and hospitals. The more money you earned, the more tax you paid."

"That isn't fair! If I work harder, I should get to keep my money!"

"And that, my darling, is the lifelong issue with tax. No one enjoys paying it, but it is necessary."

"So why is there no tax here?"

I considered that. "At some point, I think there will be. There will come a point where we need things that everyone wants and uses. It is fair in most ways, as everyone pays for something that we all use. Even shared places like libraries were built using tax."

Glancing at the sky, I noted the changing colors heralding the coming of dusk. "Come on. We need to get home, or no one will eat tonight."

CHAPTER 21

SURROUNDED BY SHREDDED PIECES of brown wrapping paper, I glanced at Cam guiltily. Rarely did we have single-use items here, but at least basic brown paper could be reused as paper for lists or notes. Like ourselves as children, our four adored pulling the wrapping off their few Christmas gifts, mostly books and clothes sourced when we were in Fremantle for that single day. Things Cam had collected in Adelaide. But each child had received a special item, something just for them. Thorsten was obsessed with the stash of Lego we had sourced and was carefully putting colored bricks together and pulling them apart. Louis had received more technical Lego, including a replica of the Sydney Opera House. Cam grinned at me. He had badly wanted to get Star Wars Lego for Louis but had finally been convinced that this was so far beyond what Louis could comprehend that it probably wasn't a good idea. Katrin had received a beautiful cloth-covered lockable diary with Australian wildflowers on the front and a set of colored pens. Xanthe, an easel, and watercolor paints. I noted the gifts hadn't left their laps as they read their new books and held up their new clothes amidst peals of laughter.

A sense of joy permeated the room. My parents would never have permitted a mess like this, even temporarily. We would have been reprimanded for chattering and squealing as our girls were doing now. My parents expected us to unwrap calmly and respectfully, never tearing the paper, but taking the appropriate time to consider each gift and giving thanks before moving on. But Cam's own Christmas mornings had been like this. Chaotic. Up early, presents first, then a family breakfast. After breakfast, he and Sorcha went to play with their gifts while the parents cleaned up. I desperately wanted that for my own children. To give them that unshakable knowledge that they were the center of our world. The sense of joy that permeated the room told me we had achieved that.

Isla and Fraser were hosting this year, for which I was immensely grateful. We hadn't recovered from our harvest festival a few months before and had spent weeks covering the pit, cleaning sheds, returning crockery and misplaced items. Each family at Roseglen took turns to host Christmas, although we were all secretly dreading Jamie and Jacinda's turn as they had recently announced that they had become vegan. While we happily catered for them, it probably wasn't reasonable for them to cater to us under the circumstances.

"It might do us all good," I had told Cam the previous week, walking home from dinner at their place as he moaned about being served yet another stir fry for dinner. "There is nothing wrong with rice and vegetables."

"I can live without meat, most of the time, but it is no eggs, no milk. Cheese is one of the great pleasures of life! How do they do it?"

"Illy would agree with you. She is adamant that cheese is one of the essential food groups."

Cam started to cook breakfast as I showed the children how to fold the wrapping paper and save it for later. They all disappeared into their rooms with their precious new items, and I smiled, watching them go.

"Merry Christmas, my love." I wrapped my arms around Cam as he stood facing the biogas, my chin pressed against his back. Lowering the heat, he turned side-on, holding me against him as he deftly flipped the waffle iron.

"Every Christmas we spend together is wonderful." He kissed me ardently before returning his attention to the blackened cast iron pan. "We missed so many. It always feels like we are playing catch-up."

"I know what you mean." I kissed his cheek and turned to fill the coffee machine with water, check the beans, and turn it on. The burring roar of beans grinding put an end to the conversation for a moment. As it quieted, I said, "We missed one because of Heidi. Lena. Do you remember?"

"How could I forget! I spent weeks in hospital and in bed. Because of her, we missed our first Christmas together."

"You aren't alone. She tried to slit my throat!" I pulled my sleeve back to display the decade-old scar running the length of my forearm, still clear against my lightly tanned skin, the fresher wounds crisscrossing. I paused, considering. "Do you ever wonder what happened to her?"

"No. I can honestly say I don't waste a second thinking about her. I will confess to asking Jamie about Jenny, Phil, Kelly, Kai, and some others. But her? No. Life is far too short to waste on people who tried to kill me."

"Who tried to kill you, dad?" Kat asked as she entered the kitchen, Xanthe close behind.

"No one. Well, actually, someone did, but it was a very long time ago."

"Why?" The incredulousness in her voice matched the hair toss and haughty stance.

"Jealousy over your mother. Long before I came here, I'm too boring now. No one would bother killing me."

"That is true enough," Kat replied in her usual forthright manner, and Cam turned to look at her in mock outrage.

"Thanks so much!"

"My pleasure," she simpered. "But seriously, dad. Your work isn't exactly dangerous, is it? You grow stuff. Not like Uncle Luca. Or even Auntie Illy. They both worked in dangerous places. Luca got shot twice! And his armored personnel carrier was blown up."

"Yes, I know," Cam muttered. We had heard this story many times. Our children were now of an age where Luca's pre-Lewis life seemed far-fetched and incredible. They loved sitting around as he regaled them with stories of life on the road, recovery missions in war zones. Helping people, living out of a tent. They thought of it as thrilling. Much like Hollywood blockbusters had seemed to us in our own childhood.

"Well, it's true, dad. You and mum went to school, which is *so* boring," she drawled with the attitude of any teenager. "Now you live here, which is even more boring. Nothing ever happens here. Luca's life must have been amazing!"

"Boring is just the way I like it." Cam smiled at her. "Now, what do you want on your waffles?"

CHAPTER 22

IT WAS THAT GLORIOUS time of year when the days were warming up, but the nights were blissfully cool. Getting in a warm bed at night was a treat made even more delicious with the addition of a warm male. The male in the bed was already dozing as I raced around, finishing a hundred minor jobs, and slipped in beside him, sighing with the relief of lying down. It had been a busy day. Lots of early spring births kept me moving, and I was enjoying not being on my feet.

Cam heard my sigh, and I saw his mouth quirk in the dim light.

"That bad, is it?" he teased.

"Not bad, just tired," I admitted. "Every year I forget how tiring spring is. But usually we spread the workload over the year. This year…"

Cam sensed the shift in my mood and rolled up onto his side, his warm arm snaking its way across my stomach. Turning to look at him, the concern in his face made me melt.

"I'm okay. I just feel so guilty that I was happy much of that time, and she was alone."

179

"That is the problem with guilt, isn't it? Often it is an illogical emotion. You know perfectly well that you weren't responsible, that you didn't even know she was still alive. But you blame yourself all the same."

"That is it, exactly."

"The guilt I felt when you went missing was indescribable," he said, a little strangled with the emotion of that hideous time. "Logically, I knew it wasn't my fault, but people blamed me. I felt so horribly guilty. I fell asleep and hadn't realized you had gone missing until morning. I didn't know where you were or what happened. Alive? Dead? I had no idea. You left for work one day and never came home."

The pain radiating from his warm body pierced me, and I rolled into his arms.

"I'm so sorry. I never meant to leave. I just wanted to warm my frozen feet. Truly. I... I called for you as it sucked me under. The last thing I remember is screaming your name, praying that you would pluck me out of the maelstrom."

"I would have jumped in after you," he breathed in my ear as his hands wrapped around my back. "I would follow you anywhere. But you can call me now. I'm here."

"Have you seen Cam?" I called. I could see Sorcha leaving the greenhouse farthest from our homes the next day. The evening sun casting long, dark shadows across the valley. A peaceful time, but I couldn't shake the feeling of unease. My arms were filled with skeins of wool from the McLarens where I had spent the day helping with their new livestock. I fervently hoped Jacinda would offer to spin them. I hated spinning and couldn't knit a stitch.

"Not since this morning," she replied, crinkling her nose before adjusting the freshly picked vegetables in her basket, the carrots about to tumble out into the mud. "He was heading out to help Luca bottle the whisky. He said something about sending whisky to Newgrange."

"It is a thank you gift for Tadhg and Jake for all of their help in cloaking us when we traveled to August. Cam took Louis, too. They needed an extra set of hands to help seal the casks and load them onto the horses. Get them down the hill and onto the carts. Louis was thrilled to miss a day of school."

"They always are. You better not tell Sam. He will be most jealous. He much preferred Di to Bridget. She works them harder than Di did."

Seeing the look of concern on my face, she softened slightly. "They will be fine."

"It is silly of me to worry, but I would have expected them home by now. The last time I arrived home to find Cam and Louis gone was when Louis ended up in the hospital. Bad memories, I guess."

Piercing screams muffled my final words. Sorcha and I looked at each other frantically as we tried to pinpoint the source in the still night air. Illy's house. We dropped our bundles and ran. My heart ran cold at the sound. Illy never screamed. We collided as she burst out her front door, and I reached out to steady her.

"What?" I asked anxiously, seeing her face blanched.

"Shot! He shot them!" she blurted in a manner very unlike Illy. Her voice was broken and garbled, making it hard to distinguish the words.

"Who shot who?" Sorcha asked, gripping her arm.

"Angus. He shot Luca and Cam. Took Louis!" She managed to force the words out as the tears streamed down her face.

"Where?"

Watching Illy stiffen as she pulled herself together, she blurted, "Sssss.... Stornoway."

The next half-hour passed in a blur. Sorcha fetched the remaining golf cart from the shed. We drove to the harbor, me seated in the back beside Illy. The first thing I remember with crystal clarity was rounding the corner to the harbor and seeing Luca and Cam lying in a pool of their own blood on the concrete dock. The moonlight reflected its gleaming white surface in the puddles which spread around them both, joined in places. Through my daze, I heard Illy's cries. Sorcha jumped from the cart before it even came to a complete stop, frantically checking them both. She had brought her small bag, the only thing she had at home and had time to grab. Luca was closest. Sorcha's grim face was illuminated in the moonlight.

"Torch!" she bellowed, and in my fog, I fossicked around in the cart for the large torch we carried for emergencies.

I watched in a daze as she moved across and checked Cam. "He is alive! Barely. He has lost a lot of blood."

"Luca?" Illy cried, drawing my attention to her kneeling in the puddle as she held him in her tiny arms. *She looks like a child clutching a giant*, I thought abstractedly. I glanced across at Sorcha as she swore and emptied her small bag on the ground, grabbing at items on the ground.

"Help me!" Sorcha barked, and I jerked in action, helping her drag Cam to the empty cart and lay him across the back seat. All the cotton pads from her medical bag were rammed against his stomach. The other, larger cart, parked alongside, still had whisky barrels laden in the back.

"Go," I ordered, and she did. Illy needed me now. Cam was unconscious, and I could be with him soon. Sorcha would fight to the death to save her brother. I knew that as surely as I drew breath. Crouching down on the opposite side of Luca's still form, I placed a hand on Illy's shoulder. She looked up, shocked, not realizing I stood there.

"He can't be dead," she choked. "He can't leave me."

Even in my haze, I knew Sorcha would have been thorough. She would never leave Luca behind if she thought he could be saved. Even under the yellow light of the torch and the well-lit night sky, his skin was gray and lifeless, his dull eyes wide open and staring. Regardless, I lifted his shredded, blood-stained shirt and lay a hand over his chest. Cold. No movement. I checked his pulse. Nothing. Looking at the entrance wound by torchlight, even I could tell that wound was fatal. Delivered at close range, it had struck him in the heart. I could see the damaged aorta through the open wound. Likely, he had bled out within minutes. An irreparable wound, even if he had been in a hospital. He would never have survived that. Illy curled up beside him, sobbing. I sat behind her and held her as she cried. There was nothing I could say. Nothing I could do. I just sat there, feeling helpless and numb. After an eternity, she sniffed and lifted her head.

"Help me."

I nodded. Despite the dark, the full moon cast enough light for us to see. Luca was an enormous man, and Illy, a tiny woman. But somehow, we emptied the cart of the full barrels, dumping them on the dock. We dragged his body to the cart and onto the back seat, and an abstract thought popped into my head. *This is what they mean by dead weight.* Illy sat on the back seat, his head resting on her lap. I watched as she stroked his hair from his face, and we began the slow journey to the medical center in the dark.

"How did you know Angus did it?" I asked when my words had returned, and I was able to assemble them in some semblance of order. Illy took a while to speak, making me wonder if she hadn't heard me, but finally, the clipped words filtered through the blackness.

"I got home and saw that the proximity sensor had been tripped."

"Really? I heard nothing."

"Nor did I. The light was flashing. It has been happening lately when strong wind buffers the sensors. Luca was going to check today to see if some parts needed replacing. So, I took my time checking the footage, thinking it was another false alarm."

I was too scared to ask what she saw.

"They arrived at the dock at the same time as the *Selkie.* I saw Angus, clear as day. Luca and Cam argued with him. Luca was tense. He wasn't happy. Then Angus pulled a gun from the back of his pants and just shot him. The camera is on the old light pole behind Angus, so I saw him pull the gun, and I watched Luca fall and the stain of blood growing in the front of his shirt. I could see Luca's face. He looked surprised, then he dropped and didn't move again. Cam was standing beside him. Cam turned slightly to protect Louis, and Angus shot him too without even a pause. Louis looked terrified and froze. Angus grabbed him and bundled him onto the yacht with Nate's help. He was kicking and thrashing. They dropped him on the deck and sailed away without looking back. All I could see was the two of them lying motionless, bleeding out on the dock. Alone."

"When?"

"Late afternoon. About half an hour before I saw the footage."

Half an hour. My brain whirred. It had taken us another half an hour of travel to get there. An hour Cam had been lying there, bleeding. But Luca was dead. Killed in cold blood. By someone he and I once considered a friend.

"We need to go after Louis. Tonight." Illy spoke in a low but firm voice.

I glanced back at her, my mouth agape. In my shock at Cam's injury and Luca's murder, I had forgotten about Louis.

"Did they sabotage the *Eurydice*?" If they did, we would never find them. Even now, they had a significant head start and a larger, faster vessel.

"Not that I saw. They had only just pulled up as Luca and Cam arrived. They took off in a rush after they took Louis, so no. I think we still have a good chance of pursuit. If we don't take too long."

We arrived at the medical center in Garynahine to find Sorcha, Hamish, and Hamish's wife, Morwenna, operating on Cam. Sorcha's face was dark, and I couldn't read her expression as she focused on her work, not even glancing up to acknowledge my presence.

"I have to warn you, it doesn't look good," Morwenna cautioned me as she pushed me out of the room that served as an operating theater. "The bullet is still inside him, and he has lost a lot of blood. If it is in his spleen, he stands a chance. But … any of the other major organs… If he survives the surgery and the night… We will be in a better position tomorrow to tell you."

Tomorrow. But tomorrow was a long time away, and my child was being held captive on a yacht in the middle of the ocean.

"Can I see him? I need to go after Louis, and I can't go without first seeing Cam."

Morwenna looked at me, then over at Illy, looking like a ghoul drenched in Luca's blood, and relented. "Let me check with Sorcha."

A few minutes later, Morwenna's head popped out of the small operating theater.

"Wear this." She handed me scrubs, a scrub cap, and gloves. I donned them quickly and followed her.

Cam was laid out on the operating table, his stomach cut open from pelvis to chest. The skin was pinned back with surgical clamps, exposing the extensive damage to his abdomen. Blood-soaked cotton pads filled the stainless-steel surgical trolley beside her. Sorcha looked up at me.

"I will do my best. But Freyja, it isn't good. The damage looks fixable, but he has lost an awful lot of blood. Do you know how long he was there?"

"About an hour before you reached him."

Sorcha nodded gravely, calculating. My patients were animal, but basic anatomy was not so different. I understood the risks.

"I need to go after Louis. Can I say goodbye?"

Sorcha nodded grimly; her gloved hands paused temporarily above his abdomen, tools in each hand. I walked to the head of the bed, crouched down, and spoke softly.

"Angus took Louis. I am going after them, now. Tonight. Illy is coming with me. I wish I could stay, be here when you wake. But I know you would want me to go after him. I will bring him back, but you need to be here when I return. Promise me."

Closing my eyes, I kissed his forehead on the tiny, exposed piece of skin between the draped white sheets and the navy cloth holding back his thick, dark hair. I barely heard Sorcha whisper, "I promise."

CHAPTER 23

"ARE YOU SURE YOU want to come?" I asked Illy for the third time as we entered her home so she could change and take a quick shower, drenched as she was in Luca's blood. Although a quick glance proved that my own state was little better. "The girls…"

"Positive," she growled. "I want an audience with Angus MacLeod. I won't rest until he pays for what he has done. Besides, I would never let you go alone."

Picturing Cam lying in the hospital bed, Sorcha's worried face lurking in the background, I knew exactly how she felt. Except I didn't. Luca was dead. Summer and Ally were without a father, and she wouldn't be here to bury him. *Please, please let Cam survive*, I begged the universe. I couldn't lose him. Not again. But for now, I needed to focus on Louis. He would be terrified, being kidnapped by a stranger and taken outside the dome. This was the only world he had ever known. Oh God. A thought occurred to me. He knew this was what had happened to his mother, Laetitia. Evil men came and took her away. He had told me once, unprompted, as we had been out walking. "They took her out there," he had whispered, gesturing toward the dome with the wide-eyed innocence of a young child. "And they killed her." Holy shit. Now history had repeated itself. The difference this time was we knew who had taken him. The question was, *why*?

"You are wondering why." I looked up to see Illy studying me, her head tilted as she unlaced her boots. "I would have thought that was fairly evident."

"First, can you please stop that? Second, why on earth would Angus want Louis? Surely if his motive was to get back at me, taking one of *my* children would be a better choice. Unless it was to get back at Cam. But what did Cam do?"

Illy rolled her eyes, exasperated, as she stripped off and dropped the blood-stained clothes in the sink. "Well, aside from Cam ending up with the girl of Angus' dreams, shagging around the clock and having beautiful children then living happily ever after, I suppose Cam did nothing at all." Illy's voice dripped with sarcasm, but she continued, "I suspect this is more than revenge. Louis is related to Angus, isn't he? Didn't you tell me once that Angus was Laetitia's uncle? Louis is direct kin to Angus. He has no children of his own, does he?"

I looked at her, agape. I hadn't even considered the possibility. "But he's only ten!" I protested.

Illy shrugged. "If that *is* the motive, and I suspect it is, then it is actually good news. He is unlikely to harm him."

It made sense. Illy was a genius at reading people and motives. If she thought Angus would want Louis as he was blood-related, that was likely the case.

"So Clava then?"

Illy pondered that for a moment. "I'm not sure. I know Ashton reasonably well. Even he would have qualms about kidnapping a child. There is a good chance that Angus is doing this of his own volition."

"Where would they go?"

Illy sighed as she walked into her bathroom and turned on the shower. "That is the million-dollar question. I have absolutely no idea."

"Please, let me help." Bridget burst into the kitchen as I paced, trying to maintain my poise. News traveled fast here. I could hear Illy still in the shower. Even after Jorja's impromptu surgery, I had kept my distance from them both. I knew they hadn't orchestrated what happened there, but they had both been aware of the forced breeding program, and I couldn't forgive that lightly.

"Well, unless you know where Angus took my son," I responded crisply, "or you can miraculously heal my husband and bring my friend back from the dead, I don't think there is much you can do."

"I can't do any of those things. But after all you have done to help us, we will do anything you ask."

I thawed slightly. She was only trying to help. "Well, if you have any contacts and can find out where Angus has taken my son, I would very much appreciate it."

"Consider it done. I will head up to Aidan's and make some calls. You realize that if Clava and Auckland are behind this, then they likely won't tell me anything."

"But if they *aren't* responsible, they may tell you that. And Bridget?"

"Yes?"

"Can you take Illy's girls tonight? Send mine over to Di. Tell Di that Sorcha likely won't be home."

"Are you sure?" Bridget objected.

"Yes." Illy's voice fired over my shoulder as she moved from bathroom to bedroom to dress. "If you would take my two, I would very much appreciate it. I will tell them about their father. But then I must go."

"When are you leaving?"

"Now. Frey, go home and pack a bag. I'll pick you up shortly. We are going."

I stared at her, open-mouthed. "You have just lost your husband. Don't you want to be with your children? At least for a few hours?"

"I will be with my children when you are reunited with yours. Luca isn't here anymore. I will mourn later. Grief doesn't need a timeframe. Go home. Pack a bag. Let's go."

"How do you even know where to go?" The sounds of crying children still echoed in my ears as we approached the *Eurydice*. Fortunately, it didn't appear they had sabotaged the vessel. That would have slowed us significantly, there being nothing else here remotely fast enough to pursue them.

"While you packed, before I spoke with the girls, I checked the satellite," Illy spoke bluntly, her voice coarse. "The *Selkie* is headed east toward the north coast of mainland Scotland."

"Clava then. Possibly Edinburgh," I murmured, my brain whirring. "Angus lived there for many years and loved it. He considered it home. I've been to his house."

Illy considered that. "Well, we still need to travel via Inverness. If he has gone to Clava, we will spot the *Selkie*. It isn't like they can hide a vessel of that size. I also have Tadhg checking his satellite feed, but it is hard in the dark. I agree. It is more likely he has taken Louis to Edinburgh. Could you find it again?"

"Certainly. It was quite close to the house Cam and I stayed in."

As we cast off, I caught Illy staring at the bloodstain on the dock. "I am so sorry..." I started before she cut me off.

"You didn't do this, Freyja. Angus did."

"But it is my..."

"No!" she snapped, more aggressively than usual. "This is in no way your fault. You made choices for your family, yourself, and your children. People make choices every single day. Those decisions impact other people. But rarely do they feel the need to shoot people."

"I rejected him," I sniffed. "More than once."

Illy lowered her eyebrows and looked at me derisively. "Women and men are rejected every day. They don't kidnap people's children as retribution."

"Maybe." I wasn't convinced. Guilt wracked me. Luca dead, Cam critically wounded.

Illy, perceptive as ever, whispered, "And that is not your fault either."

CHAPTER 24

HOURS PASSED AS WE made the journey to Inverness. We kept each other company, not wanting to be alone. Illy and I had been close for years, but I couldn't overcome the crushing sense of guilt that her husband had been killed and mine only wounded—by someone I had once trusted. Cam wasn't out of the woods yet, not by a long shot. But Sorcha wouldn't rest until Cam pulled through. I knew that without question. I was certain Isla and Fraser, Di, Jacinda, and Jamie would look after the children, both Illy's and my own. Bridget would also assist, being their teacher and knowing them well. My only goal was to get Louis and bring him home. But Illy? She would never again be with her love, the father of her children. How could she not resent me?

We stopped once for refueling, cursing we hadn't done it in Stornoway. Sorcha sent us a message late in the evening. Cam was alive but still in an induced coma. She spoke cautiously, careful not to get my hopes up. *Maybe Illy and I will be widowed together?* Anger washed over me, making my skin prickle. *No,* I seethed. Angus would pay this time. I had watched the footage at Illy's home as she showered. I had needed to see it myself, to know for sure. There was no doubt it had been Angus. The bullet struck Luca squarely in the chest. He dropped and bled out on the dock in minutes, not moving from where he lay. Cam had been lucky and had turned toward Louis, his arms outstretched to protect him.

We got an update report from Hamish as we passed through Garynahine on our way to the dock. The bullet caught him in the spleen, missing his liver and other vital organs by centimeters. Angus had paid attention when Luca and Jakob had taught us both how to fire a weapon and where to aim it. Center of mass. Now he had used that knowledge to slaughter his teacher. Cam could live without a spleen. It placed him at greater risk of infection. But for now, the enormous quantity of blood he lost was of more concern. Cam's body had gone into hypovolemic shock before we found him before we could transport him to the clinic. He faced a genuine risk of tissue and organ damage, something that couldn't be assessed until he regained consciousness. But I trusted Sorcha and Hamish. He was in excellent hands.

Nightmares plagued the few sleeping hours we allowed ourselves, too exhausted to continue traveling in the dark. Louis's sweet, childish face was scared and confused. Tortured by being outside the dome and with a stranger who he believed had killed his father. I could hear his cries, sobbing for me.

"Wait for me, Louis. I'm coming," I called, but the sobbing continued.

Waking with a jolt, I realized the sound was coming from the next room. It took me a moment to recognize the sound *was* someone crying. Climbing into bed beside her, I held Illy close as she cried. I knew from my own grief at losing Katrin that she didn't need me to speak, just to be here. Share her pain. So tiny and fragile. She curled up against me, and I held her, comforted her. I loved Luca, too. He had been my friend for years. I couldn't believe he was gone. Their children had lost a parent and in the most brutal of ways. I wished I could have comforted Cam when he lost Laetitia. He had been so alone then. He readily admitted that he wouldn't have made it back if it hadn't been for Louis. *I will bring him back to you.* I sent the silent promise to Cam as I held her sobbing form, and after a moment, Laetitia too. I had spoken to her before when Louis incurred a severe head wound. Even now, I held a sense of obligation to her. Louis may have been her child by blood, but he was mine by choice, as much my child as Kat, Xanthe, and Thorsten. I had never felt anything for him other than maternal love. *Help me find him.* I sent the unspoken wish out to Laetitia. *Please. Help me bring him home. I love your son like he is my own. Please guide me.*

Illy cried herself out and fell into a fitful sleep. Not wanting to disturb her, I held her close, kept her safe from her nightmares.

"What do you miss most about Cam?" she whispered as I brought her breakfast. She looked like she had aged a decade overnight. Her skin was blotchy and her eyes red-rimmed.

I sighed and tried to think of an answer. "That he is so dependable," I finally responded. "I trust him with my life. He is honest and loyal, and I know he loves me. There are no games. There is nothing deceitful about him. What about Luca?" I asked, wondering if this was a wise line of questioning.

"I miss the sense of peace he brought to my life," she said calmly. "I always felt like I needed to prove something. I am tiny; I know that. I tried to be more than I was. But with Luca, he accepted me in a way no one ever has. He didn't see my size, just me."

"What do you mean by something to prove?"

"Overachiever is a word that has been thrown at me quite a lot. But in my personal life too. I liked to be in control."

I raised an eyebrow.

"I had a partner for a time. He was military, too. Older than me. But he liked to play. Dominant and submissive stuff. Tying me up, handcuffs, using a riding crop. You know, games."

I froze. "Really? You?" I never thought Illy would be the bondage type.

"It was exciting, at first. Thrilling. But after a while, I realized it was all about power. Control. And he always wanted it. He didn't see me as his equal. It wasn't the lifestyle I had an issue with. It was *him*. This wasn't a man I could have children with, feel like he was my true partner. I guess I never felt that there was explicit trust. I never felt that until I met Luca. I trusted him implicitly."

I was dying to ask her about the bondage, especially after Luca's overheard comment at the harvest festival, but realized it wasn't great timing. But in typical Illy fashion, she sensed my question.

"In that case, it was about power. Have you never felt that?"

I considered that. "Not really. I must admit that I feared relationships before Cam. I usually left before sunrise."

"That is just a different way of maintaining control. Not letting them in."

"After my sister … I couldn't. I was hollow but also refused to trust anyone in case they hurt me again."

"Why did you pick Cam?"

I laughed. "Well, it had been a year, and I was lonely. Desperate for company. I was only twenty-three. But he exposed his soul to me. Told me about his anxiety and his Asperger's. I had watched him for months and knew he didn't gossip. He had ethics. I figured that if it didn't work out with him, then at least he would be discreet and wouldn't tell anyone. Truthfully, when I took him to the grotto for the first time, I was kind of looking for a friend with benefits. He was kind, respectful, and had an amazing body. Then…"

"Then what?"

"Well, I kissed him. He would never have made the first move. There we were, naked, in the prime of our lives, and he was floating and enjoying the springs."

Illy snorted as she sipped her coffee. "Really?"

"Truly. I'd stripped off and plunged into the water to give him the hint. He followed. But there he was, just enjoying the water. Floating blissfully with his eyes closed. I kept waiting for him to take the hint. He didn't. I admit to being a little frustrated. I teased him, pushed him just a little, and there was this shift in him—a powerful one. Cam is so nurturing and gentle. But that night, he took control. He took possession of me in a way I have never felt before… I still remember that first night. But it was equal—if that makes sense. He is larger than I am, stronger. But that strength has always been held in check. He wanted me, but he respected me. He has never hurt me or used his size against me."

Illy sighed. "That sounds so much like Luca. He is huge, was huge. Formidable and several times my size. But I always knew he respected me. There is something quite special about knowing that you are an equal. I hope my girls get to feel that way one day."

"Well, I had to kiss some toads before I met Cam."

"Oh, likewise. The possessive ones, the jealous ones. Those that wanted a plaything. Thought they could control me as I am smaller. But it is the sense of loyalty and partnership I will miss."

"I know it is too early to ask, but do you think you will meet someone else?"

"No. I have had my great love. I have my girls. That is enough."

"I understand. After that short time with Cam, I always knew that it would be unfair to be with anyone else. It would be settling for second best. I had plenty of opportunities. I visited many places and met many people. But none of them came close to him."

"Even though he married someone else?"

"I never really let go."

"I don't think I ever will either."

CHAPTER 25

ARRIVING AT INVERNESS MID-MORNING, we docked the *Eurydice* and refueled as we discussed our next steps. There were vessels here but no sign of the *Selkie*.

"What do you want to do?" Illy's dark sunken eyes and pallid complexion made her look nothing like my vibrant friend.

"We are here. We should visit Clava anyway, just to see if they can tell us anything. Nate could have dropped them there."

"Let's ride. We can get there faster and be on our way to Edinburgh sooner if he isn't there."

We approached apprehensively, fearful that we may not be made welcome. We had, after all, deactivated our portal and set up an arsenal of weapons capable of taking out a small country. A drone buzzing over our heads announced their rather irritating awareness of our arrival.

"No chance of being inconspicuous," Illy muttered.

People stopped to watch us as we walked up the main street toward the headquarters. It had been years since I had visited here, just once. But Illy had lived here, then later returned with Di. She knew the place and the people well. She may be given a more welcome reception.

Derek strode purposefully down the steps to meet us. He didn't even try to hide his leadership role this time as he stopped before us, a fraction closer than necessary.

"We wondered when you would turn up."

"Angus MacLeod kidnapped my son and killed her husband. Possibly mine, too." The inflection of anger was clear, even to a clod like Derek.

Illy placed a calming hand on me and turned to face him. "Can we talk, please? Perhaps somewhere more private."

He gestured with an economic movement of his head to follow him inside. Once inside, he flourished an arm toward the large meeting room on the left. Large windows spanned floor to ceiling. The room was floodlit with natural light, the spectacular scenery, shades of green visible in the distance. *The view toward the cairns,* I thought, remembering my visit there. Not wanting to lose focus, I drew my attention back to the room. I had met with Ashton several times in this room and been served delicious meals. It hadn't changed. A large boardroom space held a large oval table and black executive style leather chairs, a large screen at the end, hanging silently on the wall. The windows reflected in the black glass of the screen.

Derek poured us each a glass from the jug of water on the table. I paused, and he watched me, reading my wariness. He took a healthy swallow of his, and after a glance at Illy, I did likewise.

"We don't have your stepson."

"He is my son," I corrected, "and if you don't have him, I would like to know where he is."

Derek shrugged. "We don't know. Angus left us some months ago after some … philosophical disagreements, I guess you could say."

Just as I pondered my next question, Illy spoke. "Have you been keeping tabs on his movements?" Illy's question was so direct even Derek sat more upright. "Monitoring him?"

"No…" he stammered, mildly intimidated. "Why would we do that?"

Both Illy and I looked at him in disbelief. "Oh, come on. You have all of this equipment at your disposal, and yet you didn't watch where he went?"

Derek's face went through a remarkable series of colors as Illy noted, "Well, you know enough as you were expecting us."

Derek raised a hand, almost like a child answering a question in class, and an audible click sounded behind me, making me turn in alarm. Illy was at the locked door in a shot. Looking back, I saw Derek reaching under the table, placing a gas mask over his face, and smiling nastily as an opaque gas canister dropped from a vent that had opened in the ceiling and started filling the room with a foul-smelling yellow gas. Derek backed up as Illy and I struggled to move toward him, lifting our tops over our faces to avoid inhalation. The last thing I saw as the world went dark was Derek's grinning face sneering at me.

CHAPTER 26

THE HARD, COLD STEEL imprinted into my back woke me a fraction of a second before the sensation of my arms and legs being restrained registered in my foggy brain.

"Why do people insist on tying me up and keeping me captive?" I muttered.

The sound of Illy groaning somewhere to my right made me crack an eye open, through the dim light, to see her in a similar predicament: splayed on a sterile hospital bed with a thin mattress covered in a crisp white sheet, her arms restrained with locked cuffs to the gleaming silver bars at her sides. Her feet were shackled to the bar at the end, which had been shortened to accommodate her diminutive height. Even a glance at the secure restraints confirmed they weren't amateurs.

"It is my first time," she replied. "Can't say I am enjoying it."

"Oh, you will." A greasy voice leered from across the room as he entered my line of sight. "You rejected me once, bitch. Won't be complaining this time, or I'll gag you."

"Can't say I blame you," I said as an aside to Illy. "I'd reject him too if this is how he needs to get women."

He slipped his rail-thin and oily form between the beds and smacked me hard across the cheek, making it sting. "As for you, you stuck-up cow, you didn't even lower yourself to greet me when you were here last time."

I screwed up my nose, trying to remember. *Did we meet?* He saw the look and correctly interpreted the silence, mocking me.

"Oh, that's right. Too busy fucking your own man to notice me. We all watched. Where is he now?" I fought against the restraints as he chuckled. "Not a chance, princess. You do what I say. Maybe you want to go first." He ran his hand up the inside of the crisp white hospital gown, and I cringed, desperately trying to move away from him. The restraints were firm, and I couldn't move more than a few centimeters. He continued to cackle cruelly, stroking my smooth inner thighs with his scaly hands.

"What do you want with me, you impotent fuck-nuckle?" Anger was boiling over now, but it just seemed to rouse him more.

"Anything I want," he sneered. "You are mine. Both of you. Any time I want it, I will give it to you."

"This is the only way you can get a woman to be near you, isn't it?" I taunted. "Such a man. Your parents must be so proud."

He slapped me again, harder this time. It stung, but I refused to react.

"Dale," Illy tried to diffuse the situation, "I didn't reject you. I just wasn't ready for a relationship. It had nothing to do with you."

Dale snapped around and punched Illy in the stomach, making her cry out. "Bullshit! You thought you were better than me, you filthy whore. Thought you were so intelligent, so high and mighty. Walked around like you had a stick rammed up your ass. Well, I'll shove something else up there for you. You might like it more. I heard you settled for that grunt. I'm sure *he* likes it that way."

Illy's eyelids lowered at the mention of Luca and squirmed as Dale's hands roved up her gown. Like me, she was bound tightly and had limited space to move. Dale rammed his hand firmly into her, and she grunted.

"Luca was twice the man you will ever be," she roared, making him recoil slightly. "At least he was man enough never to force himself on anyone. *He* didn't need to."

Lights flicked on violently, making my eyes water. The double doors opened, and a woman wearing a white medical coat walked in. Dale removed his hand discretely, wiping it on his pants, and slipped away from the beds.

"Kalyan?" The relief in Illy's voice was palpable as she saw the woman's face. "Kal! It is so good to see you. There has been a mistake. I would like to speak to Ashton. Can you tell him we are here?"

"Oh, he knows." The calm response made my stomach lurch more than the words spoken. "He will drop in at some point to question you."

"He knows? That you are keeping us captive?" Illy's tone reflected her shock.

"It isn't like that."

"Well, what is it like?" My eyes bored into her. "If this is how you treat guests..."

"What did you expect us to do? You blew up the lab on Auckland and destroyed half our mapped genomes. That set our work back a long way."

"Your work?" Illy echoed. "Kal, we were neighbors. Friends. You know this isn't right."

"I have no choice, Illyria. We need to replace some of the genomes you destroyed."

"How did you know it was us?"

"Cameras. I'd recognized you anywhere, Illyria. You destroyed more than a decade's research that night. We need to get back on track."

"So, you are starting with *us*?" I could barely believe what I was hearing.

She moved the loosely untied gown from my upper arm, turning it upward as I thrashed to avoid her grip. The restraints were firm, and I had a limited range of motion. As she drew blood from my outstretched arm, she stared at the cross-hatching of scars on my forearms for a fraction of a second too long, then looked away, pretending to be engrossed in the syringe filling.

"I'll tell you about them if you let me go."

Kalyan ignored me.

"What is that for?" She had already filled the third vial, all capped with different colors.

"Just checking where you are in your cycle. So we can start the process."

As she lay the filled vials on the silver tray, I watched in horror as she repeated the extraction on my friend.

"What process?" I swallowed the bile. I needed to hear her say it. Surely not. *On conscious patients?*

"We need to replace the eggs you destroyed. It is important all the genetic sequences are replicated."

"But I have children. My DNA is in them, isn't it?"

"Yes, but we need to fertilize the eggs with different sperm to diversify the gene pool."

"Eggs?" I caught the plural and thought I would vomit. "Is that what you did with..." I trailed off, unable to say her name.

"It was much easier," she soothed. "She didn't know. I lived there. She was treated very well, I assure you."

Silence filled the artificially lit room as she continued the battery of tests, my jaw clamped shut. As soon as the door closed, the dam burst.

"I'm so sorry, Ils. This is all my fault. I never meant for this to happen. This ... clusterfuck. Dale. This..." I tried to raise my arms, resulting only in a light clang. "I am so sorry."

She turned her head and looked at me for a long time before speaking in a low, rumbling voice, unlike Illy's. "I chose to come. That murdering fucktard waste of oxygen killed the love of my life. I won't rest until he pays for what he has done, and we bring Louis home."

"What is it then?"

"I lived here." Her voice dropped even lower. "I worked with these people. Was my judgment so wrong? Were they all just waiting to keep me captive and raid my body? Rape me?"

"This is my fault." I grimaced. "We traveled to Auckland for my sister. We are here because of my son. You came because of me."

"No. It isn't. Angus would have killed Luca that day, regardless. It was my choice, and nothing that slimy lowlife can do to me will ever change our friend-ship, Freyja."

Illy changed the subject, for which I was grateful. Ever the optimist, she chatted about what our friends would be doing on Lewis. Spring planting. Animals being born. Guilt for leaving all the work for Isla struck me. Illy sensed it.

"This isn't your fault." Her tone was resolute. "We will get home, Frey. We will."

Smiling wanly, I closed my eyes in the large, win-dowless room and let sleep overtake me.

The sharp jab of a syringe jolted me from my dreams.

"Oww! What was that for?"

"You will get one of those daily until we can retrieve." Kalyan wiped the drop of blood from the injection site and capped the syringe.

"Harvest me, you mean? Treat me like a prized cow?"

"Well, we know you are fertile. You have what, two children?"

"Three," I seethed at the mention of my family.

"Ah, our intel must be a little out of date. Three is even better." She tapped away on a tablet.

"Are they healthy? Full-term gestation?"

"Wouldn't you like to know?" I growled. I would not assist these people, especially by giving away information about my children.

Illy looked kindly at Kalyan as she finished with me, and then at the woman drawing her blood. "Kalyan. Ngaire. Why are you doing this?"

Ngaire at least had the decency to turn away. Kal responded coldly. "We told you. We need to replace the material you destroyed."

"Then what? You will let us go?"

She looked uncomfortable at that, but feeling Illy's stare, finally mumbled, "That is beyond my clearance level."

Illy looked over to Ngaire. "Ny. Please. Don't do this."

Ngaire continued to ignore her, but her face flushed, unable to make eye contact.

Illy tried again. "Kal, please. You are a good person. We have known each other for years. I cared for your babies so you and Jaldeep could have date nights. I don't deserve this. Neither does she. Freyja was just trying to save her sister. Her family. Wouldn't we all do that for our own flesh and blood? We are only here to find her child. He is only ten. Angus MacLeod kidnapped him, and all we want is to take him home. I have two girls, twins. Angus killed their father, so I am all they have left. If you keep me prisoner here, who will raise my children? Do you want to be responsible for that? Leaving two orphaned seven-year-old girls? You have daughters. Is this how you would want your daughters raised? Would you want them treated like this?"

Kalyan looked away, refusing to make eye contact. Saying nothing, she finished up and left as quickly as she could, Ngaire shuffling in her wake.

Illy looked away, but I could see the distress.

"We are being monitored, aren't we?" I whispered.

"We are. No one will do anything to help us. We are trapped."

"Fuck." I couldn't contain the sickening sense of disappointment.

"Promise me something, Frey." Her voice was so low I needed to strain to make out the words.

"What?"

"Promise me you will never stop fighting. If they break you, they will have you forever. We *will* get home. We need to believe in that. We will hold our children again. One day, they will lapse … just for a second … and we will find a way home. Never give up hope. Be strong. Never stop fighting. Where there is still a tiny spark within you, they don't have you. Don't ever let them win."

Flashbacks of being restrained in that filthy shed near Inverness filled my mind, Joey licking my cheek and molesting me. This was so much worse. We knew these people. These were no bumbling buffoons. These people intended to use us as lab rats, just like my sister.

"I will," I whispered, my promise as much to myself and my children as to her. "I will never let them win."

"And Frey?"

"Hmm?"

"If you get the chance and you can't save me, promise me you will save yourself."

I didn't know how to respond to that. Leaving my best friend behind was simply not an option. But finally, I murmured, "You, too."

CHAPTER 27

MEDICAL STAFF VISITED SEVERAL times each day, checking our temperature, lifting our gowns, and subjecting us to indignities that no woman should face.

"It is like a daily pap smear, isn't it?" I said to Illy one morning as she endured her physical exam and single injection, and I was injected with my morning cocktail. Rarely did the staff speak to us, treat us like we were people. Usually, we distracted each other by making pointed, rude remarks about the medical team. Sometimes they reacted. More often, they ignored us.

"We really are pieces of meat." I sighed as they checked me over. "But I feel like cheap sausages instead of prime steak. I wonder if they treated my sister like this? Daily examinations to see if she was fertile."

"Yes, so humanizing, isn't it? Makes you realize how far we have come as a species when we treat each other like this."

"Well, I don't know about you, but I am quite enjoying having someone wipe my ass for me."

Illy sniggered. "It is the ultimate in decadence, isn't it? Though, if they are to market this place as a luxury resort, they need to work on the phrase, 'It is time to move your bowels.' Surely we can come up with something a little more glamourous."

"What, like, 'It is time to shit, ladies? Would you please oblige?'"

We both laughed hysterically, making the nurse charged with the task flush with embarrassment.

"At least we can drop one on command now," I shot over to her when I could regain control of my laughter. "We have evolved as a species."

"Well, if we have evolved, can they give me a pedicure?" Illy strained her neck to study her feet. "My nails are horribly neglected."

"Well, I need a leg wax. They feel like a forest!"

Illy laughed. "You'd never survive in the Army!"

"Likely not," I confessed. "Why, were all the women hairy-legged?"

"Of course not! It was like any other workplace. Unless we were on exercises. Then showers and razors were a luxury. But it wasn't about that. It was about team building, camaraderie, solving problems collectively. God, I miss it."

"Do you have a solution to our current problem?" I asked hopefully as the blushing nurse left the room.

"Working on it, my friend. Working on it."

"Got a nail file or some other useful tool in your handbag, darling?" Illy drawled after lunch several days later. "Did you bring the monogrammed Louis Vuitton?"

"Of course not, sweetie. I needed to choose between my Chanel, Bally, and Prada for this trip. Couldn't work out what went best with my outfit. White is so hard to accessorize."

Illy roared with laughter. "Nothing went with a khaki uniform, let me tell you!"

"It was such a thing where I lived. Prada. Bally. Gucci. Monogrammed Chanel. Even a limited-edition Spencer and Rutherford."

"But not Louis Vuitton?"

"Never. Too many fakes. I remember a girl at school getting a personalized one. The bitches teased her mercilessly for being a try-hard."

"What did you have?"

"Hedgren. Cheap, basic, functional. Much to my friends' disgust. You would think I carried a dirty street bag the way they looked at it. Though my mother had a Hermes handbag, a gift from my father. She made sure everyone knew it, too. She stored it in a soft white cloth bag. Polished it. I think she might have been prouder of that bag than she was of me. You?"

"When I went out and wasn't in uniform, just a basic black crossbody bag. I don't think it even had a brand name, or if it did, I didn't know it. Just came from a department store."

"Boutiques is where we shopped, darling," I overemphasized the posh accent of my parents and their friends. "You got personalized treatment. It was all about the *service*. I'm utterly embarrassed now by how many pairs of shoes I owned. The enormous wardrobe full of clothes, most of which I never wore. But shopping was a pastime when you have money—spending it, a social activity. Now I live in the same clothes day in and day out, and I am so much happier. Well, I *was*," I corrected, looking around the stark room that had been our home for ten days. "I would never have believed it, but I don't miss those things at all. I think of all the clothing I left behind just moldering away into nothing."

"Once, I watched a documentary on disposable fashion and its impact on the earth. It was horrifying how much textile and fabric ended up in landfill."

"Think of all of those things we owned, everything we thought we loved. Yet we walked away, and I can honestly say, I haven't thought of it since." I paused, remembering. "Is there any one thing you wish to have back?"

Illy fell silent for the longest time. "My cats. My parents. Luca. They are the only things I long for. I still hear them, my parents, and Luca. I used to see a shadow coming around a corner and think it was Max or Lily. But as for objects... well... at times, there are things I wish I still had. When you are in a rush and you wish you had a car. When you want a quiet night with your partner and wish you had a TV to entertain the kids. When you are churning cream for butter and wish you had a KitchenAid. But it is people my heart aches for, not things. You?"

"My sister. But I have missed her for a very long time. My parents too, I guess, but not as much."

"I think that is the first time I have ever heard you say that. Have you forgiven them for what they did?"

"Maybe. They did what they thought best. They couldn't have known. Likely they would have taken

Kat even without consent. The truth is, I was angry with my parents from the time they committed her. Made her someone else's problem."

"They didn't have the skills to look after her, Frey. She needed around-the-clock care."

"They had the resources. They could have paid for a nurse, let her be in her home. Comfortable, in a familiar place, and surrounded by things she loved."

"Would you really have wanted that? The shell of your sister, wasting away in her bedroom? Not wanting to bring friends or boyfriends home in case they were freaked out by the living corpse in the next room? It kind of puts a damper on a new relationship, doesn't it? 'Hi honey, can you just get a condom? Top drawer in the bathroom. Oh, and don't disturb my comatose sister in the next room!'"

"I never took boyfriends home," I confessed.

"Why? Didn't they approve?"

"Because I rarely had relationships. Some lasted a few months—most just single nights. But I didn't have a long-term boyfriend as such. Not until Cam."

"What made you stick around, then? You said that you only took him to the hot springs as a friend with benefits. He told you about his anxiety, and you figured he wouldn't blab to other people if you got it on. What changed?"

"He made me feel safe, emotionally, I mean. I had never felt that before. My parents loved me, but the way Cam treated me... I knew he was the one from the first time. It was him. It was always him."

"Luca protected me in a way I didn't know I needed," Illy whispered, tears choking her. "Like you, I can take care of myself. But he was so solid. So dependable. He completed me."

214

"Exactly."

"I will get you back to him, Frey. I promise."

As I closed my eyes, I could see him, as I always did, the last time we had been together. Lying there, his organs exposed, like a rat dissection, minus the labels. *Please, please still be alive*, I prayed silently, guilt making me flush. How could I say this in front of Illy? Luca was dead. Cam may or may not be. Consciously, I focused my mind on Sorcha. She was as willful as anyone I had ever met. She wouldn't let him die. Sorcha was the type of woman to have a list of people to haunt when she died. But, I reminded myself, she had lost two partners. Cam had told me about Sam, her fiancé in Melbourne, and Tom, her partner on Kiewa. Even Sorcha couldn't stave off death. It was Laetitia who flitted into my mind without warning. *Please. Help me,* I begged her. *Help me save Louis and Cam.* She turned like she hadn't heard me, and I saw her long dark brown hair flowing in waves over her shoulders as she looked out to sea. Peaceful but silent.

CHAPTER 28

EACH MORNING STARTED THE same. Lights switched on, forcing us into alertness. With no windows and no clocks, our bodies adjusted to the artificial light they exposed us to. Catheter bag changed, allowed a small breakfast, fed to us, sponge bath. Not once had they removed the restraints, only lengthened the metal chain to enable us to move slightly, avoiding bedsores. Illy and I had plotted what to do if they ever removed them, but that option hadn't presented itself, although several times each day, I tested them. This morning, only one tray of food had been brought in and carried over to Illy.

"Starving me now?" I asked caustically.

Dale ignored me but flashed a vicious grin. He fed Illy, slopping most of the food onto her breasts. Illy responded with her characteristic calmness, smiling at him as he groped her. Returning the spoon to the now empty tray, he wheeled me to a large operating theater, deliberately pinching my skin against the rails, gouging me with his fingernails. Still restrained, I gazed up at the large white light of the well-lit room.

Gleaming stainless steel medical equipment of all types lined the walls. But there was a window here and some natural light. Trying to sit up, I strained to see out of it but couldn't see past the trees and bushes growing in a garden bed under the window. Trees made me think of Cam, and I closed my eyes so I could erase the image of his face. Not now. I couldn't think of him now... not while this happened.

The team spoke to each other, over me, but not to me as they arranged ultrasound machines, trolleys of equipment were brought to my bedside. A tight-fitting mask was placed over my face, and the gas burned the back of my throat. I fought to keep my eyes open, straining against the wooziness that threatened to engulf me, trying to maintain control, but blackness descended, and my head rolled back.

I regained consciousness in a white, windowless room, so tiny I could have touched the walls if I wasn't restrained. A monitor bleeped beside my head, and a woman arrived, perfunctorily checking on me but not really on *me*. She just needed to confirm I had regained consciousness after the anesthetic. My stomach ached where they had used needles to extract my eggs. The cramping pain was proof I was now barren. Raided. But I couldn't even reach my hands to massage my stomach. Fighting back the tears, I remembered my promise to Illy. I would never give up.

As I lay there in that tiny room, my mind whirred. *Why me?* I kept wondering. While Illy had endured the same initial tests, it was only me they kept pumping full of drugs. Yesterday morning, an additional one. Initially, we had assumed that my cycle was at a more logical point, but as the days dragged on, they seemed more focused on me. Illy believed it was because she was a few years older than me, nearly forty. But it was punishment; I knew. Retribution for me killing Katrin. I was the priority so they could regain what they had lost. Illy was just the innocent bystander.

Drifting in and out of consciousness, I saw Cam's face watching me, worried. *Please be okay.* I sent the silent message out to the universe. I could endure almost anything if he was alive. Eventually, as the dizziness wore off, the nurse fed me quartered sandwiches and injected pain relief. Illy watched me carefully as she returned me to the shared room. Rearranging my face, I tried for reassurance.

"I'm back! Did you miss me?"

Illy instantly saw through the facade. "Oh, Frey. I am so, so sorry."

A single tear cracked through my ice queen mask. "I'm fine," I assured her, wiping it discreetly with my shoulder.

Illy kept up a steady stream of chatter. Inane things. The kids' schooling, her cats' escapades, and weeding the garden. It didn't help. I could envisage with immense detail what they had done to me while I was unconscious. Things they would have said about me. How they treated me. The finger-shaped bruises I could see on my thighs irrefutable proof that they hadn't been gentle. Payback for all the acerbic remarks I had flung their way each day. I could hear Illy's words ringing in my ears, "The only real power you have is the way you respond." Break all of their noses is how I wanted to respond.

Illy sneezed, violently and unexpectedly.

I turned to look at her and winced, my stomach cramping from the recent assault.

"Are you okay? Not getting sick? I can't imagine they would make you hot drinks and blow your nose for you."

"I'm fine." Illy smiled at me, knowing that I was just trying to keep my mind off the day's events.

"As long as you are okay. I'm not really in a position to help."

"Luca used to tease me incessantly when I sneezed," she admitted.

Tilting my head to look at her, I asked in astonishment, "Why on earth would he tease you for that? I mean, he used to tease me about many things. Called me Elsa, princess, used to change clocks on me so I would think I had woken at midday. Left a frog in my bed. Even cling wrapped my toilet once. Enormous clown he was."

Illy flushed, and I stared at her.

"What?" I asked.

"It's... it's nothing," she stammered, looking away.

Now I was intrigued. "Okay, I have just been plundered for my eggs so they can steal my children while you had a leisurely breakfast. You owe me this."

Illy mumbled, and I could barely make out the words.

"I sneeze when I am thinking about ... pleasuring myself."

I snorted, then gasped. "Is that what you were doing just now?"

"No!" she squealed. "Of course not. That was just a sneeze."

"What do you mean, you sneeze when you think about alone time? Seriously? Is that even a thing?"

"No clue. It could just be me. It took me years to work it out. I should never have told him, of course.

Luca thought it hysterical, and as soon as I sneezed, or even looked like I was going to sneeze, he would tease me mercilessly about how he wasn't man enough, and I needed lady time."

"Lady time? Is that what he called it?"

"He did." Illy's voice was brimming with mirth. "But he used to say it in that taunting faux feminine tone of his. 'Sunshine, am I letting you down again? Do you need some special lady time?'"

Closing my eyes, I could picture Luca teasing me. An enormous hulk of a man, putting on a fake girly voice, tossing his head around and ridiculing me about brushing my hair or shaving my legs when we were in the middle of nowhere, for no one to see.

"I miss him so much, Ils."

"Well, one thing is for sure, I will need a rabbit when we get home."

"A rabbit? Aren't two cats enough?"

Illy laughed raucously. "Oh God, you are so innocent sometimes. I mean, we will need to visit a sex shop if we make it to Edinburgh."

"Ohhh...." I blushed, realizing what she meant. Quietly I added, "You might meet someone else."

"No. I don't want to. I had one great love, and that is enough."

"Cam got two," I pointed out. "Sorcha had three. Maybe you will as well."

"No." Illy's tone was resolute. "No one will ever measure up. It wouldn't be fair. Sometimes I think perhaps he did so much living in his forty years that his candle burned out faster than most."

"I like that. Luca as a candle. He glowed brighter than most, but man, could he burn you."

CHAPTER 29

"**DID I EVER TELL** you that Luca loved the Dixie Chicks?" I announced several days after my surgery as the daily injections recommenced. It was getting harder to keep up our morale. Each day I was subjected to more degrading tests and examinations. We tried to support each other, chat about inane things. But there is only so much you can say when you are held against your will with your best friend, knowing it is all your fault.

"Seriously?"

"Well, okay, maybe loved is taking it a bit far. When we were traveling, we stopped at Kerguelen a few times. The team there loved karaoke. One night, Luca belted out 'Wide Open Spaces,' impeccably, with perfect pitch. It was impressive. I have to admit."

Illy giggled. "Oh, I wish I had seen that. He never mentioned it."

"He was stinking drunk, but I never let him forget it. He denied it all the next day. He claims he didn't know the song. But he sang it, word for word, from memory, complete with Southern twang. It was hilarious."

"He used to sing to the girls. Lots of different songs. Goodness, they loved it when he sang. He had the most wonderful ability to mimic different singers, even women."

"I remember him singing to you at your wedding: 'You Are the Sunshine of My Life.' There wasn't a dry eye. Every woman wanted him that day. Probably some of the men, too. Cam can't sing at all!" I laughed. "He tries, but he is off-key and off-pitch. It got to the point where the kids just told him to stop. He tried to act offended, but he was relieved to no longer have that burden. Even Happy Birthday was painful."

"I wondered why I had never heard him sing. Is he tone-deaf?"

"I don't think so. He just can't sing. But I don't know a lot about music. My parents enrolled me in violin lessons as a child, and I hated it. They forced me for a few years but finally let it go."

"Why did they force you?"

"It was *expected,* darling. They expected us to learn how to do all the important things a lady does in society. Play tennis, swim, play hockey, sail, ski—all without breaking a sweat, chipping a nail, or letting her mascara run. Playing an instrument for company was one of those expectations. Kat was luckier than me. She asked for piano, and they agreed. She was quite talented. I think that is why they let me drop it. Kat was a good musician and artist. I was the sporty one. I can barely draw a stick figure."

"I played netball," Illy mused. "I was small and quick. I desperately wanted to play goals. All the tall girls got to play goals. I was too short, of course, but at nine, I didn't realize that. I cried to my mother that they never let me."

"You are the size of a budgie now. I can't imagine you at nine. What were you, size four?"

Illy feigned insult. "Not quite, but not far off." She smirked. "When I started school, they had to order a special uniform for me as I was so small. I remember Mum being annoyed that she couldn't buy my clothes at the second-hand uniform shop."

I laughed out loud at that. "Really? I have always been tall. People asked me to help them reach things."

"I was the one who couldn't reach the top shelf in the supermarket or had to climb on the seat to reach the overhead locker on a plane. I remember on one of my last flights before I was deployed, an elderly gentleman looking so perplexed. I was traveling from Melbourne to Canberra to attend an official briefing and wearing full dress uniform, you know, with all my ribbons and paraphernalia. He so badly wanted to ask me if I needed help but was intimidated by all the colors. Very sweetly, I asked him if he would assist me. The look of relief was priceless! We ended up swapping seats so I could sit with him. We had a wonderful natter all the way to Canberra. He was visiting his daughter who had just had a baby. He had served in Vietnam and treated me with such respect."

"Didn't everyone treat you with respect?"

"In uniform? Hell, no! People fell into one of two camps. Very respectful, accommodating, and recognizing the role we performed, sometimes randomly thanking me for my service as I walked down the street. Others were blatantly antagonistic, making snide remarks in earshot about being invaders and baby-killers. It was difficult to ignore, but you got used to it."

"Baby-killers? Seriously? Why?"

"There were several high-profile international operations during the time I served and some highly politicized events where bombs were dropped on civilians. Schools, hospitals, that type of thing. Often it was our allies, not us. Or a genuine accident. It isn't always easy to tell when firing missiles and often at night. The intel can be wrong or the coordinates just slightly off. But some people take a very simplistic view of world events and see all military action as wrong. Invasive. So, they tarred us with the same brush."

"Why did you take up this project? It can't have been for the intellectual stimulation if Dale was one of your colleagues."

Dale had seen us only a few times and rarely alone since that first day, but I caught the malicious glint in his eye. He hadn't forgotten the insults. Damn. Why couldn't I keep my mouth shut? But so far, aside from choosing excessively large gauge needles and handling us roughly when we were moved to avoid getting bedsores, he hadn't had an opportunity to be alone with us.

"Because I was chosen. It was a challenge, and I relished challenges. I was single, and it gave me a chance to be moved back to Melbourne. My parents had passed, but I missed home. My relationship in Canberra had ended a few months before, but I still saw him around the base and in the Officer's mess, which was awkward. So I accepted. I've told you before I worked with Ashton daily, Angus via teleconference. But I never met Derek, Dale, or many of the others until I arrived on Auckland or Clava. The team charged with choosing the candidates wasn't necessarily the team that was deployed."

"That must have been hard. How did you do it? Knowing you are saving some people but not yourself?"

"It wasn't quite as hard as you would think. Most had families. Partners and children. They knew from the beginning that they couldn't all go and why. There was a general acceptance. Occasionally, I sensed a feeling of resentment but rarely. They knew being deployed wasn't exactly a walk in the park, either. Do you know that less than a quarter of people who qualified and were offered a place actually accepted? Many just felt that they couldn't do it. Many more thought it was overkill, an overreaction. That it would blow over, and we would find a cure."

"Well, weren't they wrong!"

The second surgery to collect my eggs was even more painful than the first, only this time I knew what to expect: nausea from the drugs pumped into me the day before and a dragging, cramping sensation afterward. Only this time the pain was extreme, feeling like I had been slashed inside. The hours I spent in recovery were longer and far more isolating.

Pretending to be asleep as I was wheeled back into the room, I could feel Illy's tenseness radiating from her bed. Only a few meters away in reality, but she felt a million miles away as I was isolated in my tiny cave, alone. *Why me?* I choked down the tears and tried to sleep off the pain.

Cam's warm breath on my cheek woke me in the dark.

"Mmm," I responded, feeling the blanket of love enveloping me before bolting awake, the restraints on my arms a rude reminder of my present predicament. A sweaty hand firmly held over my mouth and nose made me gag, unable to breathe. I wrestled against it in the darkness as the weight of the naked male body pressed down atop me. His hand pressed harder, holding my head in place as I squirmed, and he used his other hand to push apart my already splayed legs and prepared to enter me.

No. Fucking. Way.

That single thought spurred me as I fought. It had taken me months to overcome the flashbacks, the feeling of utter helplessness I had suffered after being kidnapped in Inverness. Having Joey's hands down my pants and sloppy tongue on my face had plagued me for months. *No fucking way.* My mind focused, despite the pain in my stomach. I was not going there again. I would *not* be a victim.

Summoning up as much saliva as I could, I spat the glob into his hand. Instinctively he removed it in disgust, wiping it on me, and I exploited his split-second error in judgment to screech in his ear.

"*Rape!*" I screamed, stifled by the weight on my chest. "*Help!*"

He tried to clamp his hand back over my mouth, but my head was the one unrestrained part of my body. Even with the limited movement available to me, I thrashed and bit at him as soon as his hands came near my face, catching one of his fingers between my teeth. I clamped down hard on his feral tasting hand. He slapped my cheek with his free hand, freeing his finger. I heard the resounding echo, but I scarcely felt it as I screamed as loudly as I could. *Someone must be able to hear me?* He started punching me in the head, bellowing at me to shut up. I was livid. I felt the sickening crunch as his fist connected with my nose but kept screaming. He landed another blow on my left cheekbone, making my eyes water uncontrollably. His hands found my throat, and stars danced before my eyes as I began to lose consciousness.

The sound of Illy yelling at the top of her lungs reached me, and the doors flung open. The lights were rudely switched on, revealing far more of Dale than I ever needed to see.

"You filthy raping piece of shit!" I exploded, blinking and spluttering as two male staff dragged him off my bed and away. He continued bellowing obscenities at me.

"Stuck-up whore! Think you are better than me, do you? You'll get what is coming to you, and I will be the one to give it to you. Both of you. Don't think you are special, Illyria," he sneered, stretching the syllables in her name. "You're next. You love cock, don't you? You'll love mine, plunged deep into your belly. You let that filthy beast do it. I watched. We all watched. Didn't want me, did you?"

Anger had taken hold now, and I was afire.

"How can you justify this?" I roared at the people in the room as they dragged Dale away. "Call yourselves scientists? How is beating and raping restrained women civilized? You may as well be Neanderthals. Fucking animals!"

Several more staff arrived, trying to calm me, but I was overcome with uncontrolled rage.

"He tried to rape me! He would have succeeded, too, no thanks to any of you. Is this what you have become? This is what you aspire to? You keep us captive! Treat me like meat. Stab me with needles. Harvest my eggs, and now what? You want me to have a child with *him*? Like *that*?"

The room soon filled with staff, trying to calm me, speaking soothingly to me. After the assaults of the day, I was in no mood to be placated. I fought and screamed. Seven weeks of suffering rose to the surface. I intended to make as much noise as I could. Ngaire tried to check on my nose and cheekbone, which I could tell from the pain radiating into my head were both broken.

"He did this! *You* did this!"

Two men held me down as Ngaire injected me with a sedative. I fought and lashed out as much as my restrained form would allow.

"Really? Now you are drugging me. What happens if he has another go? Are you going to protect me this time? Or just stand back and watch? Record it for your precious files?"

"He won't be back," Ngaire assured me in her best bedside manner. "You need rest. We will look at your injuries in the morning."

"All I get is fucking rest!" I bellowed. "How about not drugging and shackling me so I can defend myself? I thought you built your society on the principles of equality and respect? How scientific is this? Barbaric is what this is!"

Switching off the light and closing the door firmly ended the conversation. I exhaled forcefully, fighting the waves of heaviness pulling me down. Anger still had the upper hand. I would not let these bastards win. I would not succumb. Willing my body to stay awake, fight it, my eyelids became heavy.

"Frey? Are you okay?" Illy's voice reached me through the darkness.

I tried to calm my voice. I wasn't angry at her, but damn it, I was furious.

"Yes," I hissed through clenched teeth. "But another few seconds, and it would have been a different story. The asshole broke my nose. Cheekbone too." As I calmed, I was shocked to realize that it was *shame* washing over me with the memory of Dale lying on me, naked, his hands forcing my legs apart, and me only in a scratchy cotton open-backed hospital gown with no underwear.

Illy sensed the change in tone and didn't even bother to lower her voice.

"This is not your fault. In no way is this your fault. Be angry, Freyja. Be very angry. You have every right to be. Do not be ashamed. He is a worthless beast, trying to force himself on you. An abominable excuse for a human being. And they allowed it. You did nothing to deserve that."

"I know..."

But did I? My conscience pricked at me. *Did I ask for it? Taunting and provoking him?*

I fought the shadows, not wanting to relinquish control. Scared of what might happen, but as I screamed, the cavern opened up and swallowed me.

"*Freyja.*" It was Laetitia's voice, calling me. A sweet, lilting tone. How did I know her voice? I wondered, dazed. I had never heard her speak. "*Freyja!*" She called insistently, the voice taking on a more masculine edge. The world was vibrating, and I pulled back from her, annoyed.

"Jorgensen! Wake up! We don't have long."

My eyes shot open but couldn't focus in the darkness. The weight of the drugs pulled me down, the swirling sensation making me feel nauseous.

"I'm so sorry," the familiar voice whispered in an Australian accent. "This should never have happened."

"Ashton?" I recognized the voice, even in the dark and through fuzzy semi-consciousness. He and I had spent time together on my first visit here. A decent man, I had thought. Since we had been here, we hadn't seen him once, although both Ngaire and Kal had confirmed he knew we were here. I fought against the whirlpool threatening to drown me.

"Why are you here? In the dark?"

"The cameras are light sensitive. Dale knew that. That is why he tried to … assault you in the dark."

"He tried to rape me," I choked, the memory flooding back. "Strangle me. Landed a few solid punches, too. Broke my nose and my left cheekbone." My face had swollen. I could feel the hot tightness of my skin, even though I couldn't touch it to check.

"I'm so sorry. I never meant for it to be this way."

"If you are truly sorry, you will let us go."

Ashton paused, and I softened my approach.

"You have kept us prisoner for weeks. Conducted tests and medical procedures against our will. Stolen my genetic material to use for goodness knows what."

"We needed it for the program."

"You'll understand that is of little comfort."

"We just needed to replace what you destroyed. It is imperative. You don't understand the critical importance of…"

"She was my sister! She didn't give consent any more than I did. It was my responsibility to save her."

"I know you won't believe this, but I do understand."

230

"Please. My children need me. Angus killed Illyria's husband and shot mine. Cam is likely dead now, too. Our children are orphans if you keep us prisoner. They need their mothers."

I sensed rather than heard the slight inhalation and pressed on. "Illy has two beautiful little girls. Luca is dead. Who will care for them? Summer and Allison are their names. Sweet, beautiful girls left all alone with no parents to guide them. And my children. Angus has taken Louis, goodness knows where and why. He must be terrified. I have three other children. They have all been left without a mother. Xanthe, Katrin, and Thorsten are their names. They are my world, my everything. How do they grow up without me? Every birthday and Christmas, wondering what happened?"

Ashton tensed in the darkness.

"Please. Let me go home to my family. That is all I ever wanted. My sister. My son. My family. They are my world. I need them. They need me."

His flimsy resolve collapsed. Fumbling in the dark, he unfastened the restraints.

"Illyria too, please," I begged as I soothed my wrists, rubbed raw. I sensed the shadow move toward Illy.

Shadows swirled before my closed eyes as I fought the head spin caused by sitting up quickly after weeks of being forced to lie in a bed. I swung my legs off the bed, and holding the rail for balance, I fought to steady myself. After a few moments, I stood. I was weak, my muscles unused and wasted. My stomach protested from the surgery.

Illy was awake and alert in an instant.

"Thank you, Carl," I heard her whisper.

"I'm sorry, Illyria. I never meant for it to be like this. Go. Quickly. I won't be able to stop them from coming after you. You need to leave ... now."

Ashton steered us out of the room in the dark, and we staggered like newborn foals down a short corridor to an external door, using the walls to support ourselves. Pushing us through before he changed his mind, I heard the door close firmly behind us and an audible *click*. Illy's hand found mine in the dim light.

"Come on. See the trees? We need the cover. Let's *go*."

Moving sluggishly, our bodies weakened from weeks in a bed, we staggered down the path into the woods. My body was unresponsive, further hindered by the effects of a strong sedative. Tripping and stumbling over tree roots, I wanted to lie down and sleep, but Illy dragged me along. We couldn't be captured now. Biting my lip as hard as I could, I tasted blood through the pain. *Focus on that*, I told myself as my lip started to swell. We cannot go back there. That would break me. To come so close to freedom, but being recaptured? I vowed, even as I floundered, *I will never let them take me.*

Illy guided me to the dome, and we followed the perimeter to the hatch and let ourselves out. Dawn light started tinting the horizon a pale silver.

"We need to move," she urged as I tripped and stumbled, unable to control my numbed limbs. "They will work out we are gone soon and will send someone out to look for us. They will know exactly where we have gone, and we are easy to find. It is kilometers from the harbor. We have nowhere to hide out here."

Walking as fast as we could, barefoot, the open backs of our hospital gowns flapping around us, we watched the sky slowly change color before us as we puffed from our lack of fitness, our bodies aching from weeks of inactivity. My muscles were heavy from the sedative, but I could feel the raw sensation around my wrists and ankles, skin rubbed off in places. The crisp breeze numbed my bare back and legs, although my face was hot and swollen. My stomach ached like a knife stabbing me from the inside out, but we pushed on. Sticking to the forest edge, we moved as fast as we could, fearful of the ominous sound of a drone sent to track us.

As the sun brightened the sky, a broken-down silvered wooden fence marked the boundary of a residential property ahead of us. Fields of once waist-high grass, now brown and rotting, fenced into fields. As we neared the house site in the distance, déjà vu washed over me. The dilapidated buildings. The dead forest behind.

"Illy!" I stopped dead. "I know where I am. This is the farm."

"The one where they tried to eat you and Cam?"

"That one. We had bikes when they attacked us. E-bikes. They will be flat now. But we can ride a hell of a lot faster than we can walk in bare feet."

Illy paused. "It is a great idea, and I don't see we have much choice. Do you have any idea where they are?"

"None at all," I admitted. "We walked back to Inverness. We forgot about the bikes in the horror, just speechless that we had survived. It wasn't until later that we remembered. The risk is that Clava took them when they investigated."

Illy pondered that as we entered the wooden front gate, hanging onto the ground from one rusted old hinge. "Perhaps, but I think unlikely. They sent a forensics team. I recall reading the reports. They weren't looking for equipment. After all, they have their pick of anything they want in Inverness. Why take two bikes that aren't worth much?"

"Well, they are worth a bit to me right now. The only risk is they hit us with a slingshot. We fell and dropped the bikes. They might be damaged."

"Fair enough. But we need to try. They will soon realize we are gone."

CHAPTER 30

"SHOULD WE REST A bit and hide here for the day?" I asked as we made our way up the overgrown path of weeds and death, watching where we stood in our bare feet. "Not that I want to stay here, of course, but they might not think to look here." Even seeing the house from the road gave me flashbacks of the time spent here years ago. I had never forgotten the horrors of this place. The smells. Finding Cam hanging like a carcass from a meat hook, drenched in his own blood.

"No. If we aren't back at the *Eurydice*, they will be there waiting for us, and then we won't get away. I don't think we have it in us to walk or even ride to the next town with a decent-sized boat. I have no idea where the nearest harbor even is."

Sighing, I recognized the truth in this. "Likely Aberdeen, and that is a long way. Come on then."

Spotting the shed in which I had been kept captive, I shuddered, the memories threatening to consume me. I knew they weren't there. Exhaling fiercely through my teeth, I kept walking purposefully. Splitting up, we strained our eyes in the darkness, fighting to see the contents of the feral sheds. The stench hadn't waned; it was still unbearable and precisely as I remembered it—the reek of fear and death. I avoided the sheds with the vats, heading toward a larger one. I found an old, rusted van inside, but I knew even from looking that it would take forever to start—time we didn't have.

"Here!" Illy called, and I followed her voice to a small lean-to at the side of the house, now fully illuminated in the dawn light.

As expected, the batteries were flat, and the bikes were covered in dust, but they appeared undamaged. With our hospital gowns flapping, exposing our naked asses to the wind, we pedaled as fast as we could down the main road.

My stomach lurched at the low humming of a drone on approach. Looking up, I estimated we were less than a kilometer from the dock. I could see the marine blue of the water in the distance as it met the pale blue sky.

"Come on," Illy urged, panting as she spurred up. "For goodness' sake, Frey. *Move!*"

Drugged, weak, and in agony from my second surgery, I pedaled as fast as I could, trying to keep pace with Illy. She accelerated, and I lost sight of her. Turning the final corner, the blinding whiteness of the *Eurydice* ahead of me, I dropped my head and pushed my legs to pump the pedals. Dropping my bike beside hers on the dock, the wheel still spinning, I clambered across the bridge and felt the shudder as Illy started the engines and I dragged it up. Thank goodness we had refueled upon arrival, our quick escape from Auckland Island motivating that decision. We weren't expecting a warm welcome, but even we could never have envisaged we would depart like this.

"Do you want me to shoot it?" I called down the stairwell to Illy, where I could see her maneuvering the vessel out of its berth. I doubted the accuracy of my aim in my current condition. Normally I was an excellent shot, but right now, I could barely lift my arms.

"No point. They have seen us. They will be after us." I sensed the panic in her voice, even from down the stairwell. "Those electric cars aren't fast, but they will be on their way."

"There is no time to disable the other vessels!"

I looked around the marina, panicked. There were a lot of sailing yachts. Nothing as fast and luxurious as the *Eurydice* but plenty of motorized vessels. They could give chase.

"Do you know if they use any of the boats here regularly?" I stumbled halfway down the stairs to see Illy as she stood at the bridge. "If there is one that they use, I could try to shoot it and hit the fuel tank?" Even as the words left my mouth, I doubted my chances of success. Fuel tanks differed in location, and I didn't know the make of each vessel.

She nodded grimly and started to say something but paused as a light illuminated her face.

"Go back up and keep watch. Bellow if you see anyone. Scream like you have never screamed before."

She disappeared back into the windowed bridge, and I could see her using the radio.

Watching the bank closely, I saw no movement. The drone hovered above us, and I tipped my head to the side to get a better look. One clear shot was all it would take. Maybe the flare gun? The flares were expendable. No one was coming to save us.

"Hold on!" Illy called.

I sat on one of the white deck chairs as Illy masterfully maneuvered the craft out of the marina and headed east, picking up speed. Still feeling woozy, the drone lurked ominously overhead, and I wished fervently that I had bothered to shoot it down. It was just annoying now, buzzing around like a blowfly. The thought made me smile, thinking of summer picnics in Australia, constantly harassed by flies. The yacht shifted to full power, roaring with the sound of the water swooshing past. I jolted in surprise as Illy placed a hand on my shoulder and handed me a raincoat and a life jacket.

"Who was on the radio?" I asked, slipping the jacket on, noting that Illy was hurriedly putting hers on, too.

"Tadhg. Then Jake. Do it up. Properly and over your head. *Now.*"

Of all the people I expected, that wasn't it.

"What...? Did you encrypt...?"

"Watch." She pointed toward the marina as she zipped up her jacket, the white boats fading rapidly from view as we sped away. "Hold on to the railing. As tight as you can. Link arms with mine. Head down, hood up, and keep your eyes and mouth closed."

I scarcely saw the rush of motion. The impact of something hitting water. Hard. But the image of enormous boats flying in the air like paper airplanes, and the massive wave heading toward us I will never forget. Interlinking our arms and dropping our heads, bracing for impact, we clung to the rail as the force of the surging wave struck us and tipped the *Eurydice* sideways. The force left us hanging from our hands as the water roared past us. Digging my fingers into the slippery rail, I fought to keep hold, my weakened muscles starting to give. The vessel teetered for a moment, and I closed my eyes, knowing we would capsize. I sent out an apology to my children. To Louis. *I'm so sorry,* I thought as his face flashed before my eyes. Just as I thought I could hold on no longer, the vessel creaked and righted itself, landing with an almighty splash back on her hull. Every piece of furniture was sent flying. Chairs landed in the water. Windows shattered as objects hurtled against them. As I recovered my wits, I saw Illy hanging under the rail. Grabbing hold of her lifejacket and a handful of hair, I dragged her back under the railing. Unable to stand upright on the sopping deck, we dropped, sitting there as we caught our breath.

I had a massive lump forming on my forehead where it had struck the metal rail. Touching it gingerly, I glanced back toward the marina to see the calmness after the devastation. Broken pieces of jetty, boats, and debris floated on the surface. Some had already begun washing ashore. The drone was circling above the water's edge, assessing the damage.

Tilting my head slightly to look at her in the early morning light, I asked, "Tell the truth. How much of that was for Luca?"

"Most of it." She grinned as she sat beside me on the deck, looking across at me. "God, he would have loved watching that. But strategically, a show of force and proving that we have allies means they are unlikely to pursue us. I mean, would you?"

Suddenly everything overwhelmed me, and I let my head fall back on the wooden deck with a thwack.

"Frey. I know you are exhausted, but I need you. You can't collapse yet. You can soon, I promise. But not now. Wipe your face. We can't get water in our eyes or mouths."

Wearily, I lifted my head and took the towel out of the waterproof canister she handed me, stashed under her jacket. *Not now*, I repeated. As exhausted as I was, I was not ready to die.

CHAPTER 31

"TIME FOR A WHITE flag?" I asked, desperate for a rest after hours of keeping watch. "They aren't pursuing us." The agony was making me nauseous, feeling like someone had slashed my stomach open, my face and head throbbing in sympathy.

Tadhg had maintained secure radio contact with us for a short time. An hour after the destruction at the harbor, he advised that he had intercepted Clava's communications to Auckland and other nearby communities. A few had seen the missile fired from Newgrange. Clava had reassured them all. It had been an accident. Everyone was fine. Tadhg and Jake had been watching us via satellite. In time, it became clear that they had no intention of following us or firing upon us.

"I can't."

I looked at her curiously. "Ils, this isn't your battle. This is mine. I understand you want to avenge Luca's death, but I can do that. I need my son back. But you don't need to be here. You can drop me in Edinburgh, and I can keep going. Go home. Be with your girls."

"Did I ever tell you how my parents died?"

"I gathered it was tragically. But not the specifics."

Illy sat on the sofa opposite me and stared off into space, seeing something. She was in a place that wasn't here, unable to speak. Just as I was about to check that she was alright, she spoke.

"They had taken me to a nightclub with my high school friends. They dropped me off, kissed me goodbye, and were driving home after making me promise to call them if I needed a lift home. I was a few weeks past eighteen and didn't have my license. It was booked, but I hadn't taken the test as my birthday fell in the week of my final exams. They stopped at an intersection, waited for the light to turn green. They pulled onto the main road and were wiped out by a drunk driver. He had broken up with his girlfriend and sunk a bottle of Jim Beam. Then he thought he would go out and get more. Didn't even see them. Didn't stop to render assistance. Our car flipped and rolled down an embankment. They died there. All the while, I am dancing the night away with my friends, oblivious that my life had forever changed."

"Oh, Illy. I am so sorry."

"I arrived home at 3 AM, and they weren't there. At first, I thought the car had been stolen. Then I realized the house was empty. I panicked. Rang all their friends. Every hospital. Then the police showed up at the door. It has been a long time. But it stays with you."

"Is that why you don't drink much?" I asked curiously.

"Partly. But mainly as it impairs your judgment. In case you haven't noticed, I am a bit of a control freak."

"Did your parents know you had been accepted into the military?"

"No. At that point, I was going to be a lawyer."

"Really?"

"I knew I was good with words, and I wanted them to be proud of me. I had already been accepted into Arts/Law. That party was my celebration before I took on my summer job to help pay for it." Illy turned and vomited her breakfast into the North Sea.

"I have never been so seasick," Illy muttered as her head returned from over the rail for the third time that morning. "Then again, maybe it is anger consuming me. The blazing desire to confront that gutter-dwelling fuckwit. That keeps me going."

"It could be one of the medicines they gave us. They had no qualms in drugging Cam and me last time we were there."

Illy thought about that. "Possibly. Nothing I can do if that is the case. Getting it out of my system is the only course of action."

"Back to what I was saying: do you want to go home?"

"No. What I want is to finish what I started. I want to see Angus's face when I confront him. I want to know *why*. Why did he kill Luca? Try to kill Cam. Take Louis. I need to know. I never had answers from my parents' death. I went to the trial, but the guy didn't even remember getting in his car. I felt so empty. There were no answers to my questions. This time I need closure."

Illy's looked terrible, her usually creamy complexion tinged green.

"Do you want to stop for a day or so?" I asked, concerned equally for her, but also for the head start Angus had on us. Thanks to our detour, he had nearly two months on us.

"No," she mumbled, but I suspected she did.

"Look, let's pull into the nearest dock and let your stomach settle. I feel nauseous with all the drugs they pumped in me, too. An hour is not going to make much difference, is it? After all, it has been weeks since we left home. Clava aren't after us. Tadhg is watching. An hour or two isn't changing anything."

"Maybe..." But I could tell she wasn't convinced.

I chattered away, trying to distract her from her seasickness.

"Ils, do you think he might take Louis to Auckland? I mean, if this is retribution for what we did?" I didn't want her to think I blamed her. I genuinely didn't. But I had spent the past weeks regretting blowing up that lab. Perhaps I should have just injected Kat and left quietly? Was this payback? Had Luca died because of my sister?

"It is certainly possible," Illy considered, "but I think unlikely. He had no real ties there. If he doesn't want to reside on a yacht and live a transient life, he needs to be in a protected community if he is going to stay anywhere for a period, especially with a child. That limits the options significantly. He lived on Lewis, then with you. He is Scots. He was more likely to head to Clava. But there is no reason to believe that part of what they told us was a lie. If he were there, he would have dropped by to be a twat and act superior. He couldn't help himself. As for, is this payback, well, possibly? But why take Louis? Why not just kill Cam and Luca?" Her voice glitched slightly on the name. "There was no need to take Louis. I watched the footage a dozen times. He planned it. He took Louis deliberately. It wasn't a spur-of-the-moment action."

"You watched it a dozen times?" I echoed numbly. "Why?"

Illy was silent for a while, then responded in a husky voice. "Initially, to see what had happened. I couldn't believe he was gone, that a man so full of life had been suddenly obliterated. I saw his face, the shock kicking in. I watched him fall—the blood pooling around him on the concrete dock. Then, when I watched it again as you packed, my training kicked in. I rewound it and watched to analyze what had happened—focused on the detail. The facial expressions. The body language. I have seen far worse, you know."

"But he was *yours*," I whispered. "It is different."

"It is. But after a few times, it wasn't about me anymore. I needed to read Angus, trying to learn what I could. His motives. Make sense of what happened. He didn't intend to harm Louis. That was obvious. Taking him, or someone, was why they were there. Louis was terrified, but Angus didn't threaten him. Louis fell to his knees, sobbing over Cam. Angus made no aggressive overtures toward him. He had holstered the gun and dragged him to the vessel. It was only when I saw it the first time, when I came to tell you, that I lost it."

"Hearing you scream like that chilled my blood. I have never seen you distressed. Even when the pregnancy was complicated, and we thought you might lose the girls."

"Control is an important skill in the military. And analysis."

"What about Nate?"

"Nate was an interesting one. It was plain from his body language that he knew this was the plan, but he didn't partake in it. The only time he even got off the ship was to help Angus carry Louis. Louis was hysterical, and it took both of them to drag him aboard. But they didn't hit him or intimidate him, and no one was watching. So, while I don't know Angus well, I have to say I don't think the intention was to harm Louis. Retribution for Auckland, maybe. But I saw nothing to show he planned to hurt him."

"That is a relief. Why didn't you tell me sooner?"

"Because keeping up our spirits was the most important thing while we were there. If I started talking about what had happened, you would focus on that, and fret about how much time we had lost. Not focus on getting away. On that note, what did you say to Ashton to make him release us?"

"It is the strangest thing. I don't really know. I told him about your children and mine. I sensed a shift, so I pushed it. I couldn't even see him in the dark, but I just *felt* it, if that makes sense. Especially when I spoke about you and your girls."

"You have always had amazing instincts. Carl and I dated for a short time."

"*What?*"

"We had known each other since Melbourne. But we were so busy at that time assessing candidates and saving as many people as possible that we never had a personal conversation. Everything was about logistics, candidates. We spent some time together in the early years, on Auckland. Nothing serious, a few dinners. A movie or two."

"What happened between you?"

"It was around the time that we learned about the mass murders on Gibraltar and Great Barrier. I offered to go, to help, and I was shut down fairly abruptly. I realized he would always be more committed to the project than me, so I quietly broke it off. I doubt he ever worked out why. I certainly never told him outright. I just stopped being available. He wasn't that great with subtle communication."

"Well, that part is probably true, being committed to the project. So why did he release us? He doesn't have children of his own, does he?"

"Not that I know of. But what I know is that Carl was found as a baby, only hours old, wrapped in a filthy blanket in the women's toilets of a train station in central Brisbane. A woman went to the toilet on her way to work and found him. He told me it was all over the news. The police looked for his mother, for witnesses. But like all news, it petered out eventually, and no one ever came forward. He went to a foster home, and after a few months, he was adopted by a childless couple, both academics, who nurtured his passion for science. He was given a wonderful education, raised in a loving home. But he never stopped wondering who his birth parents were. Where he came from."

"I think I used the word orphan. I just didn't think about it."

"Well, that would have resonated. He never got over it. He told me once that his early work in genetics, mapping genomes, was to try to track down his own history. He had a book of the newspaper clippings about himself as a baby, copies of the police report, and the television stories. He would forensically analyze each photo, the blanket, the location, just to see if he could find something that the detectives missed."

"And did he? Ever find out where he came from?"

"No. It affected him more than he let on. I can imagine it is a very lonely and isolating feeling."

"I thought there was something in his tone when he spoke to you."

"Maybe. He always liked me. But I was already having doubts about the project. He wasn't someone I could confide in about those doubts, so it was easier if I broke it off."

"Did you like him, too?"

Illy's sigh was so deep that I felt it reverberate through my bones. "I did. I really liked him. He is a kind man. A good man. Intelligent and self-deprecating. He liked me, was respectful. Breaking it off was hard. I was so desperately lonely. People had partnered up, spending more time in couples. I questioned myself a hundred times. Me and my bloody ethics."

"I've told you it was loneliness that finally made me make a move on Cam," I confessed.

"The way he tells it, you two had this amazing love at first sight story. You knew each other before that night at the springs?"

"We shared a dorm but barely saw each other. They designed it that way. Different roles and different shifts. They didn't want people who worked together to live together, and they deliberately rostered us differently in the early days so we wouldn't be on top of each other. Then one night, he had a migraine, and he couldn't get the pain tablets from the packet."

"Poor Cam and his migraines. He must be having a terrible time with you and Louis missing."

"Likely," I admitted, praying he still lived.

"So, you jumped a man with a migraine?"

"No! That was well before, only a few months after we had arrived. It was the middle of the night, and I couldn't sleep. I saw him fighting to get the tablets out of the packet. He had stitches in his hand. I helped him, and we talked—all night. I liked him, and I could tell he liked me. So, I freaked out and backed off. We barely spoke again for months. I even thought he was with Di for a while. Then, one night, he slammed into me and dropped me in the mud."

Illy's blue eyes sparkled with mischief. "You two have a strange concept of romance!"

"He opened up to me, told me things that he had told no one in the year we had been there. I still don't know why I did it. I just instinctively knew that this man had ethics. He wouldn't tell anyone, even if we were friends with benefits. Besides, by that point, I had far more dirt on him. I made him change into his walking shoes, and I took him to my secret place."

"Ahh, the hot springs. Yes, I know about that part."

"So here he is, naked and floating in the pool. Blissfully unaware of me. I've not been near a man in a year, there is a rather well-built one in close proximity, and he is ignoring me completely."

"…and you were…ahem, lacking companionship?"

"Something like that. I was getting rather pissed off, realizing that he wouldn't make the first move. So, on the spur of the moment, I kissed him. His eyes popped open in complete shock, and he dropped like a stone."

"But when he came up, things took an interesting turn?"

I laughed at the memory. "When he finished coughing up a lungful of hot water. He was cranky with me. Fortunately, I turned that frustration into something else."

"Luca's face when I kissed him the first time was a picture! Sorcha spent all her time with Di, and it was a critical time in her treatment, a week or so after we arrived. We were worried. She was losing weight, and the baby wasn't growing. I could tell that Magali was concerned, but she wouldn't speak to me about it. I was followed everywhere, completely fed up with the constant surveillance. Luca and I both knew it, of course, but couldn't openly talk about it. I could sense his frustration. On this particular day, he was sitting in a chair in the office. You know the one on Clava that adjoins the main treatment room? Di was having a procedure, and we were waiting. There was a tech there, pretending to work but really just keeping an eye on us. On consideration, I think it was actually Dale. I paid little attention at the time. I just wanted him to go away so I could snoop around the files. Luca was sitting on this chair, bored as batshit, reading a book, making those grunting noises he makes when he is frustrated. I marched up, plucked the book from his hands, and dropped it on the floor. Then I sat on his lap facing him, my legs wrapped around him and kissed him."

"What did he do?"

"Froze, at first. He was petrified of me. He started to protest. I ignored him, pulled his t-shirt out of his jeans, ran my hands up his deliciously muscular sides, and kissed his neck. He was rigid, holding his breath. Just as I thought I had made a huge mistake and wondering how to back out, I felt the shudder reverberate through him. His breath started heating up my neck... let's just say that was the moment the tone changed. I was sitting on him, so I was in a position to know. The next thing I know, my top is on the floor, the windows are steaming up, and Dale has left the building."

"Poor Luca! Turning him on like that and then ditching him."

"Don't worry. I made it up to him later. While it was a bit spur of the moment, I did have fears that my experiment may not work, and he might reject me."

"But it worked? And that was it?"

"That was it. We weren't apart after that."

"What would you have done if he had rejected you?" I asked curiously. Before Illy, I had never seen Luca pay attention to any woman, and plenty had openly desired him. He could have had a woman in every port when we traveled. Several even. Muscular, ruggedly handsome, and always respectful to women, he was quite a catch.

"It simply wasn't an option. I chose him. As soon as I kissed him, I knew. It was like meeting my best friend, the one I had been missing all my life, but not even realizing he was there. He told me once, months later, when it was all too late for him, of course, that after his father abandoned him, he feared being in a relationship. In case he turned out to be a loser. But he knew when he met me that I wouldn't allow him to be a twat. I would hunt him down and kill him first."

I laughed aloud at that. "Oh, you so would. I couldn't imagine anyone better for you. Really."

"The funny thing is, I could see him with *you*. You were so close. I asked him about you. Before you and I became friends. He said that he would have loved to make a life with you, but after you left August the second time, he could see that you only ever wanted Cam. Even when that was no longer a possibility, he knew. He never wanted to be your second choice, so he never tried."

"He said that?"

"He described it to me once as 'watching someone have their still-beating heart wrenched from their chest and watching the sucking, gaping void drain the life from them. Knowing they were half a person, gasping for air, unsure if they were living or dying and not caring either way.'"

"That is a fairly apt description. Meeting Cam was like finding the missing piece to my life. Losing him was having my heart ripped out."

"I know. It was how I felt when I lost my parents. He felt it himself when his mother passed. He realized that you taking up with anyone after that kind of love would be settling for second best."

"I loved Luca like a friend. He was my wingman. No matter where we went or what we did, he was my best friend. He looked out for me, teased me incessantly, but I always knew he supported me, even if he disagreed with me. God, I miss him."

"Me, too."

Silence filled the room as we reminisced about Luca. About Cam. About all of those we had lost. And for what?

"We need to talk, Ils. About what happened. To us."

"And we will." Her tone was firm. "We will talk, analyze, cry, and deal. Just not now. We have a mission to complete. We will both need to take a very long time to accept what we went through. But not now. Now we focus on getting Louis and being grateful that we are free."

I paused. That wasn't what I wanted to hear. I needed to apologize, to make her understand how sorry I was.

"But..."

"But nothing. Nothing that happened was your fault, so you can stop that right now. And Frey?"

"What?"

"If I had to be held prisoner with anyone, I am glad it was you."

I grimaced, needing to ask one more question. "What do you think they'll do with Dale?"

Illy considered. "Likely nothing."

"Seriously?" Even through the pain relief, my face still throbbed from the abuse he had inflicted on me. I had realigned my nose and examined my cheek and jaw as soon as we knew they weren't in pursuit, as well as gingerly checking the enormous lump on my forehead, but without an x-ray, there was nothing else I could do. The bruising across half of my face was already a mottled palette of blues and purples.

"Sadly, yes. Clava is a bit of a boy's club. Auckland, too. Besides, there are no jails, no laws. And what he did, well, tried to do…"

"He tried to rape me is what he did!" I flared at the injustice. "Likely you too."

"And what do you like to see them do?" Illy asked softly.

"I can tell you exactly what I would do! Puncture his eye socket with one of those needles he loved shoving in us. Watch it deflate like a wrinkled balloon hissing air, knowing he would never leer at a woman like that ever again. Cut off his balls and ram them down his throat and watch him choke."

Illy grinned at my enthusiasm. "I would hold him down for you."

CHAPTER 32

"THEY ARE HERE," I growled, unable to keep the anger from my voice. I gestured toward the *Selkie* nestled against the far berth. It had been my home for years. Now, the halyard gusted in the wild breeze. I gently moored the *Eurydice* a safe distance away, and we climbed the stairs to stand on the deck. Long strands of hair escaped my ponytail and whipped me in the face. Illy nodded grimly but said nothing as her long dark hair obscured her vision. She had Luca's gun tucked in the back of her pants.

The wind roared, forcing us to shout at each other. Not that there was any risk of being overheard. The chilled air pierced my skin, and I reached for a jacket. Despite the years living on the *Selkie* with Luca, Nate, Angus, and Jake, outside the domes, I wasn't used to the feel of wind now, penetrating my skin with its cold, sharp fingers. Goosebumps popped up on my arms from the sudden temperature change. Closing my eyes and conjuring his gentle face, I sent a silent wish out to Cam, praying he was alive and healing. Not wanting to be tracked, we had made no further radio transmissions after those to Tadhg from Inverness Harbor. Equally, we were fearful that we would be followed, and retribution sought for the damage we had inflicted. Worse, being re-captured and returned to that sterile white hell we had endured for nearly two months. I had been out of that room only twice, for my surgeries. If we returned there, we would never see daylight again.

Images of each of my children flickered before my eyes: Katrin, Xanthe, and Thorsten. Finally, Louis's dark brown hair and soft, kind eyes came into view, and I sent out the promise. The same one I had made a hundred times since leaving Lewis. *I'm coming*, I promised him. *Hang on, just a little longer. I will find you. I will bring you home.*

Illy tapped my shoulder, pulling me from my trance. She gestured with her chin, and I followed close behind as we crept along the dock. She seemed fine, but my legs wobbled like jelly being on land again. We crept aboard, and I pointed the best path to take. Not down the main stairwell but through the access hatch. Within minutes, we realized the vessel had been emptied, both of people and supplies. I surveyed the smaller, cozy living space, needing to lean against the solid frame of the door as memories tormented me. The room where Luca and I had spent many hours together, curled up on that navy, curved sofa. Reading. Talking. I closed my eyes and pictured him, laughing. Teasing me. Memories of all the beautiful times we had spent together, playing cards, talking, flitted into my mind. This was how I always wanted to remember him. Full of life. Not how he looked when I saw him last. Closing my eyes and wishing my friend a final farewell, I turned and went to find Illy.

On a visit to Edinburgh, Angus had taken me to his home, wanting to collect some books, but I hadn't gone inside. Back when we had first traveled together, when I still called him a friend. Before we had returned to August to find Cam, before... I shook the memories from my mind and renewed my focus. We knew where we were headed. It wasn't far from the house where Cam and I had reunited, but I shook that from my mind. I turned to Illy as we climbed back onto the dock and shouted over the gusting wind.

"Getting Louis is my primary goal, but should we restock and refuel now?"

The escape from Inverness was still fresh in our minds. Illy nodded slowly. She glanced at the mid-afternoon sky, then back at me. Best to stock up now and find Angus's house fresh in the morning. While one more night wasn't changing anything, part of me felt sick for not barging in now and rescuing him.

I refueled the *Eurydice* while she emptied our backpacks and did a quick stock take. Despite the rapidly dwindling daylight, I had been here several times, both with Angus and the last time with Cam. I had a reasonable knowledge of the city's layout and could easily find the government warehouse, which had been piled high with supplies.

After Cam and I found the stash of medication in Edinburgh, Lewis residents had agreed that a visit to Edinburgh, or another coastal city once every six months, was a good idea to replenish items that we urgently needed. Hamish had led the initial raids for medical equipment, diagnostic tools, and medications.

Luca, the latter ones. One of the vets or engineers also went along to source other equipment or parts we needed. But as the years had passed, we had adapted, never losing sight of our sustainability focus. We no longer needed new medications. Cam and the team had learned to grow opium poppies from which they derived morphine for pain relief, and valerian, which had proven a mostly satisfactory alternative to salbutamol, needed to control Sorcha's asthma. Jacinda's extensive knowledge of herbs and plants supplemented the pharmaceuticals to the point where people consulted her readily. She was often called before people saw a doctor, much to Sorcha's annoyance. Jacinda had started teaching her children about natural healing, and Aroha, now twelve, was quite a capable apprentice, often treating simple cases on her own. A quiet girl, I had long sensed an underlying spark of rebelliousness masked by her studious appearance. Aroha had taken over the tasks of herb collection and distilling for her mother and could regularly be seen sitting on their doorstep of an evening with a mortar and pestle, engrossed in one of the many volumes on naturopathic medicine we had sourced over the years. Illy and I had agreed that her knowledge would soon surpass Jacinda's or that she would tire of healing. Jacinda took her vow of do no harm to the extreme at times.

Isla and I had asked for several raids on veterinary suppliers in the early years, but we too found ourselves well stocked with equipment, medicines, and general supplies. We had adapted and were quite competent in our treatment, treating most of our patients with what we had.

Initially, the traveling teams, usually led by Luca when he wasn't needed for distilling, had found some of the requests frivolous. Makeup, shampoo, and other toiletries. In a surprisingly diplomatic manner for him, Luca had introduced them to Jacinda's herbal soaps and shampoos, all biodegradable and safe to use in the recycled water of the domes. Soon those requests had dried up, too. The traveling parties went a year between visits, sometimes longer. Luca's coffee machines had been sourced on one visit, and better distilling and bottling equipment on another. Once, Luca had led a small team to France and had returned with the hold filled with cases of fine wine as well as gin stills and wine bottling and preserving equipment. Illy and I had often laughed that Luca got itchy feet between visits to the mainland, desperate for some excitement.

"Have you noticed how the last few visits have been around coffee and alcohol?" I noted as Luca had returned from one mission bursting with excitement.

Illy smiled. "He is nothing if not predictable. Always thinking of his stomach."

As we loaded the food and bottled water into the hold, I asked, "Clothes and gifts for the kids and then sleep?"

"Sounds like a plan."

"Just let me take some more painkillers. It is probably just the movement, but my stomach is killing me. My face, too. Do you want some more of Jacinda's anti-nausea stuff?"

Returning to the *Eurydice* by torchlight, we loaded one bedroom with books, toys, and clothing for the kids and some items for us.

"Every time I leave Lewis, I swear it will be the last time," I muttered as I dropped the bags I carried, laden with books.

"And each time you genuinely mean it." Illy smirked. "But then shit happens, and you keep leaving. How about I finish tidying up here, and you cook dinner? I hear canned ravioli is quite the in-thing this year. All the Michelin-rated restaurants are serving it."

I ascended the stairs into the galley kitchen, heating a can of ravioli to share. My parents would be horrified—eating food from a can. But it wasn't that bad. It kept us alive, and right now, I couldn't concentrate on cooking gourmet meals. Food was something to fill my stomach and give me one less thing to worry about. Neither Illy nor I were skilled cooks at the best of times, leaving it to our far more capable partners. *Just one more thing Illy will need to adapt to,* I thought, stirring the contents of the saucepan as it sizzled and stuck to the bottom. The guys and I had regularly eaten far worse at sea. There were only so many ways you could dress up baked beans as a meal, but we made a game of it, giving each meal a score out of ten—the cook of the worst meal needed to wash the dishes for the week. Notably, Luca seldom washed dishes.

"I miss cheese," Illy lamented into her bowl of ravioli. "There aren't many things I miss, but cheese is one."

Cheese-making was something that had taken the residents of Lewis quite some time to perfect, but now that we had, it was delicious and plentiful. I wasn't a fan of brie and camembert but loved the full-flavored cheddars and blue cheeses they produced.

"My parents adored cheese," I admitted, making Illy look up. "There was a *fromagerie* near our home in Melbourne, and each week they delivered a selection of different cheeses with tasting notes. My parents would have friends over for wine and cheese regularly, and Kat and I were always allowed to try them."

"Listen to you: *fromagerie,*" she mocked. "You know, the rest of us just called it a cheese shop, right?"

I ignored the taunt.

"Did you ever try Roquefort?"

"Oh yes, many times. Beaufort d'ete, Stilton, Pule, and even some odd cheeses, like elk and deer."

"Elk cheese?"

"Truly. It was a thing."

"Well, I'm in no rush to try moose cheese, but what I wouldn't give to have a little grated pecorino on my pasta. I'd even tolerate parmesan."

"Snob," I teased.

"Ha! Says she who ate elk cheese! You know Jarlsberg and goat cheese from the supermarket were exotic for the rest of us, don't you?"

"It was a different time." I shrugged.

"I used to think it was the lesser one," Illy said, trailing off.

"So did I. But now..." I replayed the events of the last decade. I had been held captive, twice. Been subjected to surgery against my will. My stomach twinged, and I placed a hand over the stitches beneath the table, careful not to let Illy see. My face had been broken in Dale's assault, and I bore the painful bruises. My husband and best friend shot, my son kidnapped. Then there was my sister. Laetitia. Maybe this wasn't a better time. Perhaps, when all is said and done, humans will always be self-centered animals who care more for themselves than their fellow man. Had we learned anything?

"If nothing else, I am grateful for the people this pandemic brought into my life." Illy drew my attention back to the table. "You, Cam, Luca. The kids, all of them. You mean the world to me."

"Come on." I stood, ignoring the dishes. "Stay with me tonight. Neither of us will sleep well, anyway."

CHAPTER 33

EDINBURGH AS A CITY is not that large, and the harbor at Leith was walking distance to Dean Village, a picturesque and formerly wealthy part of town. Angus's home was a stunning three-story heritage sandstone home with leadlight windows and a black slate roof with multiple chimneys. The front door was still a glossy black in the early pre-dawn light, although a thick layer of dust betrayed its lack of use.

Illy and I stood at the far end of the street and surveyed our target.

"Front door?"

"Back. They will be expecting us, but there is no value in marching up to the front door. They will have heard from Clava that we are on our way, but there is no point in making a grand entrance."

We found the laneway behind and counted houses until we located Angus's home. Like most of the others, a modern glass conservatory had been built at the back, this one extending almost to the rear property boundary. Entering the fenced yard of the neighboring house, we found a ladder in the crumbling garage and climbed onto the roof of the adjoining conservatory, then made the leap to Angus's house. I made it easily, blessed with long legs. Illy was a good deal shorter, but determination spurred her. Nothing was stopping her from completing this mission.

A skylight in the roof popped up from the slate roof. Using the new Swiss army knives we had procured the day before to replace those we had lost with our clothing at Clava, we levered it up, snapping the lock mechanism. Truthfully, I didn't care what damage we did. He hadn't cared about Luca and Cam. But I didn't want to scare Louis by smashing in the glass.

We could see the kitchen below filled with boxes of food, all clearly marked with the Scottish Government seal. They had been here a while then, and they had sourced food from the government warehouses. I thought it looked like someone had been there recently when we visited yesterday with fresh marks on the dusty floors. But not having been there myself for years, it was hard to tell. Cracking my neck and rotating my shoulders to loosen them, I set my jaw firmly.

Game on.

As we crept through the house, Illy slightly ahead of me, she looked highly capable and decidedly intense with Luca's handgun loaded and aimed. I often forgot she had been an Army officer and completed weapons training. She was quite comfortable with firearms, but I just saw her as my friend. I had never seen her as combative. *Shame he didn't have it that day*. But on his last day, he, Cam, and Louis had been loading barrels of whisky onto the *Eurydice* to take to Newgrange. He never thought it would be the last day he would hold his children.

Something was off. Rubbish was strewn everywhere, empty liquor bottles left on every surface. And the smell—like something died in here. Illy had noticed it, too. The slight shift in her posture indicated that she also recognized the current state of the expensively furnished home was at odds with its former condition. *It looked like teenage kids held a weekend-long party with their parents away,* I mused, with memories of mad cleaning up after many such parties in my own teen years. On one memorable occasion, I frantically tried to re-color grass when one of my friends, wildly drunk, had vomited on my parents' beautifully manicured lawn after binging on blue curacao, staining a rather conspicuous patch bright blue. A patch, most unfortunately, blisteringly obvious from both the kitchen window and from the pool.

We found Nate reclining with a book in the living room. His lanky frame was stretched out, feet on an antique footstool, a shock of salt and pepper hair just visible over the top of the chair. Several empty bottles lay around this room too, and the air was thick with the scent of stale alcohol. A glass of unfinished whisky balanced on his knee—the uncapped half-empty bottle was resting beside him on a small lamp table.

"Where is the cockroach?" Illy boomed in such a voice that even my heart skipped a beat. I remembered Cam calling her military budgie after she ran their briefings in Melbourne. I had heard her speak firmly to her recalcitrant children but never quite like that. Even I had recoiled, and I was expecting it. She was undoubtedly impressive. Even more than Luca, and he had taught me tone and voice projection for when I needed to be intimidating.

Nate snapped awake, dropped the book, and spilled the amber liquid all over his leg.

"Fuck!" he seethed as he mopped at his leg with the dusty lap blanket resting on the nearby couch. "I wondered when you would show up," he snarled. "Took you long enough."

Picking up the nearest solid object, a lamp, I swung and cracked him squarely across the forehead.

He bellowed and toppled sideways, half-sprawling across the black leather armchair, and grinned up at me.

"Nice to see you too, Freyja. How is your gardener doing? Or are you shagging the plumber now as a replacement?"

Illy held the gun to his temple and asked again, this time in a low but far more threatening tone, "Where are Angus and Louis?"

"Not here," Nate responded flippantly. "Nice colors." He smirked in reference to my face.

Illy continued to hold the gun on Nate, gesturing with her chin that I should search. I did. Every room, cupboard, under beds. Looking for trapdoors under rugs, hidden cupboards, and small rooms. The attic and cellar. After a thorough search of the property, I returned, catching her eye and shaking my head. Illy was tense, ready to fire, Nate grinning at her. Leering.

Seeing his face reminded me of the look Derek had given me as they had gassed us. Something snapped within me. I'd had enough. I did not want to play. I wanted my son back. I had traveled a very long way with a grieving woman who needed to be home with her children. May as well move this along. Picking up a thick volume from the bookcase, I slammed it against his ear with a resounding thwack. As he recovered, Illy pulled the rope from her pack and tied his hands and feet, forcing him into a wooden chair, much to Nate's bewilderment.

"Aren't you just going to kill me? We killed your husbands!"

Illy looked up, hearing the incredulous tone.

"Not anytime soon," she replied in such a sweet tone that even I turned to look at her.

Nate's expression changed then. "I... I..." he stammered.

"You thought we would find you here, alone, and would kill you and be on our way?" Illy spoke leisurely, menace dripping from each word. "Oh no. We are in no rush, Nathaniel. I plan to take my time. Enjoy myself. I can't wait to hurt you slowly for your role in killing my husband. Tearing him away from his children. Kidnapping a child. Oh, I plan to have some *fun*. I'd lay bets you will be begging me to end it before nightfall."

Even I flinched at the word *fun*, the precise word the two filthy men had used when they had molested me several years before. But it was the tone Illy used that skittered down my spine. "I waited so long to meet him," she continued in the same slow chilling tone. "I loved him with every breath. He was my world. Then you took him from me and my children for no reason. I can't forgive that."

Nate's face blanched. Illy continued her nasty smile as she bound his hands and feet.

"No need to gag him," she told me amiably over his head. "No one can hear him scream. At least he will let us know we are doing it right."

Nate's face reflected the look of increasing concern, and he fought against his restraints.

"So, you want to die?" Illy soothed. "I can help you there. But it won't be quick. I can promise you that. I learned lots of interesting skills in my postings. What hurts the most without passing out. How long someone can survive the most brutal of torture. Luca, too, of course. You spent many years with him before you cut him down. He called you friend. There is a special kind of treatment we reserve for those who turn on their mates. Do you know how long a person can survive without food and water? Days. Weeks, even. Let's see how long I can make this last for you. Now … where should I start? How attached are you to your toes?"

Illy sauntered into the kitchen, leaving Nate gaping at me. She returned a few moments later with the block of expensive kitchen knives. Placing the block beside the bottle of whisky, she pulled one from the wooden block and toyed with it. It was an expensive, beautifully made knife, perfectly balanced. I watched her looking at it, assessing it. She tested the edges. Razor-sharp.

"Nice," she said to herself.

Removing Nate's shoes and socks, she drew the blade delicately across the soles of his feet, making him roar.

"Oh, don't waste your breath on a scratch. I'm just warming up."

Illy's tone was soft, yet menacing. She had been my best friend for years, but I had never seen her like this. Standing in the doorway, I was petrified of this stranger. The tone, the movements. It wasn't her.

Nate closed his eyes and clenched his jaw but held out far longer than I would have thought. Illy had made quite a mess of him and the room by the time he yelled, "I'll tell you!"

"Of course you will. That was never an option."

"He ... never ... left..."

"What?" I exclaimed from across the room.

Illy maintained her poise, the bland expression on her face.

"Angus... The boy... They walked... Harris," he gasped.

Illy and I looked at each other, realizing that he spoke the truth. Harris. Angus's childhood home. All this time and we had been led on a wild goose chase. Illy placed the tip of the blade against Nate's eyeball. His shaking made me nervous. If he kept moving, she would puncture his eye.

"We saw you leave the harbor at Stornoway."

"Saw ... camera. Dropped ... up ... coast."

"What did he plan to do with the boy? Why take him?"

"Family," was all Nate could sob, dissolving into a drunken puddle of blood and tears.

Things moved rather quickly after that. Illy dispatched Nate with a single flick of the blade, spattering the bookcase containing Angus's leather-bound volumes. She dropped the knife, wiped her hands on Nate's discarded shirt, and we left via the front door, closing it behind us.

"Where on Harris did Angus live?" Illy asked gently as we walked down the street.

"Between Finsbay and Rodel on the south coast," I answered, my voice shaking as I replayed the grisly scene. "I have never been there. But he spoke of the area often enough. Reminisced about his childhood. His parents married in Rodel. It can't be hard to find."

Silence rose between us as we re-boarded the *Eurydice* ahead of our return voyage. *Is it the taking of a life?* I wondered. Surely she had killed before. But ... perhaps not, as a psychologist. She was hardly front line.

"Are you okay?" I asked as we watched the coastline drift by as we headed north.

Her head slumped, but she didn't answer. I gathered her tiny form against mine as she let go. I knew what this felt like. Knowing that you had to do it but regretting it all the same.

"If you hadn't, I would have. You should have let me."

She looked up at me. "Why do you think I did it? You told me a hundred times how you tortured yourself after Mousa, even killing those monsters at the farm. Do you think I could let you go through that again?"

"Oh, Illy. I didn't mean..."

"I had to." The thin, light voice wasn't hers. It was soulless, removed. "For Luca. For the girls. But mostly for me. He wanted to die. That was plain from the moment we first entered the house. But he could have done a lot of damage. Alerting Angus to our arrival so he could leave, and we would forever be chasing him. Warning the community on Clava. They could intercept us, detain us. So no. I couldn't let him live, but..."

"You feel horribly guilty that it was you?"

"I know this sounds stupid, but I let my emotions control me. I support people through this. One of my roles was counseling returned servicemen and women after what they had seen and done, both in the line of duty, but also in their personal lives. I know I needed to do it, but I am so *conflicted*. I feel such a mix of relief that he is gone, guilt that I did it, and absolute disgust that I took a life. I feel... I feel like an egg, floating in a cloudy swirl of negative dark emotions, threatening to break the shell and consume me."

"I think that is the best description I have ever heard," I admitted. "After Mousa, I struggled terribly. I couldn't convince myself I had done the right thing. Those men were every shade of evil. They killed Laetitia and several others, wounded Angus, and kidnapped ten women from two communities. But what gave *me* the right to take their lives? It was Luca in the end who saved me. Pulled me from the swirling cloud as you put it. He understood. Now I feel guilty that I didn't do it this time. Maybe this time, it would have been easier. They killed my friend, kidnapped my son, and tried to murder my husband."

"It isn't as straightforward as I would have thought. I thought I would feel closure, a sense of justice. But it wasn't justice. This was *revenge*."

We stood and watched the rugged shoreline for a long time in silence. Finally, I went into the galley and brought up a bottle of whisky.

"The strong stuff?" Illy joked feebly.

"You need it. We both do."

We sat on the weathered white deckchairs and stewed over our actions.

"How did you know he wanted to die?"

"He didn't want to be involved. I knew that from the surveillance video. He was there, waiting for us. As soon as we walked into the house, it was plain. He wanted to go. He was tired of this life. He had done his job. He was exhausted, sick of traveling. Couldn't even be bothered cleaning up or eating properly. He thought we would be in a rush to kill him in retribution for killing Luca and move on to find Louis."

"He didn't count on you. You were ... scary."

"I scared myself," she admitted. "There is a Jungian theory that we all have a light and a shadow side of ourselves. The shadow is the unconscious side. We don't let people see the shadow much as it is the side of ourselves that we hide, the part of ourselves that even we fear."

I thought about that for a moment. Light and shadow. I certainly had one. Well hidden, but it was there.

"Refill?" I asked as I poured myself a second glass, still jittery from the day's events.

"No, I am queasy again. Emotions, no doubt. When I was a child, and the kids used to tease me, I suffered from terrible stomach cramps. Mum took me to doctors, pediatricians, even a gastroenterologist. Eventually, they diagnosed me with migraine of the stomach. Ridiculous." She flicked the remnants of her whisky out to sea. "Anxiety is what it was. Fearful of attending school, being taunted every day."

"There is no shame in being emotional about what has happened."

"I know. Come on. Let's go to bed. Frey?"

"Hmm?"

"Will you stay with me again tonight?"

"You know I will."

CHAPTER 34

THE OCEAN WAS PERFECTLY still. We stood side by side, gazing over the glossy surface, the light reflected in the gentle waves. Layers of dead, rotting sea grasses piled up on the beach, unspoiled by footprints other than our own, no tracks of sea birds. For the first time, I realized how much I missed the smell of the ocean, the salt on the breeze, the sand, and that slight odor of rotting seaweed. As I watched the twinkle of the sun reflecting on the water, memories of home came flooding back for the first time in many years. My first life in Melbourne. My heart hurt as I longed for my life there. Maybe it was being away from Cam and the children, but in this moment, I desperately wanted my old life back. That simpler life when money paved the way, and people didn't kidnap you to steal your unborn children. Admittedly, I had left a decadent life. When I had accepted the place, I had genuinely thought we were saving humanity.

Closing my eyes, the wind blowing my hair, I could hear the sounds of home. Children laughing, traffic noise constantly humming in the background, people splashing on paddleboards and kayaks, chatter as people walked their dogs along the beach. The picture of domestic bliss. But now it was still. Deathly quiet, aside from the rustle of the wind. Opening my eyes, I took in the view. The ocean was the same. An overwhelming longing to go swimming in that familiar ocean gripped me. As Illy and I ambled along the beach, surrounded by drifts of dead seaweed and vegetation, the stench became overwhelming.

"Okay, now I feel sick too!" I joked.

Illy dashed for the water's edge as she dry-retched once again.

Watching her, a thought occurred to me.

"Ils..." I asked slowly, unsure of her reaction, "you don't think you could be pregnant?"

Her head, hung low with the vomiting, turned to look up at me in slow motion. The stunned look of amazement in her eyes showed she hadn't contemplated such a possibility.

"When was the last time... you... you and Luca..."

"The morning he was killed," she whispered. "We had wanted another child for years but had given up hope. He never said so, but I knew he wanted a son. Time was getting away from us. I'm forty next month."

"That was what, eight... nearly nine weeks ago? The first trimester was when I was dreadfully sick with my pregnancies."

"Do you think?" she said, tears pouring down her cheeks. "I just thought it was stress. Being held captive. The injections. Why I wasn't regular, I mean. I've never been regular, especially when my body was under stress. I genuinely thought they didn't want me because I was too old."

Ignoring the stench that wafted up around us, I held her in my arms as she cried.

"Is this want you want?"

Illy paused, unable to put the conflict into words. But I knew. To have a child of her dead husband would be wonderful, but to raise the child alone?

"You won't be alone," I said staunchly, reading her hesitance. "I remember every minute of being pregnant with Katrin. The overwhelming sense of isolation, of loneliness. I will be there. Everyone will support you. You will never do this alone. There is nothing certain in this world, but while I still have breath, you will never be alone."

"Thank you. That means everything."

I found a dead log and sat while Illy composed herself. Pushing her hair out of her face and still looking green, she propped next to me.

"I can't believe it might be true," she said, shell-shocked. "After all these years, why now?"

"Do you remember I once told you that you fall pregnant at the worst time possible? Well, that was Katrin. Different circumstances, I admit, but Cam and I had desperately wanted a child. Then he married Laetitia and had a child with another on the way. One stupid night, entirely my fault, and I fall pregnant. Then another year of trying before Xanthe came along. But what I can never lose, and what I can never tell Cam, is the isolation of that time. This was something I had wanted for *years*, a child of my own, with him. Then, when it happened, the timing could not have been worse. I was alone and hated. Everyone was watching and staring. Sorcha openly blamed me, and rightfully so. Di was kind, but her loyalties weren't with me. I remember all those nights, lying in bed, feeling so hollow, despite the life growing inside me. Regretting everything. Cam didn't speak to me. Barely looked at me even after she was born. He loved her. I could see that every time he interacted with her. But he was arctic around me. The woman he had once loved but loved no longer."

Illy dropped her head onto my shoulder as she stared out to sea.

"Did you know that not one person touched my stomach while I was pregnant with Katrin?" I confessed, engulfed by the misery of that time. "Not until I was in labor, and even then, it was clinical. It was, without doubt, the loneliest time of my life."

Color returned to Illy's cheeks as she rested against me. "You know that wasn't true. He always loved you. He processes his emotions so deeply and for such a long period. He loved Laetitia. One day she is there. The next, she is gone. That must have destroyed him, especially as it was the second time someone he loved had been taken away without warning. He told me he thought he was cursed, that no one would ever want him with his track record. He was fearful of ever having another relationship."

"He said that?"

"He did. If you hadn't gone after him, you likely would never have found your way back to each other. He would never have recovered. He knows that too. He was trapped and couldn't find a way out."

"Something you said or did when he came to Orkney must have had an impact. He was a lot more ready than when he left August."

"Oh, I did nothing. It was all you. So how did you do it?" she asked, a cheeky look crossing her pale, sickly face. "You never told me."

"I found him in Edinburgh, in the Office of Births, Deaths, and Marriages. He was researching Laetitia's family tree. He was asleep as I entered. He didn't want me there. He told me to leave him, to let him wallow in his self-pity. But I asked him, please give me just a few days. We had loved each other once. He tried to tell me how different he was after being with her. He had changed. But I persisted. Just a few days. If he didn't want me there after that, I would go. I pushed it, and he relented. But ... it only took one."

"One day?" she asked, a little skeptical.

"Less, actually. He asked me to tell him what I had done in the years of our separation. Then we went for a walk. He told me about Lae's family background and the children who had died on Lewis when the dome was installed. Angus's part in it. What he told me made me physically sick, and I couldn't breathe. I could picture it with immense detail. People banging on the dome, begging for them to save their children. Their babies crying in their arms. It kept making me think of little Kat. She was only a few months old when I left her to go after him. But I knew I had one shot at it. We were away from the prying eyes of his sister and the village. If I couldn't turn things around away from Lewis, I knew I couldn't stay there. I never told him, but I knew that was my single opportunity. If we hadn't found our way back to each other, I would have left for good."

"Where would you have gone?"

"Clava, most likely. I thought it was safe there. I would have had support for Kat and found meaningful work. Or rejoined Angus and Luca. They would have looked out for Kat and me."

"Wow, well, I am glad you didn't do that, for both of our sakes. But back to Cam. How did you do it?"

"You know, I didn't. He saw me struggling emotionally with the news of those people who died. I was drowning in the images of faces torturing me, and he kissed me. It was so familiar. Being with him just felt so *right*. It was a toe-curling, knee-yielding kiss." I had watched Illy and Luca kiss many times. "You know what I mean."

"I do."

"The next thing you know, we are naked under a tree in a park in the center of Edinburgh."

Illy grinned through the waves of nausea. "A rather public reunion."

"It isn't public when everyone is dead. We rarely left each other's side after that. Well, apart from the time we were held captive, and I got these. I held my marked arms out, now with fresh scars. We made a vow. We would never leave each other. Eight years, and we have kept that promise. Until now."

"Do you want to go home and care for him?"

"No. Louis is my child, too. I mean, I didn't carry him, but I promised Laetitia I would care for him. And I will. I would do this for Kat, Xanthe, or Thorsten. I do this for Louis. Sorcha will look after Cam. She won't let him go."

"You promised ... Laetitia?" she asked delicately.

"Not in real life. She and I never spoke. But after I reunited with Cam, I could feel her presence. Lingering. Not malevolently but just *there*. In our new home, the one she never lived in."

"Did you tell Cam?"

"Of course not! How do I say, 'Your dead wife is haunting me' without him thinking I was mentally unstable? It was new and wonderful, and I couldn't bring myself to tell him. I kept telling myself it was stupid. She was dead. I knew that better than anyone. But I kept feeling her when I was alone. Watching me. Judging."

"What did you do?"

"One day, after everyone had gone to school and work, I rode out to the broch, to where she was taken. I sat on the cliff edge and called her spirit. I felt her there, and I made her a promise. That I would care for him, for both of them, I told her I loved Cam and Louis. I would never speak ill of her, and I would ensure that Louis never forgot her. I swore I would always let Cam cherish his memories of them together. There was room in his life for us both. And I promised I would treat Louis the same as Katrin, with love and kindness."

"Wow. Did it work?"

"It did. Almost immediately, I felt the surrounding air lighten. Change from one of judgment to one of acceptance. You know how you walk into a room, and you can just feel people judging you? They don't need to say anything. You just sense it. That was how I felt before I spoke to her."

"And after?"

I paused, trying to think of the right word. "I guess at peace is the best way to describe it. Before, it was like the air was thick, but it dissipated. I felt lighter. Occasionally I still sense her around, but the feel is different. Cam told me she was always fearful that he would leave her for me. But he was never unfaithful to her. She saved him when he was floundering after he lost me. Then I returned the favor. Twice now, I have invoked her help with Louis. When he was unconscious with the head wound, and as we left to find him this time."

Illy turned to look at me. "That is the most amazing thing I have heard in a long time. Many people would be jealous."

"I am insanely jealous of her. She had his first child and would have had his second. He loved her when I was an empty hollow shell. But ultimately, she gave me Louis and Cam. I owe her my gratitude. She cared for them both. Now I have taken over that role."

"You are an amazing woman, Frey."

"Hardly. But one thing now makes sense. I assumed you were collateral damage or that they wanted to bleed me dry before starting on you. Now it seems likely that they knew. All the whispers and note-taking. The blood tests, fewer injections. They knew."

"I'm so sorry, Frey, for what they did to you. It is unspeakably evil to do that to any woman."

I shrugged. What was there to say? They had harvested my eggs for a purpose. We knew what that purpose likely was. I didn't want to verbalize the obvious questions: *What would they have done with Illy's baby? What will they do with my children?*

The darkness crossing Illy's face warned me she had gone there.

"Can I ask one thing?" I asked softly, drawing her attention away from the abyss. "Did you get to say goodbye that morning? To Luca?"

Illy's eyes filled with tears as she smiled. "It was a beautiful goodbye. I was in the kitchen making breakfast for the girls. He came out of the shower, his hair still damp and smelling of Jacinda's chamomile shampoo. He kissed the girls and me and asked what we were having for dinner. I teased him, telling him we were having fish and salad. He said, 'Excellent! My favorite!' I handed him his coffee and toast to take with him. Then he hugged us all and told us he loved us. Then he left, and I never saw him again."

Luca detested fish, which Illy found hilarious, her father being a fisherman. Luca also refused to eat any form of salad, insisting it was rabbit food.

"I'm so glad. One of my biggest regrets was that I never got to say goodbye to Cam. Tell him how much I loved him. He was on the early shift and had gone before I woke. I went to work, avoiding him, as I didn't want him to realize I wasn't pregnant. Then ... it was years before I saw him again, and when I did, he was no longer my husband. When Cam lost Laetitia, they fought that last morning on her birthday. It ate him up for the longest time. That was the part he struggled with, couldn't move on from. I'm so glad your last interaction was peaceful."

"That is always the risk, isn't it? When you say goodbye, you never know if it is the last time."

As I stared out to sea, I saw my sister's face, sad when I had gone to a weekend party that she hadn't been invited to. She hadn't wanted me to go, but I had gone anyway, telling her it was just two nights. I would be back on Sunday, and we could hang out the following weekend. Then she overdosed, and I never got to say goodbye, not to her. I said goodbye to her shell ... twice. Before I left Melbourne and again on Auckland. My mother, I had said goodbye to in person, but my father hadn't even come home to see me off. It was strange to realize that after all these years, I still resented that.

"I should have waited until Cam made it out of surgery and said goodbye!" I gasped, struck by the finality of it. "What if one of us doesn't make it?"

"Not … an … option," Illy said through gritted teeth, the green tinge returning. "There has been enough death. I will not allow anything to happen to you. Come on. Sitting here isn't finding Louis nor getting you back to Cam. Let's go."

CHAPTER 35

"WAIT. WE NEED TO check if he has a warning system," Illy said as we approached the dome, far smaller than most domed communities, only the size of a medium-sized farm. But a geodesic dome, regardless.

"You didn't know Angus well, did you?"

Illy tilted her head at me.

"Angus is a Luddite. Didn't you wonder why his house in Edinburgh was filled with books? The man had no tech skill. He could barely start the engine on the *Selkie*."

"Actually, that explains quite a few things."

"When Luca overheard Angus on the radio, I was surprised. Angus kept Nate on because Nate was the tech-savvy one. Nowhere near as good as Tadhg but good enough. In the years we traveled on the *Selkie*, Angus never learned to pilot it. It caused a bit of conflict with everyone else sharing the load. Initially, he insisted that his time was better spent elsewhere. What we realized, over time, was that all the controls and flashing lights freaked him out. But I was desperate to get back to Cam, so didn't kick up a fuss."

"Do you think Nate would have set up security systems here?"

"I doubt it. Angus wouldn't know what to do, anyway. He always considered himself intellectually superior. He likely believes we won't find him. It has been months."

Finding an access panel took some time, as they always did. Angus had cleverly concealed this one amidst a thicket of trees, living on the inside and dead on the outside. But there was no evidence of wiring, sensor panels, or anything else that could indicate an alarm.

"Not smart enough," I muttered, sliding the panel back. Turning to Illy, I asked, "Should we wait until dark?" I looked up to the midday sky, judging. We wouldn't need to wait long.

"No need. There is one of him and two of us, and we have a firearm, too. Besides, I have come a very long way, I am horribly nauseous, and I don't feel like waiting."

As we rounded the corner in the rutted, pot-holed road, I smiled at the blissful picture of Louis and Xanthe playing in the distance. Louis was making a swing from some rope and a flat board tied to a tree and showing her how it moved. My heart stopped momentarily as I realized it wasn't Xanthe. She was safe on Lewis. This wasn't Scarlett or Ruby, either. But bloody hell, this little blonde girl looked so much like them. I must have gasped as Illy lay a warning hand on my arm and brought a finger to her lips.

Ignoring the children, we crept around the back and entered the house via an open door. A beautiful classic manor house. Old money. Marble floors and a vast atrium greeted us, skylights illuminating the beautiful space. Expensive oil paintings hung up the ornately carved staircase encased in gilded frames. Muffled clattering led us to Angus in the kitchen. The picture of a domestic father, looking relaxed as he stirred a cast-iron pot on the black cooktop, a biogas unit visible through the window. My eyes narrowed. How dare he assume that role. Illy cocked the pistol, and he jerked, dropping the spoon. Tomato spattered across the white-tiled floor.

He smiled at me as he turned off the hob.

"Freyja. Illyria. Nice to see you."

"You had to know I wouldn't give up," I growled. "You kidnapped my son."

Angus looked at me, clearly bemused. "I didn't think you would care. After all, he isn't your son. But he is my nephew. Well, great-nephew, technically. He is no relation of yours. I remember you being rather angry learning about his birth if I recall correctly."

I had been Louis's mother since he was two. He had asked me to be his mother at my second wedding. "He *is* my son!" I roared, making him recoil in shock.

Hearing raised voices, the children rushed into the kitchen. Louis flew at me and clutched my leg.

"Mumma!"

A split-second glance at Illy showed that she had concealed the weapon and had the situation under control. I crouched down and hugged him for as long as I dared, then pulled him back and looked into his eyes.

"I'm here now, sweetheart, and we will take you home very soon. But first, I need to know, did he hurt you?"

"I was so scared," he cried, working himself into a frenzy. "He killed daddy and Luca. Then he made me walk such a long way in the night-time. He made me walk and hit me with sticks if I stopped."

The red beast rose as I envisaged my child being mistreated, beaten with sticks.

"Did he do anything else to you?" I asked, not even trying to suppress the suspicion.

"No, mum. But he killed..."

"I'm not a pervert," Angus shot at me from across the room. Illy appeared relaxed, standing beside him. She had the gun pressed to his side now, concealed under her jacket. I wasn't sure how long she could contain herself, her pale face sickly, sweat beading on her brow.

"You *beat* him?" I turned on Angus.

"We needed to hurry. We were outside the dome, and it rains an awful lot here. It was for his benefit, too. I haven't touched you since we arrived. Have I?" Angus directed this last question at Louis.

Stepping between them, crouching down to look Louis in the eye, I ignored the question.

"Darling, take ... your friend and go and play outside, please," I told him firmly. "We will leave soon. Illy and I just need to talk to Angus first."

Watching Louis take the little girl's hand and lead her outside plucked at my heart. She looked so much like Xanthe. Darker eyes, though. Goodness, she looked like a smaller version of Ruby and Scarlett, making it crystal clear who she was.

"Sit," I ordered, and Illy marched him over to a dining chair, Luca's revolver now openly held to his temple. Angus was a small man. There was no real threat of him overpowering us. But we tied him up for good measure.

"The girl? Who is she?"

"Ceridwen."

"Ceridwen?"

"She is the Celtic goddess of fertility."

Illy's eyes spring wide. "You wouldn't?"

"Wouldn't what?" Angus and I chorused.

"You planned to *breed* them?" Illy screeched, her voice unrecognizable. "They are children, you monster!"

"Well, not anytime soon," he simpered. "But when they are older, yes. It makes perfect sense. They are both of my bloodline and..."

"I'm sorry, *what* did you say?"

"The girl, she is mine. Louis is a distant relative, to be sure. But I am Ceridwen's father."

My stomach lurched. "You mean you fathered a child with my sister?"

"Not just Ceridwen—all of them," he announced proudly. "There are two other girls. I believe you have met them. Louis told me all about them."

I sat down on one of the other chairs without meaning to, the fury gone out of me in a puff of wind.

"Why?" I mouthed.

"Because you wouldn't. You and I were partnered, Freyja. You were my chosen match. We were highly compatible. I tried to get you to see that we would be an excellent pairing, but you refused to see it. I wanted to help you raise your daughter. I would have been a good father, and in time we could have had more children. We would have lived happily. Here or anywhere else you chose. I would have been good to you. But you chose to mope over that lump of a gardener rather than see the far better options in front of you. So, I took the backup plan."

There was a heavy bronze statue of a Greek deity on the lamp table beside me, and I hurled it at his head. It struck just above his eye, and he roared in pain, clutching his face. Illy didn't flinch.

"Who carried the child? The surrogate. Who was it?"

"She was."

"Who ... is ... *she*?"

"Why, your sister, of course. It was the closest I could get to you. Goodness, you look alike. It took some convincing to get permission to use her. She was their best egg producer, and pregnancy took her off the market for a few months. I used to visit her, stroke her belly while she was growing our daughter. She reminded me so much of you."

Illy's arms barely restrained me as I punched, kicked, and fought. Knocking his chair over, I kicked him squarely in the balls. He had done this to her because of me. Rage consumed me. I would kill him. Weapon not required. Even doubled over in pain, I saw his smirking grin as Illy turned his chair upright. She checked the restraints and escorted me from the room.

"Be with the children," she spoke soothingly in my ear. "They need you. I can deal with this."

I started to argue but realized she was right. In my current state of fury, I was of no use. Illy would be better to interrogate Angus, to learn what she could. Still seething, I slunk outside and slammed the door behind me. Sitting on the doorstep, I forced myself to breathe, let the cool air calm the heat consuming me. Louis came and sat across my lap, leaning against me. I stroked his hair and murmured endearments to him. Apologies it took so long to find him.

"Who are you?" the little girl whispered. She stood a few meters from me, perplexed, watching Louis interacting with a stranger.

Louis looked up.

"This is my Mumma. I told you that my mum would come. She would rescue me."

Shuffling over slightly, I made room for Ceridwen to sit alongside me. But she lingered, standing before us, studying us.

"Hi, Ceridwen. Do you like to be called Ceri?"

"I do not know," the little girl looked confused. "No one has asked me before."

"Well, I shall call you Ceri," I announced kindly. "What do you like to do, Ceri?"

"Do?" She blinked at me like an owl.

"What games do you like to play?"

"I never played before Louis came. I was not allowed to waste time. There is too much to learn. When I came to this place, I needed to read quietly, so I did not disturb Father."

"Was he ... kind ... to you?" I whispered, choked.

She looked at me, perplexed.

"He fed us, mum. He didn't hurt us. But he doesn't care for us," Louis answered. "Not like you." His arms came around my neck, and I held him against me, feeling his chest rise and fall. Ceri watched, a look of bewilderment on her face.

"Would you like a hug, too?"

She shrank from my outstretched arms like I had burned her, and I lowered them quickly.

"What do you read?"

"I can read most of Father's books," she announced proudly.

"Academic books, you mean?"

"She can, mum," Louis piped up. "She reads better than me. But there are only grown-up books here, like the ones in the library. He chooses what we need to read. We have to read all day before we are allowed to go outside. Sometimes he reads with us, makes sure we understand the tricky words. But we have to be quiet. We read from after breakfast to lunch when we are allowed a short break. Then we have to help in the gardens and do the cleaning. If we are good, we can finish in the afternoon just before the sun goes down and play a little. But only if we have finished our work."

Not wanting to dwell on Angus's use of the children as servants, I asked kindly, "What books did you read?"

"Lots of different things. Sometimes the books are hard to understand. There are no stories. I tried to remember all the stories you had read me so that I could tell Ceri. She has never heard stories."

"Louis says they are not true. Are there books with words that are not true?"

"Of course. People like to make up stories that are fun. Don't you?"

Ceri wrinkled her nose. "No. Father says that is lying. I am punished when I tell lies."

I exhaled audibly.

"Would you tell us a story, Mum?" Louis asked, looking up at me with his big brown eyes. Laetitia's eyes.

"Of course. Which one would you like?"

Ceri circled me for a while as I regaled them with my favorite stories from my childhood. Pippi Longstocking, Enid Blyton, Brothers Grimm. Highly edited, as I told them from memory, but Ceri was enthralled with the concept of pixies, fairies, and gnomes.

After a while, she sat on the edge of the step and progressively slithered closer. My heart lurched as she listened intently, leaning against me. This was Kat's child. My child. I needed to take her, keep her safe. But what if she didn't want to come? I needed to talk to Illy.

"Are there really fairies?" she whispered during a lull.

"Some people say so," I replied with a smile. "I have never been so lucky to see them, though. Maybe only special people can see them. They are magic, so perhaps they choose who they let see them."

Her eyes opened wide as she looked around the yard, taking in the stone buildings around us. It was dead in places, green in others. A small patch of pumpkins, ready for harvest. A greenhouse was visible, the door facing me. Plants covered the shelves along both walls, several rows of trees along the middle. Angus had been re-greening this place for a while. This had been his plan for some time. To bring this little girl here. To take Louis. Not wanting to scare her, but I wanted to know.

"Did you always live here?"

"No. I lived in a place with lots of people. I went to school there. Then one day, a man came and said he was my father. Then he and another man took me on a boat, out there." She waved her arm beyond the dome. "I was scared. It is not safe out there. I could not sleep, and I felt very sick. Then one day, he left me here, all alone. When he came back, he had Louis with him. He told us we are a family now."

"How long have you been here?" I asked curiously.

She looked sad. "I do not know. A long time."

"What was your home like before here?"

"There were lots of people and many buildings. But I was only allowed in some of them."

"So what did they tell you? About why you were leaving?"

"Father came one day when I was in the dormitory. They woke me up and made me get dressed. Then he took me away."

I froze. There was so much I wanted to know but didn't know where to start.

"Dormitory?" I questioned gently. "Didn't you have a family?"

"Family?" She blinked. "No. None of us had a family."

"Who looked after you?"

"The people who worked there. They made sure we ate and brushed our teeth and taught us to read and write."

"Didn't they love you?"

"Love?" she questioned, staring at me.

My eyes filled with tears.

"How many children were there? In your dormitory?"

This was a question she could answer and did so readily. "There were twelve, including me."

"How old are you?" I asked softly.

"I am six years old," she announced proudly.

Six. The same as Ruby and Scarlett. Smaller, but so much more mature, self-possessed, and she spoke so intelligently. Her vocabulary was impressive, and she spoke formally, with no colloquialisms. She didn't sound like a child. But at what cost?

"Did you say that Angus left you here when he went to get Louis?"

"Yes. I was all alone. He told me he was going to get me a friend. He left me food, and I could read anything I wanted."

"Weren't you lonely?" I asked softly.

She considered that. "I guess...." but it was clear that she had no concept of being alone or lonely.

I so badly wanted to hug her, hold her tight, but was fearful of scaring her. She had clearly never known affection. I remembered vividly when Cam had been so physically affectionate when we met, and it had freaked me out.

"Louis," I turned to look at him, pulling myself back from my melancholic thoughts. "I have some news. Dadda is okay. The last I heard, he is still in hospital, and he is very sick, but he is alive."

Louis's mouth and eyes popped wide. "Alive?" he whispered, unable to believe it.

"Yes, my darling, he is alive."

"But that man, he used a gun. Guns kill people."

"No, people kill people," I corrected him. "A gun is just a weapon. But yes, Angus tried to kill your daddy. Your daddy is strong, and he will live. But he killed Luca, I am very sad to say. Poor Ally and Summer have no daddy now because of him."

Louis was such a sensitive boy, and the conflicted emotions of joy and sorrow intermingled on his face. "That man told me to call him father, but I can't. He isn't my father. I didn't want to. But he said my dad was gone, so he was my father now."

"That is not true," I soothed, praying it was still the case.

"Poor Ally and Summer," he whimpered. "Can I be their big brother, too?"

"They would love that. When we get home, you can tell them that yourself."

"Can Ceridwen come with us?" Louis looked up at me with hopeful eyes.

As the subject of our conversation was sitting on my other side, this was a little difficult to answer. I also didn't want to alert the children that Angus wouldn't make nightfall.

"Well, that is up to Ceri. She can choose," I said carefully.

She turned an intelligent pair of brown eyes on me. Nothing at all like Kat's. Angus's eyes. I tried not to let the disgust show in my face.

"Louis tells me that the children are permitted to ... play ... where you are from," she whispered, almost too scared to speak the word aloud.

I nodded. "They do. Every day."

"And ride bicycles?"

I nodded again, seeing her brain whirring with possibilities.

"I have never seen a bicycle," she said, awed. "Or a horse. Only pictures."

"We have both," Louis said kindly. "And a cat. We can share them all if you like."

The look of sheer wonder on her face made me want to hug her, but I froze, not wanting to scare her.

"But what about Father?" she asked suddenly.

"He is not your father," Louis told her firmly before I could respond. "He took you like he took me. A father doesn't do that. A father protects you. A mother too." He glanced up at me, then back at Ceri. "I am lucky. I have two mothers. My first mother loved me very much, but she died. Wicked men took her and killed her. Evil men like *him*." He gestured inside the house with his chin. "But then I got a new mummy." He dropped his head onto my chest. "I knew when that man hurt my daddy that my mummy would come after me. She would save me. And she did," he said, sticking his chin out confidently.

"I would move heaven and earth to find you, my darling."

Louis looked back at Ceri. "That is what a parent is. Someone who loves you. My mummy helps people. Lots of people told me so."

"I do not have a mother," she said, her face crestfallen.

"You did. My sister was your mother. I am your aunt. That is why you look like me. But your mother is dead now. But ... if you want..." I couldn't bring myself to finish the sentence.

Fortunately, Louis knew what I was asking.

"Will you be my sister?" he asked Ceri earnestly. "I have two others, as I told you. And a brother. But I would like it if you would be my sister, too."

Ceri looked at Louis, then up at me for confirmation. Then she dropped into my arms.

It is like hugging a rock, I thought, as the orange glow of sunset reflected off her golden hair. A solid mass that didn't know how to be affectionate. Sitting on the step, holding them both, it felt natural that my heart would expand to include another child. Katrin's child. I just prayed I could see her in Ceri and not *him*. Realizing Illy was alone with Angus, I sat up straight.

"I need to speak to Angus about you coming with us. Ceri, do you have anything to pack? Clothes, books, toys?"

As soon as the words were out of my mouth and I saw the bewilderment on her face, I realized I had made a mistake.

"Actually, you know what?" I said breezily, "how about a completely fresh start? New wardrobe, and we already have lots of books and toys, don't we, Louis?"

"We do. Whenever mum or dad go anywhere, they bring us back lots of things."

"All for yourself?" Disbelief crept into her voice.

"Of course. I have lots of toys and books. Some I share with my sisters and brother, but some are just for me."

"Aunt Illy and I ended up in Edinburgh looking for you. Even in the rush we were in, we still found more books and clothes for you all," I said.

"More books?"

"Lots more," I assured him. "You are all becoming such excellent readers, so we got lots of new books to learn from."

Louis cocked an eyebrow at Ceridwen. "Do you want to be my sister?"

Her face betrayed the turmoil lurking underneath, but she nodded hesitantly. "I will go with you."

"How about you two have a drink and wait for us over there?" I pointed to the far field, speaking as lightly as I could. "Take your jackets and anything out here you want to bring. I won't be long. I promise. Louis, can you tell Ceri the story of when you and your sisters learned to ride a horse and Lolly ran away with Katrin?"

Louis nodded, standing, and took Ceri's hand, leading her toward where I had gestured. She scooped up their books, four large hard-covered volumes that looked much like an encyclopedia.

I returned to the house, closing the door firmly behind me and drawing the thick velvet drapes.

Illy caught my eye as I entered. I selected a knife from the knife rack in the kitchen and tested it on my finger. Sharp. Good.

Angus sneered at me. "Oh, come on, Freyja. You might throw something, but you aren't a murderer. We are friends. I know you."

"You *knew* me," I corrected coolly. "But that was a long time ago, and I was a very different person then, Angus."

"Motherhood has changed you that much, has it? Being a gardener's wife?"

"No, not motherhood." I ignored the barb. "Learning the truth. So here is how I hear it. You let your older sister be raped and banished, pregnant no less, but we will let that one slide. You were only a child yourself. Although you never went looking for her either. Then when the pandemic struck, you not only let the local residents die, children and babies, you let your own family perish, too."

Angus started to speak. I pointed the knife at his cheek, gesturing for him to be quiet.

"No, still my turn. Then when I arrived on Lewis, dazed and confused, you lied to me. You feigned no knowledge of the antipodes. But that was a lie. Pretended you didn't know who I was, but that was a lie, too. You accompanied me back to August, but you knew that Cam was already on Lewis. You were in radio contact all along, so you could have turned around and saved me that pain, but you chose not to. You then encouraged Heidi to lie to Cam about me being pregnant. He left me, which is what you wanted all along. You lied to Luca and Jakob all those years about your true mission. You were always part of it. The Collective. The Nexus. You engineered it."

Drawing the knife gently across his cheek, I continued as the blood slowly pooled.

"Then you killed my friend and tried to murder my husband. That should be enough. But to top it off, you allowed those psychopaths to use my brain-damaged sister as a surrogate to breed children for your own nefarious purposes. You kidnapped *my* son, and yes, he *is* my son, to breed him with Ceridwen when he is old enough. He is ten years old, you sick, vile monster. So, tell me, my friend, what part of this deserves leniency?"

"It wasn't for me! Everything I did was for the good of humanity!" he said incredulously.

"No, it wasn't," Illy whispered in his ear. He jumped. He hadn't heard her approach as mesmerized as he was by my speech.

"You did much of it for your own selfish purposes. Not saving those people from the pandemic? Causing Freyja years of pain when she could have been reconciled with her love? Killing Luca? All of those things were selfish, Angus, and you have no possibility of redemption. Your life has been built on a bed of lies and deception. But for Luca, for his children, I avenge his death."

The flash of silver moved so quickly across his throat that I didn't even register what had happened immediately. Angus's eyes popped wide as he felt the sting and the blood poured down his neck. A trickle at first, then a torrent. His hands flew up, and he looked at them, flabbergasted, coated in his own blood. Then his eyes rolled back in his head as he passed out.

"Let's go," said Illy, dropping the knife I hadn't realized she held.

"I would have done it," I said. "I could have spared you that pain."

"No. I was always going to do it. As soon as I saw that footage, I promised myself that I would avenge Luca, and that I have done. You were his friend once. I knew you would be conflicted in the end. It is easier this way. I have no such loyalty. I feel nothing for the man, before or now. Let's go. It is time to go home."

"You might want to your hands first," I suggested, noting the spatter of blood. "We don't want to scare Ceri."

"She is coming with us?" Illy asked calmly as she washed her hands at the sink.

"Of course. She is my sister's child. Now she is mine. Besides, I can't exactly leave her here. Not alone."

"I saw you through the window, sitting on the step with her snuggled up beside you. She looks so much like your girls."

"She does," I admitted. "But Kat and Xan have my eyes. Ceridwen has brown eyes. She is the spitting image of Ruby and Scarlett. Do you know that girl has never been allowed to play in her life? Didn't have a family before Angus took her. She has never heard a bedtime story."

"She might need some help. You can't just pluck a child from one life and transplant her into another."

"You can help me. I trust you implicitly, Illy."

"Even now?"

"Especially now."

With our arms around each other, we set off to find the children and begin the journey home.

CHAPTER 36

EXHAUSTED, I LOWERED MYSELF onto the bed beside his sleeping body, desperately wanting to wake him, tell him we were home safely. I was exhilarated just to be near him after so many weeks, but I knew he was still recovering, and rest was a critical component of that process. Ceridwen had asked to stay with Louis in his room. Louis had insisted on giving up his bed and had taken the trundle instead.

"You raised a good man," I whispered to Laetitia's ever-lurking ghost. "He is such a gentleman."

Illy had dropped me off at Sorcha's while she escorted Louis and Ceri to our home, before heading to Bridget's to collect her girls. Sorcha and Di were awake, but I had woken Thorsten, Xanthe, and Kat upon arrival, not being able to bear going to bed and not seeing them. They had staggered bleary-eyed out of their rooms, ecstatic, throwing themselves at me, chattering over each other to tell me their news and ask about Louis. The looks of suspicion indicated that Illy had been right, and they were less than pleased to hear we had brought home a new sibling. Asking a dozen questions, I waved them off, promising they could meet her in the morning. After a brief but tear-filled reunion, I asked them to stay at Sorcha's for one more night. Thorsten and Xan cried, wanting to come home. But I pleaded with them, for Louis, for this one night.

"How is he?" I asked Sorcha quietly after Di had shooed the reluctant children back to their rooms.

"He has a long road ahead," she said, switching to doctor mode. "He will survive the wound. We needed to remove his spleen and patch up several other organs. He is at greater risk of infection now, and he is in pain much of the time. But he will live."

"Thank you," I said fervently. "I can't tell you what that means to me."

"Angus?"

"He will never bother us again," I said with finality.

Sorcha nodded in satisfaction, recognizing a long story here, but now was not the time.

"Good."

Sometime deep in the night, Cam cried out in pain, and I sat bolt upright in the darkness, unfamiliar with sharing a bed.

"Honey? Are you okay?"

"Frey?" he whispered hoarsely.

"It's me. I'm home."

He gasped as alertness took hold. "Louis?"

"He is here. He is well. Asleep. You can see him in the morning."

I felt the enormous sigh draining from him as the months of stress dissolved.

"Thank you. My love, thank you." He forced the words out, emotion strangling him.

I was about to tell him to go back to sleep when he gathered me in his arms and kissed me so thoroughly I almost forgot he was injured.

"Oh, how I have missed you," he murmured as his hands ran up my back and nuzzled my neck. "When did you get back? Why didn't you wake me?"

"A few hours ago. Sorcha said you were in pain and need rest."

"Hmph. What would Sorcha know? She just keeps me drugged up and compliant."

"Pain relief, I think you call that," I teased as I kissed his chest. "I have so much to tell you."

"Tell me."

Lying with my head on his chest, I summarized the past two months. Nate, Angus, and Louis. Illy's revenge, and finally about Ceridwen.

"They did that to your sister? A brain-dead woman?"

"They did. Angus did. He and I were a breeding pair allegedly, and because I refused, they used her. This little girl is Kat's daughter. With Angus. A distant relative of Louis, but she is also a full sibling to Scarlett and Ruby."

"Fuck. Do Jorja and Bridget know?"

"Likely. Illy went straight there to get her girls. I jumped off here, woke the kids, and came straight to you. Illy brought Louis and Ceri home. She suggested that waking our kids to meet their new sibling wasn't the best idea. Seeing their faces when I told them, she was right."

"What is she like?"

"She looks exactly like Scarlett and Ruby. You can tell they are siblings. She has my hair, Kat's hair. But brown eyes from him. She looks so much like our girls I couldn't stand it. I needed to save her. But Illy says she will need a lot of time and love to adjust to her new home." Describing Ceri's life to date, I could feel the tension build.

"Who treats a child like that? Like a machine?"

"Clava did," I admitted. "Angus, too. She is only six but speaks like a well-educated adult, almost like a robot. She chooses her words with precision. It is a little off-putting. She has never known affection or love. This is going to take some work."

"Well, you have always been up for a challenge."

"And you? Are you alright with this?"

"You accepted Louis without question. When I woke and learned Angus had taken him, I knew with every fiber of my being that you would go after him, do everything in your power to save him. So yes. I will do this. She will be our child as much as the others. She will learn what a family is."

"I love you," I murmured in his ear and nearly got carried away as he kissed me.

"Why were you gone so long? Did it take that long to find Angus?"

Swallowing hard, I lay my head on his chest again, needing to be close. I told him how long we had been on Clava. The weeks of being trapped in a bed, injected daily, being prepped for surgery. Being violated. Dale's assault and Ashton finally helping us escape.

"Oh, honey." His arms tightened as I spoke and the emotion of being held captive and operated on against my will caught up with me, and I started to tremble. He touched my nose gingerly.

"Is it alright?"

"Still very sore," I snuffled, fighting back the emotion as I spoke, "but I reset it between Clava and Edinburgh. It is aligned now, and that is all that can be done. That boat has seen a few medical procedures. Many of them on me."

"I so badly want to visit Clava right now and break more than Dale's nose."

"I'm fine," I choked, not wanting the memories of that place to mar our reunion.

"Did they chase you?"

I told him about Tadhg and Jakob firing the missile into Inverness harbor.

"Seriously? It is gone?"

"It is. One shot and they won't be traveling by sea for quite some time."

"Luca would have loved that."

"He would. There is so much more, but only one more thing I need to tell you now."

"More?"

"Illy is pregnant."

Cam sat upright at that, knocking me from his chest, and bellowed from the pain.

"Pregnant? Did *they* do that to her?"

"No. They never told us they knew, but they didn't inject her daily like me after the first few days. They did physical exams. She had injections, but she had no surgery. We are fairly certain it is Luca's child."

Cam lay back down. "Is she alright? The baby? Did they do tests on her, too?"

"It was me they subjected to the daily hormone injections and surgeries. We assumed I was at a different place in my cycle or that she was too old. When I went through two cycles, I just assumed that they wanted me as the replacement for Kat. Then we escaped, thanks to Ashton. It wasn't until later that we even realized. That sent her into a downward spiral, worrying about what they would have done to her baby."

"What happened to Dale?"

"I don't know. He threatened to finish what he started, and after I screamed and alerted someone, they dragged him away. Later that night, Ashton came and released us. I guess it was Dale's assault that made him come to his senses. No one else lifted a finger to help us."

"I always thought he was a good man."

"Not good enough to release us sooner," I pointed out bitterly.

"I can't believe they did that to you."

Knowing that this topic of conversation couldn't end well, I deflected, "It is Illy we need to worry about. They were one. Now she is alone with those poor girls and pregnant. I promised her she wouldn't do this alone." Gulping, I continued. "I remember what that felt like. Having a life growing inside you but feeling empty. It is the most soul-destroying feeling, knowing you are alone but responsible for bringing a new life into the world."

Cam's arms tightened around me, squeezing the air from my lungs. "I am so sorry."

"Don't be. That was a long time ago, and now I have everything I could possibly want. But she can't be alone. I can't let her go through this by herself."

"She will never be alone. We will always be there for her. She is our family, too."

"That is exactly what I told her."

Cam's lips were soft and warm, and I felt enveloped.

"I missed you so much. For the first few weeks, all the time I was chained to that bed, I regretted not waiting until you were out of surgery, conscious, being able to say goodbye properly. I just knew if I had any chance of finding Louis, I needed to get going. Waiting around would make the search harder. Though as it turns out, he fooled us anyway."

"I cannot thank you enough for what you did," Cam spoke, choked with emotion. "He truly is your son."

"I needed to go. Illy coming surprised me, but she was fueled by anger and justice. Needing answers. I just knew that I needed to get Louis."

"He is all I have left of Lae. He looks so much like her, but I still see him as our child. Yours and mine. It is the oddest sensation to have him look like her but to know that he was meant to be yours."

I accepted his time with Laetitia, but I didn't want to discuss his former wife. Although after the events of the past weeks, I felt closer to her, too. Not that I ever knew her in life, but now I talked to her, telling her little bits about Louis, about Cam. I sensed her watching over us all. But not jealously. Instinctively, I knew she had made peace with Cam and me being a family again.

"How are you doing? Sorcha said you are still in pain."

Cam sighed. "The pain comes and goes. Shocking migraines. Sometimes I think it is my heart hurting. For Luca and Illy, for you and Louis. The pain was so intense. As I lay there on the dock, I could see Luca gasping. He was the last thing I saw before I woke up in the clinic, Sorcha nagging me. I cannot tell you how happy I am to have you both home. I need you here."

"Is there anything I can do?"

Cam stopped talking and cupped my bottom with his hands. Using his knee, he deftly rolled me on top of him, kissing me ardently.

I pulled back slightly, breathless. "I want you so much," I breathed, "but won't it hurt?"

"Let's test that theory. Besides, some pain is worth it."

"Oh God, I love you." My voice was husky from weariness and emotion, but I awakened more fully to the sensation of hands on my breasts, slipping down my ribs to my waist.

I arched my back with the blissful sensation of being loved after so long apart.

"Does it hurt? From what they did to you?"

I paused, my hands on his shoulders, wondering how much to tell him, but ultimately deciding honesty was best.

"The second was far worse. They weren't exactly gentle. They knocked me out both times. I'm not sure I would cope with remembering that."

As the moonlight streamed through the window, silence descended. Cam's lips found and kissed the raised keyhole wounds on my stomach. Four of them. Two from each surgery. Not wanting to dwell on the horrors that still tormented me, I slid down and pushed my hips against him in invitation, hungry and insistent. His tongue teased against my lips, making me moan lightly. He accepted the invitation and kissed me with so much passion that my knees would have buckled had I been standing. Slowly, we reconnected and returned to each other.

"I'm not letting you out of my sight today," I heard the honeyed murmur in my ear as the lightness in the room registered.

"Are you well enough to get up?" I was barely awake and wondering if there was any way we could spend the day in bed. Despite spending weeks restrained to one, this bed was different. Large, warm, and *mine*.

"I am. I can't wait to see Louis and meet Ceridwen. The others come after breakfast and drop in at various points throughout the day, but I want to be up when they wake. I'm sick of being an invalid."

A wave of disappointment washed over me that I was quick to conceal. Despite wanting to hide myself from the world, stay safe and warm in my cocoon, Cam needed to see Louis. Meet Ceri. Lifting myself onto one elbow, I looked down and smiled.

"Do you think I have time to shower first? It has been so long."

Not taking our eyes off each other, we squashed into the tiny shower cubicle in the private en-suite we had finally installed after years of waiting for four children in bathrooms. We had argued against it for years, feeling guilty about the additional water use, but succumbed after realizing that we were rapidly headed for teenage years with two girls.

After inspecting my wounds in daylight, tracing his fingers along my still swollen and highly colored forehead, cheek and nose, he spun me around, washing my hair with his strong fingers, taking the time to massage the delicious rose-scented shampoo in my scalp as I leaned back on him. I closed my eyes in bliss as he rinsed it out, and the suds ran down my body and into the base that caught the water, ready for recycling. I hadn't had anything other than a sponge bath in months, and a shower was heaven. After he soaped me up and rinsed me off, I felt clean. Refreshed. Ready to face anything. Cam's arms came around me as I stood there, soaking in the sensation of running water.

"I owe Sorcha my life, again," he breathed in my ear as I ran my fingers along the scars across his stomach. The jagged horizontal slash inflicted on him years ago, the fresh vertical surgical incision not yet healed. "She is making quite a habit of it. Did you know she gave me her blood? Mid-surgery, she ordered Hamish to set up a line, donating her blood to me?"

I cracked my eyes wide open to look up at him.

"Seriously? And he complied?"

"We are the same blood type. But the way he told the story, it wasn't given as a request."

"She is a force to be reckoned with," I whispered, as my fingers continued touching the still prominent wounds, making him flinch slightly.

"As are you, my love."

"What do you want to do now that you know?" Cam asked as we dressed.

"Do?"

"The girls. Ask for shared custody?"

I shook my head. "No. I spent weeks in that bed with nothing to do but think and talk to Illy. I owe her my sanity. Truly, I would have gone mad if it wasn't for her. I didn't know about Ceridwen then, but we talked about Scarlett and Ruby. They aren't mine. I am glad they are here, and I want to watch them grow up. But I meant what I said. Even though I know for certain they are all my nieces, those girls see Jorja and Bridget as their mothers. One day, we will tell them about Kat. I will insist upon that. Not so they don't feel loved, but so they understand what horrors we inflicted on each other. In the name of science."

"And Ceridwen? What is she like? Her personality, I mean."

I had only spent a short time with Ceridwen on the return voyage here. Louis had been kind but wanted to be with me, not leaving my side. Illy had spent a little time with Ceridwen, reading with her.

"She is damaged," Illy had warned me as I had seen her off to collect her own children, Louis and Ceridwen, safely out of earshot. "She has never known love. You will need to go very slowly. Don't overwhelm her. Don't startle her. She has never been shown affection, been taught how to play. Louis tried, but the concept of play was as foreign to her as teaching a jellyfish to play tennis."

Cam grinned at the analogy as he pulled on his socks. "Come on. I can hear them."

Cam and I opened the kitchen door to find Ceridwen seated, upright and rigid at the table, wearing the same crumpled clothes as yesterday. *I need to address that*, I thought as I saw her. Louis stood at the biogas cooktop, trying to make her breakfast. Louis looked up at the sound of the door opening and dropped the milk, flying into his father's arms. My heart winced as I watched Cam grimace from the impact, hugging his son protectively, then hold him at arm's length to check him over before hugging him again. Ceri, unaware I was watching, stared at the emotional reunion in amazement. *Illy is right*, I thought sadly. As she saw me watching, she assumed a blank expression. One I had perfected over the years. A mask. Never letting people see your thoughts and emotions. I looked kindly at her as I retrieved the jug and grabbed a cloth to mop up the spilled milk.

"You must be Ceridwen," Cam said, dropping to his knee in front of her.

"You may call me Ceri," she said formally, a little overwhelmed by this introduction. I wondered for a moment what she had expected.

"I'm Cam," he said softly. "Louis's dad. I am also father to Katrin, Xanthe, and Thorsten."

"Where are they?" she asked, trying to be brave. I knew the look.

Cam looked at me for support.

"Do you remember yesterday when Illy brought you here? I went to see them. They are still next door. Cam's sister, Sorcha, is a doctor. She lives in that house over there with her partner, Diana, and their children, Sam and Kendra. They looked after our children while I was away."

"They did not stay with you?" she asked innocently, looking at Cam.

I sensed his pause and jumped in. "Cam wasn't well. It was best they were with their cousins." How did I tell this little girl that the most recent father she had known had tried to kill Louis's father?

"Louis told me that fa... Angus," she corrected herself, "hurt you and killed Summer and Allison's father." She turned to look at Louis for confirmation of the names, and he nodded gravely.

Turning back to look at Cam, she asked, "Are you better now?"

Cam smiled kindly. "I am. My sister is a wonderful doctor."

A commotion outside heralded the arrival of the children, squealing again as they saw Louis and me. This time, it was a full-blown family reunion. I watched Ceri's perplexed reaction as she shrank against the wall, taking in the sights, sounds, and feel of a noisy family.

Di hugged me again. "I am so glad you are home safely!"

"You told me that yesterday! I can't tell you how good it feels to be home. Truthfully, now, how much of it is because you want to get rid of my kids?"

Sorcha eyed Cam moving around the kitchen critically.

"You must be Ceridwen," Diana said kindly, her eyes twinkling.

Ceri crinkled her nose and spoke bluntly. "You are Chinese. I have seen pictures of people like you before. Chinese culture is very old. I learned about many of the ancient dynasties."

Diana laughed merrily. "I am Australian Chinese. But now I live here, so I guess that makes me Scottish." She smiled at the girl, not letting the outburst change her bubbly demeanor.

"What am I?"

"What would you like to be?" I asked her gently.

"I do not know," she confessed quietly as the loud reunion continued around her.

CHAPTER 37

AFTER BREAKFAST, SORCHA STEERED Cam and me to the bedroom, loudly insisting on checking Cam's wounds. But as soon as the door closed, it was me she rounded on, ordering me to lift my top and lie on the bed. I scowled at Cam, knowing this was his work, but he sat silently beside me, holding my hand, guilt and concern etched in his forehead. She checked my surgical wounds forensically, her pursed lips speaking volumes. Pulling her bag from behind the door where she had clearly stashed it earlier, she removed the stitches from the two more recent wounds. As she worked, I told her about Illy's pregnancy, but she didn't take her attention from me, firing off questions. She felt along the bones in my face, palpating the breaks, asking me where I could still feel the pain, finally confirming that my cheek and nose were healing as well as could be expected. My nose was straight, but the cheekbone wasn't. It was too late now unless I wanted it re-broken to be correctly aligned. Not waiting for my response, she headed into our tiny en-suite to wash her hands as I sat up and pulled my top down, not wanting to feel a victim any longer than necessary.

"Let's take the kids for a walk and a picnic," Cam suggested as I rearranged myself, ready to return to the chaos I could hear coming from the kitchen as siblings and cousins argued.

"Want to come?" he called to Sorcha, who shook her head as she returned through the doorway.

"No. Di and I are headed into town to arrange the memorial for Luca. We have buried him, of course, but we waited for you to return to have a service. Illyria needs closure. The girls, too. It has been hard on them with you away so long."

"I should...." I started to say as we walked down the hallway toward the kitchen but broke off as Cam's warm hand lightly touched my arm. Neither of us wanted to be away from each other or our children today. *Besides, she might resent me now that we are home,* I thought sadly.

Rounding up their children, Di and Sorcha left, arm in arm, still so much in love.

"Maybe they are still happy as Sam and Kendra so compliant!" I whispered, making Cam grin, although I needn't have whispered. Our children, and particularly the younger three, were intelligent, loud, and challenging. They regularly argued, and not infrequently, got into physical altercations. The volume was rapidly escalating. I prayed they would be on their best behavior today for Ceridwen's sake. She might think she was better off with Angus.

Neither Ceri nor Louis had asked about Angus, and we hadn't volunteered anything. Illy and I swept out of the house, all smiles, and walked them to the *Eurydice*, talking all the way. It was only a few hours to Stornoway, then half an hour home. Golf carts were everywhere now. They were so prolific that no one bothered keeping track of which cart belonged to which family. They were all electric, and as Sorcha and Di's algal bioreactors had been so successful, we had as much power as we needed. Every home had a plug to charge the carts, keeping the few electricians who had initially been settled here very busy.

"Should we check in on Illy first?" Cam asked quietly, pulling me onto the couch as the kids ran around looking for socks, shoes, and hats. "Let her know there will be a memorial?"

Gratitude filled me, and I smiled. "No. Let her be with her girls today. She will want to spend time with them. But tomorrow, yes. It will all hit her tomorrow. How alone she is. Pregnant. A single mother."

"How do you know?" Cam asked curiously.

"Partly as I have been there. Mostly as I am the daughter of a psychiatrist! Mum used to talk about her interesting cases over dinner and the impact on people. Not in an identifying kind of way," I rushed to add, lest he suspect all therapists were malicious gossips. "But without using names, she would tell us things. Dangers of acting in a certain way. Things to be wary of. Cautionary tales, I guess."

"Cautionary tales? Like fairytales for teenagers?"

"Not at all. It was her way of teaching us life lessons. Describing obsessive relationship breakups, teenage girls experimenting with drugs and needing to turn to crime to pay for it. How loss doesn't always hit you instantly, owning your mistakes. The cases were always fascinating."

"Owning your mistakes?"

"I remember her describing one guy, an accountant or something financial. There was a lot more to it, but the part I recall was that every time his boss gave him feedback on his performance, he would call in sick the next day. The problem was, *he* couldn't see the issue. Likely he didn't realize that everyone else could see the pattern and were likely laughing about it behind his back. Unable to cope with criticism, he would sulk and deny it. Then take a day off. Mum would use stuff like that, non-identifiable stuff, as a lesson to us. In this case, the lesson was to learn to accept criticism, assess it, and work out whether it was valid. If it was, then acknowledge the feedback and try to improve. If not, thank the giver, ignore what they had said, and not let it affect you. But never, ever respond badly. Especially in public. Bad sportsmanship, my dad used to say. More than anything, Dad hated a sore loser. He used to say that handling criticism is like playing sport. It is so important to handle a loss graciously and with dignity. People judge, he used to tell us all the time."

"He was right," Cam admitted. "People do judge a bad sport. I've met enough of them. And not just in sports. Politicians losing an election, people missing out on a job."

"Well, it is a good thing you won me then, isn't it?"

"Angus didn't think so." Cam leaned in for a kiss, and I lay across his chest, oblivious to the riot going on around us.

"Eeewwww! Mum! Dad! Must you do that!" Kat's voice shrieked across the room.

Sitting up, I smiled at her. "Is there something you need?"

"My sneakers! I can't find them anywhere!" she wailed.

"Did you look under your bed, darling?" Cam suggested helpfully.

"Yes!"

"Wardrobe?"

"Yes!" she snapped back.

"Did you bring them back from Di's?" Cam asked, more gently than I would have after her last fiery response.

Katrin scoffed like we were imbeciles.

"Well, it is a small house," I pointed out. "There are only a few places they could possibly be."

Louis walked past at this moment, fully dressed and ready to go. Ceri was at his side, looking bewildered among the chaos.

"They are outside the front door, Kat. Where you left them."

Katrin snorted and stormed off through the door in a huff, Louis in her wake carrying the now full picnic basket.

"Goodness, she is like a hurricane," I breathed to Cam.

"She is like her mother," he retorted.

I rounded on him. "What is *that* supposed to mean?"

"Stubborn, opinionated, and unable to do what she is told."

Slapping at him, he caught my wrist and breathed into my ear. "Also, loyal, intelligent, and the most beautiful woman I have ever met in my life."

"Hmm... backpedaling, are you? Trying to redeem yourself? It is going to be a bit uncomfortable sleeping on the couch if I kick you out."

"It is all true."

Sensing that we still had an audience, I smiled up at Ceri as she watched this byplay. "It is alright, Ceri," I soothed, noticing her tense posture. "We are just playing."

"Grown-ups play, too?" she asked, her eyes popping wide.

"Oh, all the time." Cam grinned, pulling me back down to lie across his lap without warning.

"Hey!" I yelped as he lay me flat. "Watch your stitches!"

"I am fine," he protested, kissing me before sitting me upright. "Right. Is everyone finally ready? Can we go, please?"

With the children chatting happily around us, the nightmares that plagued me faded, just a little. Cam slipped his hand into mine and smiled down at me as we ambled along behind them toward our favorite place: a beautiful, secluded valley on the far side of the loch. Luca's loch. Now he was gone. I couldn't believe I was back here, and he wasn't. It felt so wrong. Luca's determined face as he gave Thorsten CPR down on that sandy bank momentarily obscured my vision. I blinked to clear it, and it was replaced by the scene as Illy held him on the dock. I doubted I would ever forget the look of anguish on her face. Snapping myself out of my melancholy, I forced myself to focus on my surroundings: stunted trees overhanging the dirt track, views peeking through as we rounded a bend, occasionally revealing hills covered in flowering heather, interspersed with fall tones, browns, and golds. All the little things I had missed lying in that bed. Tiny details that I had never paid attention to before. The scent of crisp mountain air made me snuggle down into the warmth of my jacket. Weeks of wearing nothing but a scratchy hospital gown, and I was in heaven with soft fabrics against my skin. I had never been enamored of particular trees or plants like Cam or my mother. I just took them for granted. But now, I embraced their presence with a joy that surprised even me.

Checking the children hadn't seen my inner turmoil, I forced a smile as I watched them run ahead, teasing us for being slow. They knew where we were going—a flat grassy area surrounded by a plantation of tall conifers, almost like a small football oval. Louis was carrying the basket, so we took our time, enjoying the scenery and each other. Ceri lingered behind the others, not quite as far back as us, but her discomfort was clear. Her rigid posture and awkward gait proved she had never walked for pleasure and didn't know how. The children were teasing each other, playing tag, and generally stirring each other up.

"Ceri!" I called, seeing her falling farther behind the group. "See those beautiful purple flowers? The ones growing in little clumps under the trees there. They are called field gentian. Could you pick some?"

Puzzlement crossed her face, and I watched as she squatted and squinted at the patch of flowers, pointing at them.

"What is she doing?" I asked Cam under my breath.

"You are so neurotypical. She is assessing them all."

"That isn't what I meant!"

"But it is what you *said*. Pick means to choose. So, she is choosing."

Reaching her in a few long strides, Cam squatted beside her and showed how to select flowers with as much stem as possible without damaging them. Chatting away to her calmly, he explained these flowers were found in the alpine regions across Europe, while others were native to here. I listened as he pointed out the different flowers growing in the area: yarrow, milkwort, squill, speedwell, sharing their common and botanical names, showed her the various parts, and explained how to choose a bouquet. Some just bursting into bloom, more still in bud. But not the fully open ones as they wouldn't last as long.

As I watched her, I noted she was soaking it all up like a sponge. She asked no questions but paid close attention to what Cam said, then replicated his actions. At his prompting, she handed me a bouquet awkwardly.

"Oh, Ceri, they are beautiful! Thank you!" I smiled at her, making her blush.

We showed her how to smell the scent, and her eyes widened as the earthy fragrance struck her.

"Didn't you know flowers smell?" She shook her head. "What do they smell like?" I questioned her. "Did you know they all smell slightly different? Each species has its own distinct scent." Ceri's eyes opened in amazement. "Did you not read about flowers then?"

"I know what they are," she intoned. "I believe they were used at wedding and funeral ceremonies. People paint them, too. I did not know they had a smell."

"Well, here we use them just to look pretty," I said briskly. "Also, the bees love them."

"Bees?" Ceri's brow furrowed. "The insects that make the honey?"

As we made the final descent from the rough path to the grassed valley, Cam explained about bees and their crucial role in pollination, promising to show her our hives when he did his next inspection. I carried the flowers with me to the picnic spot and laid the small posy carefully on the edge of the blanket.

"Come on, mum!" Louis called. "Come and play soccer with us!"

Not wanting to let them know I was in pain, and after checking that Cam was comfortably resting, Thorsten and I paired off against Louis and Xanthe. Kat acted as referee. Ceridwen could not be convinced to join in.

"We will teach you," Kat urged. "It isn't hard."

But Ceri shook her head violently and sat on the edge of the rug, watching intently.

After twenty minutes of laugher and running, we returned to the rug for lunch, my stomach and face throbbing, but so happy to be home.

"Ceri! Did you destroy mum's flowers?" Xanthe asked, her face dropping.

Peering over her shoulder, I saw what she meant. Every flower and stem had been shredded into tiny pieces, scattered over the corner of the rug.

Not wanting to cause a fuss, I smiled and said nothing. But Kat, ever outspoken, snapped, "Why would you do that? Mum wanted those."

Ceri, startled, refused to respond as Kat continued to needle her. Xanthe looked like she was going to cry. Cam hurriedly jumped in and changed the subject.

"Who wants a sandwich?"

After eating more than either of us had in months, Cam and I lingered under the trees, feeling blessed to enjoy the gloriously rare Scottish sun beaming down on our faces. The children had returned to play with the ball, Ceridwen lurking around the edges of the grassed pitch, pretending to be interested in the nearby bushes, growing at odd horizontal angles.

"Why do they grow like that?" I asked Cam abstractedly as I lay beside him.

"From the wind that used to gust through here. That is why there are very few tall, upright trees. They grow straight now, since we have been here, and they are protected from the gales. But goodness, the gusts of wind used to shoot right through you like a hurricane. Most of the islands don't have many established trees, only in the towns where they were protected from the wind."

"One of the few things I enjoyed when we were away was feeling wind again," I noted, not mentioning the many things that still haunted me.

"Who would have thought we would end up here?" he murmured, squirming to avoid a dripping branch, curling up behind me. "Melbourne, August ... never in a million years did I think you and I would end up here."

"Didn't you say once that you wanted to live in Edinburgh?"

"That is true. During my teens, I always dreamed that one day, I would live in Edinburgh. You asked me once if this was close enough."

"And you said yes."

Closing my eyes with the warm sun on my face, I remembered many of the places I had visited. Tropical islands with turquoise water and pristine white sandy beaches. Windswept glaciers. Bustling cities thick with pollution. But none of them felt like this place. Home.

An angry scream woke me from my pleasant haze. It was Thorsten, followed by angry chattering voices.

"What now?" I grumbled, ripped from my daydreams.

Cam was already on his feet, clutching his side from the rapid movement, trying to simmer the impending riot. With a look quelling the others and a few quick questions fired at Louis, the most reasonable of the bunch, he ascertained they had been trying to teach Ceri to play soccer. Ceri had been unable to kick the moving ball, and getting increasingly frustrated, had shoved Thorsten to the ground and snatched it. Thorsten's mud-stained pants, and the fuming faces of the others, were damning evidence.

"Is this true?" Cam asked her gently.

"No!" Ceri's voice grew high and indignant. "I didn't! He fell over."

Cam nodded, not wanting to call her a liar so soon after her arrival. The fury emanating from the other four signaled clearly enough that it wasn't true. They may be siblings and may not always get along, but heaven help someone who hurt one of their own blood.

"It is time to go anyway," he announced, to general grumbling. "We still have some chores to do at home before dinner."

Ceri said nothing but stood at the edge of the blanket awkwardly. Cam gave directions to pack up the picnic, collect the ball, grab their jackets, and start walking back.

"Have you never played with a ball before?" I asked as I stood, my stomach aching from the sudden movement.

The slight shift in posture proved she had heard me. Cam looked at me and shrugged, and I let it go, instead shaking the blanket and packing up the now much-lighter basket.

The walk home was much quieter. Our four huddled up the front, talking and kicking rocks. Ceri was a few meters behind. They weren't excluding her, I could tell, but were smarting from the perceived lack of consequences.

"Do we do something?" I asked Cam in a hushed tone.

"No. She needs to learn how to interact with others, take responsibility for her actions, and apologize for doing something wrong. She can't learn it academically. People all respond slightly differently. It can be difficult, but she needs to read the situation, respond, and assess that response. Did it have the desired effect? We can't intervene, or she will never learn."

"It is her first day. She just looks so unhappy."

"She needs to be, and they need to set expectations from the start. She hurt Thorsten, then lied about it. She needs to see that the others won't be happy about their little brother being hurt. To ignore it today and punish her next time would be even more confusing for her. She needs to learn, then maybe next time she will try a different way."

"When did you learn so much about children?"

Cam sighed. "That was my childhood. Having Asperger's, I couldn't read the situation and would always try to be the silliest, the loudest. I couldn't see that other kids were turning away from me. I thought if I could get their attention, make them laugh at me, then they would laugh with me."

"Did you ever learn?"

"Not really. I'm still not great in groups, am I? But in ones and twos, yes. Finally, a few kids gave me a chance, set clear boundaries, and told me when I was overstepping them. That helped me learn. Having siblings might be the best thing that ever happened to her. They will firmly tell her that her behavior isn't okay, like now. But they are stuck with her, so they need to work it out. They can't just wash their hands of her. It might make them a little more tolerant, too."

"I'm a little sad to say that I would have been one of those kids who would have labeled you a dick and walked away. I had no tolerance for silliness."

"Nor did Sorcha. I was lonely for a long time. I desperately wanted a friend but just couldn't connect. Then, in grade five, I made one great friend, Lil. She was wonderful to me. Lil instinctively knew my silliness was borne from anxiety and would set me straight. She liked me but tolerated no crap. Finally, I knew what it felt like to have a best friend. Then at the end of that year, her dad accepted a new job and her family moved interstate. It devastated me. But we stayed in touch. Then it wasn't until high school I met another kid with similar interests. Just having one friend was enough. It didn't remove the anxiety about everyday stuff, and I still needed help with my social game, but knowing I had one friend I could call? That made all the difference."

"I never had a good friend," I confessed. "Someone I trusted. I had lots of acquaintances. A group of people I socialized with. But after Katrin, I trusted no one … until I met you. Luca. Illy."

"You didn't have a best friend at school?"

"Not really. The girls hung out in groups, mostly along socio-economic or interest lines. The international students stuck together. So did the boarders. The scholarship kids were identified fairly early, and they stuck together. The sporty girls, the academic ones. The smokers and the partiers."

"And which were you?"

"Sporty," I admitted. "Although I did okay academically. I competed at inter-schools in a few sports:

swimming, skiing, tennis. I made nationals for swimming. A fat lot of good it does me now. When Thorsten was drowning..."

"Should we visit Illy tomorrow?"

"Absolutely."

CHAPTER 38

CAM DISAPPEARED AS I shooed children off to bed, arguing with them about teeth brushing and appropriate bedtimes. Having not seen me for months, I knew it would be some time until they felt comfortable leaving me again, each of them prolonging the bedtime separation. I could see the discomfort in Cam's movements on the walk home but knew he likely didn't want to speak about it. Talking about what happened made it real. We would discuss it at some point but not now. He was lying on the bed with his eyes closed as I entered the room.

"I've got a gift for you," I said as I closed the door firmly behind me. His eyes opened slowly, the pain making him grimace slightly.

"Really? When did you have time to get a gift? Amidst the kidnapping, rescues, and retribution?"

"When we were in Edinburgh. Before Nate."

Cam sat up against the pillows, and I handed him the black box with intricate Viking pattern embossed in burgundy and silver. "Highland Park Valkyrie?"

"Have you heard of it?"

"I've had it once before."

"Really? In Melbourne?"

Cam sighed as he held the box with one hand, tracing the pattern with the other. "Did I ever tell you about when I followed you to Lewis and then back to August? The part when I left August after I missed seeing you there? When I headed to New Zealand?"

"Parts of it. You told me about Hugh and what you found in Invercargill."

"After that. When I was on the yacht, I'd left New Zealand and drifted to Bellcamp. Did I tell you that part?"

"Not really. You just said that you were in a bad way."

"That is an understatement. I had traveled back through that hideous portal. To find you. Then you weren't there, and I heard you were pregnant and with Angus."

"I'm so sorry..."

"That's not what I meant. It wasn't your fault. Then Hugh died, and I was lost. Nowhere to go. Well, there was a bottle on the yacht. And I drank it."

"All of it?"

"I may have drunk several bottles," he admitted with a sheepish grin. "That was just the first. I don't recall the rest of them except that they were expensive and went down all too quickly. But I distinctly remember the Valkyrie. My mum loved single malt whisky. I remember thinking she would love to have tried it."

The disappointment must have shown on my face as he rushed to say, "It's fine! I loved it! It is an exceptional whisky. I can't wait to try it again."

"Thank goodness. I thought it brought back terrible memories," I said as I peeled back the black plastic, pulled the cork with a satisfying pop, and poured us both a small glass.

"What? Like the first alcohol you got stinking drunk on when you were a teenager?" Cam's eyes closed as he sipped.

"Oh, goodness, yes. For me, that was Midori and lemonade. I was fifteen and at a sleepover at a friend's house. I drank before that, of course. Alcohol was always around us at home. But that was the first time I drank to the point of vomiting, passing out, and losing control. In case you are wondering, yes, it is still green upon reappearance."

Cam smirked, swirling the amber liquid. "I was about sixteen and went to a party. Somebody had bought a bottle of Jim Beam. I drank far more than my fair share, mixed in coke, so I couldn't tell how much I had drunk. I was so sick. I can't even smell it to this day without feeling nauseous. Dad turned up and found me lying in the driveway, surrounded by my own vomit. He hosed me off, threw me in the car, and drove me home. Mum gave me the silent treatment for a week."

The smooth sensation from the whisky touching my soul made me close my eyes, feeling the warmness glide down my throat. I felt the glass being lifted from my hand as I was pushed down onto the pillow. I sighed with contentment as my boots were removed, followed by my jeans and top. The comforting weight of his body reminded me I wasn't alone anymore, and the hunger stirred from deep within me. I wanted to kiss him, but he was kissing my legs, my hips, working his way up my torso.

"Come here," I murmured, pulling feebly at his arms. "Kiss me."

"I have been visualizing this moment for months: what I would do when you were finally home. I intend to take my time."

"But you are in pain!"

"The only time I feel no pain is when I am with you."

My eyes closed, and my head rolled back on the pillow as I felt his touch, reconnecting us after so long apart. His fingers caressing my thighs and hips, his mouth setting me afire. My world exploded around him, and he followed me over the edge.

CHAPTER 39

LUCA'S MEMORIAL SEVERAL DAYS after our return began as a somber affair. Cam planted an oak tree in the memorial garden, near Laetitia's now fully established rose, and the trees commemorating the others who had passed. Oak symbolized a leader, he told me when choosing it: strong, generous, and helpful. As Cam watered it in, Josh read *The Oak* by Alfred, Lord Tennyson.

Illy stood silently beside me as Cam finished the planting. "The Last Post" was played, not on a bugle as was traditional, but on bagpipes, in honor of our home. People clustered around in small groups, forming a semi-circle in the gardens. Shuffling, not knowing what to say. Shushing children from marring the occasion. Finally, she made her way to the newly planted oak and turned to face the crowd.

"This is not what Luca would have wanted," she began to a collective intake of breath. "I have had time to think about this, and what Luca would have wanted is a party. A wake celebrating his life, not a service mourning his death. Luca loved to eat, drink, and be merry. This is my wish. Take this day. Laugh and share your favorite story of Luca. Please don't let this be a day of sorrow. Let us make it one of celebration."

A low hum spread among the crowd, followed by an uncomfortable silence as the audience didn't know how to react. Usually, there was a somber memorial planting, a reading or two, then a meal at the hall. Everyone brought a plate of food to share. People started looking at their feet, avoiding making eye contact. Sensing Illy's anxiety rise, I took the plunge, made my way to her side, turned, and spoke.

"Luca was my best friend for years. We traveled to many places together, other communities. Some wonderful, some dangerous. We were so close, shared secrets, laughed more times than I had hot dinners. The thing about Luca I will never forget was his wicked sense of humor. That man loved to tease! Me, especially. Any opportunity to tease me, and he took it. He didn't need a reason. Once I found him lying on a deck chair wearing a hot pink bikini and flicking back a long blonde wig, drinking a mango daiquiri. I have no idea where he sourced them, and he looked absolutely ridiculous, his black hairy chest poking out from under the top, stuffed with socks. I laughed until tears were pouring down my cheeks as he mimicked me, called me princess, flicking the wig around. Another time he turned up to dinner in a French maid's outfit, completely straight-faced. We were roaring with laughter as the costume was rather skimpy and didn't quite contain all of him, but he sat there, sipping his wine, acting like nothing was wrong. No one else could eat, of course, but he refused to change. Once, he turned up to breakfast in full lederhosen. The leather shorts were so tight he couldn't sit down. Not deterred, he ate breakfast standing, not breaking character once."

Chuckles rose from the crowd, and I paused before continuing, gathering my thoughts.

"No matter what I was feeling, Luca could make me laugh until my sides hurt. He was loyal, dependable, and there for me without question in the good times and the bad. I am so glad I got to see him meet this wonderful lady and have two beautiful daughters. His family was everything to him as he was to me. He saved my son's life, and for that, I will be eternally grateful. Truth told, he probably saved mine, too."

I paused as I sniffed and choked back the sobs threatening to break through.

"I will miss him until my dying breath. Luca made my life so much richer just for being in it. I am so thankful for knowing him and calling him my friend."

The stifled sob broke free from my chest, and Illy threw her arms around me as the tears flowed, and the crowd cheered, and Diana came up to speak, touching me softly on the arm as she passed me.

"Thank you," she whispered.

At the conclusion of the speeches, a party was held at the community hall in Garynahine with everyone in attendance. Food, music, dancing, and free-flowing whisky kept the mood light and jovial, and I accompanied Illy as she did the rounds, thanking everyone for coming. Most had heard by now about what had happened to us on Clava, but aside from a few comments expressing concern, a few sideways glances at my still mottled face, the day was about Luca. Everyone had a story to tell, an anecdote to recollect. Luca had touched everyone. From his early time here, to helping rescue the women on Mousa, to his later role in distilling whisky, roasting coffee, and running missions to the mainland to collect supplies, Luca was highly regarded and valued. I could feel Illy wilting at my side, but we pressed on, ensuring she spoke with everyone.

As we reached the end, I made eye contact with Cam across the room. Sometimes being tall had advantages. He pushed through the crowd and steered Illy outside, taking her and the girls home. I could finish up here, make apologies on her behalf. Her pregnancy was not common knowledge yet, and she looked exhausted.

Sorcha came over to me as I stood at the food table, my stomach gurgling and wanting to eat, but uncertain what to choose. She stood beside me as my thoughts churned, unable to decide. Berating myself, I knew it was silly. It was all food, and I liked food. There were sandwiches, pies, cakes, fruit. Why couldn't I choose?

"How is Illy doing?"

I didn't know how to respond to that and stared at the tiny meringues scattered like splotchy stars across a red plate.

"I don't know," I admitted. "Pregnant. Alone. Grieving. Relief that we escaped and guilt that we just killed two people. In turmoil, I guess, is an appropriate answer."

Sorcha nodded and stood beside me as we faced the table. *Why can't I choose?* Months of being fed small basic meals, and here I was with a smorgasbord of choice, and I was crippled.

Finally, I asked, "Are you planning to use the sample?"

Sorcha looked at me, and a series of expressions crossed her face, making me watch her, confused. She was never lost for words.

"How can I?" she whispered after a long pause.

I raised my eyebrows. "How can you ... what? I don't understand?"

Sorcha's look of scorn made me laugh.

"What?" I asked. "Really?"

"After what they did to you. How do I?"

"Did to me?" I asked, confused. "You mean on Clava? What does that have to do with you and Tom?"

"They stole genetic material from all of us, but you most of all. This is Tom, yes. But it was stolen. I don't feel right... I... I don't think it is ethical to do this."

I looked at her, stunned. "It isn't the same."

"But it is. He was an ethical man, and he didn't give consent. Nor did I. Nor did you. Using his material to father a child that he had no knowledge of? It is wrong."

I started to object, disagree with her, but the memory of those two surgeries I had endured were constantly on my mind. Waking, shackled to a bed in a tiny room, hooked up to machines. Knowing they had raided me. I knew it was unlikely that I would ever have a child again because of what they did.

Sorcha was watching as the cloud descended and steered me outside, pushing me onto a seat and sitting beside me. She was still watching as the demons fought for supremacy in my head.

"You are asking me this now as this is torturing you. I can see it. Cam can see it. You are the toughest chick I have ever known, Freyja. But what they did to you was heinous on a level I cannot comprehend. There are absolutely no excuses for what they did. I know we are not close, but I respect you, and I care about you. If you ever need to talk, I am here. Okay?"

I could feel the emotional cork pushing against the bottleneck, ready to explode, but forced the feelings back. No. Not now. Ice-queen time. "Thank you. Truly. That means a lot. Do you think you could ensure my kids get home? Ceri especially will not know how to cope with a large, emotional event. I need a little time."

"Done."

CHAPTER 40

AFTER WEEKS OF NEGOTIATION, Illy and Sorcha swapped houses. Living in the second home built in Roseglen, Sorcha and Di lived the closest to us. Sam and Kendra were mature and responsible. At seven, Illy's girls couldn't be left alone with a pregnant mother in mourning and whose first pregnancy had been dangerously high risk.

Illy lived farther down the valley, past Isla and Fraser's home, and Jamie and Jacinda, but before Jorja and Bridget. The house was built when she and Luca were newly partnered. We had teased them that they wanted to be out of earshot or just away from our noisy brood. But now, her home was too far to be within calling distance, especially at night, and we all agreed that it made sense for her to be closer to us. Cam and I had made it clear since the day we returned that we would raise this child together, all three of us.

"I miss removalists," Sorcha grumbled under the weight of a large box as she transferred it onto the back of a cart.

Illy's face fell. "I'm sorry. I am kicking you out of your home."

"Don't be silly," Diana breezed as she returned to collect another box. "She is just grumpy. No one enjoys moving. It is one of the few times you realize how much crap you have and how dirty your house is when you move furniture. How are you feeling anyway? You look exhausted."

Cam confided in me later that Sorcha was looking forward to being farther away, despite her whinging. Sorcha wasn't renowned for her tolerance and had a particularly short fuse where Summer and Ally were concerned, although she had tried to keep this in check, recognizing that they were mourning their father. Di, conversely, took everything in her stride and could regularly be seen playing with a ball or skipping rope with one of the children. I had long suspected that she missed teaching, being surrounded by cheerful chatter all day. But she was a knowledgeable and valuable addition to the horticulture team, and Cam loved working with her.

"Do you know if she will try to have another child?" Cam asked me later that night as we put the children to bed. "Sorcha, I mean. Time isn't exactly on her side."

Not wanting to betray her confidence from the night of the memorial, I replied as casually as I could, "I'm not sure."

"Maybe she is waiting for Illy?" he suggested. "She was very unwell last time, and so was Sorcha when she was pregnant with Sam. They are both forty, so higher risk."

"That is very kind of her," I admitted. "Placing Illy first."

"For all her faults, my sister is a born doctor. Bossy and opinionated, and a complete pain in the ass, but she does have her patients' best interest at heart. She is so like my mother. But I have always wondered why women go back for seconds, or thirds, when they get so sick. Every man I know would say, 'Thanks, I've done my duty,' and shut up shop."

"It is an instinctive thing," I confessed as we closed our bedroom door with a sigh, the quietness of the house making me relax after an exhausting day of carrying furniture. "Hormones, probably. You look at your children and know you would endure anything for another." Even with difficult cesarean births, my pregnancies had been comparatively easy, but I had watched Di and Illy wracked with sickness, Di's inflicted by Clava. Sorcha had still been in her Australian community of Kiewa when she had Sam with her partner, Tom.

It was thanks to Tom's extensive knowledge of bio-technology that Sorcha had set up an extensive network of photobioreactors that successfully produced much of our electricity, especially in winter when daylight hours were scarce. Each home had tanks filled with algae and biogas bladders, and the community had enormous communal walls of tanks, green and murky, but amazingly productive. Thanks to this supplementary energy, we now had the luxury of e-bikes and electric carts or buggies to get around. While we didn't have an unlimited supply, each home had some household appliances that could be operated, and life was just a little easier. But everyone knew the limitations, and families often swapped appliances when they were needed. "It is like an adult toy library," Isla had once joked as I borrowed her blender. No one owned or needed everything, but we used them sparingly, mindful of the power they used.

We had taken the surveillance equipment from Illy's former home and temporarily set it up in our bedroom, not wanting the children to see it. It was my reaction to it I hadn't expected. An icy chill crawled up my spine every time I saw the monitor set up on our chest of drawers, knowing the last time I had watched that screen, I had seen Cam lying in a puddle of his blood and Luca dead. After a few days of constant prickling down my back and waking with my heart racing to see it ominously looming over us, I draped a sheet over it. Illy wasn't convinced that Clava wouldn't come after us. We had heard from Tadhg that Auckland had come to their rescue, and together they had salvaged several ocean-worthy vessels to moor at the now partly usable Inverness harbor.

Illy had been shellshocked from the beginning when I first suggested she may be pregnant on that rocky beach, holding her hair as she heaved. She had accepted it as we neared Angus's property but was terrified of what lasting effects there may be on the baby after our time on Clava. On our second day back home, and with grim determination, Sorcha had steered us both toward the clinic, and after an x-ray on my face, had performed a dating scan. As suspected, Illy was nine weeks pregnant, confirming that the baby was indeed Luca's.

"The baby looks fine," Sorcha remarked, making Illy's chest sink, her eyes closing as I squeezed her hand.

Illy's first pregnancy had been twins with gestational diabetes but also complications because of her physical size. She was large this time, but not as large as the first time around. "Her belly enters the room a full five seconds before the rest of her," Luca had teased. As the pregnancy progressed, Sorcha monitored Illy closely but advised that she was healthy, and so was the baby. As the only two people who knew exactly what we had endured, Illy and I remained fearful of the impact on the baby, but Sorcha couldn't see anything of concern. However, she admitted it wasn't the most high-tech ultrasound equipment. Illy had readily agreed to a mid-gestational ultrasound, which confirmed that this was a single baby, and to her mixed emotion, was a boy.

"Luca would be so proud to know he finally had a son," she said as we went for our increasingly slow evening walk around Roseglen. "He desperately wanted a boy."

"He said that?"

"Of course not."

Illy was so perceptive she could pick what someone wanted for dinner.

"But you are worried about raising a son alone?" I guessed.

"I am an only child, a late in life child. A happy accident my parents always called me. All of my cousins were much older and remained on Orkney when my parents migrated. Some moved to Edinburgh or London as they got older. I lost touch with most of them when my parents died. I have limited experience with young boys. I understand girls. Boys need a strong male role model. This little guy will grow up with no father."

"That's not true. He has Fraser, Cam, Jamie, and lots of other wonderful men here. Cam will happily be his father in all ways that count. Teach him all the important things."

"Like what?" she looked up at me, curious.

Memories of Cam teaching Sam, Louis, and Thorsten flitted through my mind.

"How to rough play but not hurt the other person. Kick a ball. How to treat people with respect. Fart jokes. How to wash all your stinky bits. Teaching them to piss straight while standing. You know, man stuff."

"Oh God," she moaned unexpectedly. "Teenage boy smell! I had several army colleagues with teenage boys, and they all complained about the smell."

"Tell me about it! Sam is only thirteen, and already his room has an odor to it. Sorcha waits until he goes to school and quickly opens the windows to air out his room!"

"Did she tell you that Sam is going to take on my market rounds for me? Not forever. Just for a few weeks while I can't do it."

"No. That is a wonderful idea."

"I have promised to teach him about trade and what is a fair price. How to track what people give you and what you give others. The importance of keeping detailed records."

"He is a good kid. What about the vital bit? Reading people?"

"He is quite an intuitive young man. He will do just fine."

"When will he start?"

"He is coming with me from next week. Can you believe I am thirty-two weeks already? I am hoping to stop and take a break from thirty-five weeks. Sorcha says there is no reason this little one shouldn't go full term, being a single birth."

Her words struck me like a bullet to the chest. Thirty-two weeks since we lost Luca. It had to be her yardstick, too.

"You won't be alone. I will be there for you, every second," I said, low and calm as we walked.

"I know. I couldn't do this without you."

"You could. But I know what you mean. It is just a shame that the building teams can't build our house link before winter, but I understand they need a rest."

By long-standing arrangement, the building teams worked long hours, seven days a week for eight months of the year. Unlike most of us, who worked a five-day week, their work came in bursts, aligned to the months of the year when the daylight hours were longer. Late November to early March, there were too few daylight hours to do much outside, so this was their time to spend with their families or work on their own homes.

"You will be fine," I assured her, sensing her tense beside me. "One of the girls can come and fetch us. We will do the rest."

CHAPTER 41

THE TENSION WAS EVIDENT as soon as I approached the kitchen; Katrin and Ceri were circling each other like wildcats. Judging by the ingredients strewn around the kitchen and the cookbook open on the bench, they were baking Christmas gingerbread cookies. Katrin's frustration filled the room. The high color of her cheeks and the tenseness of her posture betrayed the fact that she was furious at her new sister. Ceri was haughtily defiant and clearly would not back down. Recognizing the volatile situation instantly, I stepped in.

"Kat." I breezed through the open door. "Just who I need. Could you give me a hand for a moment?"

Katrin mumbled something but dutifully wiped her hands and followed me into the bedroom before I closed the door.

"What's going on?" I set the tone, hoping she would follow suit and keep the volume low.

"She's driving me mad! She doesn't listen. She doesn't know how to do *anything* but refuses to take instructions either."

"You realize she's probably never baked before."

"Okay, but it's not that hard. Get the ingredients and mix them. It's just not *hard*."

"You forget, sweetheart, that someone showed you. You were new to baking once. Someone showed you how to read the recipe and follow the steps. Cream the butter and the sugar. Someone showed you how to measure the flour, how to sift it without making a mess. We all have to learn. We all need to start somewhere. So no, while it's not difficult for you, perhaps it is for her. Be kind. Please be patient."

"Fine!" Katrin stormed back to the kitchen.

Pondering whether to follow, I hung back for a while, listening to Kat's curt tones as she gave instructions. Ceridwen said little, but from Kat's humphing, I gathered she wasn't following them to the level Kat expected. Maybe this would teach her tolerance?

Lurking in the bedroom until I finally heard the oven door slam, I returned to the kitchen, peeking my head inside. Kat was sitting at the table, seething, her face bright red.

"Where is Ceri?"

"Living room."

"What are you reading?" I asked kindly, popping my head in the door.

Ceri looked up guiltily, like she had been caught in the act of something prohibited.

I smiled at her, casting my eye over her on the sofa. "A book."

"I can see that. One from here?"

"No. One I brought with me from … before. He… Father, I mean, said I could read any of the books in the library."

I nodded, not wanting to start a conversation that might lead to her asking about Angus. "What is that?" I gestured with my chin toward the crumpled brown old pages.

Ceri shrugged and handed them to me. "I found them in the lining inside the back cover."

Noting the letterhead, *Duncan McTavish, Private Investigator*, I folded them and smiled at her. "I'll read them later. Now, would you like some lunch?"

Any situation could be improved for Ceri with the addition of food. It made me wonder what she was fed when she was raised on Clava, and if lack of nutrition was why she was smaller than her siblings. Louis had already told me that Angus was no cook, something I knew all too well. While we all took turns to prepare meals on the *Selkie*, Angus's meals were tolerable, bland, and with no seasoning at all. At least Luca, Jakob, Nate, and I tried to change up a boring diet of packet and tinned meals.

The smile lit Ceri's face like a sunbeam. Discretely pocketing the papers, I steered her into the kitchen where we made sandwiches, talking about our favorite fillings. As we talked, Kat slunk out of the room, leaving me to retrieve the delicious smelling gingerbread cookies from the oven, showing Ceri how to use the oven mitt. Closing her eyes with joy as she tasted steaming gingerbread made her look so much like her mother. Katrin loved baking and sugar in any form. *One day*, I promised myself, *I will tell her everything about her biological mother.*

It was several hours before I was alone and could read the old typewritten pages, which turned out to be several letters. All addressed to "Dear Robert." The oldest, dated over fifty years before, was an investigation on Amara Kalayani Siriporn, the first wife of Angus's father. Laetitia's grandmother. It was an executive summary with promises to send a complete file. The summary spanned two pages and detailed Amara's early life as the daughter of a wealthy banker in Bangkok. She had attended the Bangkok International School and, as Cam had believed, she had indeed completed a Bachelor of Laws with Honors from the University of Sydney. Returning to Thailand after her graduation, she had worked as a human rights lawyer for a prominent international firm but had disappeared after an arranged marriage with a much older, well-connected gentleman had been negotiated. Publicly shunned, she had been eliminated from the family will.

The second was a preliminary forensic report. Amara's car had traveled off the road and down a steep embankment, ending in the ocean. A single bullet had been removed from the front driver's tire. Promises to send a full report when it became available were noted, but it wasn't included in the papers I had. Folding the letters, I returned them to my pocket. It wasn't until after dinner that I found time to show them to Cam. He read them through twice, then tucked them away in his bedside drawer.

"Are you okay?"

"I guess. There wasn't much that I didn't already know or suspect. But it was good to have confirmation. Amara was murdered then. Not too many ways a bullet ends up in a driver's tire."

"True."

"It will be good to tell Louis about her, that she was a human rights lawyer and helped people. I will need to explain what that is, of course, but it helps, a little. Just knowing."

Cam's face betrayed the turmoil lurking beneath. His eyes shadowed, brow crinkled, and lips drew tightly together.

"Is there something I can do?"

"I'm not tired. I might just take a walk."

My heart stopped. "Do you want company?"

"No, it's okay. I'll be back soon."

Cam laced up his boots silently and slipped out without saying goodbye.

The gale buffeting the shell far above me, hollow but rhythmic, kept me awake. Shuddering, I rolled over to face the empty side of the bed, closing my eyes and willing sleep to overtake me as the hole in my heart throbbed with loneliness.

CHAPTER 42

RISING EARLY, UNABLE TO sleep, I found the kitchen cold and empty. Making a coffee, I waited for his return. Finally, I woke the children, making them breakfast and slipping out to Illy's, offering to help her on my day off so Sam could go to school. One look at my face and she knew something was wrong but was friend enough not to ask. My heart sank when I realized she was headed down the valley first. But with her pregnancy now at an advanced stage, I knew I couldn't abandon her.

I hadn't seen Jorja and Bridget in the months since I had returned, other than a quick hello at public events like Luca's service. Bridget saw the children daily, but I still couldn't see those girls and not envisage Katrin lying in that bed. Me tied to mine.

Jorja broke the ice almost instantly as I stalled getting out of the cart.

"I know you likely don't want to hear it, but I need to say this. I am sorry, Freyja. Truly. For all of it. If I had known that was where you were going, I would have warned you how obsessed they are about the project and advised you not to go."

I sniffed, unsure how to respond. Eventually, Illy did.

"We have had this conversation before, Jorja. We needed to go. We thought they had Louis."

Illy and I had spoken many times over the past few months about the horrors we had endured. Held prisoner. Murdered. It still haunted me, and I knew it affected her.

Jorja nodded. "But what we did to your sister, and what they did to you. It was unforgivable. I hope one day you can forgive me for my part in it."

I paused, choosing my words carefully, not wanting emotion to control me. "I forgive you, Jorja. It took me a long time, I will admit. But lying in that bed, things became clear. If I understand nothing else, I understand that desperate need to protect your children. I don't like what you did, but I accept it wasn't easy for you either. They were very controlling, and I realize you had little choice. You took a great risk in coming here to tell me. I am grateful for that. You are part of the community here now, so unless there is anything else...?"

"No, nothing," she rushed to say. "But ... if you don't mind ... now that she has been here a while, I would like Ceridwen to spend more time with her sisters. Do you think she could come and stay for a few days? The three of them are sisters. It might help her. Illy tells me she is struggling to acclimatize here. The funny thing is, Bridget says she doesn't see it at school. She is a very attentive student."

"That would be great. My kids need me, and Cam and I want to help Illy prepare for the baby. Ceri needs a lot of time, and we don't have it to give to her right now. She loves to learn, but she is difficult, I will warn you. You can't turn your back on her. If you are sure, I'll bring her over after dinner if that suits you?"

"That would be wonderful. I want our girls to be close. I was never close to my sister, and I want this for them."

"You had a sister? You never mentioned her."

"I do, or rather, I did. An older one. Farah."

"I am assuming by the use of past tense she wasn't chosen?" Illy asked.

"I think so, although I never found out what happened to her. But I didn't go looking either. We really weren't close."

"We lived together for weeks. Bridget told us about her brothers, and you told us about yours. Why have you never spoken of her?"

Jorja sighed. "Farah was estranged from my family. She was always difficult, but she was loved and was given the same opportunities I was. Then she met her husband, and within a year, she married him. That was when the big change occurred. She became controlling, judgmental, and made it very clear that she disapproved of me and my life choices. They obviously talked, as all couples do, but it was like they fed off each other. It often felt like a tiny matter became a monumental one overnight when nothing had changed. Except that likely they had spent hours discussing it and blowing it out of proportion."

Illy and I said nothing, and Jorja continued, a wry look on her face.

"I remember a gorgeous, older family friend telling me you can't usurp the matriarch until the matriarch has died. She nailed it. That was exactly the situation in the early days. Fairly quickly after Farah married, she had children, and our brother and I didn't. Her role changed in that she became a mother, but she also thought that her role in *our* family had changed. She seemed to think that the extended family should revolve around her and her children. But our mother was the family matriarch, and she was still very much alive. Important events were always hosted at our family home, and my parents treated us as equals. Soon there were squabbles over who would host Eid al-Adha or other important events. I mulled over that for a long time, and it makes sense. In so many cultures, there is a matriarch, and always it is the oldest woman. The wise woman."

"And that was the case in your family?" Illy asked.

"We are Persian, as you know. My birth name is Gulzar, but I desperately wanted to fit in at school, so I anglicized it. Farah was lucky—her name was a lot easier. But yes, our family always centered around the matriarch. When my grandmother passed, that was my mother."

"Were you very family-focused?"

"Absolutely. My mother's children and grandchildren were treated equally in the family home. Each Friday, we all had dinner at my parents' house. They had a large house set up for family. You had to be dead or dying not to attend. Just because my sister changed from a solo woman to a mother didn't automatically make her the matriarch. She tried to take over hosting Friday dinners, but that didn't work. Christmas and Eid al-Fitr too, once she had children. We were relaxed Muslims, and after my family moved to Australia, they tried to incorporate both cultures. But celebrations were always hosted by my mother. Then she cut ties with my parents over a simple petty squabble. She had two young children by then. I mean, who does that? Cuts their grandchildren off from their grandparents for no reason at all? A misunderstanding that should have been resolved in a day. But it snowballed and became so big it was impossible to turn back. Things were said that couldn't be unsaid. Then my brother, his wife, and I got caught up in it. I'm not even sure how."

Jorja paused, and I asked, "What happened to her?"

"I don't know. Years passed. She was married with three kids by the time the pandemic struck. Wrapped up in her own life, focused on her husband and children. Once she married, they took precedence. I doubt she had any idea what I was up to. It was many years since we last spoke. I did my postgraduate study, work placements. Got a job and then accepted the role here."

"And no one said goodbye?"

"I tried to reach out to her, once, a few years after the initial falling out. It was Christmas, I felt guilty, and I sent her an email saying that fighting was silly, we were sisters, and perhaps we could get over it. But in reply, she sent me a list of demands. Things I needed to do to remain in her life. I'm no psychologist, but even I recognized it wasn't reasonable. Relationships are based on trust, not rules. You need to operate under the assumption that others will treat you with the same respect that you give them. You can't dictate what other people do. I was sad, but I let it go. At least I had tried."

"Did anyone speak to her?"

"One of my cousins. He and his wife stayed in touch. Acted as the go-between, so big family news got passed on. Births, deaths, and marriages. But I rarely thought about her, even when I was back home. After all the nastiness, Mum removed all her photos from display, cut her out of their will, and no one spoke about her. Life was busy, and, well ... she just wasn't part of it. Occasionally, I would get updates from my cousin. Nothing good, of course. She continued bad-mouthing my parents and me, which continued for over ten years after we stopped speaking. Judging my sexual preferences. Telling lies about things I supposedly did. I mean, it was all second-hand by the time I heard it, but it still hurt. The stupid thing is, if I did something wrong, all those years ago, I would happily apologize. I was young and likely made mistakes. I was no angel. But I have absolutely no recollection of the things she told my cousin and his wife that I did."

"She told them things you did *ten years ago*?"

"Apparently. More than ten years. Only I don't recall any of it. She always had a relaxed relationship with the truth, but defaming someone after so long? What does she hope to achieve?"

"Kat and I fought. We weren't always friends, but we were there for each other. I knew I could count on her if things were bad." *Except for that last time*, I thought, remembering the spiral of events that had seen me accept the place to August.

"Farah and I were never close. We were very different people, even as children. She was a party girl at uni. Scraped through on average grades and was only there for the social life. I was far more academic and not at all social. But when she met her husband, she changed completely."

Illy had been listening intently, leaning back on the cart, stroking her enormous stomach. Finally, she spoke. "You know, that speaks volumes—about *her*. It is always sad when any relationship doesn't work out. Especially a blood one. Those hurt the most. But you did your best, and you moved on. I have never heard you speak of her, and certainly not in a nasty way. Lying or even saying negative things about anyone ten *years* later is a massive grudge to bear. She must be a very unhappy, angry person. If someone killed my child, I could understand holding on to the anger for so long. But from what you have said, it was a simple disagreement. No one cheated or died. No one inflicted a serious wound on another. We all fall out with people. But we make up, or we let it go and move on. It isn't healthy to hold on to resentment and anger."

"Was she always like that?" I asked.

"No, not really. When Farah met her husband, that was the beginning. He became the center of her universe. We used to joke that she wouldn't survive if something happened to him or their marriage."

"Why *do* people change when they meet someone?" I asked Illy.

Illy smiled. "There is a fabulous psychological theory about that. Female archetypes aligned to Greek goddesses. I wrote my Ph.D. thesis about it. Archetypes and women in the military. It is a fascinating concept."

"Archetypes? Do I want to know?"

"Your sister sounds like a classic Hera. You are likely an Artemis, and Freyja here is Athena."

I raised my eyebrows at her, indicating that she may as well continue.

Illy settled in on the rock wall, resting her hands on her belly, Jorja and I flanking her.

"It is a Jungian theory, so very old, but well documented. Hera was the wife of Zeus and quite beautiful. Zeus was the chief of all gods of Olympus, and she held a prominent position of status and power. Zeus cheated terribly, but like most scorned wives, Hera refused to see it as *his* mistake, and more often sought revenge on his mistresses, not him. Desperately unhappy, but so caught up in the idea of her own marriage that she put on a brave public face and continued the pretense. In your sister's case, I assume her husband was quite successful?"

"He was. She never stopped boasting about his achievements. She spoke about him like he was a god."

"That makes sense. A Hera archetype is a woman who is desperate to be a wife. Her lifelong goal is to be married, part of a powerful partnership. The day she changes her name is the most important one in her life. She genuinely means it when she commits, for better or worse. She derives her success from that of her husband, and to a lesser extent, her children. Their successes are her successes. But he always comes first. It is what motivates her. A Hera woman makes her husband the center of her life; the bond to her husband is her major source of meaning. Everyone around her knows her husband comes first. Being associated with success and power but not achieving it for herself. A trophy wife, if you like. One that wants the luxurious life, the status, but doesn't want to earn it for herself. She stands by her man and plays the dutiful wife. It doesn't mean that she doesn't work, but his career, his prominence will always take precedence over hers."

"I knew so many of those back home!" I groaned. "Half the girls I went to school with had mothers like that. Fathers who earned millions and mothers who spent their day with their personal trainer and beautician. Turned up to events dressed to the nines with a full face of perfect makeup so he wouldn't get a roving eye and cheat with the secretary or leave her for a younger woman. Even those men we all knew to be cheating, the wife would stand by in her designer dress and smile sweetly as he accepted another award. Even if she had her own career, she always put his first."

"That's it. The risk with a Hera archetype is when they marry a Zeus. A Zeus husband uses marriage as a pretense. He marries a woman of his social class, or higher if he is lucky, and expects her to be at his side, publicly supporting him whenever it is required. He often pursues other interests, usually involving power, leaving her to manage the home and raise the children. She, on the other hand, initiates a flurry of social activity intended to present a public image of the perfect couple. Many Hera women marry Zeus men in the military, so I saw this dynamic quite a lot. Following them around on postings, waiting at home with the children when they were deployed."

This had been my friend Danica's life back in Melbourne. Getting entangled in her mess had led me here.

Illy glanced at my face and continued. "I need to point out that there is nothing wrong with any individual archetype. No one is better than another, and rarely is a woman purely one archetype; she has elements of others. One will be dominant, though, and she will make her life decisions to support that primary archetype. It is important to identify which archetypes *you* are, as well as those around you, so you can see where their intrinsic motivation differs from yours. It is often at the root of conflict between women, and particularly women within the same family."

"You said I was an Athena?"

"In Jung's theory, the seven goddess archetypes are in three groups. The vulnerable ones, or those defined by their relationships with others: Hera, Demeter, and Persephone fall into this category, although they have some key differences. Hestia, Athena, and Artemis are those goddesses not defined by their relationships. That leaves Aphrodite. She has relationships but isn't hurt by them in the way that the vulnerable goddesses are."

"Go on." I had read many Greek myths and even read the simplified versions to my children, but I didn't recall enough to identify each goddess by personality traits.

"Artemis and Athena are both achievement-oriented archetypes, whereas Hestia is inwardly focused. Artemis, goddess of the hunt, was competitive, but left civilization behind and actively avoided contact with men. She separated herself from men and their influences. Athena, the goddess of wisdom, is above all, logical. Ruled by her head rather than her heart, she joined men as an equal in anything they did. She was the coolest head in battle and the best strategist. Intelligent, quick-witted, and focused, her adaptation was to become *like* men. Freyja, you are the strongest Athena archetype I have ever met. You are rational, competent, and self-assured. You run missions, save people, and success for you is defined by your own actions. You don't need external validation. You don't measure your success by your husband's achievements, but your own. Sorcha is another excellent example of an Athena. She has taken on a traditionally male role and excelled. Imagine her in the corporate world back home? She would have worked harder to attain her success but judged herself by her achievements, not by her association with others. An Athena woman is organized, structured, and plans ahead. She is practical, uncomplicated, and confident. Someone who gets things done without fuss."

"That is *so* you!" Jorja grinned at me.

I blushed. I couldn't disagree.

"From what I know, and remember, I never met her, Laetitia was likely a Hestia. Hestia, the goddess of hearth and home, was an introvert, contemplative. She withdrew inward, tried to be anonymous in appearance, and wanted to be left alone. A Hestia daughter is likely to withdraw emotionally, retreating inward to avoid a painful family life, which we know Lae had. She often feels alienated or isolated. When a woman has a predominant Hestia archetype, she often downplays her femininity to not attract unwanted male interest. She lives quietly as she values the daily tasks that give her life meaning. From what I know, Laetitia didn't define herself by her relationships. But her home, family, her partner, her children made her happy."

I nodded. This aligned with what I knew of Lae. Intelligent but introverted. So very different from me.

"What about me?" Jorja asked.

"Artemis, as a goddess archetype, represents a sense of independence, but an attitude of I can take care of myself, rather than, I need to compete. I see you in this way, Jorja. You are independent, intelligent, successful, and self-confident, but you don't need the approval of others to recognize your own success. The

Artemis woman typically is a natural competitor, with perseverance, courage, and the will to win."

"I can see that," she admitted.

"Well, it takes one to know one." Illy grinned back. "Although I have a good smattering of Athena in me, too. Back to your sister. What is fascinating is when the women in a single family have different archetypes, it is often these that drive conflict. Strangely, you can have three daughters, and they will all be different. It doesn't appear to be inherited or learned. It is important to acknowledge that other women's motivation comes from different sources, but the key is recognizing that each archetype is valid. Your sister, Jorja, likely saw her wedding day as the most important day of her life. Her dreams had been fulfilled. I am assuming she changed her name?"

"Oh, goodness, yes. I caught her practicing her new signature even before the wedding."

I smirked, recognizing the type. Cam had never asked, and I had never offered to take his name. I saw changing my name as a sign of possession, and I belonged to no man. Although he had my heart, but that was mine to give.

"Even as a child, my sister dressed up with pillowcases on her head, pretending to be a bride, marrying a teddy bear. Waltzing around her bedroom."

"Where were you?"

"Usually with dad, my head under the bonnet or out playing with the dogs."

"I don't recognize my sister in any of those," I said as Jorja looked at me. "Tell me about the others. The other archetypes."

"Of the three vulnerable goddesses, Demeter is the maternal archetype, goddess of grain and the harvest.

Demeter is the nurturing type and has a strong desire to be a mother, but this can also manifest in caring professions, therapists, nursing, teaching, counseling. Demeter women are not competitive with other women for either men or achievements. The only jealousy she likely experiences is when she doesn't have children of her own. Di and Jacinda are both likely Demeter archetypes. Xanthe, too."

"No, that wasn't Kat. She wasn't maternal."

"I must admit, I have never fully understood the Persephone archetype. This is a split one. A child-woman, beautiful but unaware of her beauty, kidnapped by Hades into the underworld. She later becomes queen of the underworld, guiding all that go there. As an archetype, Persephone represents the young girl who doesn't know who she is. She is uncommitted to a relationship, to work, or to an educational goal. Their attitude is that of the eternal adolescent, indecisive about who or what they want to be when they grow up, waiting for something or someone to transform their lives. They are youthful, compliant, and want to make people happy."

"That is Kat to a tee. She never really grew up, though she never had the chance either. Never saw her beauty, her value. She looked for validation from others, but she had no goals of her own. She would do anything for my parents' approval or that of her teachers. She played the piano, spent hours practicing. All because she wanted their attention. To make them proud of her."

"Drug and alcohol use is more common in Persephone and Aphrodite archetypes," Illy advised. "Although a lot of Hera types in unhappy marriages self-medicate as well. They can't deal with the idea of failure, of being alone. So, they drink or use drugs to numb the pain."

"I often wondered why Kat experimented with alcohol and drugs. But now that you describe it like that, I can see she felt lost. Slowly, she withdrew. We attended an elite school of nearly a thousand girls. Girls from rich and powerful families. She didn't excel in sports, arts, or academia. She was bright but not a brilliant student. She was good at art—she wanted to be an architect—but she was never the girl on the stage at the end of the year receiving the prize. How did she differentiate herself from all those other girls in an environment that prized excellence above everything else?"

We sat in silence for a long time before Illy asked, "Did your parents allow you to drink at home?"

"They did, in small amounts. From the age of fifteen, we were allowed a small glass of wine with our meal if we all ate together. My parents believed in teaching us to try everything in moderation. They openly discussed it with us. They believed that if we had access to alcohol and could learn to respect it, drink small amounts, then we wouldn't go off and get shit-faced at the first party we attended. Mum was fearful of the risks associated with girls and alcohol. Too often, she had seen girls drugged and violated because they drank too much or accepted a drink from a stranger. Plus, alcohol was always around. The liquor cabinet was always full and never locked. Socially we were exposed to it, too. Guests drinking wine at our home. Events most weekends that always involved drinking."

"Did it work?" Jorja asked. "My parents were fairly relaxed Muslims, but they didn't allow us to drink. I did go and get obliterated the first few times I drank at parties. Fortunately, nothing happened, but I had no idea of the effects of a comparatively small amount."

"Aside from once or twice, it did for me. I could go to a party and recognized my limits. It also helped that I didn't like to feel out of control."

"And your sister?"

"Kat was wilder than me. She hid her drinking. Once I caught her sneaking a bottle of vodka from the back of the cabinet, or she drank a small amount from each bottle. That kind of thing. Besides, accessing anything isn't hard if you have the money. By the time she was sixteen, she drank heavily but managed to hide it. I was at uni by then and could drive, so I regularly picked her up, steaming drunk. Even when she was younger, every weekend we attended a social event. After an hour or two, the adults had drunk a few glasses, so they stopped paying attention to where we were and what we were doing. We were safe enough. It was always at a friend's house or the yacht club. The adults would stand around talking and drinking, and the kids would sneak off, often taking a bottle with us. Finding a quiet spot by the pool or on the beach away from their sight. Experimenting. Alcohol, drugs, sex. But she always took it a little further. I thought it was a phase and would wear off, but it didn't. Then she started smoking. I smelled it on her a few times. I just never realized that she moved onto stronger things until I found her with the syringe in her arm. I wonder now how her life could have been different if only I had said something, got her some help."

"It was unlikely to have changed anything." Illy's calm tone interrupted my thoughts. "There is no point berating yourself. She couldn't find her place. Drinking numbed the pain, and when that didn't, drugs did. There were many people like that. Some find a hobby or sport they are obsessed with. Often risky ones like skydiving or abseiling. There are also male archetypes, but that was Luca before he came here: always pushing himself, feeling inadequate, that he wasn't enough."

"He hit the jackpot when he met you." I smiled, knowing the pain was all too close to the surface. "You made him whole."

"Well, I had better get off to my little goddesses," Jorja said, standing and brushing off her pants. "Though I will assess them through a slightly different prism now. I'll see you later, Frey, with Ceri. Bring a bag. She can stay as long as you like. Who knows? She might even want to spend Christmas with us."

"Do you assess everyone you meet?" I asked Illy cheekily as we resumed our rounds. I needed to drive, Illy unable to wedge her belly behind the wheel.

"I do it all the time with my girls," Illy admitted as she leaned back, caressing her heaving stomach. "Both are headstrong and willful. They are both Artemis, I think, with a touch of Athena, too."

"Like their mother?" I teased.

"Exactly. I think that is why they drive me bananas."

"What archetype do you think Ceridwen is?" I asked Illy after a long period of silence.

"I have been thinking about her. It is probably why the archetypes were on my mind. Thinking about Ceri and how to help her. If I understand her motivations, I can support her better."

"And?"

"The problem is, I can't see any natural state in her. She is like a constructed being. She was molded, an android if you like. A robot that appears to be human.

She hasn't been able to find or express her personality because she had no opportunity to be herself for the first six years of her life. She is so utterly lost. She doesn't know who she is."

"Surely she will develop a personality now that she can? Or will she be like Kat and always feel lost?"

"Initially, I thought she would find her voice, her motivation. Express her personality. But the longer she is here, the more doubt I have. She was taught how to behave, what to do and say, and she is struggling now that her life isn't ordered and structured."

"Will she learn?" Ceri's erratic behavior was of increasing concern. Cam and I had spent many nights quietly discussing how challenging we found her.

"I don't know. But we need to be patient with her. Take it slowly."

"Will do."

"Can I ask what happened last night? Why was Cam roaming around outside until 2AM? Why you felt the overwhelming need to accompany me on your day off?"

"Did he wake you?"

"He passed by my window, and the shadow startled me."

Filling Illy in on the content of the letters, she nodded wisely.

"He will never get over her, will he?" I whispered.

Illy's arm came around my shoulder as I slowed to take a corner.

"It isn't about getting over her. He has moved on; you know he has. But he will never forget her. Do you want him to?"

Instinctively I wanted to blurt, "Yes!" but the thought of Louis's warm brown eyes seeing me as he raced across Angus's kitchen forced me to relent. "I guess not. But he didn't even know Amara. Why would fifty-year-old letters have an impact?"

"He couldn't save Laetitia, the same way Angus's father couldn't save Amara. Both died tragically, leaving behind a baby. He is likely wondering if what happened to Jasmine could happen to Louis."

"Well, of course not!"

"That is logic speaking, my Athena-friend. None of us have a crystal ball."

CHAPTER 43

AS IS ALWAYS THE way, Illy's waters broke in the dark hours of the night. She labored alone for a while but finally woke the girls—one to stay with her, the other to come and wake us.

Like all houses here, we had no locks, so Cam and I woke to the sound of tapping on our bedroom door. We jolted awake in an instant, knowing without words what was happening.

"Go home, Ally," I told her kindly. "I will be there in just a minute. Just let me get dressed."

Cam, dressing hurriedly, was dispatched to get Sorcha and hope she hadn't been called out.

As I entered, Illy was seated in the large leather chair that had been Luca's favorite. An oversized black recliner he had proudly brought back on one of his visits to the mainland. The only chair he alleged could accommodate his size. *Oh Luca*, I sent a silent wish to my friend. *I wish you could be here. To support your wife and meet your son.*

Illy's groan snapped me out of my trance, and I was at her side in a shot. "What can I do?"

"Nothing," she panted. "Just be here."

Ordering the girls back to bed, I knew they wouldn't sleep, but I also recognized that watching their mother in pain wasn't the greatest choice. Not that anything would happen to her. I had the utmost faith in Sorcha's ability as a doctor. She had undoubtedly saved my life with caesareans for all of my children.

I had no way of timing the contractions, so I tried to count, grimacing as Illy squeezed my hand until the bones grated. No sooner had the contraction passed than I heard people coming in the door. Sorcha ordered me to make her a coffee. I smiled, recognizing doctor mode.

"Cam, can you check on the girls?" I asked quietly. "I sent them to bed, but they won't be asleep." Cam disappeared up the darkened hall as I padded into the kitchen in my socks.

Three mugs of coffee later, and I returned to find Cam sitting beside Illy, holding her hand. I handed him a mug which he accepted with a grateful smile. I held Sorcha's until she finished. I had assisted her with enough surgeries over the past few months, primarily orthopedic, to read her needs and respond to them. We worked well together, and many times she had lamented my choice of profession. Initially, I had suspected asking for my help was a way to help me accept what had happened to me and move on. Acknowledge that medicine had the capacity to heal as well as harm. But as time passed, and she put more pressure on me, I realized she did call me in for my skills. After another silent prayer to Luca for the safety of his son and wife, I took my post on Illy's other side, flanking her. The contractions were coming hard and fast now, and Cam and I focused on keeping her comfortable.

"What will you name him?" I asked as Sorcha handed the tiny bundle to my friend. Cam helped Sorcha to clean up before leaving, instinctively knowing that I would stay. He needed to get home, to be there in case our children woke. With Cam's shooting, Luca's death, and me being gone for weeks, all of our children still woke during the night and checked in on us.

Waiting until Sorcha was out of earshot, Illy whispered, "How does he look? Is he ... damaged?"

"He is perfect," I assured her, stroking her sweaty hair from her face. "He is absolutely beautiful."

Illy paused, returning to my original question. "I thought about naming him Luca, but I am worried it will be too difficult. For him and me."

"Why for him?"

"Well, his father died in fairly tragic circumstances before he was born."

"So did my sister. I named my first child Katrin."

"Yes, but when you named your daughter, you weren't aware your sister was still alive. And no one here knew her. When your Katrin introduces herself, no one looks at her with pity, remembering what happened to her namesake."

"I see your point. What will you do?"

"I have been researching other variations, but they all sound similar. Lucas, Luke, Lucian. They all derive from the same Latin word. It means bringer of light."

"That is very fitting."

"I thought about using Luca as his middle name. No one uses them anyway."

Mairi, one of the women we had saved from Mousa, was a talented calligrapher. As her gift to each newborn child, she gave them a beautiful handwritten birth certificate detailing their name, date and time of birth, and the names of their parents and siblings. She also included a short Gaelic blessing at the bottom. I had one for each of my children and cherished them. But it was the only time I had used my children's middle names. Aside from a few people who went by their surname, usually where there were multiple people with the same name, even those weren't widely used here.

"Including Luca's name would be lovely," I said but went on, knowing what she was really asking me. "It was so hard, having a child, alone at that point, and desperately wanting to discuss names but unable to."

"I'm so glad I have you."

"What was your father's name?"

"Alasdair. But everyone in Australia called him Al."

"What does it mean? Do you know?"

"I borrowed a book from the library in town. It means defender of man."

"Well, I think that is a fitting tribute to his father. He was a god among men, Ils."

"That he was. My father was, too. Alasdair Luca Morgan Cadman..." She tried the name out as she gazed at her miracle.

"Do you want to try to feed him?"

"No, I just want to sleep."

Supporting Illy as she stumbled down the hallway to her bed, I set up a pillow fort around baby Alasdair so he could sleep safely and Illy could rest.

"Get some sleep," I whispered, kissing her, then the baby's head. "I will see you all in the morning."

"Goodness, she is a prickly little creature," Cam murmured, rolling over to warm me as I slipped into bed, shivering. He pulled me close, my frozen limbs thawing against his warm torso. A layer of snow coated the outside of the dome, but we were fortunate that it didn't permeate. As protected as we were in our little cocooned world, it was still bitterly cold.

"Ceri?" I yawned, snuggling in close to his warmth.

"For all their faults, none of our children could be described as prickly. Feisty and determined. Argumentative and demanding. But not prickly."

"What has she done this time?"

"When I got home from Illy's a little while ago, I found her in the kitchen. I walked in as she was cramming bread and jam into her mouth. I asked her if she was hungry. She lied to my face. I mean, she had a mouthful of bread, the slice still in her hand, jam dripping down her chin, and said, 'No.'"

"In the middle of the night?"

"Then I asked her what she was doing, and she replied, 'Nothing.' Her face turned red, so she clearly knew that she was lying to me. I told her she could have as much food as she wanted, but we just needed to be mindful that there was enough for everyone else to have breakfast. That loaf of bread was all we have at the moment, and it takes time to make more."

"What did she say?"

"She got quite hostile and argued that she wasn't eating the bread. All the while, the half-eaten slice is in her hand, hidden behind her back as she licks her lips to hide the evidence. I tried to talk to her about the value of honesty. She can have as much food as she likes, but she needs to tell the truth and remember others. But it was the next part that shocked me and why I couldn't get back to sleep. She said that all the stories we tell are lies. She said that *everything* here is a lie. Then I tried to explain to her the difference between fiction and a lie."

"How did you explain it?"

"I said that when there is intent to deceive another person, it is a lie. A story is for entertainment, to make people happy, but it doesn't hurt anyone."

"That is a wonderful description. What did she say to that?"

"She just reiterated that all the books we read her, all the songs we sing, everything here is a lie. Realizing the futility in having a moral conversation with a young child well past midnight, I told her to enjoy her sandwich and went to bed."

"She was gone when I came through just now. Illy told me she caught her taking fruit out of the greenhouse last week. She only got caught as she dropped the peach on the ground, and when Illy asked her about it, she tried to pretend that it had fallen, and she was just picking it up. Illy said that there were bite marks in it, and she had peach juice dripping down her chin. It appears our Miss Ceri has an awful lot of trouble in telling the truth."

"Agreed. How on earth do we deal with that?"

"Goodness knows. The others never had an issue telling the truth from a lie. It isn't like we starve her. I'd love to ask Illy for ideas, but not right now. She will have her hands full with the baby."

"What did she name him?"

"Alasdair Luca."

CHAPTER 44

"**DO YOU EVER FEEL** guilty that the kids don't have many toys? That they don't get lots of things to unwrap?"

"Not really," I confessed. "I often only had one or two things to open, and rarely were they frivolous."

"I just have memories of being surrounded in shredded wrapping paper on Christmas morning. Unwrapping gifts and enjoying the thrill of unwrapping each one. Maybe I didn't unwrap diamond jewelry or a Lamborghini under the tree like *you*," he smirked as I rolled my eyes, "but my parents always spoiled us."

"They may not be spoiled, but I believe our children have a far better life. Far fewer risks. They have a supportive community, aren't in danger of traffic, drugs, and many diseases have been eradicated."

"Do you think *we* are better off now?"

Recalling my conversation with Illy six months ago as we escaped, I struggled to form an adequate answer. Life was simpler here, better for the kids, but the likelihood of me being held captive in a medical facility was non-existent in Melbourne. Not wanting to ruin the mood, I answered, "They know what is important. Did unwrapping all of those Christmas gifts in our lifetime make us better people? Did it prepare us for this?"

"Of course not. I just loved it—that's all."

"They will never know any different."

"True. Christmas was the epitome of consumerism. Sales! Must buys! It went for months. Shopping, buying everyone the perfect gift. It caused me so much angst, never knowing what to buy someone. What if they hated it? Observing faces in case they showed their disappointment. Did they wear or use the item that was gifted? Then the sales after Christmas. The waste must have been horrendous."

As I placed the last of the carefully wrapped gifts under the tree, I asked, "Is there anything you want for Christmas?"

"A wish or a gift?"

Tilting my head, I looked at him suspiciously and responded, "Either."

"Well, you remember that black lacy set I got you for our wedding?" he said with a little too much enthusiasm. His face flushed.

"That was years ago! I've had two more children since then! What makes you think it will still fit? Besides, you got me more when we stopped in Adelaide."

"That one is special. You haven't changed in the years since I picked it out. Tonight?" he asked hopefully.

I exhaled. "Maybe. Surely one of the newer ones is better."

"Why not that one?"

I exhaled, not wanting to explain. Concern crossed his face, and I relented. "That one is very skimpy. It shows ... well, everything."

"That is kind of the point."

"I mean, you can see my scars," I whispered. Three caesareans and now more recent wounds to add to the mix, and I looked like a patchwork quilt.

"Oh, honey." His arms came around me as I stiffened my spine and swore I wouldn't fall apart. "I don't mind. I don't even see them."

I sniffed.

"But you do?" he asked gently.

I nodded, not wanting to open the floodgates. We had been back six months, and I had held it in. Not let him know how much that time was always foremost in my mind.

"You still have nightmares." It was a statement, not a question.

Burying my head farther into his chest, I didn't respond. Damn. I had woken him then.

"It's okay, honey. You don't need to wear anything if it makes you uncomfortable."

My head snapped up, and I looked him in the eyes. "That isn't it. One is love. One was assault."

"Then what is it?"

"I just felt so helpless. I have never felt like that in my life. My mind was fighting, but my body couldn't. Everything was out of my control. What we ate, when they bathed us, the surgeries. Him. I was utterly powerless."

Cam's arms tightened. When he spoke, it wasn't what I expected. "Speak to Isla."

"What?"

"Speak to Isla. She can help. She knows what that feels like, remember? Better than anyone, she knows. She might have some ideas."

Instinctively, I wanted to argue, but logic took hold. Isla did indeed know what it felt like to be held against your will. Helpless. Powerless. To feel like a victim.

"I don't want to cause her any trauma. Bring back old memories."

"Well, you can't speak to Illy. She is likely still coping with her own trauma—Luca, Clava, and now Alasdair. Isla is stronger than you think, and she would do anything to help you. You just need to ask."

"I will," I promised. "But after Christmas. I can wait a few more days."

Illy, with two-day-old Alasdair and the girls came for Christmas Eve. Summer and Ally were unusually subdued. Then I caught the glare Illy shot in their direction and had to hide a smirk. Clearly, they had been threatened with punishment if they misbehaved, although Cam and I didn't mind. Katrin was hardly an angel with no filter between brain and mouth.

After dinner, we sat on the couches as she held him, sleeping, and we watched the children sing the carols they had been practicing with Bridget at school, amidst raucous laughter. Ceridwen was looking increasingly uncomfortable if someone got the words or timing wrong.

"It is okay," I whispered to her as they argued over what to sing next. "No one minds."

"It is a mistake," she protested. "We should always strive for perfection."

"Sometimes. But it is Christmas. We are here to have fun with our family. It isn't about being right or wrong."

She nodded but plainly wasn't convinced.

Cam returned with the bowls of popcorn and chocolate milk, a particular treat made from blocks of chocolate Illy and I had found in Edinburgh. With the children seated on the floor and the three adults on the couch, we took turns reading Christmas stories by lamplight. I watched Illy surreptitiously as she gazed at the miracle in her arms as she fed him. An enormous baby, he already had traits of his father; I was thrilled to see Luca's dark hair and honey-colored skin as well as his massive hands and feet. Even this early, there was no denying his parentage.

Ceri sat with her arms folded and a scowl on her face. Perhaps she didn't like the book Cam was reading: 'Twas the night before Christmas. It was one of our children's favorites. I leaned forward and whispered, not wanted to disrupt the other children who were listening intently, lying back on cushions, eating popcorn.

"What is wrong? Don't you like the story?"

She paused, unwilling to say anything.

"What is it?" I pushed.

"It is all lies," she muttered.

Cam, overhearing her words, turned to look at me behind her head, not breaking his reading.

"It is a story, sweetheart. It is just for fun," I assured her. "Just listen and enjoy."

Letting the children stay up late was a special treat and one we secretly hoped would allow us a tiny sleep-in Christmas morning. Every year we tried this trick, usually to no avail. It was late when we wished Illy and her girls goodbye, all yawning madly, promising to save gift unwrapping for when they arrived after breakfast in the morning.

"Merry Christmas." I hugged my friend goodnight. Her first Christmas without Luca was undoubtedly going to be difficult for her and the girls.

The sound of terror woke me. Groggily, I stirred as I sensed Cam bolt upright beside me, sniffing the air. The waft of smoke hit my nostrils simultaneously, and we fell out of bed. I hadn't smelled smoke like this in years, and this wasn't the clean smell of wood smoke, the type produced by a campfire. This was an acrid smell of something burning that shouldn't be burned. The smell of an industrial fire.

Flinging open the bedroom door, we were struck full in the face by billowing black smoke, choking and blinding us temporarily, and the roar of flames. Cam grabbed two heavy wool blankets from the bed, threw one over me and another draped over himself as he called for the children. Xanthe's shrill screams cut through the still night air, trapped in her room. We felt our way through the blinding, acrid smoke and opened her door. As the faint light filtered through her window, I could just make out her silhouette, sitting on her bed, arms around her knees, screaming hysterically.

Cam bellowed at me over the roaring of the flames. "*Get out!*" I watched him scoop her up, and she clung to him, petrified.

I started for the door but turned back to bang on Louis's door. Since she had arrived, Ceri had only been able to sleep in Louis's room. We had put two single beds in there, but knew it was temporary. Coming from a dormitory, she preferred not to sleep alone, telling us she had been scared for the months she had slept alone living with Angus. Baby steps, Illy had suggested. Slow and steady.

"*Louis! Go out the window!*" I screamed between coughs, the ash burning my gullet. "*Smash it. Get out now!*"

I heard the thumping on the wooden floor and a few bangs.

"I can't!" he called, panicked.

"Get a boot. A chair. Something heavy. Throw it through!" I spluttered. "Use a blanket to protect yourself as you climb through. Look after Ceri. Stay safe!"

A few seconds later, I heard the shattering of glass. Katrin appeared at my side, clutching my hand as I fought to see through the haze. Coughing and choking, I dragged Kat out the kitchen door into the night, and we gasped for breath as the night sky was illuminated with the glowing orange of our home. My lungs were singed from the acrid smoke. Kat doubled over, choking. Louis and Ceri appeared beside me in the dark, looking petrified.

"Are you okay?" I croaked, and I checked them both over, my throat burning from the ashes.

They nodded, and I pushed them away.

"Go around the other side of the greenhouse," I urged. "Stay out of the smoke. Take Kat. Help her. She has inhaled a lot of smoke."

Watching the three of them dart around the greenhouse, I saw Sorcha and Di, Illy, Jamie, and Jacinda appear from their homes, horror on their faces illuminated by the glow of our home. Their children behind them, baby Alasdair screeching in Illy's arms.

Our houses were so close. If our roof caught fire, there was a good chance it would ignite Illy's, even though there was no wind here. I felt the movement of the air from the turbines in the distance.

"Please don't be blowing this way," I prayed.

"Come on!" Sorcha yelled and started filling buckets, pots, and anything they could with water from the tap outside the shed, tackling the base of the fire but making little impact. As I grabbed a bucket, I saw Jamie disappear into the greenhouse, making me cross. Couldn't he help? Were his precious plants more important? It isn't like the local fire brigade were on their way. We had no way of controlling this if it reached the roof. The roof frame would burn, and the entire building collapse. Between bucket loads, I bellowed for Cam as the gray-black smoke billowed out, making me cough. Soon there would be nothing of our home left.

Cam's silhouette appeared in the doorway, staggering with a child in each arm. I rushed forward and took them from him as he doubled over, coughing like he would die.

Jamie appeared with the greenhouse hose and rushed into the house, the hose spraying everywhere. Years ago, Cam had hooked up a hose from the nearby loch to his beloved greenhouse to supplement the watering system. I issued a mental apology to Jamie as I watched him tackle the heart of the blaze as the rest put out spot fires with buckets.

When dawn arrived, we surveyed the damage. Half our home was gutted. Our children sat on the small rock retaining wall near the greenhouse, tears streaking their soot-smeared faces. I turned to Cam to say something but noticed him looking at his feet.

"Your feet are charred!" I exclaimed, attracting Sorcha's attention. "You have burns up your legs and arms!"

"I'm okay. I can't feel them."

"Fuck. That is bad, Campbell. Full-thickness burns kill the nerves and will need grafting. Come with me. Now!"

I watched as Cam trailed behind her, the blanket still wrapped around him. For the first time in my life, I wished we both slept in full pajamas. *At least we may have something left,* I thought as I looked down at the long t-shirt I wore, pulling it self-consciously past my hips. A cry from Xanthe pulled my attention away from my state of undress.

"It's okay," I soothed. "It is only things. You are all alive. Everything else can be replaced," I choked, remembering the items, the photos we could never replace.

Illy's spare arm slipped around me as emotion took hold, calming me. Not since I had left Melbourne had I held such attachment for a place, for possessions. Suddenly it was all too much. "We've lost everything!" I sobbed. "And it's Christmas!"

"No, you have lost nothing," she soothed. "Everyone you care about is fine."

"Cam's photos of Laetitia, of his family. My family. They are all gone," I cried, feeling foolish. After all, she had lost her husband. Here I was, crying over objects. Cam's burns may be severe, but he would live.

Illy stiffened, and I pulled back to look at her. But she wasn't watching me. She was watching Ceridwen, sitting stony-faced on the wall.

"Is there something you would like to tell us?" Illy asked firmly.

Ceri looked away.

"Ceridwen!" Illy barked, and we all jumped. "Why did you do this?"

"I... I don't know..." The tiny voice, barely above a squeak, came from the angelic-looking child with the soot-smeared face.

Louis rounded on her. "You did this? To my home? To my family? You burned down our home! You nearly killed us! Do you not know how dangerous it is to light fires under the dome?"

Ceridwen shrugged and looked away.

"They are not *my* family," she mumbled.

Louis's face broke, shooting pain into my heart. He felt responsible for her, I knew. He had asked her to come here, be his sister. He turned away, unable to look at her. Illy purposefully handed me the sleeping bundle, and firmly gripping her shoulder, marched Ceridwen off to her house as the other children fired off angry questions.

Leaving Di with the children, I followed Cam into the vet shed and, waiting until Sorcha went to collect medical supplies, told him what Illy suspected.

"What are we going to do?" I asked over the sleeping baby in my arms.

"Oh, honey, only you can answer that. Do we ask her if she wants to live with Jorja and the other girls?"

"I don't think Jorja would trust her after she broke Ruby's arm last week, then lied about it. Sorcha and I needed to pin the bone; the break was so nasty. That has put an end to that relationship for a little while. Bridget was seething when she brought Ceri back. I've never seen her so angry."

Silence rose between us as he sat on the stainless table, wrapped in the singed blanket.

"What do we do? She tried to kill us, Frey. All of us. I get that she is traumatized. Had a difficult life before she came here. I am prepared to forgive most things. But in the months she has been here, she has hurt children, lied, and stolen. Now we find out she is homicidal? I can't let her put our children in danger. She could have killed them. Us too. If Xanthe hadn't woken us when she did…"

"I know. I'll speak with Illy."

CHAPTER 45

LEAVING CAM AND AVOIDING the children who were fossicking through the charred remains, I carried baby Alasdair home.

"Where is she?"

"I sent her to clean out the chook pen."

I smiled through the exhaustion and distress. Illy firmly believed in children doing chores in consequence for poor behavior choices.

"Why did she do it?

"She can't explain it. She has no words to describe this complicated cocktail of emotions raging through her. Honestly, I suspect it is several things. Wanting to destroy what belongs to others. Confusion about this new life, one that encourages what she sees as idleness and imperfection. A fascination with fire. Resentment that she is now part of a family, one among a group. She doesn't feel special. And jealousy, an incredible amount of jealousy, particularly toward your girls. She knows they are yours, and she isn't."

"How did she even do it? We have no matches here."

"She read in a book about starting a fire with flint. She found some and practiced. Then she waited until you were all asleep and set fire to the gifts under the tree."

"The tree? That is what she set fire to?"

"The gifts specifically. If you think about it, they are the symbol of her not belonging."

"But there were gifts there for her!"

"I know, but she sees Christmas as a lie. The songs, the stories. 'They are all lies,' she kept telling me. She saw all the gifts, and two were for her. She is used to being treated as an individual, not one of a group. She doesn't see herself as an equal. She is a challenging child," Illy admitted. "I'm no pediatric specialist, but she is likely permanently affected by the lack of love she was shown for the first years of her life. There are studies of children in orphanages who fail to thrive because of a lack of physical contact. I am not saying she is evil, but she has no compassion. She doesn't know how to be part of a family. She can't see what she did was malicious and dangerous. I'm sorry to say Freyja, but I think the best option is to ask her if she wants to go back to Clava. It is all she knows. Likely she will be happier there."

"But she is my niece. She is Kat's baby."

"I know that. But she nearly killed you and your family. Can you really ever trust her again? Had the fire taken hold, she could have killed my children, Frey. Can you forgive that? Because I can't. After everything I have lost, I can't lose them, too."

Silently, I wandered outside to find Cam, his arms and feet wrapped in bandages, poking around the rubble to see what was left of our life.

"I wish Laetitia were here," I mused aloud, making Cam's eyes pop. "Well, you said she was a pediatric psychologist."

"She was training to be."

"Would she know what to do with Ceridwen?"

"Possibly. She did volunteer work with challenging children. But you don't think that would be a tough situation? 'Hi honey, here is my first wife. Her niece is displaying some challenging behaviors. What do you recommend we do?'"

"Perhaps a little awkward."

"She would have helped, though. What did Illy say?"

"Illy readily admits that she is no pediatric expert, but her professional and personal opinion is that we send Ceri back to Clava. She is likely to get the support she needs, and it is a lifestyle she is used to. Being here is stressful for her, too."

Seeing Thorsten crying, I rushed to comfort him. "It's alright," I soothed. "We are all alive. We have each other. We can build a new house."

"But it's Christmas!" he howled. "Everything is gone."

"Not everything." Kat smiled at him. "Look over here. Most of your toys are okay. We need to wash them and fix a couple, but most are okay."

I looked where she stood. She was right. The heart of our home, the living room, and the kitchen were burned beyond recognition. But being a converted barn, the walls were solid and still stood, blackened. The bedrooms were newer and farther away, and although parts were a little charred, wet and smoky, most things would be salvageable. Tears filled my eyes as I watched Cam pull the wooden boxes and bags, slightly damp, from under our bed. Our photos. The one thing we had that we couldn't replace.

"Mummy, I don't want to be a fireman anymore!" Thorsten wailed.

"Duly noted," said Cam seriously.

By mid-morning, all of our friends had visited after learning what had befallen us. There had never been a fire on Lewis, and many people expressed concern about the long-term impact on the dome's fabric. Everyone brought food, but many brought empty boxes and bags to package up what could be salvaged. Isla oversaw the removal of the equipment from the vet shed and taken up to the other clinic in town. What furniture could be saved was aired, cleaned, and moved into the shed. "You can live there until they build you a new house," she announced. "Mitchell has already rallied the crews. They start next week."

"Thank you." I threw my arms around her, and she froze, not used to me showing affection. But her arms came around me and squeezed me tight.

"We'd have you with us, but this might take a few months. I'd likely kill ye."

Cam and I hadn't had time to talk about what we would do while we rebuilt, but we couldn't cram our family of six, seven if you counted Ceri, into anyone else's home. Homes here were deliberately small—partly as they were easier to heat and clean, but mostly as no one needed a large home. Knowing that a new house would be built soon, not waiting for spring, was an enormous relief. We could survive almost anything for the short term, even living in the vet shed. One solid wall was constructed of mudbrick, but the remaining walls were metal with no insulation to keep us warm.

"Xan, how did you even know?" I asked her gently as we sifted through the charred remains of the kitchen, placing salvageable items in a box.

She looked at me guiltily. Katrin could lie bald-faced, but Xanthe hadn't mastered the art.

"What?" I ordered.

Xanthe looked down at her soot-covered feet, and tears started to fall. "I was bringing Lambie inside," she whispered, waiting for the lecture about how animals don't sleep in bedrooms, especially now that Lambie was a full-sized sheep. "It was cold, and it is Christmas, and..."

"It's okay." I wrapped my arms around her shoulders and pulled her close. "That sheep of yours may have saved all of our lives. That doesn't mean she can live with us in the shed, though," I warned. "It will be hard enough with all of us in there without a sheep as well."

"Mum, Jam got out when I went looking for Lambie. I looked and looked, and I can't find her anywhere. I'm so sorry!"

"That's okay, sweetheart. You likely saved her life, too." Now that Jam was old, she enjoyed living inside more but occasionally liked an overnight stroll. I hadn't thought about her during the fire or aftermath. But she would turn up when she was ready.

By midday, we had moved our undamaged belongings into the shed, partitioning off a sleeping area and a small section for cooking. Bodhi had brought us a new biogas cooker, and Sorcha and Di had spent the afternoon moving our old algal tanks that had survived the blaze. Jam, much to everyone's relief, came strolling out of the woods like nothing had happened, demanding food.

"I'm so sorry for ruining your Christmas," I kept telling people, genuinely remorseful. This was one day people spent with their families. Celebrating. Instead, they were all here helping us.

Finally, Sorcha stopped dead in her tracks and barked at me. "Will you just stop it! You would help anyone else in the same situation, and you know it. Besides, what did you do to be sorry for? Nearly dying? It is that little bitch who needs to apologize."

Di glared at her warningly, and Sorcha scowled and returned to her work, hooking up the biogas to the bioreactor.

"I think Illy is right," Cam admitted as we ambled through the forest later that evening, seeking solitude from the craziness of the day. Cam's feet had been singed but not severely burned. Illy had donated a pair of Luca's boots, which, several sizes too big, fit over all the bandaging. Even the injuries to his arms were superficial. If kept clean, there was little risk of permanent damage. Running on adrenaline was the likely reason for not noticing the pain sooner.

"I don't think I can sleep with her in the house. She nearly killed our children, Frey. We can't turn her back on her. Besides, they know what she did. They won't forgive her in a hurry. If ever."

"Let me see if there is somewhere she can stay. Let's see Bridget. Get her to radio Clava. Can you walk that far?"

CHAPTER 46

"TELL ME ABOUT HER."

Ashton flinched slightly at the brusqueness of my tone. I was in no mood for small talk. Bridget had been sent to greet him as he arrived at Stornoway Harbor, a place I rarely visited with flashbacks of Luca and Cam still tormenting me. I hadn't seen Ashton since he had released us, and I was surprised at how much seeing him made my skin crawl.

Bridget had brought him to Sorcha's home as a neutral space. Sitting in what was previously Illy and Luca's home, on Sorcha's lounge, made me feel sick, fighting the flashbacks that threatened to over-whelm me. As Ashton settled and Di served him tea, the atmosphere was thick with tension. Shuffling and mumbling filled the space as we braced ourselves, fearful of what we might learn.

"The child..." Ashton quickly corrected himself as he saw the color rise in my face, "Ceridwen," he said pointedly, "was born to a surrogate and raised by the community on Clava."

"She was born on Clava?" I asked, surprised. That wasn't what Angus had told me.

"No. She was born on Auckland. She was raised on Clava."

"Did my sister give birth to her?"

Ashton paused, assessing the risk, but responded. "She did."

"Were there others? Kat's children, I mean."

"Yes."

I sniffed, desperately wanting to know more, but knowing that he had spoken the truth. Right now, Ceri's welfare was the most crucial factor. Information about Katrin could wait.

"When did she get taken to Clava?"

"She was a few weeks old."

"You seriously put a baby through *that*!"

"We have refined the process over the past few years. It is far smoother now."

"It would want to be. But why on earth would you do that to a baby?"

"She was one of the first. The chosen ones. We had a clearly defined program for her."

"Chosen ones?" I snapped, frustrated. This would take forever, extracting information line by line. Ashton looked at me cautiously but spoke more freely.

"Ceridwen is one of a small group of children who will ensure the survival of our species. Within sixty years, her descendants, and those of the other children like her, will be able to live outside the domes."

"Outside? How? You told us nothing could survive out there," Di interjected.

"We are working on re-greening the planet, thanks to the moss Campbell discovered. But we have no way of remaining safe out there ourselves. But these children. They will *live*. This is a monumental step forward. It will lessen the reliance on the domed communities and ensure we won't overpopulate."

"I thought the breeding program was the reason we were all chosen?" Sorcha asked.

"That program was phase two. Ensuring that all genomes survived and were carefully matched to ensure all genotypes and genetic material was passed on was critical. The third phase, and the most important part, was to modify a genome to be resistant to the protozoa."

"Resistant?" Cam asked.

"Immune, I guess you could say. It took us a lot longer than we expected to find the key to changing the DNA sequence. Finding candidate zero, the woman who possessed the genome that could be modified, took us many more years than we thought. We were starting to worry that we would never find it within the limited populations we have. When we found the candidate … your sister," he corrected hurriedly, "we knew we had found what we were looking for. Then, as we perfected the technology, we modified the egg and tested the zygote."

Jorja had mentioned genetic engineering once but had never said why. Possibly she didn't know herself. Scanning the room, I saw her standing back with Bridget, listening intently.

"How many babies did Katrin have?"

Ashton looked at me blankly. I doubted he had ever known her name, had ever seen her as a person with a family who loved her.

"My sister. Her name was Katrin. The original donor from whom Ceridwen, Scarlett, and Ruby came?" I enjoyed deliberately provoking him with the use of their names. "How many children did she have?"

"I don't know. But quite a few."

"Where are they?"

"Mostly, they didn't survive the testing phase."

"Testing?" Cam echoed as the bottom dropped out of my stomach. I knew what he had meant. We all did.

"You tested on babies?" Sorcha asked incredulously.

"We had no choice. When we thought we didn't have the right candidate, we thought perhaps one of the next generation would be immune. We were wrong."

"Fuck." I was still reeling from the confirmation that Kat was Ceri's mother in more ways than just donating her genetic material. She had been her birth mother. For months I had hoped that Angus had lied to me, taunting me for rejecting him. That she was their biological donor was clear. I saw Ruby and Scarlett as related but removed. Kat had donated half of their genetic material, albeit changed, as it turns out, but Jorja and Bridget had carried, nurtured, and cared for those girls. They were parents to them in every way. But Ceri? How did I give her up now, knowing for sure she was my niece?

"Who raised Ceridwen?" I queried. "Jorja and Bridget said they had never seen her before she came here." I glanced at them for confirmation, and they gave it.

"That is true. After her birth, she was raised in a special facility with other children from selected partnerships."

"You didn't want us to know?" Bridget asked.

"You may have asked questions if you noticed a child looking very much like your own. Questions we didn't want to answer."

"Who is their father?"

"Angus MacLeod is father to all of them. The three of them are blood siblings."

I heard Bridget's sharp intake of breath. Bloody hell. So that was true. Ceri was not only my niece but was related to Louis, too. Louis's great-grandfather was her grandfather. Was that right? My head started spinning.

"Why would you want to reproduce that asshole?" Sorcha sneered.

"All genomes needed to be reproduced, including his. When the first zygote was successful, we thought we needed the same parents. Over time, we worked out that it was the mother only. But that is why the other embryos at that time had the same parentage."

"And you used Katrin because I wouldn't?" I asked, feeling sick.

Ashton looked miserable. "You and he were a pair. That is why you were originally placed in opposing communities. He told me once that he nearly fainted when he heard your name when you first arrived here. He knew *your* name, of course. He was part of the original planning team. He knew you were his chosen match, genetically. I gather he was quite taken with you."

"Who wouldn't be?" Cam's voice beside me made me flush with embarrassment. "She is hot."

"Quite. Well, all three children are resistant to the Vienna Virus. There were five, of course, but now only three remain. There is something about you and your sister. You have the only profile we tested that could be manipulated."

"What do you mean, the only profile? How many did you test?"

Ashton looked at me directly, making me uncomfortable, although I refused to let him see how much he affected me. "Do you want me to answer that?"

Cam cut in. "No, she doesn't. It achieves nothing. Move on."

"Let's just say that you are unique. You have the only genome that we could manipulate so that the offspring were resistant."

"You tested on ... babies?"

"Embryos."

I looked away. I couldn't bear to think of all of those children being tested on. Infected with the protozoa.

"And what about me? My eggs?"

Ashton sighed. "When you destroyed the lab on Auckland Island, you destroyed the other embryos before they could be implanted. Your sister..."

"Say her name!" I barked, and he blinked.

"Katrin..." he whispered.

"Tell me what you did."

"Her body started shutting down. We couldn't put her through the cycle of hormone treatment and harvesting very often. By the end, we could only collect two or three at a time, and only once every six months. But from all the specimens we tested, she was the only one that we could change successfully. Those girls were from the last collection. We kept trying but couldn't retrieve more."

"So, you used me instead?"

"You walked into Clava. We were desperate. We spent the months after you destroyed the facility trying to find another candidate. All over the world, we looked. Tested every sample we had, but none of them were successful. We needed to continue the program. You need to understand, at some point we will outgrow these communities. We need to find a way to survive. In all the testing, all the experiments, it was only your genetic material that was resistant. Yours and your sisters. You will be the mother of the future human race."

"So why did you keep me, Carl?" Illy asked softly.

Ashton looked at her, and I saw what she did. He cared for her.

"I wanted to let you go, but you would have alerted others to Ms. Jorgensen's location. We couldn't do that. We needed her. She was critical to the success of everything we have worked so hard to achieve. Then we learned you were pregnant. We thought it was best to monitor you both. It was only nutritional supplements you were given."

"Monitor?" Illy was incredulous, Alasdair asleep in her arms. "You kept me captive for no reason? Didn't even tell me I was pregnant? Do you know the stress that caused me? Wondering what damage you had inflicted on my child? Dale would have attacked me next. You know that, right? He didn't care I was pregnant. So, forgive me if I don't thank you."

He looked out through the window to the hills beyond, his shoulder slumped.

"If you needed me so much, why did you let me go?" After a period of uncomfortable silence, I said, "That's okay... I don't need to know. I need to ask one thing, though. You said I would be the mother of the human race. How many eggs did you harvest from me?"

"Thirty."

"What happened to them?"

He turned back to look at me. "They were all adapted, fertilized, tested, and implanted in surrogates."

"I have thirty more children?" I croaked.

"Only twenty-four survived the modification process. But they aren't yours."

"How can you say that?" Anger consumed me and erupted. "They are my children as much as those I raise are. What will you do with them?"

Cam's arm pressed on my arm, forcing me to control my outburst.

Ashton paused, checking for danger before proceeding.

"That is why I asked to come here. After what happened with Ceridwen, we recognized that children need to be nurtured, raised in a family."

I nodded in agreement.

"I came to ask if you would take them."

My mouth dropped.

Ashton rushed to press his case. "We need them to survive but also to thrive. We need them to grow up socially adjusted and part of a community. We need these girls to partner up and have more children—to whom they will pass on their immunity. Over time, they will form the basis of a new civilization."

"Twenty-four?" I still couldn't quite comprehend what he was telling me.

"Well, there are twenty-four now, most not yet born, others only a few days old, and there are your sister's three, all of whom are already here. So, twenty-seven children we know will be resistant. While we would have liked more, that is enough to kick-start a new species of human, genetically resilient to the protozoa. Between these children and the moss you discovered Campbell, we have accomplished what we set out to do."

"Twenty-seven?" I croaked. "What about our children?"

"No. Not them," Ashton warned. "Only the zygotes that were genetically modified to reject the protozoa are immune. Those you conceived naturally were not."

"How would you know?" Sorcha asked suddenly.

"We have refined the processing. It is a simple blood test now."

We all noted the word *now*, but no one chose to bite.

"So, you are telling me that with a blood test, you can tell if those children are safe to go out there?"

"I am."

"And all of these children ... passed?"

"They did. These girls can all drink or be exposed to infected water, and it doesn't affect them."

"They are all female?" Sorcha fired at him. "Why?"

"We gave that a lot of thought. Once they were out there in the world, we couldn't stop people from pairing up. There is always the risk that two siblings would inadvertently pair, if not in this generation, in the next one. The modification is on the X chromosome, and as you know, the female carries two X. It made the initial modification easier and would ensure it would be passed on to every offspring. So, we only created female embryos."

The world began to spin, and I dropped my head, willing myself not to faint. Cam's concerned face swam before my eyes as darkness moved inward from the edges of my vision. The woozy feeling took hold as I saw him shoo people away. I heard Sorcha's crisp voice ordering everyone to leave as I struggled to focus on Cam's cerulean blue eyes as he ordered me to look at him.

"Twenty-four," I croaked. "I have twenty-four more children? Daughters?"

I felt Cam's arms scoop me up and carry me out the door as I tried to wrap my mind around all of those new babies. All mine. Who was the father? I couldn't possibly care for that many babies. But how did I leave them with scientists to raise, knowing what they had done to Ceri?

Cam laid me gently on the bed in the corner of the vet shed and ordered the children away. I was tired, he told them. I needed to rest. Grumbling, they disappeared out of the shed, the sounds of their voices reverberating around the walls.

"Are you okay?" he asked as he lay beside me.

Fighting the drowsiness, I tried to smile, but it came out as a grimace. "I am. But holy fucking hell. They stole thirty children from me."

Cam watched, not saying anything.

"And Illy? She was only kept captive because I was. Collateral damage. How can she ever forgive me?"

Cam exhaled sharply.

"I need to hear it. The rest of it. Arrange it, please."

Cam sighed, recognizing the futility in arguing, and left the room.

When we reconvened the following morning, Ashton was more open with the facts, recognizing that no one planned to harm him. He had told us the worst of it. Now I just needed the detail.

Clava and Auckland each had twenty-five surrogates designed to assist any couple, selected or a
love match, who couldn't have children of their own.
I thought of Magali and Nasir, now with two young
children of their own. She had contemplated using a
surrogate but eventually conceived naturally.

"So, you used the Clava surrogates?"

"We did. We wanted to keep them together, keep
a close eye on them. Especially after you escaped, we
needed to protect them at all costs. We were lucky
that we had all available surrogates at the time. We
don't use them much anymore. Most people have at
least one child, often more. Fewer babies are being
born now that we are nearly fifteen years into our
new lives. Each desired partnership also only had
one child."

"Don't the surrogates want to keep the babies?"
Sorcha asked.

Ashton didn't respond.

Remembering the cross-hatched scars across
Katrin's belly, I asked, "They aren't exactly consensual
surrogates, are they? As in, they aren't conscious?"

Sorcha's mouth dropped, and Ashton nodded.

"So, the women held in the facility on Auckland.
The one we destroyed. They were all surrogates?"

Another nod.

"Ceridwen said that she lived in a facility with eleven
other children. Were the surrogates their mothers?"

"They were."

"You said that of the thirty eggs you took from me,
only twenty-four survived?"

"That is correct."

"Are twenty-seven immune children enough?" I
asked softly, making Cam look at me, his mouth open

in astonishment. "I mean, if thousands of people survived, and that original population has now more than doubled, are twenty-seven girls enough?"

"It is. We would have liked more, but those chosen ones will partner up and hopefully have at least two children per couple. So, fifty or so in the next generation. The domes are likely to last for hundreds of years if they aren't breached, so we are safe until the resistant gene can be passed on. Too many children born now, from the same mother, may cause in-breeding within a few generations."

"I don't want to think about how many children you sacrificed in the name of science," Sorcha spat.

Ashton shrugged uncomfortably.

"What do you want to do?" I whispered, despite knowing we were alone. With no insulation, it was freezing in the shed, and it was a bitterly cold winter. Recognizing we couldn't keep them here for months in the inhospitable weather, we had billeted the children out to each of our neighbors to sleep, but they came back for breakfast. Despite the cold, I loved it, snuggled under the weight of several quilts and blankets and sharing the cocoon with a warm-blooded man. Cam lay in the dark beside me, but I knew from his shallow breathing that he wasn't asleep.

"Oh, honey, don't ask me that. They are yours. I want you to care for them. But twenty-four? How on earth do we look after, feed, and educate twenty-four more children? The four we have drive me to the brink of insanity most days."

I smiled in the darkness. Louis was a compliant child, but our three were challenging. Not to mention Ceri, and her fate was as yet undetermined. How could we introduce so many more? But they were special. Children who would ensure the survival of humanity once we could build outside. Would survive even if the domes were breached.

"Do you want Clava to raise them?" he asked softly.

"No... I... maybe... oh, I don't know."

"My darling, I would never give up any child of yours. But there are so many!"

"They aren't *yours*," I probed gently.

"I know that. But does it matter? Louis isn't yours, and I see how much you love him. You risked your life and a lot more to save him. Parenting is more about choosing to love a child. It isn't about whether or not you are related. Many people raise children not their own. Conversely, many people who are blood kin detest each other. So no, that doesn't bother me."

"I know. But so many! And all roughly the same age. Bloody hell. Imagine a birthday party!"

"If they were born via surrogate, they weren't all born on the same day."

"That is true. But close enough."

Cam rolled me into him, and I snuggled against his chest, inhaling his masculine scent.

"Not that I wouldn't have twenty-four of your babies," I murmured. "I would just space them out a little."

"Well, one thing is for certain, you have done *your* bit for humankind."

"I have, haven't I? Oh, how I wish they were yours," I whispered in his ear. "I would take them all in a heartbeat if they were yours."

Sensing I was about to go down the rabbit hole, Cam's mouth found mine in the darkness, putting an end to that conversation. Pressing his lips to mine, crushing. As his mouth became more demanding, more urgent, I melted into him, my limbs softening as his hands touched me. I forgot everything as our souls collided, pushing further inside until we clung to each other, panting and sweating.

CHAPTER 47

THE GOLDEN GLOW OF morning radiated through the single window. Rolling over, my arm struck the empty pillow beside me.

"Mmmm," I groaned, not wanting to be alone this morning, but equally not wanting to leave my warm cocoon to track down my missing husband. Dozing in the dim light, I lapsed in and out of sleep until the metal door closing jolted me awake, and the enticing aroma of coffee aroused me from my stupor.

"I'm sorry, darling," he breathed in my ear as he slipped into bed beside me. "I didn't mean to wake you."

"Where were you?" I asked. "I woke, and you were gone."

"Just a quick errand. But I brought you coffee."

Struggling to force myself up, I let Cam fluff the pillows behind me so I could sit upright in bed, pushing my bedraggled mass of hair out of my face. A wooden tray Luca had made from a fallen birch tree spread across my legs. I stared at it for a moment, remembering the Christmas he had presented it to me. So many times he had teased me about my inability to function first thing in the morning.

On one raiding trip outside the dome, Luca had encouraged the team to bring back industrial coffee machines taken from a warehouse that supplied cafés. But Luca's pride was the roasting equipment. After years of experimentation, Cam and his team had finally learned to grow coffee in one of the new hothouses, with different varietals being grown. Luca oversaw the harvest of the coffee, which he was pedantic about, ensuring the ripeness was the same so it didn't spoil the flavor. He had set up a small shed near the hothouses and, over a period of months, taught himself to remove the parchment layer and roast the green beans in small batches. After a few failed attempts, he had perfected the art, with three different styles available via Illy's trade. Cam and I preferred the darker style, which we found much richer in flavor. Now we consumed our own beans, grinding them daily, and I regularly awoke to the low burr of the grinder in the morning. Our machine had burned in the fire, but a replacement had quickly been sourced from one of the warehouses. Luca always thought ahead and had obtained replacement parts.

"Just because we live in isolation doesn't mean we can't enjoy small luxuries." Luca had grinned at me as he had demonstrated his new toy.

Blinking away memories of Luca, with three sips of steaming coffee, I could string a sentence together coherently.

"Where did Ashton go?"

"I have no idea," Cam admitted. "And I honestly don't care. He isn't here. That is all I know. I know he released you, and I am thankful for that. But he kept you and Illy prisoner. He allowed them to do unspeakable things to you. Likely he ordered it. Does it make me a bad person if I don't want to be around him?"

"Not at all. I blame him, but sometimes I wonder if he hadn't set us free, would we still be there? They would have kept repeating the cycle on me until they killed me."

I realized as soon as the words left my mouth that I had confirmed his suspicions.

"You need to speak with Isla."

I didn't want to respond to that, seeing the look of concern etch his features. So I had woken him last night. The door had rattled, and I had seen the door slam behind me in the meeting room. So many nights, I had woken in the dark, and for a moment, panicked that I was still there, bound and tied to the cold, metal bed frame. Even sometimes, lying in bed, I could feel Dale's sweaty hands insistent on my thighs. At least the panic attacks that had woken me every night in the early days had lessened. Waking in a sweat, my heart pounding, remembering waking from the surgery, knowing what they had stolen from me, but not knowing why. Cam had seen me wake in a panic enough times to know that time still haunted me. Likely always would.

"Frey." He looked at me, his head tilted to the side. "Do you want to know who the father is? The father of these girls?"

I pondered that as I sipped and stared out the window at the bright new day. *Do I?*

"I think so," I admitted. "Not that I care, but I will always wonder. If they do come here, and I am not saying I want them to," I hastened to say, "I would watch them and try to guess who they look like. It is a feeling I can't quite describe. Knowing that I didn't sleep with anyone. I didn't grow these children. Yet apparently, they are mine. I remember every second of what they did to us in that place. I know what they stole from me. But it doesn't feel quite real. Does that make sense?"

"It does."

"But then I wonder, what if the father is someone like Dale? Will I ever be able to look at those children and not see him? Remember what he did to us? Maybe it is better to know of their existence but not know *them*."

"Have you thought any more about what you want to do?"

"How do I care for that many children? But conversely, how do I not? They are mine, but they aren't. I don't know what I want. Maybe I need to talk to Ashton again. Work through the options."

Cam sipped his coffee and changed the subject to seasonal planting, a topic he could rabbit on about for hours, allowing me to zone out and not pay attention but appreciate the companionship. *Twenty-four more children.* That was more than our tiny school could accommodate, and here we were, homeless. How on earth did you feed or change nappies for that many babies? Maybe it was best that Ceri had siblings? Other children on Clava to play with?

The children arrived, looking sleepy, seeking breakfast. Cam made them toast and chattered away, leaving me to my thoughts. *How many of Katrin's eggs did they harvest over all those years?* I wondered. *What happened to them all?* After I told her what had happened to me at Clava, Jorja had admitted that they had conducted many retrieval procedures on Kat, but she never told me what happened to the embryos. Now I knew. By the time Ceridwen, Ruby, and Scarlett were born, and they learned that only Kat's embryos could be modified, they had realized there weren't many eggs left to harvest. By necessity, they had slowed down. Then I had taken a hand. As I finished my coffee, I realized that if they had harvested ten to twenty of her eggs in a cycle, they must have tested on hundreds of babies before they worked out the successful method. Kat had been there for over twelve years. Katrin's babies, those that had been sacrificed, had paved the way for my own to survive. But were they mine?

"I must go," Cam announced, with groans and mumbling all around. "I'll drop in at Juliette's and get some bread."

"I'm going to have a shower at Isla's," I told the children. "I won't be long."

Returning somewhat refreshed, I saw Louis turning on the biogas to cook porridge for the younger ones.

"You are such a good brother. Always helping others."

"I couldn't help Ceridwen," he said sadly.

"That had nothing to do with you. She had a challenging life before she came to us. She needs some time. She is safe with her sisters for now."

He nodded and turned away. I knew that Ceri leaving would hurt him terribly. He felt he had failed her. But the truth was, Auckland and Angus had failed her. Was that what would happen to these children if we didn't take them all? I hugged each of mine, and they looked at me suspiciously, instinctively knowing something was wrong.

"What is it, mum?" Katrin asked, her face screwed up in puzzlement.

"What do you mean?" I feigned ignorance. "I hug you all the time."

"You do. But something is up. You look weird."

"Gee, thanks. I'm fine. Now, what are we having?"

After sending the children to school, I spent the day pottering around the makeshift house, tidying up, but my mind churned over these children. How could I care for them all? There was no way we could accommodate them all. Even at four to a room, we would need five more rooms. We would need to get a building. A bunkhouse, by the looks of it. But what about Cam? I picked up his jacket, discarded carelessly on the back of a chair. How did I do this to him? I know what he said. But Louis was different. He was Cam's child. Laetitia's admittedly and not mine, but I had been in his life since he was a year old. We knew his parentage. His mother had passed, tragically. These children were manipulated. Would it affect them? *No*, I realized as soon as the thought crossed my mind. Ruby and Scarlett were normal little girls. There was nothing unusual about them. Ceri was highly intelligent, but cold and calculating. But that was nothing to do with her genetics. She had lived a life devoid of love and care for six years. I wondered if it would take another six for her to overcome her early years—if she could overcome it at all. The enormity of what I was contemplating struck me. I loved my children with every fiber of my being, but they were exhausting. Dealing with disagreements, being challenged over every little thing. Every request being met with an argument or a negotiation. How on earth could I manage more?

How did you do it? I silently asked Laetitia's ghost. How did you let another woman raise your child? I couldn't possibly expect Cam to adopt that many children, mine, but not his. And not mine by choice. They had been stolen from me, manipulated, and grown by strangers. Perhaps Ashton was right. They weren't mine.

Cam returned early afternoon, looking exhausted but very pleased with himself.

"What?" I asked suspiciously.

"Nothing."

"Nothing, my ass. What is it?"

"Really, it is nothing. But get changed, will you? There is a town meeting tonight in Garynahine. Ashton is going to speak."

I pursed my lips in annoyance. I wasn't ready for everyone to know.

Cam saw the look. "It is okay. Really. Sorcha and Di will be there. Illy too. We won't let people gossip about you."

Looking around as we entered, I thought the entire community appeared to be here. There was little room to stand. Shoulder to shoulder, people stood, jostling for a view of the small stage—the stage I had stood on several times to address the group.

"We need to build a larger community space," I murmured.

Cam grinned. "We do."

Ashton took the stage with Jorja, I noted with some surprise. She introduced him and spoke about the key phases of the project. Ensuring that we, the healthiest specimens, survived. Ensuring all genotypes and phenotypes were replicated in the selected breeding program. They spoke about the testing they had conducted, their findings. With some hesitance, Ashton advised they had commenced phase three, learning how to modify the genetic makeup of some embryos, and ensure that they were resistant to the protozoa that still raged around us. I felt the chill of the crowd turn against him. *Please don't tell them they are mine.* But he kept speaking.

"There are now twenty-seven children who are resilient. Immune."

The shocked silence spoke volumes. *Are these mutated little beasts?*

"It was quite a shock to learn yesterday, but my children," Jorja said, looking out across the crowd, "are resistant. Ceridwen, too. But now, there are more. Twenty-four more. All girls. Some newborn, some not born yet. Each will form a crucial part of our future. A future that will see our children's children able to live outside these domes once more. Be able to resettle our world. It is essential that these children survive, reproduce. Clava has recognized that these children need a home, a family. Freyja and Campbell can't take them all. The question now is, how do we raise them?"

Murmurs rose like a cloud and hung above the seated heads.

A loud voice cut through the thrum. "I'll take one."

My head spun around in shock to see Illy's hand high in the air, not looking at Jorja, but watching me, a beaming smile on her face. Baby Alasdair slept in a sling strapped to her front. "I would love another child, especially one that will secure the future for all of our children."

I looked at her, my mouth agape. I had avoided her since Ashton had confirmed that she had only been held hostage because of me, not knowing how she would respond. But ... this. I never expected this.

"So will we." I would have recognized Sorcha's crisp, rational tone anywhere, and a tear rolled down my cheek as I realized what was happening.

"And us." I saw Jamie, his arm around Jacinda with his hand up. "What is one more?" He shrugged.

"We would love another child," a familiar voice spoke. I followed the sound and saw Isla and Fraser beaming at me.

"Liar," I mouthed across the room at her. Isla grinned back.

"Count us in!" Josh and Orla called across the room.

"And the rest?" Jorja asked Cam, knowingly.

"Nine will travel to Newgrange," Cam spoke clearly, ignoring the crowd's rising chatter.

I gasped. "Newgrange? Why?"

"You have friends beyond Lewis, you know. Callie and Tadhg, Makayla and Jakob, Kevin and Nadia, Nasir and Magali, and several other couples have all asked to parent one of these children."

"Really?"

"Truly. Everyone recognizes that although they didn't come about in the most ideal of circumstances, these girls are special. They will be the mothers of humanity. If these children can be spread a little more widely, then they will probably choose partners from those communities and help ensure more than just this one survives. Then another six will travel to Orkney. Do you remember those women you saved? They are desperate to return the favor. Raise a life in return for the ones you were responsible for saving. The children they have had since returning are all because of you. As Alize phrased it when I asked, 'Freyja saved many generations of Orcadians. We would be privileged to return the favor by nurturing these special children.' The remaining children will live here, plus Ruby and Scarlett. Ceri will return to Clava with Ashton. Mairi and Lucie's families will take one each. Hamish and Morwenna have offered to raise a child as well."

Nodding, I ran the numbers in my head.

"Another daughter for us?" Cam asked beneath the rumble of the crowd. "Thorsten is six. There isn't going to be a better time."

I choked back the tears, knowing that he had arranged this. Called in favors across several communities. But they had all agreed.

"There is one condition, though," Ashton warned, breaking my bubble.

"What?" I asked suspiciously, my heart sinking. Of course, this was too good to be true.

"We need you to reactivate the portal. When the time comes, we need to ensure that these children have the widest range of potential partners across all communities. This is why we needed so many. To ensure they spread out and choose diverse partners. While they can travel overland, their partners cannot. Via the antipodes is the safest way, using the Nexus."

I looked around the room, taking in the apprehensive faces. We had lived in isolation for years. Our experiences with the outside world had been overwhelmingly negative. Laetitia's kidnapping. Di's illness. The murder of Luca was fresh in many people's minds.

"That isn't my decision to make," I said warily as a hushed silence fell across the room.

It was Sorcha who broke the uncomfortable silence. "What role will Clava and Auckland play now? Now that these children exist. You always wanted to control our society, our trade, and our children. What has changed?"

"Everything. This was always the end goal. To ensure all communities were interlinked, to ensure each genome was replicated, but the ultimate goal was to raise children who can survive outside the domes, immune to the protozoa. We will play no further role in the reproduction of humans."

"Just like that?" The cynicism dripped from her words.

"Just like that," Ashton repeated. "As hard as it will be to let go, this is what we need to do. We can't control people or who they partner with. We can assist with trade, but most societies are doing perfectly well on that front themselves. So, while we still have medical expertise and can assist where there is need, we want to focus on living our own lives. The years have been intensive for us, too."

"What reports do you want on these children?" Illy asked.

"With your consent," Ashton looked at me, "we would like to visit once a year. Supervised, of course. We would like to do a quick medical check just to ensure everything is okay. But for the most part, nothing for you will change."

"You won't keep trying to produce more immune people? A vaccine?"

"I will readily admit we would have liked more. Fifty would have been perfect. That would allow a margin of error, just in case some didn't survive to maturity or chose not to have children of their own."

Feeling the glares piercing him from across the room, Ashton hurriedly continued, "But we have crunched the numbers. Twenty-seven will be enough. Not in their lifetime, and not in their children's, but in fifty years, when the domes start to feel the burden of their population, their grandchildren will be able to live outside. Rebuild and start expanding our settlements when it is likely we can start over. We have achieved our goals. Chosen genomes carefully and eradicated diseases. We have preserved all genetic material by ensuring that it is replicated. We have found a way to save humanity, sustainably, and for the long term. We have ensured that this gene is dominant so that it will be passed on to all subsequent generations."

"Why not more? Our population has more than doubled. You said there were tens of thousands of survivors. How is twenty-seven enough?"

Morwenna caught the glare from Sorcha and Illy and rapidly revised her statement. "Not that I meant Freyja having more! But can you keep trying?"

"Twenty-seven isn't too bad. I know it doesn't seem like a lot, but it is dangerous to rely on too many children from one mother. Future generations could end up inbred, and that is risky. Limiting the numbers, having a long-term plan over hundreds of years and several generations is the most sustainable approach. Back to Dr. Mackintosh's question. Now our focus will shift. Our role from here is to re-green the planet. Ensure that all the vegetation we saved can grow again, outside. If you don't mind," he looked at Cam, "we might be in touch. You are still our best food security expert."

Cam nodded at the request, although I sensed the reticence. It might be all positive now, but he hadn't forgotten what they had done to me.

"The other task we have set ourselves is to repopulate the native wildlife we lost. There are some within the domed communities and many more genes cryopreserved. We have planned an extensive project, and Ms. Jorgensen, you may wish to assist with this. We kept two breeding pairs of most animals at a dedicated inland facility, so we slowly need to increase that population. We can't deal with a population explosion, but it is critical that they all survive."

Understanding, I nodded. "But people had to come first?"

"They did. We have limited resources and space. We always knew we would eventually find the key with humans, and then we could focus on wildlife. I am pleased to say that we have secured the future for us. We can return the world to the way it was, only much more sustainably this time. We will keep all animals under surveillance, ensure that no species replicates too fast and has an adverse impact on the eco-system or on other species."

Chatter filled the space. People were excited with this news as they poured out of the hall. The children had homes. Our relationship with Clava was tenuous but the most stable it had been in a decade. There was a good chance that one day, our ancestors could reclaim the earth.

"Is this what you want?"

I glanced up and saw the concern ingrained in Cam's face.

"I can't believe you did this. In a day."

"It was easy. As soon as I asked, everyone said yes without hesitation. You have touched so many people's lives, Frey. Returning the favor was something they are all willing to do. So, I need to ask you again, are you sure this is what you want?"

As I gazed into his eyes, I realized that this was the best outcome imaginable. All of my children here, or safe with friends, raised in loving homes. Homes I would happily have chosen for them. I could watch them grow up, be part of their lives. They would be safe, part of our extended family. Protected within the Caim.

BOOK CLUB QUESTIONS

1. When Freyja finds her sister Katrin, she turns off the life support and destroys the facility. Would you have done differently?

2. Freyja blames her parents for Katrin being used for scientific breeding. Was she right to do so?

3. Who are in your personal Caim or circle of protection?

4. When Cam tells Freyja about Isla's childhood and her sister drowning, she is even more embarrassed to learn that Isla sees her as fearless.

5. Freyja tells Katrin about her life in Melbourne, and describes her parents as helping others, but in a specific way. She describes homeless people as, "People looked after themselves, their own family and friends. I guess there was a feeling that we couldn't care for everyone, so we didn't. Everyone just looked after themselves."

Katrin asks, "But if each family helped one person, would that have fixed the problem?" Is it that simple?

6. After Louis is kidnapped, Cam injured, and Luca murdered, Freyja and Illyria go after Angus. What were they trying to achieve? Should they have let someone else go?

7. When Illy and Freyja are held captive in the medical facility in Clava, how does it impact their relationship?

8. Why does Ashton finally let them go?

9. When Freyja and Illy find Nate in Edinburgh, Freyja is stunned by how Illy acts, and is even more upset when she realizes her friend killed for her. Do we all have a shadow side?

10. When Angus confesses to using Katrin as a brain-dead surrogate to gestate his daughter Ceridwen, he admits it was to be as close to Freyja as possible. How would this make you feel?

11. Ceridwen's upbringing is not one of a typical child. How could this affect her?

12. Illy describes the concept of Jungian goddess archetypes to Jorja (Chapter 42). This concept is discussed better here: https://www.where-wonderwaits.com/feminine-archetypes/#feminine-archetype-quiz

   Which archetype are you? What about the women in your family? Does this idea help you to understand them better?

13. After Ceri sets the house on fire, she is sent to Clava. Can a child who has been shown no love or sense of family truly learn these values?

14. Freyja learns that she and her sister produce immune children, and that those twenty-seven girls will form a critical role in ensuring the survival of the human race. Was what Clava did to her for the greater good for many generations to come?

AUTHOR BIO

T.S. SIMONS IS AN Australian author of Scottish heritage. Living in the alpine region of Australia, she believes in the values of sustainability and community in a world where we place greater value on possessions than people. The Antipodes series addresses the question—if we gave young people the opportunity to start over, would we replicate the mistakes of the past?

She holds Bachelor and Master's degrees from Monash University and enjoys strong coffee, traveling, mythology, and snow skiing, while attempting to live as sustainably as possible. She is owned by two rather bossy standard schnauzers and two rescue cats who co-manage her household.

The Antipodes series includes Project Hemisphere, The Space Between, Infinity, Circle of Protection, and Sessrúmnir. She is now working on a related series, The Latitude Series.

Discover more at
4HorsemenPublications.com

www.ingramcontent.com/pod-product-compliance
Lightning Source LLC
Chambersburg PA
CBHW020520110726
47899CB00004B/1179